Miss Julia Throws a Wedding

ALSO BY ANN B. ROSS

Miss Julia Takes Over
Miss Julia Speaks Her Mind

Miss Julia Throws a Wedding

Ann B. Ross

Bookspan Large Print Edition

Viking

This Large Print Edition, prepared especially for Bookspan, contains the complete, unabridged text of the original Publisher's Edition.

VIKING
Published by the Penguin Group
Penguin Putnam Inc., 375 Hudson Street, New York, New York 10014, U.S.A.
Penguin Books Ltd, 80 Strand, London WC2R 0RL, England
Penguin Books Australia Ltd, 250 Camberwell Road, Camberwell,
   Victoria 3124, Australia
Penguin Books Canada Ltd, 10 Alcorn Avenue, Toronto, Ontario,
   Canada M4V 3B2
Penguin Books India (P) Ltd, 11 Community Centre, Panchsheel Park,
   New Delhi-110 017, India
Penguin Books (N.Z.) Ltd, Cnr Rosedale and Airborne Roads, Albany,
   Auckland, New Zealand
Penguin Books (South Africa) (Pty) Ltd, 24 Sturdee Avenue,
   Rosebank, Johannesburg 2196, South Africa

Penguin Books Ltd, Registered Offices:
Harmondsworth, Middlesex, England

First published in 2002 by Viking Penguin,
a member of Penguin Putnam Inc.

ISBN 0-7394-2770-9

Printed in the United States of America

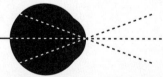

This Large Print Book carries the
Seal of Approval of N.A.V.H.

This book is for
Chuck Colhoun, Michael Martin,
and Jennifer Ross—
Miracles by marriage

Miss Julia Throws a Wedding

Chapter 1

I've a good mind to sell this house. The thought came to me, full-blown, as I looked out my front window at the absolute mess across the street. A haze of red construction dust hovered in the air, while a layer of it had already drifted over the sidewalk and covered my porch and front yard. A huge flatbed truck loaded with pallets of bricks had just come to a brake-grinding stop, blocking the street and my driveway, while men high up on scaffolding waved trowels and yelled instructions. You could've heard them all the way to Main Street.

Fifty years, or close to it, in one place is long enough for anybody. Especially when a three-story brick monstrosity, courtesy of the high-flying aspirations of Pastor Larry Ledbetter, was being built right in front of my eyes. Then there was Hazel Marie on the road to rack and ruin, taking Little Lloyd with her, and Coleman so besotted with Binkie that he hardly ever stayed in the rented rooms upstairs, and I was right before being left high and dry in this house with nothing but reminders of Wesley Lloyd Springer to keep me company. Any of which I could do without and never miss.

"Lillian," I said as I heard her push through the door to the dining room, the strains of gospel music from the kitchen radio going up a notch. She needed to turn that thing down.

"Lillian?" I said again.

"I'm listenin' hard as I can," she answered, standing there with her arms full of folded towels on her way to the downstairs linen closet.

"I've a good mind to sell this house."

She put the towels on the sofa and walked over to the window. Looking out with me, just as a worker threw a clanging shovel into a wheelbarrow, she said, "You not gonna do no such a thing, Miss Julia. That Presbyterium church buildin' get built one of these days, then things quieten down, an' you be over yo' upset."

"Not likely," I said. "Things won't ever be the same as long as that thing is standing over there right in front of my eyes, with people coming and going all the time, doing first one thing and then another just to get in shape. A Family Life Center, of all things. All it'll be is a glorified gymnasium. And I'll tell you what's a fact, the church ought not to be in the physical fitness business. Its number one concern, to my mind, ought to be *spiritual* fitness."

I turned away from the window, just sick at the sight of that brick wall going up not two feet from the far sidewalk. Turning away didn't help, though, for what I had to face inside the house was an even worse mess.

"Lillian," I said again, holding my head in my hand, "I don't know what to do about anything anymore. I declare, I'm so tired of fighting losing battles I could just sit down and cry. And I may do just that."

"You think that gonna he'p anything?"

I looked up toward the back of the house as the sound of Hazel Marie's humming and singing the few words she knew of some country-western song came from her bedroom. Happy as a lark, packing suitcases and getting ready to move out of my house and into Mr. J. D. Pickens's. Without benefit, again, of marriage, I might add. You'd think after her decade-long experience as my husband's paramour, a situation that left her with a child and not a red cent to her name when he up and died right out there in my driveway, that she'd know better than to take up with another man of similar ilk. Not that Mr. Pickens was already married, as Wesley Lloyd Springer had been to me, but he'd told her he was not the marrying kind, at least, not at the present time. But if not now, when? She was playing with fire, I'd told her. But did that stop her? No, it did not, as the click of suitcase latches testified.

"I've got to talk to her again," I said. "I can't let her keep on ruining her life like this."

"You might ought to keep out of it," Lillian cautioned, ready as usual to offer advice, whether it was wanted or not. "She a grown woman, an' she ain't never been so happy in her life."

"But she could be happier! She doesn't know what she's missing." I stopped then, recalling my own less-than-satisfactory marriage. I wouldn't wish the same on my own worst enemy, and Hazel Marie was far from that.

"Here come Little Lloyd," Lillian said, as

she moved the curtain aside to look out the window again. "That heavy ole book satchel gonna break that chile's back one a these days. He gonna want a snack with nothing but one a them school lunches on his stomach, which he don't hardly eat anyhow."

As she padded toward the kitchen, the run-down heels of her slippers flapping with every step, I went back to the window. My heart wrenched as I watched Little Lloyd walk toward the house, his head turned to watch the workmen across the street. In spite of my and Lillian's every effort, the child stayed skinny as a rail. His little thin legs looked like sticks poking out of his long shorts. A striped tee shirt just emphasized his puny chest, while a soft spring breeze lifted his fine hair, blowing it first one way then another. I could see him squint through the thick glasses, entranced as every child is with the activities of workingmen. As he reached my driveway, he turned to walk backward to watch the bricklayers on the scaffold, the Game Boy in his hand temporarily forgotten. Mr. Pickens had given him that electronic thing, now banned in the classroom, and he fiddled with it walking to and from school, and every other chance he had.

"Oh, Lord," I moaned under my breath. "How am I going to get along without them?" All I could think of were the long, lonely days stretching out in front of me, while I rattled around by myself in this empty house until I got too feeble to be of use to anybody. I could picture everybody going on about their lives, doing whatever popped into their heads to do—Coleman still carrying on with Binkie without the least hint of impending nuptials, and Hazel Marie living in sin with Mr. Pickens, and that child learning who-knew-what from their association, and Sam, well, who knew what he'd be up to. And here I'd be, old and forgotten, laid up in bed with my mind gone and my hip broken and needing a bedpan and nobody around to care if I got one or not.

Lord, I'd miss that boy, and him not a lick of kin to me, except for being my husband's child by way of Hazel Marie before I knew anything about it. Took nine years and Wesley Lloyd's demise for me to hear the first word of what he'd been up to. But that was all water over the dam or under the bridge or wherever it went.

I raised my head when I heard the screen door in the kitchen squeak as Little Lloyd came in, and Lillian's welcome and his laugh. Get hold of yourself, Julia Springer, I told myself, straightening my shoulders and tightening my mouth. Then I marched down the back hall to Hazel Marie's room, determined to give it one more try. Well, one more try today.

"Hazel Marie," I said, brought to a halt in the doorway at the sight of dresses piled on the bed, suitcases standing already filled, and shopping bags full of personal paraphernalia, like hair rollers and dryers and one pair of shoes after another. I recalled the night she'd shown up at my door, battered and bruised after a run-in with Brother Vernon Puckett's minions, without a stitch to her name except what she had on. And that was torn and mud-spattered and not fit to wear. Things had changed for her once Sam Murdoch, my onetime lawyer before he retired, and Binkie Enloe, my present-day lawyer, had straightened out Wesley Lloyd's two wills, so that now Little Lloyd and I shared and shared alike. Although his half was in a trust fund, which Hazel Marie and he benefited from, and mine was where I could get my hands on it anytime I wanted to.

"Oh, Miss Julia," Hazel Marie said, looking up from her packing, her face flushed and her eyes sparkling. "I didn't know I had so much. J.D.'s going to send me back home." And she laughed like that was the least likely possibility in the world.

"Hazel Marie," I said again, trying to keep myself together, although it was all I could do to keep from pitching a fit like I'd done a time or two before. "I wish you'd reconsider. What you're doing is just not right. What kind of example are you setting for Little Lloyd? To say nothing of what you're doing to yourself. Why, it wouldn't surprise me a bit if Mr. Pickens didn't think the less of you for not making him marry you."

We heard the telephone ring in the kitchen, and we both stopped to listen for Lillian to call one of us. When she didn't, Hazel Marie turned away, hanging her head—from shame, I like to think—so that her regularly touched-up blond hair hid her face.

"Miss Julia," she whispered, "you know how stubborn he is when he gets an idea in his head. And he's got this idea that everybody will think he's just after Little Lloyd's inheritance if we get married. He says we can have a good life together without bringing in all the legalities."

"Well, of course he would say that. What man wouldn't if he could get away with it? And you know that neither he nor anybody else can get at that inheritance. Binkie and Sam have it tied up tighter than Dick's hatband."

"I know." She nodded. "But I get a nice income from it to take care of Little Lloyd, and J.D.'s got his pride."

"Pride!" I threw up my hands. "If that's not just like a man! What does he want you to do, pauperize yourself so you'll be dependent on him? Hazel Marie, you are asking for trouble."

She looked away and refolded a dress that she'd already folded three times. "I know you think I haven't given it enough thought, but I really have. For one thing, Little Lloyd needs a masculine role model, all the books say so, and you couldn't find anybody more masculine than J.D. is."

I rolled my eyes at that. I knew what masculine meant to Hazel Marie. Well, and to me, too, at times. However. She had a point about the boy needing a man to look up to, since his own father hadn't exactly been an ideal for any child to emulate. Thursday night visits with the child and his mother hardly qualified as quality time, in my book. But, for the sake of my argument, I wasn't about to concede a blessed thing.

"Well, it just seems to me that if you're bound and determined to do this, the least he could do is make it legal." But I knew as well as she did how hardheaded the man could be.

Except for that one flaw in his character, Mr. Pickens was a good and decent man. Well, except for the fact that he was constitutionally unable to keep himself from flirting with every woman he met. And except for the fact that he'd never set the world on fire, financially speaking. I mean, how much can you make chasing down missing persons and investigating insurance fraud and the like? I'd told Hazel Marie that it looked like a woman had to make a choice between a good man and a rich one. The two didn't go together in my experience, limited though it was.

Well, then there was Sam, but he was another one who couldn't be counted on.

I'd come to that conclusion after I realized how scarce he'd been making himself lately.

I sighed then, because she'd heard all my arguments more than once, and they hadn't done any good. But, I thought, Mr. Pickens hadn't heard them, and I determined then and there to give him a piece of my mind the next time I saw him. Turning away from the packing frenzy, I said, "I just hope you know what you're doing."

Then, shocking me speechless, she ran over and hugged me, a demonstrative gesture I rarely, if ever, encouraged. "Oh, thank you, Miss Julia, thank you," she said, as the Joy perfume Mr. Pickens had given her nearly made my head swim. "I've wanted your blessing ever so much."

Blessing was not what I'd had in mind; resignation was more like it, but before I could disengage myself and answer, we heard Lillian's shoes flapping down the hall toward us.

"Miss Hazel Marie," Lillian said. She stopped in the door, holding a dish towel in her hands. "Mr. Pickens, he jus' call an' say to tell you he can't come pick you up today. He'll let you know when he can move you out, but for now, he want you to stay here with us."

"Oh!" Hazel Marie moaned in disappointment. She plopped down on a chair, then shot straight up again. Her sewing box had gotten there first. Rubbing her backside, she said, "He didn't want to speak to me?"

"No'm, he say he in a hurry. An', Miss Julia, you better take off that long face you been wearin' all day. You got comp'ny in yonder, an' they not gonna be happy seein' you mopin' 'round like you jus' lost your best friend."

That was exactly what I had lost, or was about to lose. Two or three of them, in fact, but I refrained from pointing that out to her.

"Who is it, Lillian?" I asked, turning away from Hazel Marie to face my duty. Lord, I didn't feel like entertaining company, but when you're known for your hospitality, you pull yourself together and do what you have to do, regardless of how you feel.

"Coleman and Miss Binkie, that's who. An' they say they got a 'nnouncement to make."

Chapter 2

"Married?" I couldn't get my mind around what they were telling me. When you've waited and hoped and prayed for something for so long, it's hard to believe that it's finally at hand.

Lillian, however, didn't have that problem. Standing by the dining room door, she let out a whoop that startled me so that I almost levitated from my chair. "It come to pass at last!"

Hazel Marie bounced in her chair. "Oh, that's wonderful! I'm so happy for you!" She all but clapped her hands. Little Lloyd stood beside the Victorian chair where she was seated, taking it all in. He was never far away when Coleman was around, and I intended to remind Hazel Marie that if she was so concerned about role models, the boy already had one.

Binkie was sitting on my Duncan Phyfe

sofa under the crook of Coleman's arm, both of them with smiles that kept breaking out into grins. Coleman, broad-shouldered and professional in his deputy's uniform which he filled so admirably, could hardly keep his eyes off her. And she, with that curly hair springing up all over her head, could hardly sit still. She kept glancing up at him and then at each of us, as they made their announcement to legalize what they'd been engaged in for ever so long.

"You're getting married?" I repeated.

"I finally got her to say yes," Coleman said, looking down on her. He'd make about two of her, she was such a little thing. "Took me forever to do it, too."

Such a handsome young man, I thought as I had many times before. And Binkie, that tiny ball of fire who could hold a jury spellbound and bend an Internal Revenue agent to her will, was transformed by the glow of happiness. It was a wonder to me why they'd waited so long, but I wasn't about to look a gift horse in the mouth.

"Well, it's not a moment too soon, I must say. And nobody's happier about it than I am."

"I'm real happy about it," Little Lloyd

said, his eyes rarely leaving Coleman. "But I thought y'all were already married."

"Things're not always as they seem, Little Lloyd," I said, glaring at Hazel Marie over his head. But her attention was fixed on the happy couple and she didn't notice. Which was just as well, since she already knew where I stood as far as her own less-than-acceptable situation was concerned.

"Oh, I can't wait to tell J.D.," she said. "He'll be thrilled."

"Let's hope so," I said. "And let's hope that he takes a lesson from their example. Now, you two," I went on, turning to Binkie and Coleman, "what are your plans?"

"Quick and easy," Binkie said. "We just wanted you to be the first to know, Miss Julia. Coleman and I met the first time right here in your living room, remember?"

Of course, I remembered. She'd come in out of a thunderstorm, soaked to the skin, and Coleman'd been lost as soon as he set eyes on her.

"When is it?" Hazel Marie asked. "Have you set a date?"

"Next Friday, at the courthouse," Binkie said. "And we want you all to be there."

"Oh, no," I said, gasping with dismay at

such an unseemly plan. "You can't do that! Binkie, what're you thinking of? Your folks won't stand for it, even if they have retired to Florida. There're too many things to do to get ready for a wedding—ordering and addressing invitations, picking out your dress, reserving the church, planning the reception, selecting your china pattern and I-don't-know-what-all."

Binkie waved her hand, dismissing the best part of any young woman's wedding. "We aren't going to worry with all that, Miss Julia. My folks're not in good health, and they're not able to travel. So we're going to do it without all the trimmings. Just cut to the chase, huh, Coleman?" She gave him a friendly nudge with her elbow.

Lillian grinned. "Sound like to me the chase already over."

"It better be," Coleman said, giving Binkie a squeeze. "I've been after this woman so long, I thought I'd never catch her. It can't come too soon for me."

"Well, Coleman," I said, "the groom should be eager; that's only right and proper. But, Binkie, a bride deserves a big church wedding, a dress with a long train and bridesmaids and flowers and all your friends celebrating with you. Queen for a day. Well, for longer than that with all the weeks of planning you'll need. You just can't have it at the courthouse in a week's time. Why, you wouldn't have any memories, much less any wedding pictures."

"Well, I know, Miss Julia," Binkie said, looking down at her lap and then up at Coleman. "But we're both busy, and my workload is just so heavy. I can't take the time. . . ."

"I have to take her when I can get her," Coleman broke in with a smile. "And besides, we've been, well, keeping company so long, as you keep reminding me, Miss Julia, that we don't think it'd look right to have a big church wedding."

I certainly appreciated Coleman's sensitivity to my feelings on the subject, and his careful wording of what everybody in town knew, namely, that they'd jumped the gun some time ago. In such cases, though, the best thing to do is just ignore the facts and go ahead and do what has to be done. Although I'd draw the line if Binkie wanted to wear white.

Still, I was dismayed at the thought of a hastily arranged and hurriedly accomplished civil ceremony without benefit of clergy, so I said, "I can't believe you'd want to do it at the courthouse; you need a minister at the very least. And you can keep it small. An intimate wedding would be lovely and perfectly suitable. You wouldn't need to use the sanctuary; you could have it in the chapel. It's perfect for a small wedding. Oh, Binkie, I just can't stand the thought of you two taking a few minutes between making a will and making an arrest to run down to the courthouse to get married."

"I don't know, Miss Julia," Hazel Marie chimed in. "It sounds real romantic to me."

Of course, in her situation I guessed it would, since any sort of ceremony would be better than what she was getting. And if she could've gotten Mr. Pickens as far as the courthouse, even I would've been willing to forgo the blessings of the church.

"It got to be next week?" Lillian asked.

"Yes, because the following Monday and Tuesday're the only time we can get a long weekend together," Binkie told her. "I can't take off any longer, with all the cases I have pending. But that's honeymoon enough for now."

"Oh, my word," I said, leaning my head

on my hand. "Coleman, you've got to do better than that. You're both going about this the wrong way. You ought to be making some memories that'll carry you through the years and the bad times. Not that I think you'll have any bad times, but you never know. And if you have a lovely wedding to look back on, it'll certainly help."

"I understand what you're saying, Miss Julia," Binkie said. "But we either do it next weekend or it'll have to wait until fall. And neither of us wants to do that. And as far as even a small church wedding is concerned, with my schedule, I just don't have the time to make all those arrangements."

Lillian said, "Miss Julia got the time."

No one said anything for a minute, as the grinding of the gears of another loaded truck pulling up across the street and two dozen voices shouting directions made us all cringe. When Lillian's words had a chance to sink in, a smile spread across my face. I jumped up from my chair, marveling that I hadn't thought of it myself.

"Why, of course! That's what we'll do! Binkie, Coleman, you've got to let me do it. Why, it'd be no trouble at all, would it, Lillian? It's the perfect solution!"

"Oh, say yes," Hazel Marie said, looking as excited as I felt. "Miss Julia is so good at organizing things, and I'll help her. I'd love to help; it'll be so much fun, and you wouldn't have to do anything but show up."

"She's right, Binkie." I pushed my case hard, wanting so much for this young couple to get a good start in life. Even though they'd pretty much already started. "I'll make all the arrangements, if you don't mind having it at our church. I know everybody over there and I can get things done. Oh." I stopped, remembering that Pastor Ledbetter was out traipsing around the Wailing Wall or the Dead Sea or some such thing on a tour of the Holy Land. Wouldn't you know he'd be gone right when I could've used him. "Well, our senior pastor's halfway around the world and won't be back in time. Ordinarily, it wouldn't matter a hill of beans to me where he was, but this is certainly an inconvenience."

"Pastor Petree is here," Hazel Marie reminded me. "He may be an associate, but I think he's a full-fledged minister in spite of it."

"Well, I guess he'll have to do. Now, Binkie, just say the word and we'll get you married in style. You won't have to do a thing but pick out your dress."

"Well," Binkie said, looking up at Coleman. "What do you think?"

"Up to you, honey," he said.

"Oh, please," Hazel Marie said. "Let us do it."

"Well, if it won't be too much trouble. . . ." Binkie was trying not to smile, but I could tell that she was pleased. And why not? Every young woman wants a wedding to remember, so I determined in my heart to do the best I could with what I had to work with. Although who ever heard of putting on a memorable wedding in a week's time?

"Wonderful!" I said, pacing now in front of them as one plan after another went through my head. "Binkie, I declare, if you could possibly give us two weeks. All right, all right, we can do it in one. It won't be much, but it'll be something. Now, I know young people these days like to do everything together, you know, pick out their invitations, their china pattern and such, but there's no time for that. You'll just have to let me have a free hand. Oh, my, invitations should go out at least four weeks before the wedding, and they should be engraved.

Well, it can't be helped. Start your list, Binkie, and you, too, Coleman. We'll invite by phone. It may not be the correct thing, but it'll have to do. Besides, we're not inviting Amy Vanderbilt, so our etiquette doesn't have to be perfect." I stopped in mid-pace, thinking of the wedding I could've put on if they'd given me enough time.

"Binkie," I started up again, "you'll need to pick out your china pattern. And your silver and crystal."

"I've got all of mother's. She wanted me to have them when they moved to Florida."

"Good. She has lovely taste, and that's a few less things to worry about. But you need to go out to Belk's and get on their bridal list, and anywhere else that you want people to shop for you. If they're going to spend the money, they might as well get what you want."

"Hold on a minute, Miss Julia," Coleman said. "This is sounding pretty complicated."

I gave Binkie a long look, trying to read her feelings, and what I saw was a rosy flush on her pale face and a sparkle in her eyes. I knew I was right to push this, because every bride deserves all the attendant festivities at least once in her life, although I knew a few who'd done it more than once. I'd even heard of one twice-divorced woman who'd gone down the aisle in full white regalia with four bridesmaids behind her. An example of the worst possible taste.

"Coleman," I said, "here's the first lesson for you. Pick out your groomsmen, order your tuxedo—although you really ought to own one—and the flowers for your bride, pay the preacher, plan the honeymoon, and leave the rest to us. Oh, and show up on time. That's all the groom has to do."

"Yes, ma'am," he said, then pulled Binkie closer to him. "What do you say, sweetheart?"

"I don't know how you're going to do it," Binkie said to me. "But, I guess it could be fun. At least, let's make it fun. Not something dreary and formal, with all that traditional rigmarole. I don't want us to get carried away with trying to do everything by the book. Something small and simple and happy will suit us fine. But, I warn you, Miss Julia, I can't be much help; my schedule next week is so full I get tired just thinking about it."

She was telling the truth, for I noticed as she was speaking that she'd begun to look a little green around the gills. Lord, there was nothing worse than a bride getting sick right before the wedding.

"You ought to be gettin' some rest," Lillian said, frowning at her. "You an' Coleman, neither one, don't get enough rest, an' you don't eat right, neither."

"You ought to listen to Lillian," I said, nodding in agreement. "And I want you to put everything out of your mind, and leave it all to us. We'll get it done, and done right. Oh, I wish there was enough time for me to give you a party, a tea or something, and I know your friends would like to give you a shower. Although, I'll tell you something your mother'd tell you if she could. Don't encourage showers; suggest a luncheon instead. People'll give you nicer wedding gifts if they don't have to buy half-a-dozen shower gifts beforehand. See, this is the kind of thing I can help you with."

"There's just one thing," Coleman said, and he pointed his finger at Little Lloyd. "*You* have to be in it, bud."

If the child had smiled any wider, his face would've split wide open. He nodded, too overcome to speak.

"Thank you for wanting to do it, Miss

Julia," Binkie said, leaning her head against Coleman. "But please don't put yourself out; I just want to get it done."

That was Binkie all over. She'd always had a mind of her own, and it was usually different from what you'd expect from a girl raised as well as she'd been. Why, she'd even refused to make her debut at the Governor's Ball in Raleigh when she'd been the only girl in Abbotsville to've been asked. It'd nearly killed her mother. But Binkie had me to reckon with now.

"It's settled then," I said. "So don't give it another thought."

"Uh-oh," Coleman said, as he fiddled with some little attachment on his law enforcement belt. "Use your phone, Miss Julia?"

"Of course. You know where it is. Now, Hazel Marie," I said, as Coleman headed for the kitchen phone. "You're just going to have to make the sacrifice and put off your move until this wedding's over. I'm going to need you, and Little Lloyd, too. In fact, I'm not sure I can do it in this short amount of time if you're not here to help me."

"Wel-l-l," she said, her eyes darting

around. "I guess I could. I mean, it's only a week, so maybe J.D. won't mind."

I could've cared less whether Mr. Pickens minded or not. This wedding was having added benefits, as far as I was concerned.

As Coleman came back into the room, he said, "Binkie, Miss Julia, sorry to break this up, but I have to go. They're calling everybody back on duty—a little problem at the jail. Come on, sweetheart, I'll drop you off and get on down there."

"Wait, wait," I said, as Binkie got up from the sofa and followed him to the door. "We have to discuss, oh, I don't know what all, a million things. Come to dinner tomorrow night, and we'll get it all done then. And bring your invitation lists and, Binkie, both of you need to ask somebody to stand up with you. That's the law, you know; you have to have two witnesses."

They were on the porch by that time, but Coleman turned back. "Lord, Miss Julia," he said with a teasing smile, "if the two of us don't know the law, I don't know who does."

Chapter 3

"A week!" I turned back to Lillian and Hazel
Marie and threw up my hands. "Have you
ever heard of such a thing? Well, let's get
started; every minute counts. Hazel Marie,
when you talk to Mr. Pickens, invite him for
tomorrow night. Now, let's get a pad and
pencil and start making a list."

"What kind of list?"

But my mind had already run ahead. "I'd
better get over to the church before that associate pastor goes home. Lance Petree,
have you ever heard of such a name? What
was his mother thinking of, I ask you. Lillian,
you help Hazel Marie think of all we need to
do, and I'll go over and reserve the chapel
for Friday night. Oh, I know, let's do it Saturday afternoon. An afternoon wedding
would be nice, don't you think? Yes, I like
that, and Binkie could get a good night's
rest beforehand. And people could wear

tea-length, the women, I mean. Oh, Lillian, we've got to think about the reception. Where'll we have that?"

"We could have it here," Hazel Marie said, without giving one thought to the jumble of construction across the street that our guests would be subjected to.

"I wish we could," I said. "But the Inn in the Pines would be easier on us, and it doesn't have an eyesore to deal with. Well, I'm going to run on over and get this wedding on Pastor Petree's dance card."

As I crossed the street, I fumed at Pastor Ledbetter for being off in a foreign land, leaving a beginner in his place. Untried ministers of the Gospel didn't generally worry me since I was always willing to give them a chance, but this one was hardly to my taste. Too young, for one thing. And too pious, for another. I couldn't say much for his sermons, either, since they sounded like academic papers he'd gotten A's on in seminary. He'd stand up there behind the pulpit and read them off to us, word by word. And if he ever looked out at the congregation, his pale complexion turned red from the neck up and he'd quickly look down at his paper again, losing his place in the process.

Well, I thought, as I walked down the sidewalk past that soon-to-be-permanent eyesore, one preacher's as good as another for my present purpose. I paid little mind to the workmen crowding the sidewalk, wiping dirt and sweat from their faces and preparing to leave for the day. With the noise level of the construction work easing off, the pigeons that roosted in the steeple were circling the church overhead. I could hear the flutter of their wings as they came in for a landing and congregated on the roof before slipping through the louvers on the steeple for the night. Something needed to be done about the unholy mess they made up there.

Putting pigeons out of my mind, I entered the church through the back door of the Fellowship Hall, and headed for the pastor's office at the far end.

And there was Norma Cantrell, the pastor's secretary, her teased hair frosted to within an inch of its life, sitting at her desk, guarding access to the preacher. Even though he wasn't there. The woman could stop anybody less determined dead in their tracks, but I knew how to deal with her.

"Why, Miss Julia," she said, giving me a smirk that tried to pass for a smile. She was paid to be nice to the church members, but she didn't keep that fact uppermost in her mind most of the time. "What brings you out this late in the day? You know I can't do anything about the noise those men are making; that's all part of building a building. I guess we'll just have to put up with it, won't we?"

"I'm not here to complain about that, Norma, although a few well-placed complaints would not be uncalled for. But, no, I've come to see Pastor Petree."

"You have an appointment?"

"No, I don't, but I need to see him."

"He's busy." And she shuffled some papers to show that she was, too.

"Norma, I know that he leaves just about this time to make hospital visits, so he's going to stop being busy in about two minutes. Now, if you're not going to punch that button to summon him, I'll just knock on his door myself."

I turned and started across the hall to the associate pastor's office, leaving Norma sputtering behind me. I just hate officious people, don't you?

Giving a sharp rap on the door, I opened it and stuck my head in. "Pastor Petree?"

Startled, he looked up from the magazine he was reading. "Yes?"

"Pastor, I'm Mrs. Julia Springer, remember? I had you for Sunday dinner a few weeks ago when you first got here."

"Oh, yes, of course. Come in, Mrs. Springer." He came to his feet, brushing his wispy blond hair off his forehead and smoothing it in place. Then he checked the knot in his tie. "Now, Mrs. Springer, I've done all I can do about the noise and dust from that construction work. They have to have trucks and cement mixers and cranes to get their work done, and I don't know what else I can do."

"That building's not on my mind today, Pastor, you'll be happy to know. No, I've come to schedule a wedding."

"Oh?" His eyebrows went up, then came together in a frown. "Are you sure? Perhaps we need to discuss other ways to deal with your loneliness. Widows, especially, are so susceptible, so eager to remarry that they don't always make good decisions." Then he smiled.

I stared at him until the smile faded from his face. "I hope you don't think loneliness is the only reason a widow would remarry."

But he probably did, being unable to imagine older people in the throes of passion. He had a lot to learn. "Besides," I went on, "it's not my wedding we're talking about."

"Ah, I see," he said, his eyes sliding away from mine. "Well, I hope it's no time soon. The church calendar is full for the next two months." He reached for his appointment book and frowned at it as he flipped through the pages.

"I don't want the sanctuary; this will be a small wedding. The chapel'll do us fine."

"What date would that be?"

"Next Saturday, the first weekend in June."

He shook his head, and kept shaking it. "I'm sorry; the chapel is already taken for both Saturday afternoon and evening. This is the busiest time of the year for weddings, you know."

"Oh. Well, what're we going to do? My two young friends only have next weekend, and if I don't get a church and a preacher, they'll go to the courthouse, and I just can't have that."

A smile started at the corners of his mouth, but he had himself in so much control, it didn't get much further. I declare, with that pale complexion and the strained and pious look around his eyes, all I could think of was what a world of good a purgative dose would do him.

Then he straightened his shoulders and tried for a professional look. A dried shaving nick on his chin somewhat detracted from the effect. "Well, if I may suggest . . . well, as I said, the church is busy next weekend, but other ministers will be conducting those weddings. So, if you'd consider another place to have the ceremony, it just so happens that I will be free."

That brought me up short, so I stood there cogitating. Having the wedding in a church was not the be-all and end-all. It could be held somewhere else, anywhere else, if that was the best we could do. I'd read of skydiving weddings, underwater weddings and, locally, there'd been a wedding in a Burger King restaurant, of all things, written up on the society page and everything. I'd always wondered if they'd reduced their Whoppers to a miniature size for the reception.

And there'd been perfectly lovely garden weddings and home weddings. . . . A smile broke out on my face, quivered and stopped at the thought of construction clutter detracting from a wedding in my home. Then I stiffened my spine, vowing to bear the burden of a less-than-attractive vista from my porch. Besides, having it in my living room, Binkie and Coleman's meeting place, would be most apt and fitting.

"Good," I said, making up my mind. "Put five o'clock next Saturday on your calendar, Pastor. We'll have it at my house, and you know where that is. And I'd appreciate it if you'd have those workingmen sweep the street and the sidewalks before they take off from work Friday afternoon."

"I'll speak to the foreman about that. But," he said, frowning, "five is not good for me. Could we possibly change to an earlier time?"

I pursed my mouth at another hitch in my plans, but I nodded my head. "I guess we'll have to then, won't we? Let's say four o'clock. At least that way people won't expect a full meal at the reception."

"Good. It's settled then," the pastor said, making a note on his calendar. "I'll look forward to conducting the ceremony." He looked up and ventured another small smile. "It'll be my first wedding here. Well, I must admit, it'll be my first wedding ever. Something for my scrapbook."

I took a step back, wondering if I was endangering Binkie and Coleman's legitimacy. "You are legal, I mean, licensed to marry people, aren't you?"

"Oh, yes, ma'am, absolutely, by the presbytery, the synod and the state. Now," he said, moving his magazine to search for a notepad. "I'll need the names of the parties concerned, and we'll have to set some times for the required marital counseling sessions."

"Counseling sessions?" I had a swift image of Binkie and Coleman being counseled by this wet-behind-the-ears, unmarried and unassociated associate pastor, and I almost laughed. They could counsel him about a few things. "I wouldn't worry about that if I were you, Pastor. Binkie's a lawyer and Coleman's a deputy sheriff, recently promoted, so I don't know that they'll have time for any counseling sessions. But, since they're both counselors of a sort themselves, I doubt they'll need your full course, don't you?"

"Well," he said, somewhat taken aback. He glanced out the window, seeming torn between following church policy and wanting to put this wedding in his scrapbook. "I don't know, Mrs. Springer. Rules are rules, so I must insist. It's imperative that as an ordained minister, I satisfy myself that this decision for holy matrimony is within God's will."

I bit my tongue to keep from saying what I thought, which was that he wasn't the one who had to be satisfied. The idea that a perfect stranger, even if he was clothed in a black robe every Sunday, would take it upon himself to pass judgment on two people's readiness for marriage. Take it from me, Binkie and Coleman were past ready.

So I said, "We'll work it out, don't worry. I'll write down their names for you, so you'll know who you're joining together. Now, Pastor Petree, is everything settled? I don't want to have to be worried with this again."

"Yes, I think that's it," he said, taking the slip of paper from me. "Oh, one more thing. I trust there's no, uh, problem here? I mean, is there a reason for the haste?" Spots of red bloomed on his pale cheeks.

"Not a reason in the world. Don't worry your mind about this being a hasty decision; I assure you it is not. Those two have been seeing each other for, I don't know, a good long while by now." Well, everybody uses euphemisms every now and then, so if he didn't take my meaning, all the better.

I said my good-byes, mixing in my gratitude, and turned to go, relieved that I'd retained a preacher, such as he was.

"Ah, Mrs. Springer?" He cleared his throat as I raised my eyebrows. "If you don't have your music already set, you might be interested to know that I can help you with that, too."

"Oh, yes? What I know about music could be put in a thimble, so I'm going to need some help. What do you have in mind?"

"Well," he said, a flush spreading up from his neck. "I play the guitar and sing a little. I've done it a number of times for friends' weddings."

A quick image of Pastor Petree leading Binkie and Coleman in their vows, then hooking a guitar over his shoulder and presenting a musical rendition before he pronounced them flashed through my mind. I didn't know whether to laugh or cry at the spectacle that would be.

"I, well, I'll have to consult with the bride. She may've already asked someone. I appreciate the offer, though, and we'll keep it in mind." And I left before he could come up with another unseemly suggestion.

A *guitar,* I thought with a shudder. I just couldn't go along with all the modern ideas cropping up in church services everywhere these days. If it wasn't guitars strumming "Kum Ba Ya," it was dancers cavorting in the aisle waving chiffon scarves. If they ever started that in my church, that'd be the day I'd take my membership elsewhere.

And it wasn't just regular church services that'd suffered from the bending of the traditional rules that'd served us well for centuries. To my mind, weddings were where the worst seemed to come out, with people making up their own vows and such as that. Thank goodness Binkie was going to be too busy to think of doing such a thing. I'd hate to think of what she'd come up with.

Crossing the street on my way home, I thought about the strange ideas that some people had of what constituted a wedding. As far as I was concerned, a wedding was supposed to be a ceremonial rite of tradition and high intent. But most of all, it was supposed to be a sedate and formal act, conducted with the utmost seriousness, and I intended to see that this one was exactly that.

Chapter 4

"Well, Lillian," I said as I marched into the kitchen where she was preparing supper. "I've got it arranged, not exactly as I wanted it, but I think it'll work. Where're Hazel Marie and Little Lloyd?"

"They upstairs in his room, gettin' him halfway packed up for when Mr. Pickens come. She plannin' to stay for the wedding, though; she tole me she was."

"Well, I'm not one to question manna from heaven, because we're going to need her help. Mr. Pickens can just stay busy, as far as I'm concerned."

As I began to tell Lillian my plans for the wedding, her frown got deeper and deeper. "You know what this mean, don't you?" she demanded, when I finished describing how lovely the living room would look with candlestands and flowers, and maybe an arch over Binkie and Coleman as they said their vows in front of the fireplace. "It mean we got to clean this house from top to bottom, that wall need paintin' where the door hit it when somebody sling it open, the livin' room drapes need cleanin', them dinin' room chair seats need re-coverin', and how you gonna seat everybody who gonna come, anyway?"

"Let's not worry about all of that; we don't have time. You keep this house in good shape already, and if a few things could use touching up, well, we'll hope nobody looks too closely. We'll get done what can be done, and let the rest go." I sat down to start making lists of what could be done.

"What about the food you gonna serve? 'Cause I guess you gonna have the reception here, too."

"It would be more convenient, wouldn't it? Once people get parked, they won't want to go somewhere else. We can lay everything out on the dining room table, finger food, not a full meal, which is a benefit of having an afternoon wedding. Even though it'll be earlier than I wanted, thanks to preachers who overschedule. Well," I said, with a sigh at the lack of cooperation I was running into, "it can't be helped.

"Now, Lillian, we can put the wedding cake on the tea cart and roll it out when it's time for the cutting. It'll work; I'm sure of it." And I added wedding cake to my list.

As one idea after another entered my head and a picture of a simple and elegant wedding began to emerge, I began to feel more and more excited. All my previous dark thoughts were being displaced by the happiness of the moment. Let this be a lesson, I thought, keep yourself busy doing for others. Which was exactly what I was doing.

Little Lloyd pushed through the kitchen door. "Hey," he said. "Lillian, did I leave my Game Boy in here?"

"No, honey, I ain't seen it."

"Little Lloyd," I said, my head bent over the list I was making, "Coleman wants you to sing a solo at the wedding."

His head snapped toward me, his mouth open. Then, seeing a smile at the corner of my mouth, he grinned in return. "Nuh-uh."

"Well, okay, if you don't want to. But we're going to find something for you to do. Run on now, and let us finish this."

As he left, still grinning, Lillian said, "I'm gonna need some help back here in the kitchen to serve all them folks I know you gonna have."

"Oh, Lillian," I said, laying down my pen. "You're not going to be back here in the kitchen. You know Coleman'll want you as a guest, and I wouldn't have it any other way. This is going to be a catered event. Although we'll still need somebody to oversee the table, be sure the trays're replenished and so on." I stopped with a sudden happy thought. "I know. I'll ask Emmett what's-his-name, you know, Mr. Howard Connard's man and James, who works for Sam. You wouldn't mind them in your kitchen, would you?"

"I guess I wouldn't," she said, turning her head so I wouldn't see how pleased she was at the thought of being a wedding guest instead of a wedding server.

"Good. Let's get you a new dress for the happy occasion, too. Now, where's the phone book? I need to get a caterer lined up."

Lillian handed me the thin book, and as I thumbed through to the yellow pages, she said, "I hope you don't get Miz Dolan, she not hardly able to make them party sam'iches no more. I don' know she can fix for no big bunch of people."

"I know she can't. But, Lord, Lillian, Sarah Dolan's made sandwiches for every party, reception, tea and coffee held in this town for thirty years. To tell the truth, I'm about tired of the same thing everywhere I go." I ran my finger down the listing, short though it was. "No, I'm looking for that woman who moved here from Atlanta and started a catering business. LuAnne said she does some lovely things. What's her name? Katie, Kate, something . . . oh, this must be it. Katie's Kuisine." I twisted my mouth, thinking it over. "I don't know if I should engage somebody who either can't spell or thinks such spelling is cute."

"All you in'erested in is, can she cook. If she can and she know how to set a pretty table, I wouldn't worry 'bout no spellin'. What we gonna have, anyway? 'Cause I need to know how much of them silver serving pieces to start polishin'."

"We'll all help get it polished. I'll have to look at what this Katie person offers before deciding, but certainly we need a tray of party sandwiches. Finger-size, of course, with some pinwheels and open-faced and different shapes and sizes. Something cheese, either a spread or cheese straws, or both. And, I think, since there'll be men, we should have a standing rib roast with rolls and condiments to go with it. Oh, let me put this down; we'll need someone to slice it at the table as people go around. Now, what else?"

"You need a fruit tray with some a that poppy-seed dressin' for dippin', an' that big glass bowl filled with shrimps on ice. An' some of them little tarts that make two bites for the ladies and one for the menfolk," she said, as I nodded, writing fast to keep up with her. "An' something hot in yo' silver chafin' dish, meatballs of some kind. Better put down toothpicks 'cause you ain't got but twenny-four of yo' good silver forks, which I know won't be enough."

"We'll get out Mr. Springer's mother's silver. And her china, too. I don't like the pattern of either one, but they come in handy for a big do. And that's another thing, Lillian, we've got to decide how many people we can accommodate and let Binkie know so she can make her list. She wanted a small wedding, and I'm afraid that's what she's going to get."

"I don't know why you talkin' like that. There been a hundred people in this house before."

"Yes, I know, but those were coffees and teas when we could stagger the guest list. These people'll be here all at one time, and they'll have to be seated. It's going to get crowded."

"We could always put the ceremony on the TV and set up out in the yard and the porch and the garage, like Billy Graham do."

I gasped in sudden dismay. *"Lillian!"*

"What! Law, what is it?"

"Music! I just thought of it. What're we going to do for music? I don't have an organ or a piano and, goodness knows, I couldn't play either, if I did. What in the world are we going to do?"

"Why, just rent one."

"Can you do that?"

"I don' see why not. You can rent everythin' else."

"What about somebody to play the thing? With all those weddings scheduled at the church, I expect the organist and the pianist and the choir director have already been taken."

"You can ast 'em, see if they know somebody else and, if they don', Miss Mattie Mae Morgan at the Harvest House AME Zion church could do it for you. She a good piano player, I don' know how she do with no organ, though. 'Course you might not want a ebony person playin' in yo' house."

"Don't be silly, Lillian," I said, waving my hand. "If she can play any kind of instrument, I want her. Just no accordions."

I bent over my pad, jotting down the various ideas as they came to us. I always say that if you want things done right, you have to get yourself organized.

I lifted my head with a sudden thought. *"Lillian!"*

"What!" She jerked upright from the counter where she'd been leaning. "Law, what is it?"

"I just thought of something else. What kind of beverage should we serve?"

"Why, tea and coffee, same as always. And maybe some punch, lemonade or somethin', in yo' silver punch bowl, an' I wisht you'd stop scarin' me to death, yellin' like that."

"Punch," I said, tapping my teeth with the pen. "I know what some people'll expect at a wedding, at least for the toasts. And I do want something festive, but they're going to have to be disappointed if they expect anything stronger in my house. Wesley Lloyd would turn over in his grave." Not that I gave two cents for any disturbance of his eternal rest.

"Why don' we serve some kinda punch that go with Miss Binkie's color scheme? That what you us'lly do, anyway. You got recipes for pink, green and orange for when you have them Ladies of the Church meetin's. And red for Christmas."

"Yes, and I'm sick of them. None of them are special enough for a wedding, much less this one which has been so long in coming. Think about it, Lillian, they're all made with ginger ale. For the pink, you put in strawberries; the green is made with limeade and food coloring; the orange is just ginger ale poured over orange sherbet until it's a mushy mess. I mean, they're the kind of things you serve to children and old ladies. I want something different and, well, special."

Hazel Marie and Little Lloyd pushed through the swinging door into the kitchen. "I didn't know you were back, Miss Julia," Hazel Marie said. "What can I do to help?"

"Have a seat, and help me decide what to serve to drink at the wedding."

Hazel Marie started smiling, then she said, "Well, I know what Binkie'd want."

"What?"

"Beer. She loves that stuff."

"Think of something else," I said, knowing when I was being teased. "Your hands washed, Little Lloyd? Lillian's ready to put supper on the table."

"Yessum, I just washed them." But who could tell the way he was working that Game Boy thing, both thumbs flying?

"I know what you can serve, Miss Julia," Hazel Marie said. "What about that sparkling grape juice they have in the grocery store? It looks like champagne and tastes real good. Miss Mildred Allen served some at her Christmas tea, remember?"

"You mean that wasn't champagne? And here I've been thinking bad thoughts about her ever since."

"No'm, it's nonalcoholic, but I expect a lot of people wouldn't know the difference if you wrapped the bottles in a towel."

"Then that's what we'll do, if you're sure we won't be leading some poor soul astray.

Far be it from me to be the cause of anybody's downfall."

I wrote down sparkling grape juice and hoped nobody'd make the mistake I'd made at Mildred Allen's Christmas tea and think the worst of me.

Chapter 5

"Car turnin' in," Lillian said, as Hazel Marie and I straggled in for breakfast the next morning. She wiped her hands on a kitchen towel and looked out the window. "I better put on some more eggs; it's Coleman in that deputy car of his."

"Wonder what he's doing here so early?" I asked, making sure my bathrobe was presentable. "Although I'm always glad to see him. In fact, it'd suit me to see a little more of him around here."

Hazel Marie tried to hide her smile behind her coffee cup, but I knew what she was thinking. Coleman was supposed to be living right upstairs in the room and sleeping porch he rented from me, but rarely used. Sam had been worried about me being alone after the terminal departure of Wesley Lloyd. So, since Coleman Bates had just moved back to Abbotsville after getting his law enforcement training on the streets of Atlanta, Sam had talked me into taking him in as a boarder. Coleman was pretty much alone in the world, a fact that had reassured me about having his family and friends in and out of my house. Even so, I'd had my doubts about taking in a boarder, but it'd worked out fine until Coleman'd met Binkie Enloe, and from then on, we hardly ever saw him. Oh, he showed up now and then to have one of Lillian's meals, and occasionally he'd spend the night to justify, I guessed, the rent he kept on paying. I try not to think about where he spent the other nights, although I am on record as strongly disapproving. But far be it from me to pass judgment on what other people do.

I didn't have to worry about that any longer though, since, thank goodness, they'd be safely married, come Saturday afternoon.

"Morning, folks," Coleman said, as he came in the back door looking shined and polished in his dark navy deputy's uniform with official badges and insignia on his shirt and leather-creaking law enforcement equipment dangling from his belt. "Lillian, you look good enough to eat."

She laughed and ducked her head. He was her favorite, except for Little Lloyd. "I'm fixin' yo' breakfast, so get yo'self set down and ready for it."

I cleared a place at the table while Hazel Marie set out a place mat and silverware for him.

"How are you, Coleman?" I asked, and received a beaming smile in answer. My goodness, his uniform certainly set off his trim physique. I'm not too old to appreciate a fine broad-shouldered young man, especially one with blond hair and deep blue eyes and good manners. And one whose happiness glowed on his face. That's the way a bridegroom should look, I thought.

Still smiling, Coleman held out his hand for Little Lloyd to shake. "How you doing, bud?"

"Real good," Little Lloyd said, hero worship glowing on his face. As the boy shook Coleman's hand, it did my heart good to see how he'd picked up on so many of Coleman's manly virtues. Although I needed to speak to the child about offering such a limp hand.

Then Coleman took a chair and held his cup for me to pour coffee. While he waited for Lillian to fix his plate, I brought him up to date with the wedding plans. "Be ready for some serious dinner table discussion tonight. You and Binkie come on along about seven. Hazel Marie, be sure and tell Mr. Pickens we're expecting him, too."

"You heard from him lately?" Coleman asked Hazel Marie. When she shook her head, Coleman went on. "Binkie's keeping him busy, I expect. She's hired him to investigate some case she's just taken."

"Well, I'm glad somebody knows what he's doing," Hazel Marie said, a little sharply, too. "I haven't heard a word from him."

I wanted to tell her that, given Mr. Pickens's type, she'd better get used to his independent ways.

"I saw him this morning for a minute at Binkie's office," Coleman said, as I passed the cream pitcher to him.

"They're working on Saturday?" Hazel Marie asked, obviously disappointed. "I thought sure he'd be off."

"Yeah, well, Binkie's got a bee in her bonnet about that case. Anyway, I said something about dinner tonight. Was that all right, Miss Julia?"

"Of course. Is he coming?"

"He said if that slave driver I'm about to marry will let him, he will." Coleman shook his head, smiling. "That girl's a pistol."

"I can't wait to see him," Hazel Marie said, brightening considerably.

"Y'all heard the news?" Coleman asked, as he set to work on the plate of bacon, eggs and grits that Lillian set before him.

"What news?" Lillian asked, standing over him to see if he wanted anything else. "I don't never turn on the radio or the TV till Miss Julia outta the kitchen."

Coleman grinned and said, "That little spot of trouble we had at the jail yesterday was an escaped prisoner."

"Oh, no!" Hazel Marie said, while Lillian turned her face to the ceiling and said, "He'p us, Lord."

"Who?" I asked.

He glanced up at me, his eyes smiling. "Dixon Hightower. Remember him?"

"Well, I should say I do. I thought that little rascal was locked up for good."

"We did too. He was put away as a habitual violator, a three-time loser, a few years ago. But some liberal lawyer wrangled him a new trial, which is how he escaped.

They transferred him from Raleigh to our jail for the hearing, and, well, he got away from the jailer." Coleman just shook his head. "Embarrassing as hell, you want to know the truth."

"That sounds just like him," I said. "Dixon Hightower's nothing but a nuisance, but you have to watch him like a hawk."

"Yes, ma'am, we learned that the hard way. A couple of deputies may lose their jobs over this. Problem is, we haven't caught him yet."

"You mean he's still loose?" Hazel Marie's eyes widened at the thought. "The jail's not but four or five blocks from here. Why, he could be right under our feet, and us not know it. I can't stand the thought of somebody sneaking right up on me."

"Oh," Little Lloyd said and put his fork down.

"Hey, it's okay," Coleman said, noticing the child's peaked look. "Dixon's not going to hurt anybody, just pester us to death, that's all. We'll have him back behind bars in no time. But, Miss Julia, you should take some reasonable measures, like keeping your doors locked. You know how he is."

"Well, my Lord," I said, thinking to myself

that I didn't need this worry added to the full week's worth I already had. "He ought to have a good whipping, with all the turmoil he's put this town through. I remember Pastor Ledbetter going out of his way to help him and bring him into the church. Talked until he was blue in the face about the vice of stealing, for all the good it did. The pastor told Dixon that he should be trusting the Lord to provide for his needs and not be stealing what belonged to other people. Problem was, though, Dixon didn't *need* any of the things he stole; he just picked up whatever took his eye."

I sighed, recalling the many futile efforts so many had made to reform the unreformable. "And Dixon's poor mother tried her best with him, but some people just can't be helped. I can't remember a day of his life when he wasn't stealing something from somebody. Why, you couldn't put your laundry out on a line without half of it being gone when you went back."

"It wasn't just laundry, Miss Julia," Hazel Marie reminded me. "He was bad for sneaking into people's houses, when they were home, too, and taking anything he could pick up, although I never heard of him taking anything of much value. He liked odds and ends. But there're people who've sworn their doors were locked, then looked up and saw Dixon inside the house." She frowned at the thought. "I don't know how he does it, but he can get in anywhere."

"And out, too, it seems," I said. "As the sheriff has so recently found, no offense to you, Coleman."

Little Lloyd was taking this all in, his eyes wide behind his glasses. Coleman reached over and ruffled his hair. "Don't you be worrying about Dixon. He's holed up somewhere, laughing at us. Soon as he sticks his head out, we'll snatch him up so fast he won't know what hit him."

"I sure hope so," Little Lloyd said. "If anybody can catch him, I know you can."

"Just let me at him." Coleman laughed, then laying his napkin beside his plate, he got to his feet. "Got to get back to it. 'Preciate the breakfast, Lillian, it ought to hold me till I get some more of your good cooking tonight. Now, you folks keep your doors latched. I don't want anybody dropping in on you."

As he started toward the door, he turned back and said, "Almost forgot. Binkie asked me to give you this, Miss Julia. It's our invitation list."

"Good. We'll get on the phone right away."

Lillian stuck a Ziploc bag filled with cookies into Coleman's hand, as his radio erupted with static. He gave her one of his quick grins, waved to us and jogged to his patrol car, his head turned to speak into the radio on his shoulder.

"Lock that door while you're there," I said to Lillian.

"That's what I'm doin'," she said, but I hardly heard her for thinking of Dixon Hightower, the town thief, now a man on the run. I remembered him as no more than a child in his mind, although he had to be at least forty years old by now. Dixon had never gotten his full growth, his mother having to buy his clothes from the Belk's boys' department. Not that it did any good. Dixon didn't like to bathe, or change clothes, either. He had a sly way about him, always scuttling along from one end of town to the other, picking up bottles for the deposit. He kept a smile on his face, though, just as friendly as he could be while he was robbing you blind.

"His poor mother," I said. "It's a good

thing she's dead and gone, and not having to witness what Dixon's up to now. But I'll tell you one thing, he'd better not mess with me while I'm busy with this wedding."

Thinking about that possibility put me on edge, especially when I saw Little Lloyd press his hand against his stomach, which occasionally got queasy on him. He was a nervous child. I patted his arm, and glanced out the window half-expecting to see that little pest tiptoeing from one boxwood to the other.

"He better not try stealing anything 'round here," Lillian said, brandishing the heavy iron pan that she cooked cornbread in. "He gonna meet this arn skillet, if he do."

Then Little Lloyd said, "Mama, I'm supposed to go to a meeting at the church this afternoon."

"Oh, honey," she said. "I don't think you ought to go anywhere today. I don't want to take the chance of you running into Dixon Hightower. Let's wait till they get him back in jail."

"He wouldn't hurt you, Little Lloyd," I said, entirely agreeing with his mother but not wanting to give him nightmares. "All he'd do is sneak up on you and scare you half to death. Then he'd pick your pocket clean as a whistle."

After a while Little Lloyd looked from one to the other of us. "Mama? I don't think I can miss that meeting. Miz Ledbetter'll be mad as thunder at me."

"Emma Sue Ledbetter!" I said. "What kind of meeting is she having?"

"She wants to start a young people's group. She came to our Sunday school class last week and said she wanted everybody between nine and twelve years old to show up today and not be late. She meant it, too." He rubbed his stomach.

I heaved a sigh that would've blown out a candle. "Wouldn't you know, she's at it again. I declare, I don't know why the pastor didn't take her with him." I stopped, because I knew why he'd left his wife at home while he led a church group on a tour of the Holy Land. The both of them poor-mouthed around for months, making sure every member knew that his salary couldn't cover two airline tickets. They wanted the deacons to give him a bonus or raise his salary or, barring that, they would've accepted a love-offering for her expenses. But the pastor already had every member, except me, pledged up to the hilt to pay for that Family Life Center he was so determined to build. The man could get blood out of a turnip, so there were a number of fairly anemic-looking people in the congregation who weren't at all interested in providing an expense-paid vacation for his wife. Even if it was an educational trip and they planned to get rebaptized in the river Jordan.

"Not that I'm against a young people's group, you understand," I said to Little Lloyd. "I think it's a good idea. But Emma Sue Ledbetter is known to have spells of do-good activities which she can't seem to help. I remember the time her heart was burdened about the babies in the nursery on Sunday mornings because they needed grandmotherly attention. She went around badgering every white-headed woman in the congregation to sign up for nursery duty. As if, by the time you're sixty, you'd be thrilled at the opportunity to change diapers again."

I propped my chin on my hand, remembering the havoc she'd created with that proposal. "The pastor was gone then, too, at General Assembly, I think. You wouldn't believe the hornets' nest he came back to, because Presbyterian women, and men, too, for that matter, don't like both the pastor and his wife getting calls from the Lord. It's confusing, to say the least."

I stopped then, because I'm not one to criticize either the pastor or his wife in the presence of young children. Even when one or both needed it.

"Don't worry about the meeting, Lloyd," Hazel Marie told him, patting his hand. "We're just being careful so, if you have to miss it, I'm sure Mrs. Ledbetter'll understand."

"I hope so," he said, not at all convinced. "She said she expected me to be there, come what may. Come what may, that's what she said right in front of the whole class."

"It'll be all right," I said, smoothing down the cowlick that was standing straight up at the back of his head. He needed to be sleeping in a stocking to tame the thing. "I'll call and tell her that today's not a good day. Besides, I think your stomach's feeling a little uneasy."

I didn't mention the fact that when Emma Sue Ledbetter got on her high horse, she put my stomach in the same state of contention. Emma Sue and I had never seen eye to eye on a number of matters. For instance, if she was in charge of a Women of the Church meeting, as she usually was, she never failed to call on me to offer the prayer. I just hated to pray in public and she knew it, since I'd told her time out of mind not to call on me.

"Julia," she'd once told me, a note of exasperation in her voice at having to instruct me again. "As Christians, we should always be ready to pray, preach or die."

"You may be ready, Emma Sue," I'd said, "but I'd just as soon wait on all three. Call on somebody else from now on."

But from then on, she'd been concerned about my prayer life, giving me books and tracts to read, offering to have one-on-one prayer with me, wanting to be my prayer partner and warning me that prayer was the way to sanctification which, if I didn't watch out, I'd never reach.

Don't you just hate to be given spiritual advice from somebody who needs a bigger dose of it than you?

Chapter 6

"My word," I said as I looked over the invitation list Coleman had given me. "They haven't given any thought to this at all. I'll just have to add some names to it; I can think of a dozen right off the top of my head who should be here.

"Now, Hazel Marie, and you, too, Lillian, help me with what else we have to do today. Florist, for one thing. I'll call The Watering Can, and get them lined up. Who else?"

"Photographer?" Hazel Marie said.

"Oh, goodness, yes. I'll give that job to you, Hazel Marie. Call around until you find one, although with all the weddings scheduled for next weekend, it may take you a while. But stay on it until you do; we have to have pictures. What else?"

"You call that catering lady?" Lillian asked.

"She's on my list to call this morning. And

I'd better put down Emma Sue Ledbetter and tell her to cancel that meeting Saturday afternoon," I grumbled, jotting down her name. "Who ever heard of having a church meeting on Saturday? The church takes up enough time as it is."

"What you want me to cook for tonight? An' how many people you havin'?"

"Well, let's see. Coleman and Binkie, of course. Hazel Marie and Mr. Pickens. That's four, and I make five. Five, Lillian."

"You not gonna ast Mr. Sam? That way the table be even out. Man, woman, man, woman, man, woman."

That stopped me because I had to think about it. Coleman and Binkie both thought the world of Sam, and ordinarily I wouldn't think twice about inviting him. But it'd been ten days since I'd heard from him, and two could play that game. So I said, "I hadn't planned on it. Besides, Little Lloyd can even out the table if that's all you're worried about."

"Don't make no difference to me. But you gonna get yo' nose stuck so high up in the air, you won't see what right in front of yo' face, you don't watch out."

Continuing to grumble under her breath,

she banged a pan on the stove, and Hazel Marie and I left to start making our phone calls. For the first time I saw the sense in Hazel Marie having her own line, when all the time before I'd thought it was an unnecessary expense just to be able to talk to Mr. Pickens in private.

"Well, Lillian," I said, pushing through the swinging door into the kitchen a little while later. "I hope you're happy. I've invited Sam, and a good thing, too, because Coleman has asked him to be the best man. So now we'll have an uneven number at the table because I want Little Lloyd, too. Let's put the boy opposite me at the foot of the table. Binkie on my right and Coleman on my left, since they're the guests of honor. Then Hazel Marie and Mr. Pickens opposite each other in the middle. Sam can sit on Little Lloyd's right, opposite nobody."

"Guess that'll fix him," she said, half under her breath. "If he notice."

"Don't give me a hard time, Lillian. That man's made my life a misery lately, blowing hot and cold like he's been doing. Now, what're we going to serve?"

"I already took that tenderloin roast outta the freezer."

"That'll be good. Let's do oven-roasted new potatoes, and see if you can find fresh asparagus; call Mr. Wheeler's store and have it delivered. If you can't get fresh, get the canned and make that casserole with the cheese on top. A nice salad and some of your yeast rolls. And whatever you feel like making for dessert. You know I don't eat dessert, so whatever you want will be fine. The men will love anything you fix."

"What about that lemon chiffon pie what Coleman like so much?"

"Perfect. I might even have a small piece myself."

Hazel Marie, in her downstairs bedroom, and I, on the upstairs line, spent the morning hours on the telephone issuing invitations. In between calls to guests, I managed to line up the florist, the caterer and a rented piano. On top of that, I spent futile time looking for someone whose piano playing was better known to me than Lillian's friend from the AME Zion church. Half the people we called were not in or closed on Saturday. I declare, planning a wedding was a lot more involved than planning a tea, which I could've done in my sleep.

On my way downstairs, I looked in on Hazel Marie. She was talking on the phone to someone, so she waved happily at me as I went on to the kitchen.

"Lillian," I said, "where's Little Lloyd?"

"He settin' on the back steps ruinin' his eyes with that Gametoy."

"Boy," I said.

She glanced at me, frowning. "What boy?"

"Game Boy, not toy." I opened the screen door. "Little Lloyd, I have a job for you, if you don't mind."

"No'm, I don't mind."

"I want you to take the hose and wash off the front porch, the front walk and the driveway. There's brick dust and plaster dust and every other kind of dust everywhere you look from that construction site. Hose off as much of it as you can, and give the boxwoods a good spraying. They're coated with it, too. We want it all looking nice for our guests tonight."

He got up from the steps and put his Game Boy in his pocket. "It sure does need it. And I better weed the flower beds some, too." He cut his eyes at me and grinned. "That's what I get the big money for, isn't it?"

"Your allowance is plenty adequate, you little rascal," I said, smiling back. "But, Little Lloyd, stay in the yard. Your mother'll worry about you if you wander off."

And I would, too. Not that I was concerned about Dixon Hightower, who was probably already back behind bars, but I always felt better when I knew where the child was.

As he got the hose from the garage, I went back in to set the dining room table for Lillian. Before I got out of the kitchen, though, Hazel Marie came running in.

"Miss Julia, guess what!"

I'd never seen her so excited, so I guessed: "Mr. Pickens wants to get married!"

"Oh!" She had a momentary drop in her excitement level, but it didn't last long. "No, that's not it, but I just talked to Binkie. You know, just to be sure that J.D.'ll be here tonight. And he will, but she said she was about to call me. Miss Julia, you won't believe this, but she wants me to be her bridesmaid! Should I do it, Miss Julia? What do you think?"

I couldn't bring myself to say what I really thought, which was that Binkie was headstrong and gave little or no thought to how things would look. So I mentally bit my lip and said, "Why, of course you should and I think it's fine."

Hazel Marie was all of forty and maybe a little more, to say nothing of the fact that she hardly qualified as a maid. If that meant what I thought it did.

"Well, see," Hazel Marie said, "I thought she maybe ought to ask somebody she's known longer. You know, one of her college friends or someone she works with."

"I wouldn't worry about that, Hazel Marie. She wouldn't've asked you if she hadn't wanted you. Who else is she asking?"

"Just me! And Coleman'll have Sam to stand up for him. Oh, this is so exciting! What do I wear? What does a bridesmaid do? I've never been one before."

Hazel Marie looked for all the world like one of those skinny little models, except for being uncommonly large above the waist. I thought to myself that all my lessons on hair treatment and correct attire had taken root and grown. Although some of them had grown in directions I was unprepared for, like hemlines halfway to Christmas. But she was as pretty as she could be, and if Mr. Pickens could've seen her in her present state, he would've married her in a minute.

"Binkie'll decide on your dress. Lord, I hope she'll have time to do at least that. All you have to do is get it fitted if it needs it. As for what you do, we'd better get out Miss Vanderbilt's etiquette book so we don't forget anything. Ordinarily, the bridesmaids give a party for the bride, but there's no time for that. Let's see, I think they help her dress for the ceremony, and just be available for whatever she needs."

"I'm just so excited. But, Miss Julia," she said, leaning close with a frown on her face. "You don't think I'm too old, do you? I mean, to be a brides*maid*? That just means somebody who's never been married, doesn't it? And I haven't but, well, there's Little Lloyd, does he count?"

It took all I could do to keep from rolling my eyes. Of course he counted, but if you wanted to be legalistic about it then maid did mean unmarried and that's what she was and might continue to be. Unfortunately.

"Times change, Hazel Marie, and we

have to change with them. This wedding's going to be one of a kind already. So I say let's do what Binkie wants, within reason, of course, and she wants you."

"Oh, that's such a relief," she said. "You always know the right thing to do, and I so wanted you to say it was all right. I'm so thrilled I don't know what to do. Oh, I know, I'll ask Binkie to go to lunch next week. That'd be a correct thing to do, wouldn't it, Miss Julia?"

"Perfectly correct and a lovely thought. You can offer to run errands for her or do whatever she needs doing."

"Oh, this is wonderful!" She ran over and gave me a less-than-welcome hug. Being around Mr. Pickens so much was making her more demonstrative than I was accustomed to.

Then she headed for the door. "I can't wait to tell J.D.; maybe I can reach him on his car phone. This is going to be so much fun!"

When the door closed behind her, I sank down into a chair and sighed. "Lillian," I said, "there went the oldest living bridesmaid, and thrilled to death about it."

"You jus' let her have her enjoys, an' don't say nothin' to bring her down."

"Have I said anything?" I demanded. "All I'm trying to do is keep this wedding within the bounds of propriety."

"I don't know 'bout no bounds. Le's jus' get Coleman and Miss Binkie married an' worry 'bout bounds later on."

"That's exactly what I intend to do. I declare, Lillian, have you ever heard of so many people living together without benefit of marriage, just as bold and brazen as they can be? I really think I'm doing my civic duty, to say nothing of my spiritual duty, to get those two publicly married so everybody in town will know it. And as for Hazel Marie, well, she and Mr. Pickens know how I feel about their situation. But they've both been burned before, so I'm trying to understand that they want to try it out first.

"But I'll tell you this," I went on. "If everybody tried it out first, there'd be a lot fewer marriages in the world."

Lillian laughed, nodding her head. "Yessum, and if I'd knowed what I was gettin' into, I'd a never got into it."

"Well, at least she can be a part of

Binkie's wedding and that may do her and Mr. Pickens some good. Maybe they'll see what they're missing. Oh, my goodness," I said, looking at the clock. "I've got to call Emma Sue Ledbetter. That child'll worry himself to death until I get that meeting straightened out."

Emma Sue answered her phone with a questioning "Hello?", like she wasn't sure anybody'd be on the other end.

"Emma Sue, this is Julia Springer, and I'm calling to tell you that Little Lloyd won't be at your meeting today. He's needed here at home."

She sighed in that martyred way of hers. "You're the fifth person this morning to cancel out. I guess I'll just have to call it off."

"That's too bad," I said, not meaning it at all. "But maybe that tells you something about having it on Saturday."

"I don't know, Julia," she said in a soft whine. "I try so hard, you just don't know how hard I try, and people let any little incident get in the way of the Lord's work. Why, for example, I've misplaced my favorite tortoiseshell hairbrush, can't find it anywhere and I've looked this house over for it. Put it on your prayer list, Julia, if you will." She paused to gather herself, while I tightened my grip on the telephone. "I know a lot of people would let something like that distract them from their daily walk, but I just make it a matter of prayer."

"Good for you, Emma Sue," I said, anxious to distract her from the subject of praying, which she didn't think I did enough of. But what did she know? Just because I didn't talk about it all the time, much less air my business for the titillation of the prayer chain, didn't mean I wasn't doing my share of it. "But what does a hairbrush have to do with anything?"

"Well, it's just an example of how we let little things divert us from our main business. And another example is the fact that everybody's scared to death of Dixon Hightower when they ought to be trusting in the Lord. That's why they're keeping their children home, and that's what I know you're doing, too, Julia. Well." She sighed. "I guess I can't blame you, but it's setting a bad example for the children and, who knows, maybe starting a dozen more Dixon Hightowers on their way."

"Oh," I said, waving my hand even

though she couldn't see it. "That's most un-likely, Emma Sue. Besides, I couldn't give a flip for Dixon Hightower; if he's not back in jail by now, he's hiding in the woods or, most likely, he's up in the mountains where he'll stay until the snows come."

"I don't worry about him, either, because my trust is in the Lord. But I guess I can't expect everybody to be like me." She sighed again, like she'd all but given up on the human race, and I had to struggle to keep from giving in and sending Little Lloyd to her meeting.

Before I could assure her that she wasn't alone in her faith, she sniffed and blew her nose. Oh, Lord, I thought, she's going to start clouding up, which she did when-ever anybody in the congregation disap-pointed her.

She sniffed again and murmured, "I was really counting on Lloyd being there. He could be a leader, I know he could, if he'd buckle down, and our little group could be just the thing to bring him out."

I sat up so straight I almost pulled my back out. Emma Sue was a fine one to be making critical comments about how any child was raised.

"Little Lloyd's already been brought out as far as he needs to be, Emma Sue. Now, he'll try to be at your next meeting and, if he likes it, we'll send him every time."

"Oh, Julia." And I had to wait while she fought her disappointment in me, swallowing a sob as she did so. "You can't let a child decide what's right on the basis of whether he likes it or not. You have to tell him what to do and see that he does it. Of course," she said, "you wouldn't know that, since you've never had any children of your own, would you?"

I got off the phone after that little jab as soon as I could, so mad I could've spit nails. There she was, telling me how to raise a child when her own were walking examples of how not to. Her two boys were grown by now, one off in Los Angeles somewhere looking for himself, and you know what that means. And the other, the last I heard, was working for the Democratic Party in Washington, D.C., which in the eyes of the pastor and Emma Sue was worse than being in California.

Chapter 7

It's a settled fact that when you have more than enough to fill your day, something unexpected will come knocking at your door. Or in this case ringing your telephone. I had just put the phone down after making several more calls to extend invitations to the wedding, when it rang under my hand.

"Mrs. Springer?" It was a voice that I didn't at first recognize, but she went on to firmly and forcefully identify herself. "This is Etta Mae Wiggins. You know, I was Mr. Sam Murdoch's home nurse that time he broke his leg? And I rent a space from you in the Hillandale Trailer Park? Well, I'm calling to let you know that we're having some trouble out here."

I was silent for a minute, trying to place the Hillandale Trailer Park. I had no trouble placing Etta Mae Wiggins. Her image immediately flew into my mind, and I just as immediately was on my guard. Yes, I remembered the small, curly-headed, dyed-blond little snip; the one who was all over Sam pretending to take care of him, and the one with the checkered marital history. And some even more garish unmarital history, as well, if the tales told around town were true.

The trailer park was another matter. I had vague recollections of the list of properties that Wesley Lloyd had owned, none of which I'd known about until he was dead and gone. I'd been amazed at the number and variety of businesses that he'd invested in: convenience stores, gas stations, an office building, retail buildings, a car wash, untold numbers of undeveloped acres and yes, a couple of trailer parks. He'd never said a word to me about any of them because, I later learned, he didn't run them, just collected rent. Which I still did, although it all came to Binkie's office through Mr. Willis Carter, my so-called properties manager. He was supposed to handle these matters, because I didn't want to be bothered with them.

So why was this woman calling me about trouble out there?

"Ah, yes, Miss Wiggins," I said. "I believe you want to get in touch with Mr. Carter. He manages things for me, and he'll know how to take care of any problems you might have."

"I've tried that, Mrs. Springer, and I can't find him. In fact, we can never find him unless somebody hasn't paid their rent on time, then he finds us. I've also called the sheriff's department, and I might as well not've found them, either, because they haven't done a thing."

"The sheriff's department! What on earth made you call the sheriff?"

"There's a thief out here! I tell you, Mrs. Springer, something has to be done." The woman's voice was getting more heated by the minute.

"You mean somebody living there is a thief? Why, I'll have him evicted first thing Monday. Who is it?"

"No, ma'am, it's not anybody living here. At least, we don't think so, since everybody's been here for so long and this has just started." She'd calmed down by this time, but I could hear the concern in her voice. Still, she had a nerve calling me over something even the sheriff couldn't handle.

"Well," I said, "if you don't know who it is, what can I do about it?"

I heard her take a deep breath, then she said, "I would think that, as the owner of this place, you'd want to take some measures to increase security. The pole lights're out all the time, so that it's pitch-black at night. There's no fencing anywhere, so that anybody can come in anytime they want to from any direction. Why, when I have to go out at night to see one of my patients, I never know who's going to be hiding in the bushes. It's dangerous out here, Mrs. Springer, and, well, we need something done about it."

"I'll have Mr. Carter replace the lights as soon as I can reach him, and I'll tell him to keep them in good repair. But, as far as a fence is concerned, Miss Wiggins, I believe there're several acres out there. Do you know what it'd cost to enclose all that?"

"Mrs. Springer," she said, and I could hear her voice getting tighter. "I just know that everybody out here has had things stolen from them, and I know that sooner or later somebody's going to get hurt. And a lawsuit against you would cost more than any fence, I don't care how many acres it went around."

"A lawsuit! Young lady, are you threatening me?"

"No, ma'am, I'm not. I'm just passing on what I've heard others say who live here. Just come out here, Mrs. Springer, and see what we have to put up with."

"All right, I will," I said, determined to stop this little matter in its tracks. Just nip it in the bud, before she disrupted my already busy week with more phone calls. "I'll come right now, even though I have my hands more than full here. How will I find you?"

She gave me directions to her trailer, and I put the phone down with a trembling hand. A lawsuit! I declare, everybody and his brother was suing people right and left. But, to sue *me*? The idea of being threatened with civil action made my blood boil. Mr. Carter had a lot to answer for, and believe you me, I intended to see that he did.

———

By the time I drove to Delmont and beyond, out Springer Road toward the Hillandale Trailer Park, I was even more incensed. Little Lloyd accompanied me, sitting in the passenger seat, occasionally cutting his eyes at me with concern.

"Little Lloyd," I said, "I'll tell you one

thing. It is a heavy responsibility to own things. If it's not a roof leaking, it's a furnace that's out. And as the owner, you are responsible for seeing that it's fixed, even when it's an act of God, as the insurance people say. And does it come at a convenient time? No, sir, it does not. Just let yourself get busy with something important, and here comes another complaint. Or insurance bill. Or tax bill. Well." I sighed. "Heavy hangs the head that bears the burden."

"Ma'am?"

"I'm just saying that I'm glad you came with me. It'll be good for you to see what you're in for as a property owner. Eventually, you'll be taking care of what you own, and maybe mine as well. In fact, if I remember right, this is one of the properties that belongs to both of us. So take note."

I turned in at the gravel road that ran through the middle of Hillandale Trailer Park. Gravel had run off the side, leaving ruts and ridges in the road, and I had to slow considerably. Dust boiled up behind us, settling across the trailers as we passed.

"I guess," I murmured, "I ought to have this scraped and more gravel put on."

"Yes, ma'am," Little Lloyd said, as he

looked out his window at the grassless yards and the metal trailers baking in the sun. Lord, it was barely June. What would it be like in August?

"Maybe," he went on, "you could have the road paved, and cut down on some of this dust."

"That'd be nice, I'm sure. But an owner has to balance out his income with his expenses, and not get too carried away." I leaned over to look through the side window. "I believe this is where Miss Wiggins lives. You remember her, don't you? She was visiting when the power went out in that last ice storm we had." The one who'd made a fool of herself over that race-truck driver, I almost said but didn't.

"Yessum, I do. She was Mr. Sam's nurse who he liked so much."

"Huh," I said under my breath. Then, "Now, Little Lloyd, you must learn to treat all people with respect, especially those who don't have as much as you do. This young woman apparently has nowhere else to live but in a tin trailer on rented property, although I must say her place looks better kept than most of them." I turned in behind an old, sagging car that I recognized as

Miss Wiggins's, and looked around. There was a plastic awning over the door on the side of the trailer that threw a green shadow over a poured concrete porch. An aluminum chair and a pot of geraniums decorated the entrance.

"Well, let's see if we can get through this without too much trouble," I said, opening the car door.

Little Lloyd followed me to the shade of the awning, but before I could knock on the door, Miss Wiggins opened it and stepped out to meet us. Right there, she made her first mistake with me. She should've invited us inside, unless there was something or somebody she didn't want us to see.

"Miss Wiggins," I said, acknowledging her with a formal nod of my head. "I've come to see what the problem is, and I sincerely hope that there'll be no more talk of a lawsuit."

"Yes, ma'am, but it's not me that's talking lawsuit. I was just passing on what I'd heard."

She looked ill at ease, standing there clasping her hands together. I imagined that she was remembering the run-ins we'd had at our other meetings, from which I'd always come out the better.

"Well, tell me what's going on. Oh, excuse me," I said, taken up short for forgetting my own courtesies. "You remember Little Lloyd, don't you? Say hello to Miss Wiggins, Little Lloyd."

He smiled and held out his hand, making me proud. "Hello, Miss Wiggins."

"Hi," she said, a broad smile lighting up her face. It pained me to admit it, but she was not unattractive. Her personality, though, was another matter. Grating, I'd call it. She shook the child's hand, and asked about his mother. I kept forgetting that Hazel Marie had grown up around this part of the county, and that Miss Wiggins was surely familiar with Hazel Marie's long-term attachment to my husband.

For that matter, she knew who Little Lloyd was, too. That meant she could see right through me. Suddenly I didn't feel at all comfortable in her presence.

"Now, Miss Wiggins, we don't have all day, so tell me what's going on."

"Well, everybody in the park, just about, has been missing things." She turned and pointed down the graveled street. "The Barnhardts in that second trailer over there are missing a yard chair. The Crenshaws're missing a barbeque grill, and Miguel Martinez's remote control is gone. And that was from *inside* his trailer." She turned and pointed in the other direction. "Carrie Munson, who lives about five trailers down, lost every bag of Fritos and potato chips she had, and she'd just gone to the Wal-Mart super store to stock up. And I'm missing two bags of hard candy that I keep to give to my elderly patients. A lot of them don't have enough teeth to chew, but they love the hard kind that'll melt in their mouths. Now it's all gone."

Her shoulders seemed to slump with the injustice of it all. Then with renewed energy, she said, "Just all of a sudden, seems like, things're missing from one trailer or the other. Oh, and my neighbor across the street there, her son's bicycle is gone. And it had a flat tire. I mean, who would want it?"

"Well," I said with some relief, "it doesn't seem that anything of value has been stolen. In fact, a lot of what you mentioned could just be lost."

"No, Mrs. Springer," she said, shaking her head. "We formed like a search party, and looked all over, in and around all the trailers. Those things aren't just lost; they're gone." She closed her eyes for a second, as if she needed to gather strength. Then she looked at me straight on with her hard blue eyes, and said, "Those things may not sound like much to you, but they're things that people spent money on and not many of us can afford to spend twice on something. But the worst thing is that we never know when or where whoever it is, is going to strike next. At first we thought the same as you did, that they'd just been lost. But would everybody start losing things at the same time? I think not. And I didn't even tell you everything that's been stolen. I have a list inside. I'll get it for you."

"No need, Miss Wiggins. I understand the problem, and I'm trying to figure out what to do about it. I'll certainly see about replacing the lights, and I'll dress down Mr. Carter for his negligence. In addition, I'll speak to someone at the sheriff's department about putting a regular patrol out here. But a fence around all of this is out of the question. I think a better solution would be to assign some of the residents here to set up a watch at night. You people need to take some responsibility for looking after yourselves."

A flush spread across the young woman's

face, and I realized that *you people* might've been a poor choice of words.

She lifted her head and gave me another hard look. "I told the others we couldn't expect you to do anything and I was right. So I guess *we people* are on our own. Thank you for coming out; I'm sorry I bothered you." And she turned on her heel and went inside the trailer, closing the door firmly behind her.

"Well," I said, pursing my mouth. "If that isn't the rudest thing. Come on, Little Lloyd, no need to stand here any longer."

We got back in the car, and I drove slowly through a cloud of dust until we were on a paved road. Somehow, the farther away we went, the more troubled I was about the exchange. I knew I was right. I mean, what could I do? Still, I felt that I hadn't come off in the best light.

"Miss Julia?" Little Lloyd looked over at me. "We could hire somebody to stay out there for a while. I mean, like an off-duty deputy. Coleman told me that a lot of them take extra jobs like that."

"You think we ought to?"

"Yessum, I do." He was quiet for a minute, thinking over the problem as he usually did. "The worst thing, I think, is not knowing who's sneaking around. If I lived there, I don't think I'd ever get to sleep at night."

It'd never entered my head that I would ever live in such a place, so it surprised me that the child could picture himself doing it. "What else would you want done if you lived there?" I asked.

"I'd want that street paved. And, let me see, I guess I'd want a fence around the park. Did you see down at the end of that street? Looked like a dump on the other side of that line of trees. I'll bet there're stray dogs and, maybe, some tramps or something that pick through the trash. They could just walk right into the trailer park anytime they wanted to. And I'd want Mr. Carter fired. He's not taking care of things, Miss Julia. He should've been the one to notify you of the problems they're having."

"I declare, Little Lloyd," I said, with an approving glance. "Here I was thinking you were too tenderhearted, but I see you have a businessman's mind. All right, I think we've just had a board meeting. First thing Monday, I want you to call all the fencing companies in town and get some estimates.

Then, as soon as the wedding's over and things calm down, we'll contract for a fence. It'll cost us, but I expect we can take it off our taxes as a capital improvement. In the meanwhile, I'll deal with Mr. Carter. Just as soon as he replaces those lightbulbs, and I find somebody to replace him."

We smiled at each other, both of us pleased with our management strategy and how well we worked together. It's never too early to teach a child the ins and outs of business. Although Little Lloyd's first lesson was going to cost me an arm and a leg to fence the place in. Still, there was some satisfaction in knowing that I was thinking of doing something that Wesley Lloyd wouldn't've done in a million years.

We were on the other side of Delmont by the time Little Lloyd worked himself up to another worry.

"Miss Julia? I bet I know who's doing all that stealing."

"Who?"

"I bet it's that ole Dixon Hightower, don't you?"

Chapter 8

That night, as Lillian cleared the table before serving her lemon chiffon pie, I brought my guests up to date on what Hazel Marie and I had accomplished during the day.

Then Binkie got down to business. "So what's left to do, Miss Julia? Sounds like everything's about done."

"Not even halfway," I said. "We've been on the phone all day, and everybody we've talked to is coming. But, I'll tell you something, Binkie, there're people you've overlooked, like the sheriff, for instance. And what about a county commissioner or two and some of the judges you know? You have to think of your future, both of you. You may not be particularly close to these people, but they'll consider it an honor to be asked and they'll remember it. They can do you good down the line."

Binkie twisted her mouth, but finally gave

in. "I hate to ask them just because I'm supposed to, but okay. That'll bring the count
up to fifty or sixty, though. Can we get all of
them in here?"

"I'm sure we can. The living room will be
a nice-sized room, once I have the furniture
moved out. You'll be surprised how much
space we'll have with that heavy sofa gone,
the chairs and that huge desk. And the
whatnot that I've been wanting rid of ever
since Wesley Lloyd insisted on putting it in
there. I intend to move everything out to
make room for the chairs and piano. That
rental place closed at one o'clock today and
I had to track the man down at home. He
was pleasant enough when he heard what
all I wanted to order."

Hazel Marie, her face glowing in the light
of the candles on the table, said, "We're
going to set up the chairs so there's an aisle
for you to walk down, Binkie." Mr. Pickens
sat across from her, his black eyes watching
her every move. "It's going to be lovely."

"Where will I walk from? The kitchen and
through the dining room or from the porch?"
Binkie laughed. "Or maybe I'll swing in
through the window on a vine."

"Oh, Binkie," I said. "From the stairs, of

course. The only problem with that is if you have a dress with a train, every time you take a step down the stairs, the thing'll come swishing down around your feet and be a hazard to life and limb."

"Little Lloyd could help with that," Sam chimed in, surprising me that he knew the first thing about weddings. "He could hold it up for her as she comes down the stairs, then spread it out at the bottom. Isn't somebody supposed to do that, anyway?"

"Yes, they are, Sam," I said. "And that's an excellent idea. Little Lloyd, don't look so anxious, you'll do fine."

"I'm not going to have a train," Binkie said. "So forget that little chore, Lloyd. No, we're both going to wear jeans. Coleman's going to wear a Duke sweatshirt, and I have a Wake Forest one that'll look great with a veil."

"Oh!" I gasped. "Binkie, you can't."

"She's teasing you, Miss Julia," Coleman said, laughing.

They all joined him, laughing, and so did I after a while. Though with Binkie, you could never tell.

"Rest assured, Miss Julia," she said. "I won't shock you. In fact, I'm going to the

Asheville Mall tomorrow afternoon and look for something to wear. I'd better find it, too, because it's the only free time I'll have."

"What kind of dress will you look for?" Hazel Marie asked.

"Something plain and simple. No Southern belle type for me, all lace and satin and beads and veils. And certainly not one with a cathedral train or even the smaller one, whatever it's called."

"Chapel," I said.

"Huh?" Coleman said.

"Chapel train, the short one."

"You'll be beautiful in anything," Hazel Marie said, leaning toward her. "What're you going to wear in your hair, if you don't want a veil?"

"Oh," Binkie said, squishing up her curls with both hands, which didn't do them a bit of good. "Probably put a paper sack over it. It's just awful."

"I like it," Coleman said, smoothing down what she'd left sticking up.

"Let me fix it, Binkie," Hazel Marie said. "I'm good with hair and I'd love to do it. You know I almost went to beauty school, so I know a few tricks of the trade. We could pull it up and back from your face, leaving a few little tendrils hanging down in front. Then, maybe a little circlet of flowers right where we gather it all up. What do you think?"

"If you're willing to work with this mop, I'll be happy to let you do it. Thanks, Hazel Marie."

"If everybody's finished," I said, getting to my feet, "let's adjourn to the living room."

That was a cue for Mr. Pickens to get up and hug Lillian and give her outrageous compliments on the meal. Coleman wasn't far behind him, taking a tray out of her hands and heading to the kitchen with it. They were going to spoil her, if they didn't watch out. But I shouldn't've worried, since her favorite was still Little Lloyd, whom she invited to help her put the dishes in the dishwasher.

As we settled ourselves in the living room, Hazel Marie said, "I'm so happy to be in your wedding, Binkie. It's going to be so much fun." She reached over and put her hand on Mr. Pickens's arm. "Isn't it, J.D.?"

"Sure is," he said, and stifled a yawn.

"So," I said, as Sam scooted his chair closer to mine. I fingered the glass buttons on the bodice of my gray silk, and paid no attention to him. "You have a best man and a bridesmaid. Who else is in the wedding party? You'll need some ushers, Coleman, to show people which side of the aisle to sit on."

"All settled," Coleman said. "J.D. and Little Lloyd're going to usher, along with a couple of guys from the department."

"Oh, excellent. But tell them not to wear their uniforms. Cutaways would be the thing for the time of day. Hazel Marie, we'll have to get Little Lloyd fitted for his, first thing Monday."

"If we have to dress up," Binkie said, "I'd rather have dinner jackets. They'll look nice on a warm afternoon."

I took a deep breath, not wanting to contradict her, but it was my duty to point out the obvious. "Binkie, white dinner jackets are very handsome, but they're not worn until after seven o'clock, and since we've decided on four, I'm afraid they won't be appropriate."

"Let's do it anyway," she said, smiling as if inappropriateness was all the more reason to do it. "Nobody will know the difference. Coleman, tell them who else you've asked."

Coleman put his arm across the back of the sofa and smiled at her, then looked up at me. "Miss Julia's going to love this. I've asked Lieutenant Peavey to be the soloist."

"Coleman!" I said, nearly choking. "You can't be serious. The man can hardly open his mouth, he's so rigid and uptight. I can't imagine he can sing." All I could picture was that cold, hard face with the black sunglasses reflecting my frightened face. Lieutenant Peavey and I were not exactly what you'd call congenial.

"He can sing, all right," Coleman assured me. "He's the soloist at his church, and he's sung at the weddings of several deputies. He's good, Miss Julia, I promise. He'll surprise you."

Telling myself again that it was their wedding, but doubting that Lieutenant Peavey would add any gaiety to the occasion, I said, "That brings up something else. I'm having trouble finding somebody to play the piano. Every trained musician in town is already engaged. Could Lieutenant Peavey bring his own accompanist?"

"I'll ask him," Coleman said, which allowed me to put that little problem on hold without bringing up Miss Mattie Mae Morgan.

Mr. Pickens stifled another yawn, making

me want to smack him. That seemed a signal to the others that it was time to go. While Hazel Marie went to the kitchen to have Little Lloyd come out and say goodbye, and Coleman was asking Sam where he could rent formal wear, I pulled Mr. Pickens aside.

"Mr. Pickens," I said, "does any of this ring any bells for you?"

"What?" He leaned his head closer, a frown on his face. "What kind of bells?"

"Wedding bells, Mr. Pickens. What do you think we've been talking about?"

He began to grin then, shaking his head, while I yearned to shake him to within an inch of his life. I said, "Let me remind you that Hazel Marie's uncle, Brother Vernon Puckett, has come close to taking Little Lloyd away from her, not once but twice in times past. And he had nothing to go on but rumors, *false* rumors, I remind you, that Hazel Marie was living a loose life. Now, what do you think he'll do when he finds out about that child being brought up in a house of sin? I'll tell you what he'll do, he'll be in that courthouse getting a protective custody order before you can turn around."

"No, he won't." Mr. Pickens shook his

head, hiding a smile under that bushy mustache. "You worry too much, Miss Julia. I can take care of Hazel Marie and Little Lloyd, and Brother Vern's not going to be a problem."

"You don't know him like I do. He's a snake in the grass, and if he sees any way to get his hands on that trust fund, he'll go after it in a flash. And if you and Hazel Marie keep on with this unseemly plan, it won't be rumors that can be disproved. He'll have the facts this time, facts that'll prove to any Republican-appointed judge that Hazel Marie doesn't have a family value to her name."

Mr. Pickens had the nerve to put his arm around my shoulders and say, "Trust me, darlin'; I've got it taken care of. And if you have to know how, I'll just tell you that Brother Vern doesn't have the cleanest hands in the county, and he knows I know it. He's not going to make a move against the boy, so put your mind at rest."

Lord, the man had a way with women. No wonder Hazel Marie was under his spell. It was all I could do to keep from leaning my head against his chest and letting him take care of everything.

I knew better than that, of course, because no man needed that kind of power. They get carried away and start thinking they can boss you around.

So I pulled away from him and said, "You're a good man, Mr. Pickens, but I still don't like what you're doing. You ought to marry Hazel Marie, and not toy with her like this."

"*Toy* with her?" He threw his head back and laughed. "You have a way with words, Miss Julia. But you can stop worrying and leave it to me."

"Well, I guess I'll have to, won't I?" I stepped farther back so I could keep my head. "But I warn you, Mr. Pickens," I went on, shaking my finger in his face, "if you hurt her or cause her trouble in any way, you'll have me to answer to."

"Don't think I don't know it," he said, grabbing my finger and kissing it, laughing at me all the while.

If I hadn't known it before, I would've then. Hazel Marie had her work cut out for her.

As Binkie and Coleman left together, headed for a night in the same state of togetherness, and Hazel Marie lingered on the porch with Mr. Pickens, I sent Little Lloyd to bed and turned to find Sam nowhere near far enough away.

"I'll drive Lillian home for you," he said. "She's just finishing up in the kitchen."

"That's good of you, Sam. I appreciate it." I moved away from him. "I'm going to owe her a fortune, with all the extra time she's putting in this week."

"Well worth it, Julia. It's a fine thing you're doing." He took a step, standing much too close again, making me uneasy with the thought that somebody would walk in on us. "And I'd like to help you, if you'll let me."

When he leaned in close, I said, "Well, we've got a pile of silver that needs polishing. . . ."

Chapter 9

Sunday morning, and Hazel Marie said she didn't think she could make it to church. That's what happens when you're contemplating a jump into sin as she was; you lose your taste for sermons on the subject. If you're honest, that is, and Hazel Marie was as honest as the day is long. In a back-handed way, I admired her for staying home. I had known and still knew any number of people who could lie, steal, cheat, betray, embezzle and take part in all kinds of illegal and immoral activities and still sit in church every Sunday morning with smiles on their faces.

"Let me comb your hair, Little Lloyd," I said as I ran the comb under the faucet. He stood still as I parted his hair and put enough water on his cowlick to make it lie down for a while.

We walked over to the church in time for

Sunday school, and by the time I'd passed the Family Life Center in its state of half-completion, I needed some lessons in patience and forbearance.

After Little Lloyd went to the young people's class, I took my place in the Lulu Mae Harding class and put my dollar in the basket when it was passed. LuAnne Conover, a friend for too many years to count, leaned over my shoulder to tell me how much she was looking forward to the wedding.

"What can I do to help, Julia?" she whispered while Alma Claxton, the class president, made announcements and asked for volunteers to take casseroles to a member who'd just come home from the hospital.

"We have a lot of silver to be polished," I whispered back. "I could use some help with that."

"Oh," she said. "Well, you know how hard that polish is on your manicure. But I'll try to come by and help out. You just call me, now, if you need anything else."

I don't remember what the lesson was, something about the first miracle that occurred in the city of Cana, I think. My mind was busy making more lists and thinking of all the things that still had to be done. I should've listened more carefully to the lesson, though, since the miracle had to do with wedding preparations. I could've picked up some pointers.

After Sunday school, I met up with Little Lloyd and we found our usual place in the sanctuary, fourth row from the front on the aisle.

I gave about as much attention to Pastor Lance Petree's sermon as I had to the Sunday school lesson. The man was a droner, on and on and on until my head was nodding and my eyes drooping, so overcome with the tedium I could hardly bear it. Pastor Petree was not a stirring speaker. One thing I can say about Pastor Ledbetter, he'd raise his voice now and then to keep the congregation awake, even somewhat on edge since we never knew when he was going to cut loose.

Emma Sue Ledbetter caught up with me in the narthex as the congregation filed out. "Come over here, Julia," she said, "I want to talk to you a minute. Lloyd, you can wait for us on the steps." She guided me out of the press of people anxious to get out where the sun was shining and dinner was waiting at home.

"What is it, Emma Sue? I've got a million things to do today." I hated to be short with her, but I didn't have the patience to put up with her whining. Emma Sue and I had not been the closest of friends ever since she'd taught a Sunday school lesson on the effectiveness of prayer, and prayer alone, regardless of the problems facing us. I'd piped up and said that it stood to reason that we should also take advantage of modern medicine and technological advances. "We're Presbyterians, Emma Sue," I'd reminded her in front of the whole class. "Not Christian Scientists." She'd been worried about my spiritual state ever since.

Now she wanted something from me or she wouldn't have pulled me to the side to speak in private.

Leaning in close, she said, "I know just what you're going through, Julia, and I'm so happy about that young couple. You've had a time with them, haven't you? You're putting stars in your crown, but that's not what I wanted to talk to you about."

I waited, biting my tongue, to hear what she had to say. Emma Sue was a short, fleshy woman who made her own clothes and they looked like it. I happened to know the salary Pastor Ledbetter made and knew she didn't have to scrimp the way she did. She didn't use makeup, either, other than a little dusting of powder to take the shine off. Her eyes looked weak and red-rimmed behind her glasses, as if she never got enough sleep. Of course, they teared up at the drop of a hat so maybe that's what was wrong with them. Either that, or pinkeye.

"Two things burden my heart, Julia," she whispered, looking over my shoulder to see who was close enough to overhear. "One is the young peoples' meeting, which I've rescheduled for tomorrow right after school. We have to get the young ones active as early as we can, you know, if we're going to keep them off drugs and welfare. And I'll be heartbroken if Lloyd is not there. He's such a fine little fellow, in spite of his background, don't you think?"

I gripped my pocketbook and nodded.

"And his mother has turned into a real asset to the church, even though I've had to ask the Lord's forgiveness for thinking so harshly of her at first. All that eye makeup, you know. But, Julia, there's something that's weighing so heavily on my heart that I have to share it with somebody." As I wished she'd chosen someone else to share it with, she pulled me farther into the corner and whispered, "I had to go into Larry's office this morning, and there's something missing from it."

"What?"

"Have you ever noticed that little miniature clock he keeps on his desk? You know, the one with the tiny brass balls that go around as it keeps time? That was a gift from his mother when he finished seminary, and he thinks the world of it. Well"—she leaned closer and hissed into my ear—"it's not there anymore, and that office is supposed to stay locked when he's away."

"Maybe he took it to the Holy Land with him."

"Why would he do that? I packed his travel clock, so he wouldn't need another one. No, somebody's taken it."

"Well, who, Emma Sue? I mean, who has access and who'd want it?"

"There're three people who have keys, besides Larry." Her face darkened with suspicion. "I have one, and so do Lance Petree and Norma Cantrell."

"Oh, surely you don't suspect them."

"Norma's always admired that clock." Emma Sue's eyes welled up and she dabbed them with the handkerchief that she always kept handy, knowing how often she'd need it. "You're so capable, Julia; would you talk to her? Would you do that for me?"

"Not on your life, Emma Sue. Norma Cantrell and I've crossed swords too many times for me to go and accuse her of stealing from the pastor."

"Oh, you wouldn't say *stealing.* That's too strong and it'd hurt her feelings."

"I don't know what else you'd call it. Look, Emma Sue, I think you ought to wait till the pastor gets back. Who knows, if he thinks that much of the clock, he may've locked it in a drawer or a cabinet before he left. I mean, you're treading on dangerous ground, suspecting either his secretary or his associate. And I'm not about to be drawn into such a thing. Besides, I have enough on my plate right now, so I can't be investigating a theft, if there even was one. Come to think it, though, I do know a private investigator if . . . , but he's busy now with another case, so forget about that. Wait till

Pastor Ledbetter gets home. That's my advice."

"It just hurts me so, Julia, to think that somebody would do that to us." She sniffed wetly, as the last of the congregation gave us a wide berth. They all knew that when Emma Sue started overflowing, she wanted something she wasn't getting, and they didn't want to be caught up in whatever it was.

"Well," she went on with a heavy sigh, "if you won't help me, I'll just put it in the hands of the Lord. I'm going right home and start the prayer chain."

"Oh, Emma Sue, don't do that. You know what'll happen. By the time a dozen people get called to pray about this, it'll be all over town that Norma Cantrell's a thief. Every person who gets called will add a little to it, and first thing you know, the prayer request won't sound anything like it started out sounding."

"You don't have much faith in prayer, do you, Julia?" A hard look came into her eyes, flooded though they were, and I took a step back.

"I have enough faith to stay away from a rumor mill, which the prayer chain has come to be. Remember when Hallie Trent asked for prayer because the doctor told her if her womb dropped any further, she'd have to decide between surgery or a pessary? And by the time the story was told a few times, they had that poor woman unable to pass her water or even walk, her womb had fallen so far out, and six people showed up at her house with casseroles. So, if you're going to start the chain about Norma, just take my name off the list. I'm not going to be a party to circulating such a story.

"Now, Emma Sue, I have to get Little Lloyd home; he needs his lunch." And I stepped away and out of the narthex as quickly as I could, leaving her stunned at my lack of spirituality. Nobody, as far as I knew, had ever resigned from the prayer chain, so I took a certain amount of justifiable pride in being the first to turn my back on that hotbed of gossip.

"You did the right thing, Julia," Sam said.

We were sitting in his car late that afternoon at Walter's Ice Cream Stop, eating butter pecan cones. The windows were rolled down to catch the warm spring breeze and so I could watch Little Lloyd, who was sitting at a picnic table, licking chocolate ice cream dripping down his cone and playing with his Game Boy. Sam had come by to give us a break from the telephone—we were phoning last-minute invitations—and unwrapping stored china and stacking up silver serving pieces and flatware on the dining room table. "Take a break, Julia," Sam had said. "I've had ice cream on my mind all day."

So, as we ate ice cream in his car, I'd told him of Emma Sue's suspect in the Great Church Robbery, omitting any mention of the prayer chain for fear he'd think I'd fallen into apostasy, and he'd laughed. "She'll calm down when Ledbetter gets back and shows her where he put it."

We spent a pleasant hour discussing the wedding and how relieved I was to know it was fast approaching, even if I was about to break my neck getting ready for it.

I leaned my head out the window. "Come on, Little Lloyd. We've got to be getting back."

As the boy dropped his chocolate-covered napkin into the trash and came to the car, Sam said, "You in a hurry, Julia?"

"Well, yes. I have things to do. Get in, Little Lloyd, and buckle your seat belt."

When Sam pulled up in front of my house, there were two cars taking up all the curb space.

"That one's Mr. Pickens's car," I said. "But I don't know the other one. Just pull into the driveway, Sam, and come in for a while."

"That's a big ole Cadillac, Miss Julia," Little Lloyd said. He'd sat up straight as soon as he'd heard me mention Mr. Pickens. The child had admired Mr. Pickens ever since we'd run all over the state with him a few months back, and he wasn't at all unhappy that his mother admired him, too.

The light blue full-sized Cadillac parked in front of Mr. Pickens's flashy Firebird was neither the newest model nor the oldest, but it took up an inordinate amount of space. I noticed a wooden cross and a rabbit's foot dangling from its rearview mirror. Covering all the bases, I guessed.

When we walked into the living room, Mr. Pickens stood up to greet me and to shake Sam's hand. Hazel Marie was in a chair across the room from where he'd been sitting, and I wondered if they'd had words.

Then I saw the owner of the Cadillac in the other Victorian chair, and I knew why Mr. Pickens and Hazel Marie had been on their best behavior.

"This is Miss Mattie Mae Morgan, Miss Julia," Hazel Marie said.

Miss Morgan heaved herself out of the chair with the most glittering smile I'd ever seen. Two gold teeth added their luster, and the big gold hoops in her ears flashed an accompaniment. The woman had to be a size 22 or 24, somewhere around there, and there was enough turquoise satin around her to make Omar's tent. She was an ebony person, as Lillian had described her to me, and there was a lot of her.

"Miss Morgan," I said, shaking her hand. "I'm sorry I wasn't here when you came, but I didn't know you were coming."

"Oh, I don't 'spect you to be settin' 'round waitin' on me, Miz Springer," she said, just as pleasant and friendly as she could be. "Miss Lillian tole me I ought to drop by and see where you havin' the wedding, and see what kind a instrument you want me to play."

"Well, it's not exactly here yet. I'm having to rent a piano and it won't be here until sometime Friday. Is there any particular kind you'd prefer?"

"No'm, I can play anything with black and white keys on it, even a pump organ, if you want to go that far. But I never have learned on one of them keyboards with pipes that run up through the ceiling and foot pedals and all."

"We won't have one of those, I assure you. But take a seat, Miss Morgan. And you, too, Sam. Mr. Pickens, sit back down. We might as well plan the wedding music while Miss Morgan is here. And I don't know a thing about it, so what would you suggest, Miss Morgan?"

"Call me Mattie Mae, Miz Springer. I don't hardly know who you talkin' to when you say Miss Morgan." Laughter rolled up through the turquoise dress in waves. "Now, who that fine lookin' little man come in with you? That got to be Miss Lillian's baby, Little Lloyd Puckett. Come on over here, honey, an' let Mattie Mae get a look at you."

Little Lloyd walked over to her, hanging his head, just hating to be made the center of attention.

"Why, you fine lookin'," she said. "Jus' the spittin' image of . . ."

"Come over here, son," Mr. Pickens, bless his heart, broke in before Miss Morgan could bring up the boy's father and embarrass us all. "Let me see how you're doing with your Game Boy." Little Lloyd hurried over to sit by Mr. Pickens on the sofa, relieved to be out from under Miss Morgan's scrutiny. Children don't like to be made over in public, don't you know, especially when they're told who they favor.

"Now, Miss, I mean, Mattie Mae," I said, feeling somewhat trapped into accepting this pianist of questionable talent. "What do you usually play at weddings? Lillian speaks so highly of you that I may have to rely on your suggestions."

"Ma'am, I can play most anything you want from 'Rock of Ages' to 'Rock Around the Clock.' The Lord done blessed these hands of mine. But I 'spect you don't want neither one of them, so we got to get in between. I usu'lly play a nice mixture of church music while the guests is coming in. Then when you or somebody give me the high sign, I bust out with the wedding march, an' I do it real joyful like so the bride, she get a happy smile on her face. Then I go along with whoever's doin' the solo, if you have that. Then when the ceremony be over, I come down hard on the recessional so the bride an' groom feel like runnin' on out and startin' they wedded life right that minute."

"Well, I say," I murmured, frowning at Mr. Pickens, who looked as if he was about to have a seizure. Sam wasn't in much better shape, but he'd had more practice keeping a straight face in polite company.

I tried again. "Well, Mattie Mae, what I have in mind is a very sedate and, well, proper wedding; it's a serious thing they're undertaking, you know. Maybe . . ."

"Honey, don't you worry about it," she said, laughing off my hesitation. "I can play the strings offa that piano, an' play it any way you want it played."

"There is one other thing," I said, hoping this would dampen her enthusiasm. I'd searched the town over for a capable pianist without finding one, but now I was beginning to think that a student in training would fit the bill better than Miss Mattie Mae Morgan. "The soloist will be Lieutenant Peavey of the sheriff's department. He might need you to play for him, and I don't know that you'd want to tackle that."

"Wayne Peavey!" She leaned out of her

chair, stretching the seams of her dress. "Why, I been playin' for that man ever since he sing his first solo down at the community center. I never let him forget it, neither, how his pants legs quivered all the way through four verses and a chorus." And she threw her head back, laughing at the memory.

Mr. Pickens put his arm around Little Lloyd and pretended to whisper something to him, but I could tell it was to keep from laughing out loud. I could've smacked him, and Sam too, who was gazing up at the ceiling, whistling under his breath.

"Well, I declare," I said, not knowing what else to say.

"Now, Miz Springer," Mattie Mae went on. "Don't you fret yo'self about that ole Lieutenant Wayne Peavey. I know how he be, and he don't worry me none. I jus' reach 'roun' an' smack him good, he start gettin' ahead of my music. I keep him straight, don't you worry."

"Well, I declare," I said again, resigning myself to accepting the last available piano player in Abbotsville on Binkie and Coleman's wedding day, but not without a considerable amount of fear and trepidation for the outcome.

Chapter 10

"Guess what!" Hazel Marie pushed through the kitchen door Monday morning, jangling my nerves as I tried to get myself together for the day. I needed my coffee before hearing any kind of news, good, bad or indifferent.

"What?" Lillian turned away from the stove, spatula held high.

"Binkie just called to say she found a dress yesterday. She wants me to go over today and try on the bridesmaid's dress. And she found some she thought you'd like, Miss Julia. Come go with me; we'll have so much fun."

"I guess I ought to," I said, setting my cup in the saucer. "Though I haven't given much thought to what I'd wear. I'd surely like to see what Binkie's picked out, though, so I'll have time to get used to it by Saturday."

Little Lloyd came in then, still in his pajamas, his hair sticking up all over his head. His face looked pale and naked without his glasses.

"Come 'ere, baby," Lillian said. "You 'bout to starve this mornin'? Lillian's got you some hot oatmeal and cinnamon rolls. Set on down, while I fix 'em for you."

"Mornin'," he mumbled as he took his place at the table.

Hazel Marie came over to the back of his chair and hugged him, and told him we'd drop him off at school on our way to Asheville. "Just think," she said. "Only five more days and you'll be out for the summer."

When she left to get ready for our shopping trip, I sat in easy silence with the child. We were alike in wanting a quiet time early in the morning.

"Miss Julia," Lillian said. "You seen my good can opener?"

"Lillian, you know I don't bother things in the kitchen."

"Yessum, but I can't find it nowhere."

"Use the electric one, why don't you?"

"I don't like that thing. It whir 'bout halfway 'round a can, then drop it off an' you have to start over again. I like that one what goes in my hand."

"I haven't seen it, Lillian. Maybe it's in the dishwasher."

"No'm," she mumbled. "I done looked."

"Well, it'll turn up." I rose from the table and walked past Little Lloyd, smoothing his hair as I went. I would've lingered with him if I'd had time. "I'm off to get dressed," I said. "Hurry up now, Little Lloyd, you don't want to be late."

———

Hazel Marie and I got to the bridal shop, or The Bridal Shoppe, in the middle of the mall in Asheville, not long after it opened for business. I was more than a little uneasy by the time we walked in, fearing what Binkie had chosen. That young woman needed a mother's hand, although she'd been more than her own mother could handle.

We were greeted by one of those professional saleswomen; you know the kind, blond hair pulled back in a bun, black dress, hose and shoes, and a pair of glasses on a pearl chain around her neck. She took us to a spacious fitting room that was furnished with brocade upholstered chairs, tiny tables with satin pincushions on them and an elevated platform in the middle for proper viewing in the floor-to-ceiling mirrors.

The woman smiled at Hazel Marie and said, "You must be so excited to be the matron of honor."

I was immediately affronted on Hazel Marie's behalf, but she didn't turn a hair. Didn't even notice the insult, I don't think.

"Oh, no," Hazel Marie said. "I'm the bridesmaid, the only attendant Binkie'll have, so maybe I count as the matron of honor, too. Or"—she giggled—"maybe the maid of honor. I'm not married yet."

The woman raised her eyebrows, but left the subject alone. "I'll bring out your dress; I know you're going to love it. Would either of you like coffee or a glass of wine?"

"I should say not," I said, noting that it was not yet eleven o'clock in the morning, not that I would've accepted at any time of the day. "Thank you all the same, but we're pressed for time and need to get on with it."

She studied me for a minute. "Let me guess. You're the mother of the groom, right?"

"As near as he has, I guess. But no, just a close friend and the director of the wedding, which is an honor, too."

"Oh, I should say. Well, we need to find something outstanding for you, and I'm sure we will. We have some lovely things. I'll be right back with the bridesmaid's dress and a selection that Miss Enloe wants you to look at."

While she went to get the choices, I wandered around the room, looking at the bridal gowns hanging in the open closets.

"Hazel Marie," I whispered, impressed in spite of myself with the elegant surroundings. "Come look at this. Think how you'd look in this one if Mr. Pickens gave you the chance." I pushed aside the other dresses to show her a beaded satin creation that was fit for a princess or a movie star.

"Oh, it's beautiful. Look at that train, would you? Wonder how much it is?" Hazel Marie felt along the sleeves until she came up with a price tag. "Oh, my goodness! Is this right?"

I glanced at it and nearly lost my breath. Eight thousand dollars for one dress to be worn one time, and not for very long, at that. I straightened the hangers and stopped looking just as the saleslady came back carrying a thin, filmy garment.

Holding up the pale lavender dress by its hanger, she said, "Isn't this the most elegant thing you've ever seen? It's handkerchief linen in lilac."

I looked at it, then reached behind me, feeling for a chair. I collapsed on it with a sudden shortness of breath.

"Tell me," I gasped. "Tell me Binkie didn't pick that one. Why, it's hardly more than a slip."

"Oh, Miss Julia, it's beautiful," Hazel Marie said, which didn't surprise me at all, considering her natural taste in clothes. "Just look at the little spaghetti straps and the way the skirt flows from the Empire waist. And these darling little roses in the same material right where the bodice dips down low in front."

"I see them," I said, fanning myself with a magazine. "And so will everybody else. That's why I'm about to have a heart attack here. Hazel Marie, there's not enough on top to cover what needs to be covered. What is Binkie thinking of? It's entirely inappropriate."

Paying no attention to my palpitations, the saleslady unzipped the dress. "Go ahead and try it on," she told Hazel Marie, "and I'll be back in a minute with the fitter."

"Oh, wait," Hazel Marie said. "I know the

groom shouldn't see what the bride will wear. But can we?"

"We altered it just a little yesterday while she waited, and she took it with her. But I can tell you that it's similar to yours, only in blush."

Blush, I thought as I leaned my head back against the chair. All I could picture was Binkie in that next-to-nothing dress standing before a temporarily sanctified altar in my living room in front of God and everybody. Whatever happened to pointed sleeves and high necklines and veils that cover head and shoulders, suitable for a detailed write-up on the society page? I should say, *blush.* That's what we'd all be doing.

When the saleslady left, I whispered to Hazel Marie, "How in the world does anybody wear such a thing? Why, your underwear straps'll show."

"No, they won't," she said, beginning to unbutton her blouse. "You wear a strapless."

"A strapless?" I didn't own such a thing.

"Well, actually, most people don't wear anything underneath."

"Well, I hope you don't plan to go half-naked." I sat up then with a sudden thought. "Hazel Marie, you don't think we can talk Binkie into something else, do you? That thing looks like something you'd wear to bed."

She didn't answer me, just held up that wisp of a dress, her eyes shining as she turned it this way and that. "I think I'll just try it on. It'll probably look a whole lot better when it's on. And, Miss Julia, I'll get out in the backyard for the next few days and get a tan. You don't look near as naked when you have a tan."

I held my head and moaned under my breath as Hazel Marie commenced coming out of her clothes right there in the main fitting room.

The saleslady came bustling back in about the time Hazel Marie got down to her step-ins, and they both acted like it was the most normal thing in the world. I would've been mortified if I'd been either one of them.

"Here we are," she said, hanging up two long purple garments. "Now, this is the one Miss Enloe liked the best." And she took one, holding it by the hanger and spreading the skirttail out on the carpet. "Why don't you try it on?"

"Me? Binkie picked that one for me?" I couldn't take my eyes off the thing.

"Yes, once she chose her dress and the bridesmaid's, she decided it'd be nice if you blended in with her pastel color scheme. See how the lilac dress is just a shade lighter than this lavender one."

"I thought it was purple," I managed to say, my eyes still on the dress. All I could see was a long purple crepe with a cowl neckline that draped halfway to the waist and no sleeves, making it entirely unacceptable. When you get to a certain age, there're areas of the body that cry out to be covered, and the neck and upper arms are two of them.

"She liked this one, too," the saleslady said, reaching for the other purple gown.

"I'll take it," I said before she could whip out another bare-necked one. It was much more to my taste, a purple, I mean lavender, lace with a high neck and long sleeves, and I figured I'd better get it while the getting was good. No telling what else Binkie might've had her eye on.

"Oh, you have to try it on, Miss Julia," Hazel Marie said, as I averted my eyes from her state of undress.

Not wanting to put on a public display of nudity, I retired to a private space that was no more than a closet and stepped out of my dress. Putting on the lavender lace, which I was happy to note had tiny buttons all the way to the neck, I looked in the mirror. It fit, Lord, did it fit. I was not accustomed to anything binding me around the waist, but that thing started binding from the bustline to the hipline. Then it flared out enough to allow a few medium-sized steps.

I went out into the main room, hesitantly, because I wasn't accustomed to all the swirling around my ankles the skirt was doing. Hazel Marie was standing on the platform, modeling her dress, and I must say she was a picture in it. Even though I wanted to throw a stole or a sweater around her shoulders before Mr. Pickens and half the town saw her in it. Emma Sue Ledbetter was going to have more to criticize than a little blue eye shadow.

"Oh, you're beautiful, Miss Julia!" Hazel Marie cried. "Don't you just love it?"

"It'll do, I guess."

The saleslady snuck up behind me and seized the back of the bodice. "We need to take this in; it's too loose," she said, turning me toward the mirror as she pulled the fabric tight enough to strain the seams. "See how much better that looks?"

Before I could disagree for the sake of taking a breath, Hazel Marie chimed in. "She needs a better bra, one that'll give her some uplift."

"I have all the uplift I want, thank you all the same," I said, but they weren't listening to me. Hands unbuttoned the bodice, reached around and noted my underwear size, and someone was dispatched to that intimate apparel shop that ought to be ashamed of the catalog it sends to unsuspecting homes.

The next thing I knew, I was back in the closet, refusing help from either of them, with the promise of at least trying on a wired-up, padded contraption the likes of which had never been on my person.

By the time I'd snapped, rebuttoned and ventured out again for their inspection, I was feeling some better about Binkie's choice. When the fitter pinned the back of my gown, I finally dared to stand beside Hazel Marie and look in the long mirror. As Hazel Marie exclaimed over the fit and how the color of the dress complimented my hair and complexion, I marveled at the difference certain foundation garments can make in a woman's general appearance. They can make a new woman of you, if you didn't need to sit, walk, turn around or take a deep breath.

"Well, Hazel Marie," I said, as we drove back toward Abbotsville. "It looks like I'm breaking with the tradition for mothers of the groom, even substitute ones, as I guess I am for Coleman."

"I didn't know there was a tradition."

"Oh, yes, it's an old saying but most mothers of the groom try to follow it, as well they should. Anyway, the tradition is that the mother of the groom should wear beige and keep her mouth shut. That's exactly what I intended to do, but with that lavender dress Binkie wants me to wear, I guess I'm just throwing that part of the tradition right out the window."

Hazel Marie turned her face away from me, her shoulders shaking and a strangling sound coming from her throat. I reached over, keeping one hand on the wheel, to pat her on the back so she could get her breath. She was often affected that way when I instructed her in the traditional graces of refined living.

Chapter 11

"Did you reach everybody on your invitation list, Hazel Marie?" We were driving through town on our way home, and the burden of all we still had to do was weighing heavy on my mind.

"Yessum, I got through to the last one this morning before we left. And everybody I called is coming. What about your list?"

"I still have two I haven't reached. I declare, you'd think people'd stay home just one hour a day to receive their calls. I must've called the Bentons and that girl who works in Binkie's office a dozen times yesterday. So, I still have them to invite, plus everything else we have to do." I pulled into the driveway. "Here we are."

"Lillian," I said, as Hazel Marie and I came into the kitchen. "As soon as we change our clothes, we're going to start on that silver. Will we be in your way if we use the table in here?"

"No'm. I'll put some newspapers on it an' get out the polish for you. But 'fore you go upstairs, that phone been ringin' off the hook. The florist lady say do you want baby's breath in all the 'rangements, an' do you want some ferns hanging on the porch. The rent man say when he bring them little chairs, do you want him to set 'em up or do we want to do it. Miz Conover, she call an' say do you need to borry her good china, an' that Miss Etta Mae, she call an' say nobody doin' anything 'bout the lights where she live, an' Mr. Sam, he call an' say he waitin' to he'p any way he can. Oh, an' Miz Mildred Allen, she say she had to be away from her phone an' she wonderin' if she miss gettin' her invite to the weddin'."

"Oh, for goodness' sake, that woman, she doesn't even know Binkie and Coleman. Lillian, help me please. Call the florist, the number's on the pad by the phone, and tell her baby's breath is fine and so are the ferns, but that I'm counting on her to make these decisions. And tell the rental man that I certainly do want him to set up the chairs, and that I expect them to be in place no

later than ten A.M. Saturday morning." I
stopped to think a minute. "No, tell him Friday afternoon, and he can bring the piano
at the same time and it better be in tune.
Oh, and I need to see about having the furniture moved out of the living room. I'll do
that as soon as you're off the phone. Call
Sam back and ask him to pick up LuAnne's
china. I don't think we'll need it, but better
safe than sorry. And Etta Mae Wiggins'll just
have to hold her horses till I have time to get
to her. That woman's going to give me a
case of heartburn with all her complaints.
And Mildred Allen can keep on waiting.

"Come on, Hazel Marie, let's get out of
these shopping clothes and get to work."

"I'm coming," she said, then turning to
Lillian, she asked: "Did J.D. call?"

"No'm, but he might've tried and not got
through."

"I hope he will," Hazel Marie said. "I can't
wait to tell him about my bridesmaid's
dress."

"Binkie's keeping him busy," I reminded
her. "And I'll tell you something else, Hazel
Marie, you can't expect a man to be interested in a dress." Or non-dress, I added to

myself. But on recalling how little she'd be wearing, maybe he would.

———————

As it turned out, we didn't get far with the silver that afternoon. By the time we all got off the phones, Hazel Marie left to pick up Little Lloyd at school. We'd heard a news broadcast on Lillian's kitchen radio that Dixon Hightower was still eluding capture, so Hazel Marie didn't want the boy to walk home by himself.

When they returned, Lillian put a glass of milk and a peanut butter sandwich in front of Little Lloyd. "You eat all that," she told him. "I know you hungry."

"Yessum, but I've got to hurry and get over to the church for Mrs. Ledbetter's meeting."

"Law, you ain't goin' over to the church by yo'self. Miss Julia, he can't go by hisself. That ole Dixon could reach out an' grab at him."

Hazel Marie gasped at the thought, but I said, "Dixon's nowhere around here, Lillian. The boy's perfectly safe to walk half a block. But," I went on, seeing the stricken look on Hazel Marie's face, "I'll walk over with him and wait for him till the meeting's over. I need to talk to Emma Sue anyway, and see what she's done about that missing clock."

"Oh, thank you, Miss Julia," Hazel Marie said. "I'm hoping to hear from J.D., so I want to stay by the phone. I'll keep on with this silver while you're gone."

"What clock?" Lillian asked.

"Oh, the one with the brass balls of the pastor's," I said, waving it off. "Emma Sue thinks Norma Cantrell took it, but that's the way false rumors start. Now, don't any of you say a word about it, because I don't believe in passing on gossip."

As Little Lloyd and I walked across the street toward the church, I said, "Now, Little Lloyd, it's good to be active in a young people's group and be involved in wholesome activities. But if it's too much for you, you don't have to stay in it. You already go to church and Sunday school, and you have your schoolwork to consider, so don't feel like you have to add anything else if you don't want to."

He said something in reply, but I didn't catch it. The noise as we passed the construction site was so loud I couldn't hear myself think. The sidewalk was covered in

mud from hoses snaking around wheelbar-
rows and pallets and one kind of power tool
after another. Why, we even had to leave the
sidewalk and walk in the street to get past
them all. I'll tell you, Pastor Ledbetter was
going to have a monument to family values
to beat all other monuments. The thing was
huge, stretching up some three stories and
spreading out to cover most of what had
been the parking lot. From what I'd heard,
although I tried not to listen when the subject came up, they were putting in a gymnasium, a running track and an exercise room
with all kinds of muscle-building machines
that would create ripples on your stomach,
and who would want such as that, I'd like to
know. And a sauna, of all things. Plus office
space, meeting rooms with up-to-date
sound and video systems and a snack room
with a microwave. Now, don't tell me that
Presbyterians needed such luxuries, especially since what we really needed was more
space for the day-care center the church
ran during the week for working mothers. Of
course, we'd been the last church in town to
open a day-care center, since Pastor Ledbetter didn't believe in working mothers.
The diaconate and the session finally over-

ruled him, though, since most of their wives and daughters were now running the town's professional offices, hospital, retail stores and city and county bureaucratic departments, in spite of what the pastor didn't believe in.

When Little Lloyd and I finally got into the relative quiet of the church, closing out the din of construction, he joined several other little boys and girls who were on their way upstairs to Emma Sue's meeting.

"Tell Mrs. Ledbetter that I'll be waiting down here in the Fellowship Hall for you," I told him, hoping that would make her hurry things along. I'd brought along my lists to rearrange while I waited, and I didn't want to wait long.

A lot of good that turned out to do, because an hour and a half later, after I'd made a completely new list and read every pamphlet in the rack and was reduced to reading a hymnal somebody had left on a table, the children finally came straggling downstairs. They all looked somewhat dazed, although a few ran out of the building as if their lives depended on it. Little Lloyd was one of the last ones, coming down the stairs carrying a long box full of papers of some kind, a bewildered expression on his face.

He walked over to me, holding the box across both arms. "I've been elected chairman of home missions," he said, looking up at me. "I didn't want it, but Miz Ledbetter said it'd be good for me. She said I was the perfect one for the job since you had all the time in the world to help me, and it'd be good for you, too."

"Well, I never," I huffed, taken aback at having been appointed to a committee at a meeting I hadn't even attended. But that's the Presbyterian way of doing things. If you're not on your toes every minute of the day, they'll slap you on a committee so fast it'll make your head swim. "What're we supposed to do on this committee?"

"Knock on doors and hand these out," he said, setting the box on the floor and handing me a pile of pamphlets entitled "The Power of Prayer," and stamped with the phone number and address of the First Presbyterian Church of Abbotsville. I glanced inside one of them and saw that it was little more than a list of what to pray against. Our nation would be saved, it said, if we united in prayer against liberal forces that wanted to extend the welfare state, secular humanists who wouldn't allow little children to pray at football games and tree-hugging groups that were trying to under-mine free enterprise.

Before I could gather myself, so outraged at the thought of sending children to pass out such propaganda that I could hardly get my breath, Little Lloyd said, "And we're supposed to put these on as many cars as we can." He handed me a stack of slick red and blue bumper stickers.

I held one up and read PRAY WITH US, which put me in need of prayer myself, to keep from going upstairs and smacking Emma Sue Ledbetter to kingdom come.

"My Lord," I said. "What has got into that woman? Little Lloyd, there's no way in the world that you're going door-to-door to pass these things out. What does she think you are, a Jehovah's Witness or a Bob Jones student? I'm going up there right now and give her a piece of my mind."

"She's already gone," Little Lloyd said. "I saw her go down the hall toward the front stairs by the chapel."

"Well, of course she would! She knew I was waiting for you down here, and she didn't want to face me. I tell you, Little Lloyd, I know why she gave this job to you; she's getting back at me. I don't have a doubt in this world but that she's got that prayer chain humming again. She'll have everybody on it praying for my soul!"

Little Lloyd's glasses slid down his nose as he frowned. Then he said, "Why's she worried about your soul, Miss Julia?"

"Because she has to have something to worry about," I said, then seeing the worried look on the boy's face, I went on. "It's only because I don't agree with her on every little thing, and because I took my name off the prayer chain. I'll tell you one thing, Little Lloyd, spreading rumors about somebody under the guise of praying for her is not my idea of a Christian activity. And I'll tell you something else, being a Democrat does not put anybody's soul in danger, either, and don't you listen to anything anybody says to the contrary."

"No'm, I won't."

"Now, bring that box and come on," I said, heading for the door. "We're going to see Sam."

Chapter 12

We picked our way through the obstacle course by the construction site and, for the first time since they'd dug the foundation, I didn't pay it any mind. I was too intent on doing something about the preacher's wife who was intent on using a child to put me in my place.

Pointing Little Lloyd toward the car, I stuck my head in the kitchen door to tell Lillian where we were going. She called after me as I headed to the car, "You better watch out for that Dixon Hightower."

"I'm not worried about Dixon Hightower," I called back. "I'll deal with him if I have to. Right now I have other things on my mind."

In ordinary circumstances, we'd've walked the four blocks to Sam's house, but I was in too much of a hurry to get there and get something done about that meddlesome woman. Besides, that box of one-sided political tracts and religious bumper stickers was heavy. So I drove.

I pulled into Sam's driveway and turned off the motor. "Come on, Little Lloyd. Grab a few of those things to show Sam, but just leave the box on the backseat."

Sam came to the door as we walked up on his wide veranda that was lined with white rocking chairs and ferns hanging from hooks between the porch columns.

"Well, Julia," he said, smiling at us as he held the screen door open. "This is an un-expected pleasure. It's been a while since you honored me with a visit. Hello, Little Lloyd, I've been missing you around here, too. What've you got there?"

"Just wait till you see, Sam," I said, fol-lowing him into his comfortable living room. The room was a testament to Sam's long widowerhood, filled as it was with heavy leather furniture grouped around the fire-place. A dark Oriental rug covered the floor, and overstuffed bookcases lined the walls. If it hadn't been for the French doors, open now to the veranda, you'd've felt smothered in books and magazines and papers of all stripes and kinds.

"Look at this, Sam," I said, taking the

pamphlets from Little Lloyd and poking them at Sam. "I want you to just look at this."

"Have a seat, Julia. Make yourself comfortable and let me see what James can offer us from the kitchen."

"Nothing for us, thank you all the same," I said, holding up my hand. "That reminds me, though, I need to ask James if he would help us at the reception."

But I had other things on my mind at the moment. "Sam," I said, "that woman's got her sights set on me, and I'm not going to stand for it."

"What woman?"

"Why, Emma Sue Ledbetter. Who else would do something as sneaky as this? She's gone all the way around Robin Hood's barn to get back at me. Just look at this stuff." And I thrust the pamphlets in his hand.

As he skimmed one of them, his eyebrows went up. "Interesting. What do you want me to do about it, Julia? If this reflects her views, there's nothing we can do to change them."

I almost stomped my foot. "That's not the point! I don't care what her views are, as long as she doesn't push them on me! But worse than that, she's told this child to distribute them. And to top it off, she expects *me* to help him do it!"

I took a breath and ranted on. "And as far as what you can do about it, you can go to the session and show them what she's doing and have them put a stop to it."

"I'm not on the session anymore. . . ."

"I know that, but they'll listen to you, Sam. And if that's not enough to shake you up, look at this thing." I took a bumper sticker from the boy and waved it around. "She wants this child to glue these things on every car he can, and she wants me to help him. Can't you just see us, sneaking up on parked cars and slapping on bumper stickers? Furthermore, she didn't even tell him to ask permission first, did she, Little Lloyd? That's called *vandalism* in my book, and this child is not going to be a party to it. If she wants to cover every car in town, let her do it. But she'd better not come within ten feet of *mine*!"

"Now, Julia," Sam said, beginning as he usually did to dampen my fire. "Sit down and cool off. Of course, Little Lloyd's not going to do that, and, of course, I'll make sure that somebody on the session knows what she's doing. But let me remind you, a good eighty percent of the elders will agree with her and the other twenty percent won't want to make waves with the preacher's wife."

"That just makes me so mad I can't see straight," I said, finally sinking onto the leather sofa, which creaked under me. "Especially since you're probably right. But, Sam, she's deliberately aiming this at me. Hold that thing up, Little Lloyd, so Sam can see it."

The boy stretched out the bumper sticker, and Sam read aloud, "'PRAY WITH US.' Well, Julia, if people want to encourage prayer, that's their privilege. I don't see any reason to get upset about it, but I agree that you and Little Lloyd ought not to be pasting them on parked cars." He smiled at the thought, but I was not amused.

"I should say not. Now, I'm a firm believer in prayer, Sam, as you well know. So if anybody wants to stand on a street corner and make a public fool of himself, why, I say that's his right, but that doesn't mean I have to do it. And, furthermore, I don't think it's necessary to announce to the whole world that you're praying, or advertise that fact with a bumper sticker, either."

"They don't see it that way, Julia," Sam said with that easy smile of his. "I expect they see it as a witness to others and as a testimony to their faith. I can't imagine that this is aimed directly at you."

"Sam, I declare," I said, jumping to my feet again to pace between stacks of books on the floor. "You are so blessed tolerant that you're going to wake up one morning and find that you don't stand for anything. My problem is not with people who want to paste these things on their bumpers or with people who want to pass out tracts from door to door. It's still a free country after all, as long as they don't expect *me* to join in. And that's exactly what Emma Sue Ledbetter's doing with this." I stopped in front of him and put my hands on my hips. "And I'll tell you why. It's because she's been exercised for months that my prayer life's not up to par, and it didn't help when I resigned from the prayer chain."

"Slow down, Julia." Sam put his hands on my shoulders, and for the first time, began to take me seriously. "You don't need to let this upset you so."

So I reminded him of why I'd opted out of the prayer chain, which I was sure Emma Sue had then started buzzing on my account, as well as Norma Cantrell's.

"She as good as told me," I went on, "that my soul's in danger because I refused to be a party to it. She'll have the prayer chain praying for me, and you know what that means. By the time her request for prayer is passed along to every nosy woman on the chain, no telling what the end result will be."

By that time I noticed the pale face of Little Lloyd as he listened and took in all I was saying. "Little Lloyd," I said, turning to him, "I'm sorry you had to hear all of that. But don't you worry about it. Some people just get carried away, and Mrs. Ledbetter is one of them, even if she is the preacher's wife. Just because somebody enjoys a certain position doesn't mean they're always right, or that they're above criticism." Wesley Lloyd Springer sprang to mind, but I refrained from mentioning him. Then, having reassured the child, I turned back to Sam. "I'm going to set that woman straight, Sam, if it's the last thing I do."

"Now, Julia," Sam said. "All you have to

do is tell Emma Sue that Little Lloyd can't do it. Both of you have too much to do with this wedding coming up and, besides, isn't Lloyd going with his mother when she moves?"

"Oh, Lord, don't bring that up! I can hardly bear to think of it, much less tell Emma Sue. Why, Sam, imagine what she'd send out along the prayer chain then. Little Lloyd, why don't you run to the kitchen and speak to James; you don't need to hear this. Ask him about coming to our house on Saturday, and tell him that I'll confirm it with him as soon as I get my ducks in a row. Hurry, though, because we need to go and let your mother know what's going on. Just leave that stuff here with Sam. In fact, why don't you bring that box in and leave it here. I don't want to be carting it around. Sam, you can throw it out or burn it or do whatever with it. Well, wait. Leave me one of each to show Hazel Marie. And leave two more for Coleman, so he'll know to go after Emma Sue if there's a sudden spate of bumper stickers around town."

Little Lloyd started toward the door to get the box from the car. "Wait," I said, stopping the boy as he left the room. "Leave another set for Binkie; she needs to know what's going on. Sam, thank you for your help, although I expected a little more concern from you. You just never take anything seriously enough."

"Oh, I do. You just don't notice what I'm serious about. Now, Julia, don't let Emma Sue get you down; you have enough on your plate right now. The pastor'll be back before long, and he'll calm her down."

"I know." I sighed. "I just hate the thought of what the prayer chain's passing along about me."

Before I could continue bemoaning my fate, I was distracted by Little Lloyd, who was running up the steps and across the porch. He snatched open the screen door and let it slam behind him. Before I could reprimand him, he ran up to me, breathing hard. "It's gone! Miss Julia, that box is gone!"

"What do you mean, it's gone?"

"I mean it's not there!" His eyes were almost as big as his glasses. "I left it on the backseat like you told me to, and it's not there! It's not anywhere in the car or around it! I looked all over and it's not there!"

"Well, this is a pretty come off," I said,

holding Little Lloyd's hand so he'd stop waving it in my face. "It's of a size you could hardly miss. Sam, who in the world'd come along and take a box the likes of that one out of my car? In broad daylight, too?"

"I bet I know who, Miss Julia," Little Lloyd said, still hardly able to get his breath. "I bet it was that ole Dixon Hightower, don't you?"

Chapter 13

"Lillian!" I called as soon as I stepped into the house. Little Lloyd and I had jumped out of the car and scooted across the yard as quickly as we could in case Dixon was hot on our trail. Not that I was scared or anything, but the boy was. Besides, having something stolen right in front of your eyes can make you a little jumpy. We were both breathless by the time I got the door locked behind us.

"Lillian," I said, as she turned from the refrigerator holding several eggs in her hands. "Have you heard from Coleman?"

"No'm. Why? What's the matter?"

"What's the matter! I'll tell you what's the matter. It's that Dixon Hightower who stole a box of Emma Sue Ledbetter's political views right out of the backseat of my car. Where's Hazel Marie?"

"She takin' a bath. Mr. Pickens, he fin'lly

call an' say it be a while 'fore he move her out, but he might have a minute to come by later on. And the upholstery man come an' he moved ever' stick of the livin' room furniture out. I been dust moppin' ever since. But how you know it was Dixon that got in yo' car? An' what that stuff you say he take? Little Lloyd, that bad ole man didn't hurt you none, did he?"

"No'm," the boy said. "We didn't even see him. But it had to be him; nobody else'd do such a thing. Miss Julia was going to give those tracts and bumper stickers back to Mrs. Ledbetter and now she can't. And I bet we'll all be on the prayer chain now." He put a hand on his stomach, which always acted up on him when he got worried.

Lillian frowned. "What you say?"

"I'll explain later, Lillian. Right now I've got to report this," I said, my nerves strumming from our close encounter with the thieving rascal. Dixon didn't really scare me, but he made me mad enough to wring his neck. "Sam's not convinced it was him, but I am and I'm not going to put up with it."

Hazel Marie walked in then, all freshly bathed, dressed and hot-rollered. "Not going to put up with what?"

So Little Lloyd told our tale in detail, and Lillian and Hazel Marie were suitably impressed with our narrow escape.

"Law!" Lillian said. "That ole Dixon gettin' bold as brass."

"Well," I said, having had time to think a little more clearly. "We don't know for sure that it was Dixon. But whoever it was, I'm just glad that I didn't send Little Lloyd to the car just as somebody was in the process of stealing that box. You've got to stay within our eyesight from now on, Little Lloyd."

"Oh, baby," Hazel Marie said, putting her arms around him. "I don't want you to take any more chances. Miss Julia, do you think he knew it was your car?"

"I have no idea. It could've been anybody's, as far as I know. On the other hand, Sam had every window in his house open, so who knows who was sneaking around, listening to every word we said? I've got to report this."

I went to the phone and dialed the sheriff's department, which gave me no satisfaction at all. First of all, Coleman was on patrol and unavailable for a personal call and, second of all, Lieutenant Peavey, the only other deputy I could think to ask for, was in the same condition.

"Well, I have to speak to somebody," I told the man who'd answered the phone. "I have reason to think that I know where Dixon Hightower is, or *was* not thirty minutes ago."

He perked up at that. "You've had a sighting?"

I paused and looked down at the receiver. Then I said, "I'm not reporting a UFO here. However, we just missed seeing some little sneak. I'm pretty sure it was him because something was stolen from my car, a box that was on the backseat, and we'd just walked in to tell Mr. Sam Murdoch what was in the box, which shouldn't've been coming from the church, much less the preacher's wife. And I think you'd agree with me on that. Sam certainly did."

"Uh, ma'am, would you run that by me again?"

"It's perfectly plain. A box was stolen from my car, which was parked in view of the whole world in Sam Murdoch's driveway, and absolutely nobody would want the thing, considering what was in it. So I'm thinking it had to be Dixon. I mean, who else in town would steal something not worth stealing?"

He sighed, then said, "Give me your name and address, and the address where the perpetrator is alleged to be."

I did, and hung up, somewhat uninspired by the deputy's response to a clear lead toward the most wanted man in Abbot County.

"Well," I said, "I've done all I can do. It's in their hands now, unless I get mine on Dixon. Imagine stealing something from *me,* who's always done the best I could for him."

"He crazy, Miss Julia," Lillian said. "He don't half know what he do."

"That's no excuse as far as I'm concerned. When he steals from me and puts Little Lloyd in danger, he's going to have to suffer the consequences."

"I couldn't agree more," Hazel Marie said, but the ringing of the doorbell diverted her attention. "Oh, that's J.D.!"

She hurried out, with Little Lloyd and me right behind her, in case it wasn't. I stopped in the dining room, watching as she swung open the front door, her face glowing with expectation. Before she could say a word, Mr. Pickens stepped inside and wrapped her in his arms and gave her a kiss that would've made me throw caution to the winds. As Hazel Marie's response clearly showed she'd already done.

My goodness, some men had a way with them. It wasn't the way he kissed her that affected me so much, but the way he held her—like he was holding something precious that would just kill him if he lost it. I'd never seen anything like it, or been the object of it, either.

Being reassured that Hazel Marie was in safe hands, or arms, I motioned to Little Lloyd to follow me back to the kitchen.

"Miss Julia," Little Lloyd said as the door swung to behind us. "You reckon we could ask Mr. Pickens to move in with us for a while?"

"Why, whatever for?" I could picture myself sitting up half the night listening for footsteps between bedrooms.

"So Dixon won't come stealing something again. I'd sure feel better if Mr. Pickens was with us."

"Me, too," Lillian said. She stood by the sink wringing out a dishcloth that didn't need it.

"You two, you're getting all worked up over something that's not going to happen. All right, I know," I said, holding up my hands to ward off their responses to that. "I know that Dixon was the one who probably took that box from my car, but let's face it. He did us a favor, now that I think about it, since I was trying to get rid of it anyway. But he's not going to come here to the house. There're too many people in and out all the time and, if he's still around, which I doubt very much, he's not going to risk some of us seeing him and calling the sheriff. So the two of you need to stop worrying about it."

"Yessum," Little Lloyd said. "I'll try."

"Run on and play then." As he left, I walked over to the sink and took a glass down from a cabinet. Turning on the faucet to fill it, I whispered to Lillian, "Lillian, we don't need to be making this worse than it is. You know how that child can make himself sick with worry over practically nothing. Which, I'm convinced, Dixon certainly is."

"That easy for you to say," she told me, frowning her disagreement. "Don't nothin' ever scare you, but me, I done seen too much not to know what some peoples can do."

I put my hand on her arm. "I know, Lillian, but I really don't think he's going to come around here. He's probably got a hideout up in the woods somewhere, a long way from here. All I'm saying is that we need to keep our heads and not agitate Little Lloyd any more than he already is."

She grunted and turned away. "Jus' look like to me we ought to be takin' some of them *measures,* like Coleman tell us to. Not jus' set around an' say Dixon not gonna bother us."

"Well, that's fine," I said. "If you want to take a few measures, it's all right with me. Maybe it'd cut down on the child's worrying if he knew Dixon couldn't get in. Just don't lock me out of my own house if I walk out in the yard."

She turned back to me, relief obvious on her face. "You mind if I spend the night? Me an' Little Lloyd got lots to do to make us feel safe."

"Of course, spend as many nights as you want to. I'm sure having you around would relieve his mind as much as anything."

"Do it matter what we do? I mean, some of them window locks not too sturdy. We might need to put a stick of wood in the windows to keep 'em from bein' pushed up."

"I don't care what you do. In fact, I think it's a good idea to keep the child's mind occupied and his hands busy. If he's doing something, he won't have time to worry.

"And speaking of that," I went on, putting down my glass. "There's something worrying me, and I need to do something about it. I can't let this business with Dixon, or whoever, put it on the back burner."

"What you up to now?"

"Oh, Lillian, you won't believe what Emma Sue Ledbetter expected Little Lloyd and me to do." And I told her of the child's home mission project. "Can you see us doing that?"

"Well, no'm, I can't see you doin' it, but they's people out there think mission work a good thing."

"I know that," I said tartly, working up a head of steam. "But there's mission work, and then there's mission work. But each of us is called to what we're suited for and, believe me, I am not suited for squatting behind a car and gluing on a bumper sticker. And that's what I'm going to tell Emma Sue Ledbetter."

I rubbed my hands down the side of my dress, dreading the coming minutes. Reaching for the telephone, I took a deep breath and gathered my thoughts. I declare, you have to walk a thin line when you need to tell somebody off, yet do it without making an enemy for life. Especially when it's the preacher's wife you're dealing with.

When she answered her phone with a questioning "Hello?," I went straight to the point. "Emma Sue, I don't mean to hurt your feelings, but Little Lloyd can't go door-to-door or do any pasting, either."

"Julia?"

"Of course, it's Julia," I said, determined to get said what needed to be said. "Now, Emma Sue, don't get upset, but what you've asked that child, *and me,* to do is entirely unacceptable. In fact, I'm surprised that you'd even consider me for such an activity."

"Oh, Julia," she said, somewhat wetly. "I thought you'd be glad to help. I know you've been having trouble with your own prayer life, and witnessing to others about the power of prayer would strengthen you spiritually."

I bit my lip to keep from letting her have it. Then, with a mighty effort to soften my tone, I said, "Emma Sue, I appreciate your concern for my spiritual health, but right now I have too much to do to worry with it.

I'm just letting you know that you'll have to get somebody else for your home missions. Or, even better, come up with another project since we Presbyterians generally keep a low profile when it comes to accosting people in their homes or crawling around cars parked on the street."

"Oh, Julia," she said again, along with a few sniffs and swallows. "Excuse me. Let me get a Kleenex." When she came back to the phone, she went on. "I can't help but be disappointed. I thought you'd be so good at this and, Julia, you know we must share our faith with others. It's incumbent upon us."

"I share plenty every time they pass the collection plate," I reminded her. "Don't think I don't."

"I know you do," she whimpered. "But, Julia, there's so much work to be done, and nobody wants to do it. Well"—she sniffed loudly—"I guess if you won't do it, I'll have to take it on myself. Although you wouldn't believe how many times this sort of thing happens."

I probably would, but I didn't tell her that. As long as she came up with such outrageous ideas, people were going to scatter every time they saw her.

She blew her nose, then said, "Well, Julia, I wish you'd reconsider, but if you won't, there's nothing I can say to change your mind. Except pray for you, as I always do. Just drop off the tracts and bumper stickers at the church, and I'll get them as soon as I can. I'll just have to do the best I can with them."

Oh, Lord, how was I going to drop off something I no longer had? My head started spinning trying to think how to explain the situation, considering the state of sorrow I'd already put her in.

"Uh, Emma Sue," I said. "We may have a little problem with that. We're so busy; the wedding, you know. I'll get them to you just as soon as I possibly can. And, speaking of the wedding, I'm so glad you're coming. It wouldn't be the same without you." And I kept her on that track for as long as I could, turning her mind away from prayer tracts and bumper stickers, as well as their current unknown whereabouts.

When I finally got off the phone, I turned to Lillian, who was standing there, shaking her head.

"Don't say a word, Lillian," I said. "Not one word."

Chapter 14

After a light supper, during which Lillian and Little Lloyd discussed their burglarproofing strategies and Hazel Marie ate in the semi-dream state Mr. Pickens had left her in, I realized that I had had enough for the day. Dealing with both Emma Sue and Dixon in one day had left me as limp as a dishrag.

"I'm going to excuse myself and go to bed," I said, laying my napkin by my plate and rising from the chair.

Hazel Marie looked at me sharply, and Lillian said, "It not even dark yet. You gettin' sick or something?"

"Not at all. I'm just tired. This would've been a busy day even without having to put up with Emma Sue Ledbetter. That woman just saps my strength. And tomorrow'll be busier, so I'm going to get a good night's sleep."

"You sure you're all right?" Hazel Marie's

look of concern as she started out of her chair gave me a great deal of comfort. "You want me to get you some aspirin?"

"No, really. I'm not sick, just tired. Don't worry about me; I'm just going to crawl in and put this day behind me." It was all I could do to keep from yawning in their faces.

"If you're sure then," Hazel Marie said, sitting back down. "I'll be sleeping upstairs with Little Lloyd so he won't be scared, so if you need anything during the night, I'll be right across the hall."

"An' I'll be right next door to you," Lillian said. "You 'member I'm gonna spend the night."

"Yes, thank you both, but I won't need anything. I plan to sleep at least ten hours and get up in the morning ready to get this wedding in high gear."

And off I went, climbing the stairs slowly and stiffly. A good long night's sleep every once in a while did me a world of good, and I looked forward to closing my door and my mind on all the things yet to do.

After preparing for bed and taking a last look at my lists, I drew the curtains and crawled under the covers. For a little while,

I could hear the murmur of their voices downstairs and of the television turned down low. None of it bothered me; in fact, it was soothing to know that the people closest to me were safe inside my house, and there if I needed them.

Later, when the room was completely dark, I roused enough to hear the shuffle of feet in the hall outside my door and a few whispers as the three of them came upstairs to go to bed. I smiled to myself, knowing that they were trying to be quiet for my sake. Then, as the house settled into the quiet of sleep, I drifted off again.

Sometime way up in the morning, I sat straight up, a noise like the end of the world jerking me out of a sound sleep. With my heart thudding like a drum, I jumped out of bed, as a crashing and banging and yelling and cursing echoed throughout the house.

"My Lord!" I said, trembling so bad that I almost stumbled over my gown as I ran for the door.

Little Lloyd, his hair standing straight up and his eyes bulging out of his head, opened his door at the same time and we stared at each other across the dark hall.

"It's Dixon!" he yelled. "Help! It's Dixon!"

Hazel Marie grabbed him from behind and I turned, only to run smack into Lillian, who'd dashed into the hall from her room. I screamed and she screamed. Then Hazel Marie shrieked like a banshee, while Little Lloyd jittered around, yelling, "It's Dixon! It's Dixon!"

Lillian and I clasped each other, both of us trembling as more clashing and banging came from the stairwell.

"Do something, Lillian," I gasped. "Somebody's breaking in."

"I got this here arn skillet," she whispered hoarsely. "Le's go get him." She raised the heavy iron pan, which she'd apparently slept with, and we crept to the head of the stairs.

The racket Hazel Marie and Little Lloyd were making almost drowned out the blue streak of curses coming from the foot of the stairs. In between the fearsome swear-words, the clashing and banging continued unabated.

"The light," I whispered, reaching for the switch.

"No!" Lillian whispered back, grabbing my arm. "Le's sneak up on him."

"Lord, Lillian, it's dark down there."

Across the hall, Little Lloyd was dancing up and down, his arms flailing, as he screamed, "Call the sheriff! Call the sheriff!"

"Wait! Wait a minute," I heard Hazel Marie say. "Calm down, Lloyd, honey, calm down. It's all right."

And suddenly I knew it was all right. I flipped the light switch and looked down the stairwell at a man curled up at the bottom of the stairs, pots and pans and metal trays and an ironing board piled up, on and around him.

"Oh, Jesus!" Lillian bellowed. "We done kilt him!"

"Who!" Little Lloyd screamed, as he finally freed himself from his mother and came running to us. "Is it Dixon? Is it Dixon?"

An arm of the man rose from the pile, swiping away several pans that clanged away across the floor. Mr. Pickens pulled himself to his feet, looking somewhat stunned and disheveled. "What the hell!"

"J.D.!" Hazel Marie screamed, running past us in a thin nightgown. "Are you hurt?"

I raised my eyes to heaven, both relieved and done in to see Mr. Pickens leaning against the wall, as pans clanked around his feet. "Well, Mr. Pickens," I said. "I guess you've learned that your sins will find you out. What are you doing sneaking up my stairs in the middle of the night?"

"I was sneaking *down* the damned stairs," he said, holding his head with the hand that wasn't holding on to the wall. "What the hell did I run into?"

I stared at Lillian, then at Little Lloyd, both of them looking somewhat chastened. "We made a barricade," Little Lloyd whispered to me. "So Dixon couldn't get in."

"Thay Lord," I said, then turned to more important matters, as I watched Hazel Marie croon over Mr. Pickens, smoothing his hair and asking where he hurt. Her nightgown left little to the imagination, and I was tempted to either throw a sheet around her or turn off the lights.

"So," I said, crossing my arms. "Tell me, Mr. Pickens, just what you were doing up here before you tried to go down?"

"Oh, Miss Julia," Hazel Marie said. "I told him he could use Coleman's room. That was all right, wasn't it? You were asleep and I didn't want to wake you. J.D. had to come in late and leave early on Binkie's case, and I hated for him to have to drive back and forth from Asheville. He'd hardly've gotten any sleep at all. Oh, honey," she said, running her hand over his face, "why didn't you use the back stairs?"

"Wouldna done no good," Lillian mumbled. "We got them barry-caded, too."

Little Lloyd stood beside me and I could feel him trembling as he gazed down the stairs at what he and Lillian had wrought. "I'm sorry," he murmured, half under his breath. "I'm sorry; I'm sorry."

I put my arm around his shoulders. "It's all right now. No harm's been done."

"Hell and damnation," Mr. Pickens mumbled, but loud enough for me to cover Little Lloyd's ears. "I was checking the house before I left, be sure everything was locked. And, by God, it nearly killed me."

"Mr. Pickens," I said, and right sharply, too. "I'd watch the way I talked, if I'd nearly met my end like you did."

"Jesus, woman," he said, flashing those dark eyes at me as he felt for sore places. "I *did* meet my end. Rolled ass over elbow all the way down."

Chapter 15

There was no more sleeping after that frightful awakening, so some of us pitched in and helped pick up the pots and pans. Lillian and Little Lloyd had denuded the kitchen cabinets to put up their barricades, so it took a while to gather what we needed to prepare breakfast.

Mr. Pickens wasn't a bit of help, nor was Hazel Marie, since she had to soothe and baby him. There he sat at the kitchen table, holding his head and moaning every once in a while, looking pitifully at her as she petted him. Then when he'd had enough of it, he got to his feet, fully recovered and ready to undertake whatever investigation he was conducting for Binkie. He gave Hazel Marie a quick kiss and took himself off, while she was still begging him to go to the hospital.

"Hazel Marie," I said, shoving a Dutch oven in a cabinet, "don't worry about him.

The only thing hurt about that man is his pride."

"But he hit on his head." She wrung her hands worse than Lillian could do.

"Well, see? With as hard a head as he has, he couldn't be hurt much." And I started laughing at the thought of Mr. Pickens going head over teakettle down the stairs. Lillian held on to the sink as she laughed with me, and finally Hazel Marie joined in.

Little Lloyd came in, already dressed for school, and looked from one to the other of us as we wiped tears and doubled over with more spasms of laughter.

He gradually began to smile as we began to get our breath and tell him what we were laughing about. "I hope Mr. Pickens won't be mad at me," he said, worry overtaking any humor he was able to see in the situation.

"Of course, he won't," Hazel Marie said, straightening his collar. "In fact, he told me that you and Lillian had put up the best burglar alarm he'd ever run into."

"He mortally run into it, didn't he?" Lillian said, and that started us off again.

We hardly stopped the rest of the morning, although it seemed that all I did was make more lists. I left a loud, slow message on my yardman's answering machine asking him to cut the grass first thing Friday morning. Raymond never answered his phone, since he couldn't speak much English and I certainly didn't speak Spanish. Then I double-checked with the rental place so that the chairs and piano would be delivered on time, and changed my order from a three-tiered to a four-tiered wedding cake.

"You think that'll be big enough?" I asked Lillian as I hung up after talking with the caterer.

"Prob'bly so," she said. "I'm gonna save two slices for the freezer, so it be ready for they first anniversary. Even if somebody don't get any."

Hazel Marie fixed sandwiches for our lunch, then went out into the backyard to get some sun so she wouldn't look so naked in her bridesmaid's dress. I doubted the efficacy of that kind of covering, but I kept it to myself.

After an hour or so, she came into the kitchen looking flushed and sweaty from all that baking.

"Miss Julia," she said, "I've been trying to

think of what to give Binkie and Coleman for a wedding gift. Have you thought what you're going to give them?"

"You need something to drink, Hazel Marie," I said, going to the refrigerator to pour her some lemonade. "And, yes, I've given it some thought. The groom's parents, which I guess I'm the stand-in for, are supposed to give a silver service. But, I declare, I can't see Binkie ever using one. She's not the formal entertaining type."

"No'm, she's not." Hazel Marie took the glass I handed her. "She might use a gas barbeque grill, though."

"Well, I'm not going to give that. No, what I've decided to do is give them the silver pitcher my aunt gave me when I married. You know, that ornate one in there on the sideboard. It's quite old and, since it's sterling, which they hardly make anymore, very valuable. I know Binkie won't use it as a serving piece, but she can put flowers in it and enjoy it that way. And they both can enjoy the check I plan to put in it, too. What're you going to give them?"

"I don't have anything as nice as your pitcher," she said, sipping the lemonade and cooling off. "But I think I'm going to give them a set of sheets. I know they'll need them, since Binkie said they're going to buy a king-size bed and they don't have any sheets to fit. In fact, I'd planned to get them two sets until I priced them. They're awfully high, so I think I'd rather get them one really good set, instead of two ordinary ones."

It pleased me that Hazel Marie had learned that quality was better than quantity. Now that Sam had made sure she had an income from Little Lloyd's trust fund, Hazel Marie managed it with a pleasing amount of frugality, taking lessons from me.

"What about you, Lillian?" Hazel Marie asked. "Have you thought what you're going to do?"

"Yessum, I have," Lillian said. "I already started making up a bunch of things for they freezer, so they have something to eat for a while. Miss Binkie don't do much cookin', an' Coleman, he a hungry man."

We all laughed at that, and I told her that they'd probably appreciate her gift more than all the sheets and silver pitchers they might get.

———

Hazel Marie, still concerned about Dixon, drove to the school about two-thirty to pick up Little Lloyd. For myself, I didn't have time to worry about Dixon Hightower. I figured he wouldn't dare bother me again, and if he had to bother me in the first place, he couldn't've taken anything I'd rather him have. Maybe Emma Sue's tracts and bumper stickers would do him some good.

Hazel Marie and Little Lloyd came in the back door, and I thought to myself that the child looked more worried and bedraggled than usual. Still had Mr. Pickens's stairway exit on his mind, I guessed.

"Hey," he said, as he shrugged off his book bag.

"Hey, baby," Lillian said, "come give me a hug. You hungry, sugar?" She headed for the refrigerator. "I got some lemonade an' cookies jus' waitin' for you."

He thanked Lillian, then sat down at the table. Then, nibbling at an oatmeal cookie, he said, "Wonder what Coleman's doing parked around the corner?"

"Why, I don't know," I said, looking up from the guest list I was counting for the third time. "Was he in his patrol car?"

"Yessum, I saw him when we pulled into the driveway, just sitting there. He didn't see us, but it looked like he was on duty so I didn't bother him."

"Parked around the corner?" I repeated. "Why, something must be going on. Maybe he's on the lookout for Dixon, although that little runt better not be around here. Or another prisoner they've let escape. More likely, though, he's waiting to lead a funeral procession. A good thing you didn't interrupt him, Little Lloyd; that was thoughtful.

"Lillian," I went on, "do you remember the time a prisoner escaped from the courthouse right before his trial began? They looked everywhere for him, got the dogs out and everything, and finally found him up in that big tree in front of the courthouse."

"I 'member. An' I 'member when some woman tried to go through a courthouse window an' got stuck in the screen."

As we laughed, we heard footsteps on the back porch and Coleman walked in. His face was so stiff and drawn, my first thought was that Dixon was on top of us. Then I saw a suitcase and a duffel bag in his hands.

"Coleman?" I asked, as we all stopped what we were doing and stared at him.

"Mind if I move back into my room, Miss Julia?" he asked, not meeting anybody's eye, as he crossed the kitchen and headed for the back stairs. His shoulders were slumped even worse than Little Lloyd's. "If it's a bother, I'll find an apartment as soon as I can."

"No bother," I mumbled, stunned at this sudden announcement. Then, standing to go after him, I called, "Coleman, what's the matter?"

He didn't stop, just continued up the stairs. "The wedding's off, Miss Julia."

"No, Jesus!" Lillian cried, smacking her hand against her chest.

"Oh!" Hazel Marie cried, then propped her elbows on the newspaper-covered table and covered her face with her hands.

I sunk back into my chair, rendered speechless by this turn of events. Little Lloyd stared, open-eyed and -mouthed, at me.

The sound of more footsteps on the back porch and the squeak of the screen door opening couldn't shake us out of our shock.

"Here comes the Spode," Sam sang out, to the tune of the wedding march, off-key and completely inappropriate in the present circumstances. "Where you want this box of china, Julia? Lillian told me to pick it up, and

I always do what she tells me to." He winked at her as she smiled weakly at his foolishness.

"Anywhere. Put it anywhere," I mumbled. The placement of china was the last thing on my mind. "Sam," I said, turning to him, "you've got to do something."

"I'm here to help; just tell me what to do." Then, looking at each of us in turn, taking note of the stricken looks on our faces, he put the box on the counter and said, "What's wrong?"

"Oh, Sam," I wailed. "Coleman's moving back in. He said the wedding's off. You've got to talk to him, because he just can't do this. If he's left Binkie in the lurch, with our dresses bought, invitations out, the caterer and the florist ready to go, and Lieutenant Peavey practicing his solo, why, I . . . I don't know what we'll do. Talk to him, Sam. See what the matter is, and tell him he can't do this to Binkie."

"Called it off? Any idea why?"

"No! He didn't say one word about why. That's why I want you to talk to him."

"I don't know, Julia. He may not want to talk to anybody," Sam said, touching my arm to calm me down. "These things happen, you know, what with the stress of the wedding. I expect they've just had a little tiff, and they'll work it out themselves."

"You didn't see him, Sam. He looked like he had the whole world on his shoulders. Whatever's happened, it's not a little tiff. I tell you, we've got to do something before Binkie is shamed before the whole town. Oh, Lord," I said, holding my head, "left at the altar. She'll never live it down."

"Why don't you call her? Get an idea of what's happened before I try to talk to Coleman."

"Well!" I cried, throwing up my hands. "That's the whole problem right there. I should've known it. Binkie's too busy to straighten this out. Too busy with her cases to even take part in her own wedding. That's it," I went on, nodding my head as I felt sure I'd nailed down the problem. "Coleman can't stand the competition of her job. Men! They choose smart, accomplished women to fall in love with, then when they marry them, they expect them to turn into happy little homemakers with nothing in their heads but what closet to clean or what floor to mop. I declare, you'd think if that's what they want, they'd choose an airheaded blonde in the first place! Oh, sorry, Hazel Marie, that was not a reflection on you, just a figure of speech."

I dropped back into my chair, just done in with the thought that the lovely wedding I'd planned was now in tatters. "Go talk to him, Sam. Please."

Sam patted my shoulder. "Look, there's no use speculating on who's at fault. Maybe nobody is; maybe they've both decided that they aren't right for each other."

"My Lord, Sam, they've been right for each other for, lo, I don't know how long! Now is a poor time to be thinking otherwise. Especially since I have everything planned down to the last sprig of baby's breath. Go on upstairs, Sam, and find out what's going on, so we'll know what to do about it."

"I'm not sure it's a good idea," Sam said, frowning, as he headed for the stairs. "But I'll try."

"That's all I want," I said, thinking that if everybody tried as hard as I did, there'd be a lot less heartache around this house.

Chapter 16

"No good, Julia," Sam said as he came back downstairs, shaking his head. "He just says he can't talk about it right now. We'll just have to leave them alone and let them work it out themselves."

"How can I do that?" I stormed. "Sam, you don't seem to understand! Here it is just days before the wedding and the whole town's set to see it take place."

Sam gave my exaggeration a brief smile and said, "Let's not worry about the town, Julia. Coleman's the one we ought to be concerned about. And Binkie, if she's in half the shape he's in."

Hazel Marie's eyes began to overflow at the thought. "I just can't stand it," she sobbed. "Everybody's breaking up and hurting each other and, oh, nobody, just nobody cares about anybody else." And down went her head onto the table. She'd been listening to too many country music songs, in my opinion.

"Well," I said, ready to throw up my hands. "I don't know what to do. Should I start canceling everything on Coleman's say-so? I've ordered enough food to feed an army, so if there's no wedding, who's going to eat it? And my furniture's gone and the silver's polished. And wedding presents are coming in, stacking up like you wouldn't believe." I looked wild-eyed around the room, hoping an answer would be forthcoming from somewhere.

"Hazel Marie," I said, my eyes lighting on her. "Stop crying and help me out here. Should we carry on and hope those two will mend their fences? Or should we start calling everything off?"

She raised her head and wiped her face with her hands. Little Lloyd handed her his napkin and patted her on the back. "I don't know, Miss Julia," she said. "It just hurts me so bad for this to happen. I don't understand it. Here, they both wanted to marry and they've let some little thing come between them. While J.D. won't even . . ." Down went her head again as the tears gushed out.

"It's all right, Mama," Little Lloyd said, patting her again. "Don't cry."

"Why don't you call Binkie before you do anything?" Sam said, the voice of reason as always.

"I'll do better than that," I said, determined to get to the bottom of the problem. I'd thought it was Binkie who was being left at the altar, but now I realized I was the one left holding the bag. But over and above a houseful of guests and a mountain of food and a preacher and a soloist and a pianist on my hands, Binkie and Coleman *ought* to get married.

"She'll just put me off if I call," I said, turning to look for my purse. "I'm going to her office and I'm going to sit there until she tells me what's going on."

"Hold on, Julia," Sam said. "You might ought to stay out of it."

"I'm already in it, Sam! Besides, I can't stand the thought of Coleman up there hurting and refusing to talk about it. Somebody owes me an explanation, and I'm going to get it. You want to go with me?"

"No," he said, shaking his head. "It's not my place to question their decision. She wouldn't appreciate me sticking my nose in.

But, you, yes, maybe she'll talk to you since you've worked so hard on the wedding."

"I should think so," I said, about to build up a head of steam to shake some sense into Binkie, who I'd decided was the one at fault. The idea, hurting that sweet man upstairs who wanted nothing more than to legalize their situation. Both of them needed some straight talking.

As I headed for the door, Lillian untied her apron and said, "Lemme go with you. You might need some help if she in bad shape, too."

"Come on then. I'm heading out."

With my pocketbook dangling on one arm and the other arm swinging in time to my steps, I marched down the sidewalk, Lillian in her white uniform puffing along beside me. Lord, it was hot, with that heavy, muggy feel of a thunderstorm on the way. I wasn't about to let a little heat and humidity delay me, though, as I stepped out right smartly on my mission of reconciliation.

"Don't walk so fast," Lillian said. "You gonna wear yo'self out 'fore you get there."

"I can't help it, Lillian. I'm so agitated I don't know what to do. I declare, I've been trying and trying to get those two married, and just when I thought it was going to happen, they call it off. No," I said, stopping on the curb to wait for a light to change. "I'll bet it was Binkie who called it off. What is the matter with that girl?"

"You don't know that, and it might not be nothin'," Lillian said, wiping the perspiration from her brow. "Maybe jus' a little tiff, like Mr. Sam say."

"It's got to be more than a *little* tiff. Binkie knows what's involved in planning a wedding. She wouldn't call it off at the last minute without a really good reason." As the light turned green, I stepped off the curb and started across the street. "At least, I hope she wouldn't." Then again, Binkie'd hardly done anything a normal bride would do.

We walked into her office and into the waiting room. Mary Alice McKinnon, such a pleasant young woman, looked up from the paperwork on her desk and smiled. "Afternoon, Miss Julia. Can I help you?"

"Yes, you can. Tell Binkie that I need to see her."

Mary Alice frowned and glanced toward the closed door of Binkie's office, the one that Sam used to occupy. "I don't know, Miss Julia. She's awfully busy and, well, to tell the truth, she's not feeling too well today."

"I don't doubt it, but that's why I'm here. Please tell her that I intend to wait till midnight, if that's what it takes for her to talk to me."

"Well, let me just see." Mary Alice punched a button on her phone, as I turned away to give her a little privacy.

She hung up the phone and, with a worried look, said, "Binkie says she has a minute or two. You can go on in."

Lillian and I exchanged glances, although Lillian didn't understand mine. But telling us to go on in was a glaring clue that something was bad wrong. Always before, when I'd made a professional call on Binkie, she'd come out into the waiting room to personally conduct me into her office.

I opened the office door and walked inside, Lillian right behind me. Binkie was sitting behind her huge paper-strewn desk, although she didn't strike me as having been working very hard.

"Have a seat, Miss Julia. You, too, Lillian. I know why you're here." Binkie leaned back in her executive chair and blew out her breath, like our visit was just something she had to put up with.

"Binkie," I began, propping my pocketbook on my lap and resting my hands on it. "If you know why we're here, I wish you'd let me in on it. Coleman said the wedding's off, and I just can't accept that."

"You'll have to, Miss Julia," she said in a small voice, as she looked out a window. Or would have, if the blinds hadn't been closed. "I'm sorry you've gone to so much trouble for us, but I'll reimburse you for what you've spent."

It just flew all over me that she thought my only concern was the cost and inconvenience to me. "Binkie," I said, "forget about that. I don't want any reimbursement. What I want is a reason for this sudden change of heart when you and Coleman have been getting along like a house afire right up to this very last minute."

She bowed her head and fiddled with some papers. "It just wouldn't work, Miss Julia. I realize that now, and so does Coleman. We both know it."

"Coleman doesn't know anything but the fact that his heart is breaking in two. You should've seen him when he walked in a little while ago. Looked like death warmed over when he told us the wedding's off."

She stirred some papers on her desk, her eyes lowered. "What else did he say?"

"Not another word, no explanation or anything. He wouldn't even talk to Sam, and you know yourself that Sam's as easy to talk to as anybody. Binkie, you make your living talking, so talk to me. What happened? Did Coleman do something or say something that he could undo or unsay? Is it just second thoughts on your part? You ought to know that every bride has a few, but it usually doesn't stop them from going right on down the aisle." I stopped, thinking to myself that maybe even a few second thoughts should've stopped them.

"Miss Julia." Binkie sighed and rested her arms on the desk. "It's like this. Coleman and I are on opposite sides of the law. Wait," she said, as my mouth dropped open. "I mean he tries to put people in jail and I try to keep them out. We're at cross-purposes all the time."

"But, but," I sputtered. "That shouldn't matter a hill of beans. Besides, you ought not to take your work home with you. Wesley Lloyd never did." It flashed through my mind that Wesley Lloyd wasn't the best example to bring up.

"Well," she said, tapping now with a pencil on her desk. "It's come to a head now. See, I'm Dixon Hightower's attorney and I'm convinced that he shouldn't be in prison. He should be getting care and treatment, not be locked up like a criminal. He's just not responsible for his actions. Coleman, of course, doesn't agree with me. And it's caused . . . difficulties between us."

"Oh, Binkie, for goodness sakes," I said. "You can't mean you've let that little no-account sneak thief break up your wedding! Why, I never heard of anything so ridiculous. Believe me, he's not worth it. And, for my money, Dixon ought to be locked up somewhere so he won't be rummaging through other people's things."

"I'm not going to argue with you, Miss Julia. I've been round and round with Coleman about it for days," she said, looking everywhere but at me. "That, and other things. Coleman got upset when I hired J.D. to find Dixon; said it showed I didn't trust the sheriff's department to do its job. And I said that the deputies were so mad at Dixon for escaping and hiding so well that there was no telling what they'd do to him when they caught him. And Coleman said I was a liberal lawyer. And, well, it just escalated from there."

Lillian, sitting beside me and listening to this pitiful excuse for a reason, crossed her arms over her breast and nodded to herself. "Uh-huh," she said under her breath.

"That is nothing you two can't resolve," I said, leaning forward and grasping the edge of her desk. "You love each other, and you both knew what the other did for a living before things got this far. Binkie, I tell you what. Let's go ahead with the wedding since it's so near and already planned and everything, then you and Coleman'll have all the time in the world to straighten this out."

"Miss Julia, I, oh, . . . excuse me." She jumped up from her chair and ran for the door. I heard her hurried footsteps outside the office, fading as she went down the hall. A door slammed somewhere in the depths of the building.

"Well, whatever was that about?" I turned to Lillian, my eyebrows raised. "If she's too upset to talk about the problem, she could at least be courteous about it."

Lillian put her hands on her knees and

leaned on them. "She with chile, Miss Julia."

"That still doesn't . . . she's *what*?"

"She pregnant or I ain't never seen pregnant before." Lillian nodded her head decisively.

"But they're not married!" I said, even as I realized it was probably the silliest thing I'd ever said. "I mean, how can you tell?"

"I see it 'round her eyes. It don't never fail. A baby in the womb show up first 'round yo' eyes. She down yonder right now throwin' up ever'thing in her stomach."

"Well, I never!" I was too done in to question Lillian's diagnosis. She'd never been wrong before, and had predicted a number of little arrivals long before any announcements had been made.

Lillian stirred in her chair, ready to rise. "We might better go see 'bout her. She prob'bly need a wet washrag on her head."

"Wait, Lillian. I'm not sure I can stomach . . . well, you know how suggestible I am. Maybe we should leave her alone. She hasn't seen fit to confide in us, so she might not appreciate us knowing her secret. Although, obviously, it won't be a secret for long."

I got to my feet, unable now to sit still. "Oh, my goodness, I can't believe this. Lillian, if this is so, and I don't doubt you, it's all the more reason to get those two married." I stopped in mid-pace and turned to her. "You reckon Coleman knows? It'd be just like her to keep it from him, too, just like she's done with us. She can be too independent for her own good sometimes. Come on, Lillian, let's go tell him, and tell him he's got to make Binkie see reason."

"Well, I don't think it our place—" she started, but to keep up with me she had to step lively.

"Mary Alice," I said, pausing beside her desk on my way out. "Tell Binkie not to worry about a thing. It'll work out, or I'm going to know the reason why."

Mary Alice nodded, her eyes wide as I sailed out the door, Lillian close behind.

"The first thing we have to do," I said, switching my pocketbook to the other arm, "is tell Coleman that expectant mothers don't half know what they're doing. He just has to overlook her and carry on without getting his feelings hurt. And the next thing we have to do is make Mr. Pickens hurry up and find Dixon Hightower. Then Dixon'll just have to get himself another lawyer. That'll solve a whole lot of problems right there."

Lillian's shoes flapped on her heels as she hurried to keep up with me. "I don' know we oughtta be doin' all that."

"It can't hurt," I said, stepping off the curb. "I mean, what could be worse than the mess they're already in?"

Chapter 17

It was close to suppertime by the time we got home, and the sky had darkened considerably, with the threat of rain hanging heavy over the town. The house smelled of the green beans that Lillian had left simmering on the stove. Hazel Marie had started the chicken frying, then she'd gone to her room as soon as Lillian took over. She was still in mourning over Binkie and Coleman, and in no shape to hear even more bad news. Little Lloyd was upstairs finishing his homework, and I began to set the table, after determining that Coleman had taken himself off while we were gone.

"Wonder where he went?" I said to Lillian. "He needs to be here with people who care for him and he needs to eat something. He's had a shock to his system, and he ought not be wandering around by himself."

I carried on in this way for some little

while, talking and mumbling half to myself and half to her. I was so perturbed by the thought of another illegitimate child on the way that I forgot the place mats. Just put everything on the bare table.

"I declare, Lillian," I said, folding a napkin into tiny pleats and wrapping it around my finger. "I'd think Little Lloyd would be enough."

"What you talkin' 'bout?"

"You know." I walked around the counter and lowered my voice. "Enough children out of wedlock. I mean, can't those two see what a handicap it'll be? Binkie ought to know better, being a lawyer and all. But, I declare, I don't think I can bring it up to her, face-to-face. I'd be so embarrassed."

She dried her hands on a paper towel, and said, "Don't look like it hurt Little Lloyd none, an' I know lotsa chil'ren in the same boat."

"Well, I know it happens." I shuddered and turned away. "I just can't bring myself to think about it. In detail, that is. There're things that just shouldn't be done without a marriage license, or even discussed."

"Miss Julia, that kinda goin's-on been done without no license for long as people been around. An' you know it. You ain't gonna change people, so quit worryin' it to death." She picked up a long fork and began turning the chicken in the hot grease. "An' ain't no reason for you to talk to 'em about it, neither."

"Well, *some*body has to! This is a small town, Lillian, and everybody'll know. I tell you, I've suffered from that situation with Hazel Marie and Mr. Springer, knowing that every time anybody looks at her they see them together. And no telling *how* they see them together." I shuddered again, then pulled myself together. "But I'm over that now and hardly ever think of it. But, imagine Binkie raising a child in this town by herself while everybody knows its daddy is driving around in a patrol car. She can't even pretend she's a widow or divorced." I stopped again as an errant thought entered my mind. "Wonder which Pastor Ledbetter'd think is the worst, to get divorced or to give birth out of wedlock? That's a theological dilemma, right there, don't you think?"

"I don't think 'bout them things, myself. What I think about is we got a few more days 'fore the weddin', an' lots can happen 'tween now and then." She began lifting the chicken pieces to drain on paper towels before putting them on a platter. "You go call Miss Hazel Marie an' Little Lloyd to the table. This rice 'bout ready, an' I'm startin' the gravy now."

As we sat at the table, I saw that Hazel Marie's eyes were still red and teary from her earlier bouts of crying. She said she could hardly swallow for the lump in her throat, so not wanting to start anything up again, I put off telling her what Lillian suspected about Binkie. Plus, I didn't want the boy to hear about such things at his tender age. Little Lloyd didn't have much to say, affected as he was by the sudden change in all our plans.

I finally broke the silence. "Wonder where he is?"

"Who?" Hazel Marie asked.

"Why, Coleman, of course. All I can think of is how hurt he is, and how hungry he must be. I wish he'd come eat something."

"Maybe he's over at Binkie's." Hazel Marie perked up at the thought. "Maybe they're getting back together."

"You reckon? Oh, I hope so. Put them both in your prayers tonight. You too, Little Lloyd."

"Yessum, I will." The boy stirred his rice and gravy, then looked up at me. "Maybe we ought to start the prayer chain for them."

I dropped my fork with a clatter. "Don't even think such a thing! Why, if Emma Sue Ledbetter got wind of this, there's no telling where it would end." And, thinking to myself but not wanting to tell him, I had a sudden image of Binkie, heavy with child, being gossiped about all up and down the prayer chain. "There's nothing wrong with the prayer chain, Little Lloyd, but some things need to be offered up within the family. And this is one of them."

"What're we going to do about Saturday?" Hazel Marie asked, as if she'd suddenly come out of her daze.

"I don't know yet. I keep thinking that they may decide to go through with it, and I'd hate to have everything canceled if they do. Besides, if we start calling and telling all the guests that the wedding's off, they'll want to know why. And what're we going to tell them? I certainly don't want to go into details because nobody'd believe they broke up over Dixon Hightower. I can hardly believe it myself."

"Dixon Hightower?" Hazel Marie stared at me.

"That's what Binkie said. She's defending him in his new trial. If, that is, they can find him to even have one. She's upset because Coleman thinks he ought to be in jail, and she thinks he ought to be in a hospital or a home for the helpless. And that's what Mr. Pickens is doing, trying to find Dixon for Binkie before the deputies do."

"That's what he's doing? Oh, I hope J.D. hasn't made things worse for them by working for Binkie. You know how good he is, Miss Julia. Why, I don't doubt that he'll find Dixon first, and give Binkie a chance to keep him out of jail. That might make Coleman real mad."

"I don't think Coleman would get mad about that. He sure isn't mad now, although Binkie seemed to think he was. She doesn't know how to read people. Lawyers never do; they have their minds on the written page and that's all. But Coleman is cut to the quick over her feeble excuse to call off the wedding. No, there's something else going on with that girl, but I can't figure out what."

"Maybe they'll work it out. I just hope

they do before Saturday, so we can have the wedding. I was so looking forward to being a bridesmaid. Looks like . . ." She stopped and blinked her eyes. Then she cleared her throat. "Looks like that's as close as I'm going to get to the real thing."

"Oh, Hazel Marie, honey," I said, reaching over to put my hand on her arm. "Don't say that. Mr. Pickens will see the error of his ways sooner or later. Now, let that all go and let's think about what we ought to do. We have two choices: we can go ahead and cancel or we can let things ride in hopes that they'll want to get married by Saturday."

Lillian said, "Why don't y'all keep on with yo' plans, an' have either a weddin' or a party, however it work out? That way, if it turn out to be jus' a party, you be too busy to answer nosy people's questions 'bout not havin' no bride nor groom. An' you cut down on the gossip time since nobody'll know about it till the weddin' day."

"Why, Lillian!" I said. "That's a brilliant idea. Let's do that, Hazel Marie. Of course, none of us will be in a party mood if there's no ceremony, but at least we won't have to make dozens of phone calls to explain why there won't be one."

"That would be a relief," Hazel Marie said. "And having a party would at least get the food eaten up. Maybe Miss Mattie Mae Morgan can play some dance music since the living room's cleared out. But, Miss Julia, what're we going to do about all their wedding gifts? They're piled up high on your tea table."

"Yes, and on my best cutwork linen cloth. I called Mary Alice yesterday to tell Binkie she'd better get over here and pick them up. She needs to get started on her thank-you notes right away. Six months is all a bride has to write them, you know, and even that's too long, to my way of thinking."

Hazel Marie frowned, and I remembered she'd been reading Amy Vanderbilt's eti-quette book, dreaming no doubt about her own wedding. If she ever had one.

"The correct thing, I believe," she said, "is for Binkie to send them all back. If there's no wedding at all, I mean. Maybe we ought to offer to help her. It'll be a big job."

"I'll do no such thing," I said. "What I aim to do is load them up in the car and dump them in her office. Let her suffer the embarrassment of returning every gift to every giver and try to explain herself to each one. Maybe that'll give her a taste of her own medicine." I don't believe in taking vengeance into my own hands, but Binkie had to shoulder the consequences of her failure to observe the accepted social customs. Like not getting married when you say you're going to.

Hazel Marie nodded with some hesitation, then gazed off into the far corner of the room. After some little silence, she said, "You think Binkie and Coleman would want to come to the party, even if they're not getting married?"

Chapter 18

That hardly warranted an answer, but I said, "We can at least let them know that we'll be ready even if they're not. Maybe they'll decide to go through with it for appearances' sake alone. There're worse reasons for getting married, in my opinion. Now, Little Lloyd," I went on, turning my attention to him, "if you've finished your supper, why don't you run upstairs and get ready for bed?"

"But, Miss Julia," he said, "it's not bedtime yet. It's still light outside."

"So it is," I said, taking note of the yellowish light in the yard as the wind picked up and a spatter of rain hit the windows. Thunder rolled in the distance. "Well, homework then, but if you've finished that, you can watch television if the lightning's not too close. And speaking of that, if it rains Saturday, that'll be the last straw. Run along now; your mother and I have some things to discuss."

"Oh, I get it." He folded his napkin and placed it beside his plate and grinned at me. "You don't want me to hear what y'all say. Okay, I can take a hint."

That got a smile from Hazel Marie and a laugh from Lillian. "You little rascal," I said, smiling in spite of myself, "you can read me like a book. But this is talk for grown-ups. Your time'll come soon enough."

When he left, I turned to Hazel Marie and said, "This is hard for me to talk about, but I'm going to do it anyway. Tell her, Lillian."

"Why you want me to do it?" Lillian came to the table and I motioned for her to sit down.

"Because you're the one who noticed it first. Although, sooner or later, I would have, too."

"Sooner or later, ever'body will," she said, drawing the chair close to the table. "Won't be no surprise in that. Well, Miss Hazel Marie," she went on, propping an arm on the table, "fact is, Miss Binkie, I think she pregnant."

"What!" Hazel Marie reared back in her chair, as astounded as I had been.

"Wait a minute, Lillian," I said. "You told me she *is,* not that you *think* she is. Now, which is it? We need to know for sure, since it'll make all the difference in the world as to what we do."

"I'm pretty sure," Lillian said, nodding her head. "I nearly always can tell. It come to me when I seen her eyes an' hear her runnin' to th'ow up like she done."

"Oh, my goodness," Hazel Marie said, properly disturbed, as I'd hoped she'd be. "Then she and Coleman *have* to get married. It is Coleman's, isn't it?"

"Hazel Marie!" I cried. "Don't ask such a thing! Of course it's Coleman's. Let's don't make this any worse than it is. The question is, how're we going to get them married?"

"Does Coleman know?" Hazel Marie asked.

"I'm figuring he doesn't, or he'd be doing more than moving back here acting like a beaten child."

"I don't know, Miss Julia." Hazel Marie was getting that far-off look in her eyes again. "Binkie's got a mind of her own. But I'll tell you this, she's got a hard row to hoe if she tries to manage by herself. I know what I'm talking about, if you don't mind me bringing it up."

"That's exactly what I hoped you'd do," I said. "I think you ought to talk to her, tell her what she's letting herself in for, raising a child without a husband. Tell her about the looks and the stares and the whispers, all that you had to put up with. Maybe you can talk some sense into her."

"You don't think . . . ?" Hazel Marie started, then stopped as her eyes began to fill. "No, she wouldn't do that. Surely she wouldn't."

"Do what?"

"You know, . . . not have the baby," she whispered, as the tears overflowed.

"Oh, Lord!" I cried, jumping up from my chair. "I hadn't thought of that! Oh, no, she wouldn't! Would she? Lillian, we can't let that happen. Hazel Marie, what're we going to do? We have to get them married. There's no two ways about it."

I paced the floor, so agitated at the thought of what Binkie might do that I couldn't get myself together. I certainly supported a woman's right to choose, but to my mind the time to choose was before, not after the fact.

"I have to talk to her. And to him," I said, although I didn't know what I could say to either. "Something has to be done. I've a good mind to go over to Binkie's right now and set her straight."

"You better leave Miss Binkie alone," Lillian declared. "What I say is you oughtta sleep on whatever you plannin' to do, 'cause you might make it worse, jumpin' in like you do sometimes."

"I don't see how it could get any worse." I sighed, sinking into a chair. "But you're right. Let's all sleep on it. Although I doubt I'll close my eyes all night long." I went to the window and peered out at the pounding rain. "I hope they've covered that half-finished building over there. Not that I care if it washes away, but it'd be a lot of people's money down the drain."

I went upstairs feeling bruised and battered, so undone with what the day had wrought. Before getting in bed, though, I called Sam to lean a little on his shoulder and share the burden I carried. I don't believe in passing on gossip, but Binkie's condition was hardly gossip and Sam could be trusted with it. He was a lawyer after all, even though retired, and lawyers as a general rule know how to keep secrets.

"Help me, Sam," I said. "We have to get them married before they ruin their lives."

He sighed and said, "Julia, more lives have been ruined by getting married than by not getting married. You have to let them decide what's best, then accept what they decide. Give them some time to work it out."

"I don't have the time to give!" I said. "Saturday's almost here, Sam, and the wedding's all set. If they miss that, they could just go on as they are forever. What I'm saying is, this is the perfect opportunity to make them go through with it."

"No, Julia, you don't want to do that. Making them get married is not the way to go."

"I don't see why not," I said. "A lot of marriages begin like that for a lot of different reasons. And some of them work out. At this point, I just want them married so that child will have some legitimacy. Don't you think that's enough reason for them to get married?"

"I'll have to think about that. Times have

changed, you know; it's a different world today."

"Not to me, it isn't. Now, look, Sam, I want you to talk to Coleman. Tell him what's at stake here. Between the two of us, we ought to be able to get them back together."

"What if they don't want to get back together? What if their differences over Dixon have uncovered something more basic in the way they feel toward each other?"

"I don't believe that for a minute," I told him. "I agree that there's something more going on than disagreeing over Dixon, but with a child on the way, they'll just have to overlook whatever it is and do the right thing."

After cautioning me again about interfering in the lives of other people, Sam told me to get a good night's sleep and he'd be over in the morning to talk about it again.

I tried to sleep, but even with the drumming of rain on the roof, I couldn't get comfortable, tossing and turning until I had to get up and remake the bed. Instead of crawling back in, though, I sat by the window, watching the rain glittering in the light of the streetlamps, and studied the problem. Even though Coleman had moved back in, we'd seen neither hide nor hair of him, not even at mealtime, which he wasn't prone to miss. So he was avoiding us by working long hours, then coming in after we were in bed, and leaving before we got up. I didn't know how he was functioning on so little sleep, but it was a settled fact that he was doing all he could do to keep from facing any of us, namely me.

Well, I could fix that.

I wrapped my robe around me and crept down the stairs, so as not to wake anybody else. This was going to be between me and Coleman. I took a seat at the kitchen table right by the back door where Coleman always came in. I left the lights off, except for the outside light at the back door that always stayed on.

I don't know how long I sat there in the dark, listening as the rain beat against the windows. I must've dozed off a few times, jerking awake at the least little sound until I had a crick in my neck. Finally, I heard his car turn into the drive and that brought me fully alert. I heard Coleman splash to the door and up onto the stoop, his key ring jingling softly. My eyes were adjusted to the filtered light that leaked in from the streetlamps, so when he pushed open the door, I could see his outline as he entered the kitchen. The creak of his duty belt announced his arrival, as did his tired sigh as he carefully pushed the door closed. He'd always been considerate that way, not wanting to wake the whole house with his comings and goings.

I saw his shape lean on the kitchen counter for a few minutes, thinking he was alone. I hesitated before speaking, not wanting to peel him off the ceiling if I startled him too bad.

"Coleman," I said as softly as I could.

"Huh?" He straightened abruptly and whirled around. "Who's that?"

"Don't shoot. It's just me."

"Miss Julia? What're you doing sitting there in the dark?"

"Waiting for you. Sit down, Coleman, I want to talk to you. And you need to talk to me."

I wasn't sure he was going to do it. He stood by the counter for a few seconds, as if he were considering just walking on upstairs or maybe out to the car and driving away. But I'd counted on his good manners, and sure enough, he felt for a chair and pulled it away from the table.

Then he turned back and pulled off a paper towel from the roll on the counter. Mopping at his hair and wiping down his arms with it, he said, "Let me get the lights on."

"No, leave them off, and come sit down. What I have to say is better said in the dark. At least, it is for me. I might not be able to talk about it with the lights on. Coleman, you know I'm not one to interfere in other people's business, but there's something you need to know. About Binkie."

I was able to make him out in the shadows of the room, as he sat heavily in the chair. His broad shoulders slumped in what looked like more sadness than I could bear. If I'd had any hesitation at all before this, I knew then that I was right to take a hand in matters.

He propped his elbow on the table and leaned his head on his hand. "Okay," he said with a deep sigh. "Let's hear it."

Chapter 19

"There's something about Binkie I don't think you know. And you need to, whether she's seen fit to tell you or not."

He didn't reply at first, just sat there in the dark waiting, I guessed, for more bad news. I wished I could make out the expression on his face before I went on, but all I could see was his head turned down as he looked at the table.

Then he said, "Did she tell you?"

"No. Lillian did."

"Lillian? How does she know?"

"Lillian knows a lot of things, believe me. Anyway, the thing is, do you know?"

"What're we talking about?"

"We're talking about the fact that Lillian says that Binkie's expecting a baby. Now wait," I hurried on, "I know this is a shock to you, and I'm sorry to be the one to tell you. But now you can see how important it is for you and Binkie to get over your differences about Dixon Hightower and get yourselves married as soon as you can. Like, on Saturday."

"You've lost me here, Miss Julia. What's Dixon got to do with anything?"

"Well, I don't know! It's beyond me to understand how the two of you have let that thieving rascal come between you. It doesn't make sense to me."

"To me, either. Is that what Binkie said?"

"Yes, it is. But, Coleman, let's not get off on Dixon. You don't seem to understand what I'm telling you. Binkie's pregnant. I can't be any clearer than that, and you have to do something about it."

He smeared his hand down his face, then leaned back in his chair. "I know she is, Miss Julia. That's why we decided to get married in such a hurry."

"Well, thay Lord," I said, stunned that he'd known all along, yet had let things come to such a pass. "Then what's the problem? Why in the world have you called it off?"

He was quiet for so long that I wasn't sure he was going to answer me. I declare,

getting a man to talk about personal matters was like pulling teeth.

Finally, in a rasping voice, he said, "Binkie
changed her mind. We went to the pastor's
counseling session the other night, which
wasn't the smartest thing we've ever done.
He gave us a compatibility test that made
Binkie roll her eyes. I thought she was going
to walk out when he started telling us about
a wife's obligations to her husband, and
how the husband has authority over the
wife. And how the purpose of marriage was
for each couple to have three children—two
to replace the parents and one to replenish
the earth. Whatever that means. I knew that
wasn't going over too well and, sure
enough, on the way home, she said she just
wasn't cut out to be anybody's wife. And
that having a baby was no reason for either
of us to feel we had to marry." He gave a
short, harsh laugh that sounded like it hurt
his throat. "As if that was the only reason
I . . . well, she said she didn't want me to
feel obligated to marry her, to have a shot-
gun wedding just to live up to old-fashioned
and outdated conventions. She said that a
woman could manage just as well without a
husband. And nothing I say makes any

difference. . . ." He trailed off with a world of pain in his voice.

It was my turn to remain silent. I was stunned that an expectant mother wouldn't jump at the chance to marry her baby's father. Especially this father, who was as fine a man as ever walked the face of the earth.

"Coleman," I finally managed to get out. "I don't know what to say. I could just wring Pastor Petree's neck, but Binkie should know better than to listen to him." I stopped, trying to understand this younger generation that seemed willing to throw out the baby with the bathwater, which I guessed was a bad choice of words in the present situation. Some old-fashioned notions needed throwing out, but not all of them. I recalled hearing Wesley Lloyd rant and rave about overeducated young women who got too big for their britches, demanding high salaries and benefits and so on. He'd go on a tear about a woman's proper role in life and, according to him, that role was not in positions of authority in business or in the church. And Pastor Ledbetter confirmed his views from the pulpit. To hear either of them tell it, a woman was made to be dependent on her father, then on her husband, and woe be to any woman who stepped out of line.

I was confused in my own mind. I certainly did not agree with Wesley Lloyd's views, or with the pastor's, especially after learning of Wesley Lloyd's extramarital escapades. Learning what he'd done had put a damper on everything else he'd pronounced as gospel.

But I couldn't go so far as to agree with Binkie that a woman could do it all by herself, especially if she had a choice in the matter, which Binkie certainly did. And especially now that she was in such a delicate condition.

"Let me get this straight," I said. "You want to marry her, but she doesn't want you to feel obligated just because people expect it of you both. Is that right?"

I saw his head nod in the gloom of the kitchen. "That's about it."

"Well, that's the most wrongheaded thing I've ever heard, and I'm not going to stand for it. Coleman, you get after her and don't leave her alone. It's all well and good to draw up into yourself, but not in this case. What you have to do is tell her that she promised to marry you on Saturday and that you're holding her to it, and it doesn't matter a hill of beans what other people think. First thing this morning as soon as it's daylight, I want you to start sending her flowers. Send them every hour on the hour till her office is overflowing. Put a sweet note on every one. Call her, tell her you love her, and tell her you're going to be standing in front of the arch in my living room come Saturday at four o'clock sharp. In the meantime, I'll be talking to her, too, and telling her that nobody takes the pastor's views on marriage seriously—just look at how many women run the households in town. And between us we'll get that little unborn child some legitimate parents. And have the wedding that I've made all the arrangements for."

"I wouldn't count on it," he said, sounding so hopeless that I could've shaken him.

"Stop that, Coleman. You have to have a positive attitude. You've got to show her how excited and happy you are to be marrying her. If you act like it's all hopeless, she'll figure it is, too. No, you've got to let her know that you're counting on her promise to marry you. Because, frankly, Coleman, women in her condition are known to have moods, so you just have to be understanding."

"I don't know, Miss Julia. Doing all that might turn her off even more."

"What you're doing now isn't helping, is it?"

I saw a flash of his teeth as he either smiled or grimaced. "I guess not."

"Then try my way and see what happens. Now, I want you to go on upstairs and get a good night's sleep. What's left of it, anyway. And then I want you to get up in the morning, determined to do everything you can to show her what she'll be missing if she lets you go."

"Well, she did say that I could see the baby and help with raising it. And she said that maybe in a year or so, if we still felt the same way, we might think about getting married. After it was clear to everybody that we weren't being forced into it."

"Good Lord," I said, throwing up my hands. "Binkie's the most mixed-up person I know. But that shows she doesn't want to lose you, which means she loves you. Oh, Coleman," I went on, struck with a sudden thought. "The license! Do you have one? Both of you have to sign for it, don't you?"

"We did that early on Monday," he said, rubbing his hand across his face. "Before she had second thoughts. I have it, though a whole lot of good it'll do now."

"You just hold on to it. You're going to be using it," I said with more assurance than I felt. "Wave that thing in her face, and remind her that you have proof of her promise."

"I guess I can try it," he said with a weak laugh. "Probably won't change her mind, but nothing else has, either. When she gets an idea in her head, well, you know her, Miss Julia." He got up and pushed his chair under the table. "I'd better get on to bed."

"Yes, you do that. And, Coleman, I'm glad we had this little talk. I think it's done you a world of good. You sleep well and we'll see what tomorrow brings."

"Good night, then." He started toward the back stairs, his shoulders still slumped, in spite of all my efforts.

"Coleman," I said, as he was almost out of the room. "Come back a minute. There's something I want to ask you that's been worrying me."

He turned back to face me, but didn't come any closer. I figured he'd had about enough of my questions and probably my advice. But this was important.

"Why haven't you given her an engagement ring?"

He shook his head and gave another little laugh. "She didn't want one. Said it was too conventional, and that I didn't need to spend money on what was just a symbol." He paused, then went on in a lower tone. "She said that we loved each other too much to need a reminder that we'd promised to get married. Kinda ironic now, I guess."

I got up from my chair and said, "Listen to me, Coleman. Every girl wants a ring whether she says she does or not. I mean, what's she going to show her friends if she doesn't have a ring? And you're going to get her one. I want you to go this very morning and buy the biggest and best ring you can afford, and if you can't afford it, I'll loan you the money."

He thought about it for a minute. "What if she won't take it?"

"I'm betting that she will. Especially if you give it to her in the most romantic way you can think of. Believe me, Coleman, romance can melt any woman's heart." I knew what I was talking about, because I'd never had any.

"Well, I guess I don't have anything to lose by trying it. But, you know she's not the romantic type."

"Go to bed, Coleman, and take this thought with you: every woman in the world is the romantic type."

Chapter 20

I got up the next morning, tired and dragging. Sitting up half the night, telling a man how to woo his lady love, had taken the starch out of me. But the loss of sleep was in a good cause, and there were so many last-minute things to attend to that I had an extra cup of coffee and started in on them. The fact that the rain was over and the day bright and clear helped considerably. And as far as I was concerned, that was enough bad weather until after the wedding.

I told Lillian and Hazel Marie the upshot of my late-night advisory session with Coleman, and they both agreed that I'd hit on just the right approach to changing Binkie's mind.

"You know what I think?" I said, as Lillian washed the breakfast dishes and Hazel Marie combed Little Lloyd's hair. "I think Dixon Hightower was just Binkie's excuse. I think it was Pastor Petree who turned Binkie off. I get turned off just by looking at him."

"Run and get your books, Lloyd," Hazel Marie said. "It's about time to leave for school. Just a couple more days and you'll be out for the summer." She gave him a light tap on the bottom as he turned to leave.

"About time, too," he said, pushing through the kitchen door. "I can't wait."

"Miss Julia," Hazel Marie said, with a wicked grin. "Every time I think of Pastor Petree counseling Binkie and Coleman on the intimacies of marriage I get tickled. And I bet Binkie couldn't keep a straight face."

"I wish she had laughed instead of taking to heart whatever he said. You know, Hazel Marie, even if Coleman's romantic campaign works and she decides to go through with it, there may not be enough time to get in all the counseling sessions, which, after the results of the first one, might not be a bad thing. But what if Pastor Petree refuses to marry them, and they're both left at the altar?"

"Oh," she said, "would he do that?"

"He could. He's so rigid he can hardly bend enough to sit down. We could be left in the lurch with a bride and groom and no preacher."

Lillian untied her apron and folded it. "No, we wouldn't. Miss Mattie Mae Morgan can bring the Reverend Morris Abernathy with her, and he'd marry 'em up without no questions ast. 'Course he a ebony person, too."

"That doesn't enter into it, Lillian," I said. "The main thing is to get them legally married, I don't care who does it. Why don't you give him a call and put him on standby, just in case?"

Little Lloyd came back into the kitchen, carrying his book bag and frowning to beat the band. "I can't find my Game Boy again. Has anybody seen it?"

"No, sugar," Hazel Marie said as she looked for the car keys. "But you shouldn't be taking it to school anyway. It'll turn up sooner or later."

"Not if that ole Dixon Hightower has it," the boy said. Then as the implication set in, his eyes got wider. "That means he's been in our house! Oh, no, what're we going to do?"

It took the three of us to reassure the child that Dixon had not been wandering through the house while we slept. At least, I didn't think he had. But just in case, I determined to buy a Game Boy replacement before Little Lloyd got home, so he wouldn't worry himself to death.

After Hazel Marie returned from taking Little Lloyd to school, we all pitched in to straighten and clean and move furniture around as we prepared for either a party or a wedding, whichever it turned out to be. The florist dropped by, which meant that I had to drop what I was doing to go over everything with her again. The doorbell rang, the telephone rang, visitors came by to offer help and to leave gifts, but mostly to see what was going on. Lillian gave the baseboards in the living room and the dining room a last dusting, while Hazel Marie polished the banisters, and I sprayed the prisms on the chandelier with some of that self-cleaning stuff that sure beat taking each one off and washing it in ammonia water.

Late in the morning, Sam came by to see if he could help, giving us a good excuse to take a break. I told him about the romantic campaign we'd set Coleman on, and our plans to have a party instead of a wedding if the campaign failed to win Binkie over.

"Is that what it takes, Julia?" he asked, cutting his eyes at me. "I mean, to make a woman change her mind? Maybe I should take some lessons, especially if it works." Then he leaned over and put his hand on my arm. "But don't be too disappointed if it doesn't."

"I have to try, Sam. And so does Coleman. He can't lose any more than he already has, so he might as well go all out."

"Can't argue with that. Now let me get to that rug you want rolled up."

As he went to the living room, an ear-shattering crash and the sound of men's voices came from outside. I realized that I'd been hearing big truck motors and squeaking brakes for some little while.

"What in the world is that?" I said, getting up and going to the door.

Hazel Marie and Lillian followed me out into the yard, where we stood dumbfounded at the sight across the street. Two huge dump trucks, blocking most of the street, were parked beside that half-built building, and men, yelling to each other and wielding tools, stood on top of the building, scraping up and throwing down into the truck beds the roofing material that'd been so recently put on.

"Reckon they're tearing it down?" Hazel Marie asked as she gazed up, shielding her eyes with her hand.

"It sho' look like it," Lillian said. "They takin' the roof off and it hardly been on."

"This just beats all," I said, watching as black asphalt roofing material slammed down into the trucks, leaving bits and pieces floating in the air and drifting across the street and into my yard. "They're polluting the whole neighborhood with that mess, to say nothing of the noise they're making."

Just then, a few of the men saw Hazel Marie standing there in her shorts and skimpy shirt, and you know what happens when a certain type of construction worker sees a pretty woman. They couldn't restrain themselves, even in my presence, and catcalls and whistles joined with the general level of noise.

"Get in the house, Hazel Marie," I said, "before one of them falls off the roof. Although it wouldn't be any more than he'd deserve. Come on, Lillian, I'm going to put a stop to this."

As we went back into the kitchen, a particularly large clump of roofing material slammed into a truck bed, clanging against the metal as it hit. Sam poked his head in the kitchen door. "What the devil is that racket?"

"Just one more thing to add to the troubles of this day," I told him. "They're over there, ripping off the roof of that brand-new Family Life Center. And here we are, just a couple of days from Binkie and Coleman's wedding or whatever, and there'll be cars trying to park with those trucks blocking the street, and a mess all over my yard and front porch. I'm calling Pastor Petree and putting a stop to it."

I reached for the telephone, but Sam said, "Wait a minute, Julia. You don't still have your heart set on a wedding, do you?"

"I certainly do. Those two belong together, and I'm not going to let them ruin their lives. I've decided that since Binkie has not seen fit to formally notify me of a cancellation, I'm going to keep on with my plans. Whether Binkie and Coleman show up or not." Then I added: "Maybe it'll bring them to their senses when they see that everybody's expecting a wedding."

"Julia . . . ," Sam began, then backed off.

"I just don't want you to be disappointed if it doesn't work out. But go ahead and call Petree. See what's wrong with that new roof we just spent twenty thousand dollars to put on."

When I dialed the church office, I got Norma Cantrell, of course. "I need to speak to Pastor Petree right this minute," I told her, "and don't put me off."

"Why, Miss Julia," she said with an unbecoming degree of satisfaction, "this is his sermon preparation time, and he can't be disturbed. I'll be glad to take a message."

"Sam," I said, covering the phone and turning to him. "We need a complete employee overhaul in that church. No one is ever available for people in need." Then uncovering the phone, I said to Norma, "I'm not about to leave a message and wait forever for him to get back to me. He's as slow as molasses, and this is urgent. Put me through to Pastor Petree right now before I come over there."

I'd have to remember that threat, for she quickly got Lance Petree on the line. I let him know in no uncertain terms that I wanted that work on the roof brought to a halt. "You know we're having a wedding over here this weekend, Pastor," I told him. "How could you let them create such a mess all up and down the street like they're doing? And why do they need to be doing it at all? That roof was just put on."

"It's the flashing," he said, "or something that maybe wasn't installed right. We had major leaks with that rainstorm last night, Miss Julia. Rainwater ran down the side of the building, just soaking the bricks. Part of the roof has to be replaced before the whole building is damaged."

"Leaks!" I cried. "Do you know what the church paid for that roof? I hope to goodness we're not going to have to pay double for a new one. But, listen to me now, you go and tell those men to put a tarp over everything and leave it until after the wedding. And tell them they better clean up their mess before they leave."

"Well, I don't know that I can do that, Miss Julia," he said, making me want to shake some gumption into him. "Pastor Ledbetter wanted it done by the time he gets back next week, so I don't think I ought to stop them. You know how hard it is to get workers on the job."

"I knew it! I knew he arranged to have the

work done while he was gone so he wouldn't be subjected to the mess. Now listen, Pastor Petree, I don't care what Pastor Ledbetter wants. I'm going to call every deacon and elder in the church, and let me tell you that many of them are invited to this wedding. And when they see what I'm having to put up with, well, they're going to be giving you some contradictory orders, believe you me."

I was steaming by the time I hung up the phone, but before I could let off some of it, Lillian said, "Miss Julia, who the head deacon at yo' church?"

"Lillian, you smart thing! Why didn't I think of that. Of course, Mildred Allen's husband is. I'll call and invite them to the wedding right now, then we'll get something done!"

"A little late to be inviting, Julia, don't you think?" Sam said with that little smile he saves for me when I do something he's not sure of. "And what if there's no wedding to invite them to?"

"I'm not worrying about that now," I said, "and Mildred Allen'll be so glad to hear from me she won't care how late she's invited."

That proved to be the case, especially

since I apologized all over myself, telling her that my list with her name on it had fallen behind a chair and that there were several others on the list who were also getting late calls. And she warmed my heart when she expressed outrage over what was taking place across the street. "Well, we'll just see about that," she said when I told her what Pastor Petree'd said. "I'll have Herb go right over there and make them stop. And see that they clean up the street and your yard, too. A wedding's too important to be interfered with like that."

I hung up the phone, thinking that I'd always liked Mildred Allen.

"Julia," Sam said, "I'm going to leave you with it. I left a message inviting Coleman to come have supper with me tonight. I don't expect he'll want to see all the long faces around here, if Binkie's still holding out."

"That's thoughtful of you, Sam, but you can just uninvite him. He has things to do that don't involve going to somebody's house for supper. He needs to keep after Binkie, not leave her alone to dream up some more modern claptrap like she's been doing."

"Maybe you're right. Far be it from me to

interfere with the course of true love, and when you come right down to it, it's not my business to counsel him. Look how poorly I've done in the romance department." And with a smile that both wrenched and lifted up my heart, he took his leave.

Hazel Marie and I finished our cleaning and polishing, then made sandwiches for lunch. We spread pimento cheese on bread slices, with her occasionally commenting on the futility of the work we'd done on the house. Well, what she said was: "I just hope the wedding guests appreciate what we've done, even if we don't have a wedding."

"Well, it need cleanin' anyway," Lillian said, trying to encourage us, but failing, as far as I was concerned.

When the mailman came by, I was surprised to find a scented envelope addressed to me. And taken aback to find the drawing of a kitten chasing a butterfly on the notepaper inside. Completely inappropriate for anyone but a child, so why wasn't I surprised that it was from Etta Mae Wiggins, reminding me of the troubles at the trailer park? I declare, the woman was going to drive me crazy.

I pursed my mouth and stuffed the note

in my pocket. I had too many other things on my mind to worry with her now. Besides, if she intended to document her complaints in writing, she should've used a better grade of stationery. What she'd used certainly wouldn't hold up in court.

By late afternoon, the house was quiet; the workers across the street had taken their trucks and left, Hazel Marie had picked up Little Lloyd from school, and I was in his room looking over his homework while he played with his Game Boy. I'd bought it to replace the one he thought Dixon had taken, and he'd not known the difference.

I heard Lillian plodding up the stairs, surprising me since she usually called us to supper from the foot of them.

"Miss Julia," she said, sticking her head around the half-closed door, "you looked at that fam'ly building lately?"

"Not any more than I can help," I said, glancing up from Little Lloyd's geography paper. "Why?"

"You better get up from there and look at it. Somethin' hap'ning over there."

Chapter 21

"What is it?" I got up and started down the stairs, with Little Lloyd right behind me.

"They's people over there," she said worriedly, "an' I don't know what they doin'."

"It's probably a meeting of some kind. Where's last Sunday's bulletin? That'll tell us who scheduled a meeting. Not that it matters to me who goes and comes."

Lillian frowned as I walked past her on the stairs, then she followed Little Lloyd down. "I never seen no meetin' over there like this. An' I don't think yo' bulletum tell you nothin' 'bout it."

The evening in early June was just at that time between daylight and dark when things slow down and people sit on front porches to call to neighbors walking by. But nobody was sitting out or walking by. Instead, all I could see when Lillian pointed out the front window was a group of shadows on the far side of the street next to the new brick wall of the Family Life Center. As we watched, the group broke up and individual dark figures moved slowly across the street to regather on the sidewalk by my driveway.

"See there," Lillian said, "what'd I tell you?"

"Who are they? I can't make out any faces, but they sure don't look as if they're going to the church, do they?"

"No'm, when I first noticed 'em a little while ago 'fore it got so dark, they looked like some of them workin'men that work so hard over there ev'ry day. But why they come back at night jus' to stand around? Don't make no sense to me, when they could be home restin'."

"I wish we could see them better," Little Lloyd said, as he stood in front of Lillian and me gazing out with us. "Oh, there go the streetlights. Now we can."

But we couldn't. The nearest streetlamp was on the corner, so it just threw the middle of the block into deeper shadow. All we could make out was a group of people, maybe eight or so, milling around.

"Go out on the porch, Lillian," I said, "and see if you can hear what they're saying."

"I'm not goin' out on no porch. This white uniform'd show up like a lightbulb. They'd know I was out there, listenin' to 'em."

"I'll go," Little Lloyd said, and before I could stop him, he slipped out the screen door and stood beside a porch post.

Keeping one eye on him and the other on the mass of shadows that I was beginning to see were mostly figures of men, I tried to think of reasons why they'd be there.

"You don't suppose they're waiting on someone, do you? I mean, at this time of night who would they be meeting?"

"Maybe they a search party," Lillian said. "Out lookin' for that ole Dixon Hightower."

"I don't think so," I said, straining to distinguish any familiar faces. "If they were a search party, there'd be some deputies with them. And besides, Dixon's long gone if he has any sense. Which, come to think of it, isn't very likely."

Little Lloyd eased the screen door open and came back into the living room. "Miss Julia," he whispered, "I couldn't hear much, 'cause they're mostly whispering. And they're doing it in Spanish. One of them might be Señor Acosta. He's the foreman on the bricklaying crew over there."

"I declare, Little Lloyd," I said, looking at him with interest. "I didn't know you knew any of the workmen."

"I don't, really," he said. "But Señor Acosta came and spoke to our Spanish class 'cause his son's in it. So I kinda know him and he's real nice."

Lillian said, "I'm thinkin' we ought to call Coleman. Jus' in case."

"Oh, I don't think so," I said, trying to calm her concern. "Not if Little Lloyd knows one of them. Besides, Coleman's got better things to do, at least I hope he's doing them, since the time is drawing nigh."

"Look," Lillian said. "They's two of 'em walking off down the sidewalk. I think they leavin'."

"I believe you're right. You know, if they're some of the workmen on the building, maybe they've just come by to admire what they've wrought. Although I certainly wouldn't be able to take pride in the thing." I bit my lip as I strained to see, then said, "They could also be new arrivals who want to apply for jobs."

"At this time a night?" Lillian said.

"I guess you're right, that couldn't be it." Then as another possibility occurred to me,

I went on. "Oh, Lord, I hope they're not teenagers up to some mischief."

"No'm," Little Lloyd said. "I don't think that's it. Señor Acosta wouldn't be with anybody who's up to any mischief." Then as we continued to watch, he said, "I'm maybe getting a little worried, anyway."

Lillian said, "I think we better call the sheriff."

"No, look," I said, as the group began to disperse, with one or two more drifting off down the sidewalk. "They're all leaving now. I think it'll be all right, but let's keep an eye out in case they come back."

"I'm going to lock the doors," Little Lloyd said. "Now that I think about it, my stomach's not feeling too good."

"Lord, Lillian," I said as he headed for the back door. "That child scares too easily. We have to keep our heads, even when we're concerned about something ourselves."

"Well, don't do no harm to keep the doors locked," she said. "You got all that silver settin' out in plain sight an' somebody might want some of it."

"I know it. But it's just as Coleman said about Dixon; we should take sensible precautions. And that doesn't mean booby-trapping the stairs again, either. So keep the pots and pans in the kitchen."

She didn't say anything for a minute, then we both started laughing, remembering how Mr. Pickens had tumbled head over heels down the stairs, swearing worse than a sailor.

———

By Thursday morning, I'd not seen Coleman or heard him come in during the night, so I didn't know how well his campaign was coming along. Far be it from me to wish for someone to fall into sin, but I had hopes that he'd spent the night with Binkie. Of course, they wouldn't be *falling* into sin, since it was a settled fact that they were pretty well mired up in it already.

I'd just gotten dressed for the day when the phone rang with news of the first crisis. It was Emma Sue Ledbetter calling from the church and she was in a state. You'd think she'd've wanted to avoid me after the stunt she pulled with those bumper stickers and pamphlets and such. But Emma Sue operated on a different plane from most people. A fact that she herself would tell you in a minute.

"Julia," she gasped. "You've got to come

over here. You're the closest church member, and I need some help. Drop what you're doing and come over as quick as you can."

That's all she said, just hung up before I could tell her I was still hot about her ill-conceived home mission project. But I welcomed the prospect of telling her face-to-face, and I determined to do it even if it meant laying her low with a tongue-lashing in the church itself.

Calling out to Lillian to tell her where I was going, I headed out, working up a righteous anger as I went. Workmen on the building had already started their day, so I had to run the gauntlet to the tune of half a dozen portable radios sitting around on sawhorses and windowsills. The mixture of country western and what Little Lloyd called salsa, which I'd thought was something to eat, was enough to give me a headache.

When I went into the Fellowship Hall of the church, I didn't see anyone. It was too early for Norma Cantrell to be there, and for the first time I wondered what Emma Sue was doing there so early, herself.

Walking back toward the pastor's office, I called softly to Emma Sue. A church with nobody in it can be a pretty spooky place, so I glanced through each door as I passed.

"Julia!" Emma Sue sprang out of a side hall, scaring me half to death. "You won't believe what's happened!"

"What! Lord, Emma Sue, don't jump out at me like that." Then, getting my breath back, I rounded on her. "Now, listen, this is as good a time as any to tell you how I feel about all this public witnessing and street-corner preaching and ringing people's doorbells just when they're sitting down to supper. And I want you to know I don't appreciate you getting Little Lloyd involved in it."

Emma Sue stared blankly at me, as if she hadn't heard a word I'd said. Then she blinked and said, "She's been at it again."

"Who?"

"Norma! It's got to be her. She's the only one around when Lance Petree does visitation and Larry's not here. I know it was her."

"What's she done?"

"I want you to come here and look. Just look." Emma Sue took my arm and pulled me toward a pantry-like room in the short hall between Pastor Ledbetter's office and Pastor Petree's. She threw open the door and said, "Look at that! Have you ever seen anything to beat it?"

I looked, and all I saw were black ministerial robes hanging from a rod and a row of shelves stacked with pastoral oddments. My eye was taken with a stack of the round silver servers that held in slots the tiny glasses we used for communion. The first time Hazel Marie took communion in our church, she'd leaned over to me and whispered that they looked like miniature shot glasses. I set her straight, you may be sure. On another shelf there was a stack of silver plates the deacons used for passing around the loaves of communion bread. Various other odds and ends like candles, old bulletins and dog-eared books filled the other shelves.

"I don't see a thing, Emma Sue, except what's supposed to be here."

"You're not looking," she said. And pointing to the floor under the shelves, she went on. "See that?"

"I don't see anything."

"Exactly! It's gone, and now what're we going to do?"

"Emma Sue, don't get yourself in an uproar. Is something supposed to be there?"

"Yes! The wine for communion!"

I stared at her. Wine? In a Presbyterian church?

But she was plowing on, paying no attention to my startled look. "We had almost a whole case of it, and it's gone! I know it was Norma; she has a key to the closet. It had to be her, and Communion Sunday'll be here before you know it, so what're we going to do?"

"Well, I don't see what the big upset is. Just go out and buy some more; there's plenty of time. I don't know why you'd think Norma took it. Doesn't it make more sense that we used it all last time, and it just wasn't replaced? After all, it's a long time between Communion Sundays, and what with Pastor Ledbetter getting ready to go to the Holy Land, he might've forgotten it." In our church, we only took communion four times a year, once every quarter, which was four times too many for some people who resented the lengthy time it took to pass around the sacramental elements.

Emma Sue lowered her eyebrows at me. "He'd *never* forget that. Besides, I know there was a whole half a case here. Julia, you're just not getting the enormity of this.

Now I know, *theoretically,* that it's not holy wine until Larry blesses and consecrates it, but it was bought for that purpose and ought to be held sacred." She patted her chest, as if she was having trouble getting her breath, and her eyes began to fill.

I stood there, wondering how far off the deep end she'd let herself get to. "Emma Sue, first off, I know what it's supposed to represent in the communion service, and that's miracle enough for me. But I doubt that even Pastor Ledbetter has the power to turn Welch's grape juice into wine, whether it's holy or not. I mean, what we're talking about here is something you can get at any grocery store in town."

Our church had always held firmly to the belief that its members shouldn't be encouraged in the evils of strong drink. And for that reason, along with not wanting to give recovering alcoholics the least little taste of it—which was all they could get from those tiny glasses, anyway—we'd always substituted grape juice for what the Bible called for. Which was wine, as anybody who could read knew. We'd had a preacher one time who wanted us to switch to the real thing, but it caused such an outcry, especially from the ones who proclaimed the absolute literal nature of the Scriptures, that he'd had to forgo it.

"Julia!" Emma Sue cried, her eyes bulging out at me. "It was not just any grape juice, much less Welch's! It was nonalcoholic communion wine ordered from the Church Closet Sacred Accouterments catalog at the discount price of forty dollars a case!"

I stepped back from the onslaught. "Well, if that's the case . . ."

She dabbed at her eyes and heaved a heavy sigh. "Maybe now you see why I'm so upset. Well," she went on, as she looked at me through teary eyes. "I guess I'll have to buy the ordinary kind, but I tell you, Larry is not going to like it. But, Julia, why in the world would Norma take it? You reckon she had a party or something?"

"Oh, Emma Sue, I don't think so. But I do think that you're jumping to conclusions again. There's no reason to suspect Norma of doing this, and I say that even though I don't like her and never have."

"There's nobody else who could've done it." And out came the damp Kleenex and down came the tears again. "Oh, Julia, if it's not one thing it's another, isn't it? I hope you'll join me in prayer about this."

"Well, not now," I said, determined to forestall a prayer meeting. "And don't get me started on that subject. You need to pull yourself together, Emma Sue, and lock this door up again. It's not the end of the world, and there's plenty of time to buy more. But I caution you, don't be going around accusing Norma of taking it; you could be wrong. Just don't do anything until the pastor gets back. He'll handle it without getting the church sued within an inch of its life.

"Now, I've got to go. I'm looking forward to you being at the wedding where you can cry to your heart's content. I may even shed a few tears myself." Especially, I thought, if Binkie doesn't show up.

Chapter 22

I left Emma Sue to her suspicions and headed for home. Before crossing the street, I had to wait several minutes on the corner by the Family Life Center to let a slow stream of traffic pass by. A number of pickups and vans with three or more people crowded onto the front seats crept by, as well as several cars filled front and back with people sitting on top of each other. None of the vehicles was moving very fast, but every time I almost stepped off the curb, another one turned the corner.

Finally, a shiny, red sedan with the tail of some animal hanging from the antenna slowed and stopped, the driver kindly motioning me to cross in front of him. As I waved my thanks, I noticed how similar he and his passengers were to the waiters in the restaurant where Little Lloyd and I had first met Mr. Pickens that time he ingested a whole pitcher of beer. I'd almost not hired him because of it.

I knew a lot of the hard-working people from south of the border had moved to our truck-farming county to pick beans and apples during the season. Local employers were eager to have them, and they'd blended right into the community. As I got to my side of the street, it suddenly struck me that I was one of those local employers. Raymond had been cutting my grass and pruning my boxwoods for almost two years now, and I hardly ever thought of him as a foreigner, except for the fact that I couldn't make head nor tails out of half of what he said. He seemed to understand me, though, nodding his head and saying "Sí" to everything I asked him to do, and then doing it. Little Lloyd was taking Spanish in school, so he made use of the time to practice his skill whenever Raymond came to the house. It seemed to me that Raymond enjoyed the boy's efforts because he laughed a lot as Little Lloyd tried to converse with him.

"Hazel Marie," I called as I got into the house and walked back to her room.

"Ma'am? Come on in. I'm trying to decide if I need to press my bridesmaid's dress."

Our dresses had been altered, delivered and carefully unpacked the day before. She had hers hanging from the closet door, and I had another swift palpitation at the brevity of it.

"You won't believe what Emma Sue has to cry about now." And I told her about the missing grape juice, and we laughed at Emma Sue's propensity to drop a tear at the drop of a hat.

"Harriet, from the florist, just called," Hazel Marie said. "She wants to bring the ferns for the porch tomorrow morning, and some potted plants to line the front walk. She said she'd fill the arch with greenery at the shop, and bring it, too. She'll put fresh flowers in it early Saturday morning."

"That sounds fine, just so nothing wilts or dies between now and then. Oh, Hazel Marie, I just hope and pray that we have somebody to stand under that arch. Binkie's worrying me to death. If I thought her mother and daddy could do something with her, I'd send them plane tickets to get up here and do it. But from what she's said, they're not in any shape to make any headway with her. Of course, they weren't able to even when they were in good health."

"Have you heard from Coleman?" Hazel Marie asked. "Maybe something's changed, if he's done what you told him to."

"Not one word. And, frankly, I don't want to. I'm afraid of what he'll tell me. What I'm planning to do is go right on with our plans and, if I don't hear from them, I'll call Binkie Saturday at the last minute and tell her to get herself over here for her wedding. Maybe that way, she'll be too ashamed to tell me she won't do it. I mean, look, Hazel Marie, *she* hasn't told me that the wedding's off. And it's her place to do it, if she means it. As far as I'm concerned, if I hadn't happened to see Coleman when he came in, saying it was off, I wouldn't know anything about it, would I?"

"That's one way to look at it, I guess." She stopped and gazed off into space. "Yes, you're right. It *is* Binkie's place to tell you, and follow it up with a handwritten note and some flowers. She can't expect you to cancel everything, just on the groom's say-so. Unless it was his decision, which we know it wasn't. It would be the courteous thing for her to do." Hazel Marie'd been reading the etiquette book again.

I turned toward the front door as somebody rapped on the screen door. "Who could that be?"

As I walked toward the front, LuAnne Conover let herself in. "Julia, I've had the most wonderful idea, one I bet you haven't even thought of since you've been so busy, and I want to do it for you."

"Come in, LuAnne. What is it?"

"Well, I can't stay," she said, her hands fluttering as they always did when she had a bright idea. "I'm on my way to that fabric place out on the highway. But I thought I'd better check with you first, just to make sure somebody else is not already doing it."

"What?"

"Well, you know I've been wanting to help with the wedding?"

I nodded, recalling all the silver we'd had to polish without any help.

"Now I've come up with just the thing," she went on, her eyes sparkling. "I just hope nobody else is doing them, because they're perfect for me."

"What, LuAnne?"

"Well, you know those little bags that you

put rice or something in and tie up with ribbon? You know, for the guests to open and throw whatever at the bride and groom as they leave? Well, that's what I want to make for you."

"Why, LuAnne, that's a splendid idea. I can't thank you enough."

"Well, now, listen. I've been looking through Martha Stewart's wedding book, and she recommends rose petals to fill the little bags. But, Julia, it'd take forever to pluck petals and fill bags. So, I thought maybe using birdseed would be better. Everybody says not to use rice, because it can get slippery on bricks or pavement. And, besides, birdseed's ecologically sound and feeds the birds, too. What do you think?"

"I think birdseed's a fine idea," I said, hoping we'd have some cause to throw whatever she decided to use. "How're you going to make the bags?"

"I'll just buy some white net and cut out squares, then tie up the birdseed with pink ribbon. How many bags do you think we'll need? Fifty or sixty?"

"About sixty, to be on the safe side. But, LuAnne, are you sure you'll have enough time to do them?"

"I'll work on them nonstop," she assured me. Then, leaning in close, she lowered her voice. "Besides, Julia, they're the perfect thing to work on in my lap. You know, while we're watching television or whatever. That way, maybe Leonard'll behave himself."

"LuAnne . . ." I said with a warning note in my voice.

"I know you don't like to hear my problems, but, Julia, ever since the doctor put Leonard on that medication, he can't keep his hands off me."

It hadn't been too long before that LuAnne had cried on my shoulder because Leonard had lost his taste for life. She'd complained that he never put his hands on her, moving her to consider divorce, and at her age, too. She'd even made it plain that she wouldn't be above considering a dalliance with a race-truck driver, either.

Now the shoe was on the other foot, for Leonard's appetite had markedly increased, and she spent a lot of time getting her hair done and shopping and visiting friends. Anything to get out of the house and away from him, she'd told me. "He's driving me crazy," she'd confided, and it was all I could do to keep from staring at him during church services. He was such a meek-looking man, I just couldn't imagine. . . . Well, and I tried my best not to.

"LuAnne," I said, "why don't you ask the doctor to adjust his dosage? Wouldn't that work?"

"Oh, my goodness, no. Leonard won't hear of it. Says, now that he's got it back, he doesn't want to risk losing it again. But I've found that if I keep myself busy, especially with something in my lap, like some cross-stitch with needles all around, it sort of deters him. That's one reason I want to do these bags. And to help you, too, of course."

"It's thoughtful of you, LuAnne. And we can certainly use them."

"I've got that big pretty basket that fruit came in last Christmas. I thought I'd pile all the bags in that and tie a big ribbon on the handle."

"That'd be perfect. Thank you again, LuAnne. That's one less thing I have to worry about."

She gave me a conspiratorial grin, and said, "No, thank you. You're giving *me* one less thing to worry about."

As she left on her fabric shopping trip, I

thought to myself that medical science is a wonderful thing, even if it didn't hit quite the right degree of moderation in some cases.

———

I had hardly gotten halfway back to Hazel Marie's room when the doorbell rang.

"I'll get it, Lillian," I called, wondering if LuAnne had come back for a longer visit, which I certainly did not have time for today.

But it wasn't LuAnne, it was that little snip, Etta Mae Wiggins, in a white shirt and drawstring pants like hospital workers wear. Even though I knew full well she didn't work in a hospital.

"Yes?" I said, standing with the screen between us.

"Uh, Mrs. Springer," she said, twisting her hands. "I'm sorry to bother you, but I was out this way seeing a patient, and I thought I'd just drop by and let you know that Mr. Carter hasn't replaced those bulbs yet. We're still in the dark, and, Mrs. Springer, it's scary out there with the woods all around. Especially when we have to go out or come in at night. I just thought you'd like to know he's still not doing his job."

"I've talked with him, Miss Wiggins, and he assured me that he would have those lights replaced right away. You just haven't given him enough time. He has to find a ladder tall enough to reach, and someone to help him."

We stood there looking at each other for a minute, neither knowing where to go from there. I began to feel bad for not inviting her in, but I knew she had work to do, and so did I.

"Well," she said, beginning to turn away. "I thought you'd want to know."

As she started toward the porch steps, I had a sudden mental picture of Little Lloyd watching this exchange.

"Miss Wiggins," I said, opening the screen door and stepping out on the porch. "Just a moment, please. I thank you for letting me know that Mr. Carter hasn't done what he assured me he would do. I will call someone else this very day, and let Mr. Carter know that I no longer need him in my employ."

She turned to me, her eyes lighting up. "Oh, thank you, Mrs. Springer. I hate for anybody to lose their job, but he's just not worth whatever you're paying him." She stopped and bit her lip. Then, as if determined to get it said, she went on. "We've had something else stolen, too. Blanca Diaz, who lives just two trailers from me, had her beautiful hand-embroidered shawl stolen. She brought it with her from Mexico, and now it's gone."

"I'm sorry to hear it, but Little Lloyd is in the process of getting estimates to get a fence put around the park. So, if you . . . I mean, if the residents out there can just watch out for one another a while longer, we'll have something put up that'll keep you safe."

Her eyes really lit up at that. "Oh, thank you, thank you, Mrs. Springer! I didn't think you would do it, but everybody'll be so happy to hear it."

So enthusiastic was her response that I stepped back for fear she'd throw her arms around me. "Well, good. And I hope there'll be no more phone calls or letters or visits about this matter. You have to realize that I can't have a fence put up in a day. But I assure you that as soon as this busy week is over, it'll get done. You'll just have to have some patience, Miss Wiggins."

That turned her glow down a notch, but she had my promise, which was as good as gold. When she left, I went back inside marveling at how little it took to make some people happy. Of course, it would take a great deal more than a little for me to pay for it, but I had a warm feeling, knowing how pleased Little Lloyd would be. But then, it would be just like Miss Wiggins to come up with something else she wanted done, now that I'd given in to her demand for a fence.

But I followed through on my promise and went straight to the telephone to give Mr. Carter his notice, and hoped to heaven I could find someone to replace him. Then I looked through the notes Little Lloyd had made—such a dependable child—and called the fence company with the lowest bid.

"There," I said to myself. "Maybe they'll fix it so that Miss Wiggins is fenced in for good."

Then I smiled with the anticipation of telling the news to Little Lloyd when he got home. My smile was short-lived, though, for as soon as I hung up the phone all my worries about Binkie came rushing in again. Believe me, the afterglow of doing a good deed doesn't last very long when troubles loom all around you.

Chapter 23

I had a good mind to try another good deed and, the more I thought about it, the more convinced I became that it was exactly what was called for. I'd not heard from Coleman, so who knew how his campaign was progressing, if it was at all. So somebody had to do something.

One thing was for sure; I'd never be able to rest if everything that could be tried, wasn't tried. So to that end, I decided to take on Binkie myself and tell her in no uncertain terms that it was time to grow up and get married like she was supposed to.

Having determined my course of action, I walked upstairs after supper to tell Hazel Marie I was going out for a while. Little Lloyd was taking his bath and Hazel Marie was laying out his clothes for the last day of school tomorrow.

"Hazel Marie," I said. "I just can't sit here

any longer without knowing what's going on with Binkie. I've decided to go over there and have it out with her."

She turned to me, clasping a red-and-white knit shirt to her bosom. "Oh, good! I was wondering if there wasn't something we could do. You want us to go with you?"

"No, I think it'd be better if I tackle her by myself. Not that you wouldn't be of help, but I have some harsh things to say to her and she might not want an audience to hear them."

"You be careful then, and let me know when you get back," Hazel Marie said. "I'll be waiting up for you."

She walked downstairs with me and whispered, "Good luck," as she waited in the doorway until I got in the car and backed it down the drive. I wondered if I ought to honk the horn so I wouldn't run over some of the people who had begun to congregate again on the sidewalk, but they'd left me plenty of room. After backing into the street, while a van and a chrome-laden sports car waited for me, I glanced at the gathering mass of people, noticing that a few women had joined them. You'd think they'd have better things to do than wander up and down the sidewalk. Putting the car into gear, I dismissed what other people found to do with their time—it was no business of mine—and hurried off to Binkie's town house or condominium or whatever the latest developer called it.

Her place was in a cluster of similar units at the north edge of the town. I'd only been there a couple of times, and then only in the daylight, so it took me a while to find hers, since they all looked alike. Every time I went, though, I just got sick at the thought of that beautiful house in the historic district where she'd grown up. Her parents had offered it to her when they'd moved to Florida, but she would have nothing to do with it. Too old, she'd said, and too big. So they'd sold it to somebody from New Jersey who wouldn't know a Georgian from a Federal.

So what did Binkie end up with? An architect's nightmare, full of angles and skylights and lofts and open spaces. Why, her bedroom was up a spiral metal staircase that would've broken my hip a dozen times if I'd had to climb it. And not only that, her bedroom was in the loft, overlooking the living-dining-cooking space down below. Why, when you walked in the front door, you could look up and see her bed, plain as day. I couldn't sleep that way myself. No telling who would walk in.

She opened the door to me in her pajamas and robe, looking somewhat surprised to see me at that time of night.

"Binkie," I said, marching myself inside. "I've come to see if you need any help packing for your honeymoon. Where're your suitcases?"

"Uh, Miss Julia, I'm not . . ."

I held up my hand to her as I walked toward her sofa. One of those sectional things. "I don't want to hear it. You wanted this wedding, and I've planned this wedding, and we're going to have it. And furthermore," I said, taking a seat without a by-your-leave. I wanted her to know I meant business. "It's the height of discourtesy for you to call it off without saying one formal word to me. So, I've carried on, and it's too late now to change your mind."

"Miss Julia," she said with a sigh as she sat at right angles to me. "Look, you don't know . . ."

"Of course I know, and it won't be long till everybody in town knows, too. A baby on the way can be hidden just so long, you know. You've just got to get married before it's obvious to everybody."

Binkie managed a sad smile. "That won't make any difference. They can still count."

"Let them count, Binkie. You'd be surprised at the number of seven- and eight-month babies born in this town all the time. They're the number one topic on the prayer chain for a while, then people forgive and try to forget. *If,* that is, the parents show their good faith by getting married before the baby makes its appearance.

"Now, Binkie, I've put up with your recalcitrance this whole week, and so has Coleman. It's time to think of someone besides yourself for a change. That little baby needs a daddy, and you need a husband. This is no time to be obstinate just to show people how independent you are."

She frowned and pleated her robe across her knees. "You don't understand, Miss Julia. Times have changed, and a woman doesn't have to get married just because she's expecting."

"The times haven't changed that much! Why, even that Steinem woman got married and she didn't even have to, so it wouldn't hurt you to do the same."

She got up and walked around the ell of the sofa. Leaning against it, she looked at me and said, "I, well, I've seen too many unhappy couples, Miss Julia. Doing divorce work, you know. I can't tell you how many times I've seen men who're mad and resentful because they got trapped into marriage. I don't want Coleman ever to feel that way."

"Binkie, for goodness' sake! Does Coleman *look* trapped! Just tell me one thing, do you love him?"

She looked down, her face softening as she smiled. "Oh, yes."

"Well, thay Lord!" I said, leaning back in exasperation. Then I sat up straight. "And you know he loves you, don't you? Don't you?"

She nodded, still with that smile at the corners of her mouth. I knew good and well that *love* didn't guarantee a good marriage, but I also knew that young people put a lot of stock in it. So I played every card I had to the hilt, hoping to convince her that that unstable emotion could conquer all.

"This beats all I've ever heard!" I got up and walked over to her fireplace, unable to sit still in the face of such foolishness.

"Look, you are loved and you are in love, and as pregnant as you can be, on top of that. There's not one thing stopping you from marrying a fine man like Coleman, except contrariness. That is not attractive, Binkie. Not at all."

"Well, I'm still thinking about it, but . . ."

"You don't have *time* to think about it! The wedding's this Saturday, and that baby's due . . . when's it due?"

"In about five months."

"Oh, Lord." I put my hand to my head to stop it from exploding. "Binkie, that child needs to be legitimate. Believe me, I know the consequences of having what Lillian calls yard children. You don't want to put that mark on your very own child."

"It's not that way anymore," she said, rubbing her hand across her waist, which, now that I was noticing, seemed to've gotten a little thick. "The world is a different place now, and nobody cares about such things anymore."

I could've pulled my hair out, I was so frustrated. "Binkie, wake up. This is not New York and it's not Atlanta. It's not even Chapel Hill. You just don't do such things in

Abbotsville without suffering the consequences. You and that child both."

"Miss Julia," Binkie said, looking me
straight in the eye with a lawyerly gleam in
her own. "I happen to know that your marriage wasn't the best in the world, so I don't
understand why you're so anxious to push
me into the same kind of situation."

Well, I huffed, so she wants to play rough.
"It's not the same kind of situation at all!
There's no comparison between Coleman
and Wesley Lloyd, and none between you
and me. For one thing, I wasn't expecting a
baby. But let me tell you, if I had been, I'd've
married quicker than I did and with a lot less
thought. That was the way I was raised.

"And I'll tell you something else, Binkie
Enloe, you're just being willful and selfish,
thinking only of yourself and not that little
new life that you're bringing into the world.
There're plenty of women who've married
for less reason than you have, and made the
best of it, too. You think everything has to
be perfect? Well, let me tell you, it's not
going to be. In fact, you're about at the
point of losing what you do have. You think
Coleman's going to live the rest of his life on
the edge of yours, just so you can pride

yourself on your independence? No, ma'am, I don't think so."

"He said . . ."

"I don't care what he said, and I don't doubt that he meant it at the time. But what about ten years from now, after he's watched his child grow up without him? Binkie, listen to reason."

She looked around the room as if she'd find some support somewhere in the rafters. "There're problems with our jobs. He got upset with me for taking Dixon's case. In fact, he laughed at me, said I didn't know what I was getting into. And I resent that."

I spread my arms out with a loud sigh. "Well, resent all you want to; it's not enough reason to ruin your life. You and Coleman can work out little things like that after you're married. And I'll tell you this, I'd hate to think I'd let a no-account like Dixon Hightower make my decisions for me."

"You don't understand, Miss Julia. You're of the generation that thinks a woman should submit to her husband in everything, take a backseat to him and agree with him even when he's wrong, like that minister said I should do. I can't and won't do that."

"Nobody's asking you to, especially not

Coleman. Now, I don't care what Pastor Petree said to the contrary, this whole matter of marital authority and submission ought to be dismissed out of hand. And I wish I'd had sense enough to do it when it might've made a difference. Besides, when have you started listening to what preachers say? I thought you'd given up on church. Which is another subject I mean to take up with you one of these days. Now, I grant you, I used to think that's what a wife was supposed to do, but that was before I knew what that kind of blindness could lead to." I walked over to her and put my hands on her shoulders. "Binkie, let's get you and Coleman married since everything's ready and waiting. You won't regret it, and even if you do, you can rectify it later on. And that little child will thank you for the rest of its life."

She tightened her mouth and shook her head. "I'm just not sure I want to be married. I don't think I could put up with all the complications and compromises that marriage requires." She gave a quick laugh. "Too used to making my own way and my own decisions, I guess."

"Binkie," I said, "have you thought about the complications and compromises that having a child requires? You are making a terrible mistake if you think it'll be easy handling them by yourself. Don't you know that you have a man who'd do anything in this world for you and this child?"

"I know," she said, her voice softening. "I really do know." She turned the ring on her finger, then showed it to me. I blinked at the size of it. "Coleman gave me this," she said with a soft laugh. "I didn't think I wanted one, you know, like everyone else." She gazed at it and sighed. "I guess I shouldn't be wearing it."

"Oh, wear it, for goodness' sake. Maybe it'll remind you of a sacred promise you made. Binkie, let me tell you, you won't find a finer man on the face of the earth than Coleman Bates, and he is just so hurt, thinking you don't care enough to marry him."

"I know, Miss Julia, and I hate it, I really do. But I'm just not sure enough to go through with it."

"Lord, honey, it'd take a miracle to be sure about anything in this life."

"Maybe that's what I need." She gave me a tired smile. "A miracle."

Chapter 24

I drove home, clutching the steering wheel as hard as I could, just so torn up inside I hardly knew where I was going. It was all I could do to keep from going back and throttling that recalcitrant girl. Of all the perverse ways of thinking, she took the cake.

It was hormones that was causing it. There was no other explanation for her contrariness that went against what anybody else in their right mind would do. It's a well-known fact that expectant-mother hormones can disrupt even the most level-headed woman, and Binkie had always been a little skewed to begin with. I thought of all I'd heard about the strange cravings women with child have. If Binkie kept on in her perversity, she wouldn't have anybody to send to the store when a craving for pickles and ice cream hit her.

Pitiful, is what it was. And infuriating, if

you want to know the truth of it. Half the town, well, maybe fifty or sixty, would be showing up on Saturday to witness a wedding, and how was I going to explain that the bride had a case of liberated independence and wouldn't be showing up? Claiming hormonal influences wouldn't exactly help matters.

One minute I was so mad at Binkie I could've wrung her neck. But the next, I felt like throwing my head back and howling in frustration and disappointment. Then I tried to come to terms with the fact that there might not be a wedding on Saturday, and maybe never. I was just going to have to stand by and watch Coleman and that unborn child suffer. To say nothing of the suffering I'd be put through for planning a wedding without a bride and groom, as well as Hazel Marie, who'd suffer for not getting to be a bridesmaid. And all because Binkie had some twisted notion about forcing Coleman into marriage, when of all the men least likely to need forcing, it would be Coleman.

Well, the only thing left was to pray for a miracle that would change Binkie's mind. I hadn't noticed too many miracles taking place lately, though, so it wasn't something I could put money on.

I drove slowly down the street, turned the corner onto Polk and headed toward the house. Two blocks away, I saw something that made me come to a rolling stop. I peered through the windshield, unable to believe my eyes. The crowd of people had doubled and, maybe, tripled, since I'd left. I could hardly believe my eyes as I came to a stop in the middle of the road. I sat there watching as more people came from one end of the street to the other, converging in a mass directly across from the Family Life Center. And it seemed to me that every last one of them had a candle, for I could see the flames expand as they lit one candle from another. As I watched, a considerable number of the people went down on their knees, right there on the gritty sidewalk. And half of them in the street.

Finally I eased toward the house, passing more people who were joining the crowd, and turned carefully into the driveway. Then I hurried into the house.

"Hazel Marie," I called softly, not wanting to wake Little Lloyd. Tapping on her door, I called again.

"What happened?" she said, flinging the door open. Little Lloyd was in his pajamas sitting up on her bed watching television. "What did Binkie say?"

"Oh, Hazel Marie, I hate to tell you this, but I don't think she's going to do it. I tried every argument I could come up with, but it was like talking to a brick wall. I declare, that girl may be a smart lawyer, but she doesn't have an ounce of common sense. Little Lloyd, what in the world are you watching?" He was sitting there, his eyes glued to the screen where a half-naked girl was performing calisthenics to something that passed for music.

"Britney Spears," he said.

"Hazel Marie, is that good for him? Those gyrations're going to pull that girl's back out, if she's not careful."

"It's all right, Miss Julia. Now, tell me what Binkie said. Maybe there's still hope that she'll come around. I've been counting on being a bridesmaid." She looked with longing eyes toward her bridesmaid's dress hanging on the closet door.

"Yes, well, I've been counting on a wedding, period. I don't know, Hazel Marie." I sank down into a chair, just about overcome with the effort I'd put out on Binkie's behalf, and getting no results, either. "I don't know what to do with her, but I've a good mind never to speak to her again. Although how I'll be able to manage that when her baby comes, I don't know."

"It just makes me want to cry," Hazel Marie said, then went right ahead and started. "I mean, here I am wanting to get married so bad and J.D. is too stubborn to do it. And she's got Coleman who'd give his eyeteeth to marry her, and she spurns him."

"It's worse than that, Hazel Marie," I said. "She's not exactly spurning him. From what I gathered, she expects to continue right on in the same unseemly manner that got her into this situation to begin with, but without any legal bond between them. Or between Coleman and that little . . . , don't listen, Little Lloyd."

"No'm, I won't."

"We'll talk about this in the morning, Hazel Marie," I went on, nodding and frowning toward the sharp little ears that could easily listen to me and Britney Spears, too. Then, in spite of my mind being filled with the problem of Binkie, I recalled the street gathering outside. "Those people we saw last night are back, and there're more of them. I declare, I wish I knew what they're doing. I could hardly get in the driveway for all the people. If Binkie hadn't sapped all my strength, I'd go out there and run them off."

"At least they're quiet," Hazel Marie said. "We'll see about them in the morning. I know you're tired, so you go on to bed and try to sleep. Want me to go upstairs with you?"

I shook my head. "I'll manage." She patted me on the shoulder and walked out into the hall with me. She stood there watching as I plodded up the stairs to my bed.

Friday morning, the day before the wedding, found me almost beside myself. I'd sat up half the night hoping to waylay Coleman, but he'd not come home, which both soothed and agitated me. It could've meant that he'd stayed the night with Binkie, an event I disapproved of and hoped for at the same time. Or it could've meant that his campaign hadn't worked and he couldn't face my disappointment.

On the other hand, Sheriff Frady could have had him and every other deputy out looking for Dixon, so that Coleman had no time to pursue a personal matter. As I thought about that possibility, it began to make sense to me. Earl Frady kept his fingers on the pulse of the town, as any elected official would do, and he could read the newspaper and hear the nightly news just as the voters could. This morning's headline in *The Abbotsville Press* blared out: STILL AT LARGE! with a long article on the ineptitude of the sheriff's department. With that kind of publicity, the sheriff would have Coleman out beating the bushes for Dixon Hightower instead of beating down Binkie's door as he ought to've been doing.

"Hazel Marie," I said, as we stood that morning in her bedroom looking at our wedding dresses again. "Sometimes I think I'm the most foolish woman alive. Here I am, going on with a wedding without the participation of the principal parties. I mean, when do I just throw up my hands and say, 'Okay, you don't want it, we won't have it'?"

"Oh, don't say that, Miss Julia," Hazel Marie said, pressing her fingers against her mouth. "Remember, we still have all those people coming so we'll have some kind of festivity, with or without a ceremony. We just have to set our minds on having the wedding, and it'll come about. I believe in having a positive attitude, don't you?"

Lillian, tying an apron around herself, appeared at the door of Hazel Marie's room. "Miss Julia, them people's back outside. An' they's more of 'em this mornin'.'"

"Well, for goodness' sake," I said. "What're they doing?"

"Jus' standin' 'round, lookin' like they lookin' at that fam'ly buildin'.'"

I waved my hand, dismissing the problem. "I can't be bothered with them, Lillian. As long as they're not being a public nuisance, they can look as long as they want to. Though, Lord knows, I could find something better to look at."

The firing up of a popping motor outside Hazel Marie's back window stopped any further conversation. "There's Raymond," I said, over the noise. "Right on time, too. He'll have this yard looking good in no time. I better go speak to him, and let him know it has to be perfect for tomorrow." I stopped and rubbed my forehead. "Although I don't know why I'm bothering with it now."

"Oh, please don't say that," Hazel Marie said. "Let's keep our spirits up, and maybe it'll work out."

"I'm trying," I said, "believe me, I am." I started for the door. "Well, let me go and see Raymond."

"Uh, Miss Julia?" Hazel Marie stopped me. "I think his name is Ramón."

"Why, Hazel Marie, you know I don't speak that language. I'll be back in a few minutes, Lillian, and we'll go over the last-minute things."

As soon as I stepped out into the back-yard, Raymond turned off his lawn mower, letting it sputter to a stop in a cloud of smoke. He took off his hat and smiled shyly at me, careful not to meet my eye. A spark of sunlight, glinting off the large gold cross on a chain around his neck, flashed in my eyes.

"Good morning, Raymond," I said. "I'm glad to see you. It's a beautiful day, isn't it? Now, what I want you to do is to get the whole yard, front and back, looking as good as it possibly can. We hope to have a wed-ding here tomorrow, and I want everything spick-and-span."

"*Sí.*" He glanced at me, smiled and let his eyes slide away.

"I know you'll do a good job."

"*Sí.*"

"Knock on the door when you're through, and I'll pay you. But take as long as you need to get it looking good; I don't care if it takes all day."

"*Sí.*"

Pleased with my ability to communicate with a speaker of a foreign language, I started to go inside. Then, with another thought, I turned back to him. "Oh, Raymond, do you know why there're so many people out on the street today?" And recalling the similar gathering last night, I added, "And last night, too?"

He smiled, ducked his head and said, "*Sí.*"

"Well, why?"

"*¿Por qué?*"

"What?"

"*¿Qué?*"

I shrugged my shoulders, and he shrugged his, still smiling. "Well, carry on," I said, waving my hand, and he did, reaching to pull the starter cord.

I was feeling somewhat less pleased with my communication skills as I went back into the kitchen, but maybe Raymond didn't know any more about it than I did.

Little Lloyd met me at the back door,

having just come in from a short last day of school. He held the screen door for me and said, "Miss Julia, come quick. The truck's here with the piano and the chairs. They're about to move them in."

Lillian and Hazel Marie joined us in the living room to supervise the move. The truck had been backed up into the driveway, and the back door let down to form a ramp. Two men carefully moved the spinet piano on a wheeled platform down the ramp and onto the drive. Then they maneuvered it across the lawn and up a ramp across the porch steps. Little Lloyd held the screen door open for them and, first thing I knew, they had it situated in front of the bookcase beside the fireplace.

"I hope the thing's still in tune after all that manhandling," I said, cringing at the thought of what Miss Mattie Mae Morgan might do if she hit a few clunkers in the middle of the ceremony. If we had a ceremony.

The men made two dozen trips from the truck to the house, bringing in the little gilt chairs. Hazel Marie and I got them arranged in rows facing the place where the arch would be.

"Miss Julia," Hazel Marie said, "these

chairs are awfully little and spindly. I'm not sure Miss Mildred Allen can fit on one of them. She might need two, the way she spreads out. You think they'll hold her?"

"Lord, Hazel Marie," I said. "I can't worry about that now." But as I lined up another row, I went on, "On second thought, maybe we should see that she gets one of the dining room chairs. I'll tell Mr. Pickens to watch for her, and keep her away from these. We sure don't need another catastrophe, which it would be if one crumpled up under her."

When one of the movers brought the receipt for me to sign, he said, "We'll send somebody later today to check that piano, be sure it's in tune." Which relieved my mind considerably. Then, as he gave me the carbon copy, he added, "Got a lot of traffic on this street, don't you?"

"Not usually," I said, glancing over his shoulder as we stood in the door and, sure enough, that steady stream of cars, vans and pickups was still at it.

I didn't know where they'd come from or where they were going, but it came to me that there might be some street-repair work going on somewhere and traffic was being rerouted along Polk. It didn't make much difference to me, as long as they were cleared out by the next day, but while I watched the rental company's truck ease out into the street, a bottleneck happened right in front of my eyes. The Watering Can's delivery van pulled out of the traffic and edged to the curb, just as the rental truck made a sharp turn out of the driveway, blocking both lanes of the narrow street. Between the people jammed up on the sidewalk and the cars jammed up on both sides of the rental truck, my quiet street looked like rush hour in downtown Atlanta. I stood on the porch, my hands on my hips, surveying the confusion. While the men in the rental truck and Harriet in the delivery van had a number of unpleasant things to say to each other, I noticed that a good many of the occupants in the cars seemed content to wait out the situation. They leaned out the car windows, staring and pointing at the Family Life Center. I intended to tell Pastor Ledbetter that was proof I wasn't the only person in town who thought the thing was a blight on the landscape.

I couldn't stand to watch the confusion and went back into the house. Before long, Harriet came puffing up on the porch, carrying two huge Boston ferns in hanging baskets.

"What's going on, Mrs. Springer?" she asked, putting down the baskets and wiping her forehead with her arm. "Where're all these cars coming from? My goodness, it's hot."

"It certainly is. I'll have Lillian bring you some iced tea. And as for the traffic, I think they're working on some of those potholes somewhere and have the streets blocked off. Little Lloyd, make yourself useful and help Miss Harriet bring things in."

As I went back through the living room, Hazel Marie was taking a dust cloth to the chairs, going over each one to be sure they were clean and ready for our guests.

"Harriet's going to bring in the arch in a minute, Hazel Marie. You might have to move a few chairs so she can get it in."

"Yes, ma'am, I'll help her."

I went on into the kitchen and was brought up short at the sight of milk bottles and ketchup bottles and mustard jars and mayonnaise jars and plastic bowls, with and without lids covering every inch of space on the counters. Lillian was bent over reaching into the open refrigerator.

"I'm cleanin' out this 'frigerator, if you wonderin'," she said. "I got to make room for that caterin' lady when she come tomorrow."

"Was all this stuff in the refrigerator?"

"You be surprised what was in this thing. I been th'owin' out, right an' left. If anybody want any lunch, they better grab it now, 'cause it gonna be gone pretty quick."

"I guess we better get in here, then, and get it while we can. I'll call Hazel Marie and Little Lloyd."

As I started out, Lillian said, "Tell Little Lloyd I already got him a peanut butter an' banana sam'ich made. You an' Miss Hazel Marie got to fend for yo'selves."

"Yes, well, we'll bring in something for supper, or maybe we'll all go somewhere. So don't worry about what to fix."

"I wadn't aimin' to," she said, dumping the ice tray into the sink. "Oncet I get this kitchen clean, I don't want nobody messin' it up again."

I walked back to stand beside the counter. "Lillian, when you finish here, why don't you take off early and go home. You must have a million things to do to get ready for tomorrow. You got a new dress, didn't you?"

She wrung out a dishcloth and smiled, her gold tooth flashing in her mouth. "I got the prettiest dress in town. I know Miss Binkie's colors, and I wanted to match up with 'em. My dress is hot pink satin, an' I got a matchin' hat, a little tiny thing with a veil on it."

"It sounds lovely." I leaned against the counter and bowed my head. "Oh, Lillian, I don't know how I'm going to get through it all."

"I know what you mean, an' my heart 'bout to break, too. If Miss Binkie don't marry Coleman, we gonna have to watch that pore man suffer every livin' day." Tears stood in Lillian's eyes. Then she gave the dishcloth a final wring and said, "If I didn't love Miss Binkie like my own chile, I'd say it jus' downright cussedness what make her do such a thing."

My sentiments, exactly.

Chapter 25

Realizing that I hadn't heard Raymond's lawn mower for some little while, I went outside to see how he was coming along. I found him in the front yard, standing by the crape myrtle with a pair of pruning shears in his hand. Instead of using them, though, he was gazing across the street at the Family Life Center.

"Raymond," I said, startling him so that he looked straight at me. "Have you finished the backyard?"

"*Sí.*" He bobbed his head and immediately started snipping a boxwood beneath the crape myrtle.

"Good. The front shouldn't take you long. If you need to move those potted plants the florist put out, go ahead and do it. Just put them back where she had them." I paused, looking around to see what else needed to be done. "Maybe give everything a good watering, and be sure all the weeds're pulled. Little Lloyd made a good start on that the other day. You know, Raymond, a row of annuals along the foundation shrubs would look good, wouldn't it? Impatiens would be nice, don't you think? I should've thought of them earlier in the week, but if the nursery has some in full bloom, would you have time to plant them for me today?"

Raymond was such an agreeable man, nodding and saying *Sí* to everything I suggested. It was a pleasure doing business with him, even though his eyes kept sliding away toward the building that was the bane of my existence.

"Well, carry on," I said, going back into the house to call the nursery for an urgent delivery.

Little Lloyd was finishing his lunch, so he overheard me place my order with the nurseryman. He immediately volunteered to help Raymond set them out.

"I better help Ramón," he said. "Show me where you want them, Miss Julia, so we'll be sure to get them right."

"I've already told him."

"Yessum, I know, but tell me, too."

I did and, leaving them to it, wandered

through the downstairs rooms, checking for last-minute things to do. Harriet had placed the arch of greenery in front of the fireplace with tall multibranched candlestands on each side. She'd also placed white wicker plant stands in the corners of the room, waiting for the arrangements she'd put on them the next morning.

The dining room table was shining with lemon polish and the glow of silver serving pieces. I straightened the row of linen napkins and moved a tray an inch to the left, imagining how it would look with the centerpiece that I'd told Harriet had to be spectacular. I was trying to keep my mind occupied so I wouldn't worry about there not being anything to celebrate, come the next day.

By the time Raymond and Little Lloyd finished planting a row of white impatiens in front of the boxwoods, I had to say the yard looked festive enough to change Binkie's mind if anything could. After thanking Raymond and paying him for his good work, I walked across the street and spoke to the man I assumed to be the foreman of the construction site. He was the only one standing around watching the others work, so it was a good guess.

"Sir, I want you to know that we're hoping to have a wedding tomorrow right across the street. You can see how hard we've worked on the yard, so I'd appreciate it if you'd have your men clean off the sidewalk over here before you leave today. And furthermore, if you have any brick dust or sawdust or any other kind of dust to spew out into the neighborhood, please defer it until Monday. It'll be bad enough then, but it just won't be acceptable today."

"Yes, ma'am," he said, looking at me from under his baseball cap, which he'd not had the courtesy to remove. "That young pastor's already asked us to do that."

"What a pleasant surprise. I didn't think he'd remember to speak to you. Well, thank you in advance for cleaning up the mess you've made over here."

Going back across the street, I noted that the cars and pickups, which we'd had so many of that morning, had eased off to a trickle. I hoped it stayed that way.

As the day was wearing on, I discussed with Hazel Marie and Little Lloyd where we should go for supper. Eating out was not a favorite of mine, but if we disturbed Lillian's kitchen by trying to cook, she wouldn't be fit to live with. Little Lloyd wanted to go to some pizza parlor that was so noisy it interfered with digestion, and Hazel Marie suggested Hal's Barbeque House. My choice was the S & P cafeteria, where we could each get what we wanted except, as Little Lloyd pointed out, pizza and barbecue.

While we were trying to decide where to go, the doorbell rang, announcing Emma Sue Ledbetter, laden with a casserole, salad and rolls.

"My famous dessert is in the car," she said. "I'll bring it in as soon as I deposit these in your kitchen." And she zipped past me, bearing her gifts, while I rolled my eyes at the thought of her famous dessert. A dump cake, the name of which put me off considerably, consisting of any number of cans of fruit and boxes of cake mix dumped into a Pyrex dish, stirred and baked.

"You didn't have to do this, Emma Sue," I said, following her back to the kitchen. It burned me up, knowing that she'd brought supper to make me feel guilty for jumping on her about those blasted bumper stickers. Unbeknownst to her, though, I didn't feel the least twinge. "We were planning to go out."

"No, no, you don't want to do that. I know you're all terribly busy getting ready for what I know will be the sweetest wedding, and you won't have time to cook. Now, this is a chicken and rice casserole, made with Campbell's cream of mushroom soup, and this is a congealed salad with sour cream between the layers. You won't believe what I made my dump cake with this time."

"Don't tell me, Emma Sue," I said, feeling queasy already. I never liked to know what made up the food I was eating. "Let it be a surprise. A nice surprise, I'm sure. You are so thoughtful to do this, but I wish you hadn't." I knew that Hazel Marie and Little Lloyd were going to wish the same.

"Of course I should've," she said, as she took tinfoil off her dishes. "You might want to run this casserole in the oven for a few minutes. Now let me go get the dessert."

"I'll walk out with you and get it. I know you're busy, too."

We walked out to her car, and she handed me the dish. "A little ice cream on top just sets this off," she said. "Oh, Julia, I'm so looking forward to the wedding. I just wish Larry were here to be a part of it. You know," she went on, lowering her voice, "I wasn't sure I ought to attend. I had to pray long and hard about it, but the Lord told me it would send the wrong message if I stayed away."

"Well, I'm glad He gave you permission to come. But you know, Emma Sue, times have changed, and you don't always have to stay home when your husband's out of town. A lot of wives attend things by themselves these days."

"Oh, I don't mind that. It's just that, well, I'm sure you know why those two young people are in such a rush to marry." She gave me a knowing look that made me step back a pace. "And when I heard, I really thought you should've stayed out of it and let them sneak off to marry without any fanfare like they're getting. I hope you'll forgive me for thinking you were wrong to put on a big show; I really had to wrestle with the Lord about you. But then He pointed out to me that some people just haven't progressed as far on their spiritual journey as others have. But don't you worry, you're at the top of my prayer list, because you know I love you in the Lord, Julia." She put her hand on my arm and patted it to confirm her words. "And as far as Binkie and her deputy are concerned, I've come to see that as long as two people are doing the right thing, we shouldn't judge when they do it."

"Judge not, Emma Sue. I expect you know the rest of it."

"Well, I worried about putting my stamp of approval on such a hurry-up wedding, which I would do if I attended. You know, under the circumstances."

"Just what circumstances are you talking about?" Although, with a sinking heart, I thought I knew.

She leaned close to me and hissed, "Binkie's, well, you know, *expecting*. That's what I'm talking about."

Oh, Lord, I thought, wishing He'd speak to me. Since no word came from on high, I had to muddle through by myself. "I think you're jumping to conclusions again, Emma Sue," I managed to get out, hoping my face didn't show my sinking feelings. "Where in the world did you hear such a thing?" Then with a gasp and sudden understanding: "Not . . . the prayer chain? Don't tell me it's making the rounds on the prayer chain."

She smiled. "Well, Julia, what's the prayer

chain for but to share our concerns for people in trouble?"

"Who started it?" I demanded.

"You know that young Creasman couple that just joined the church? Well, she's expecting and she saw Binkie at Dr. Crawford's office, and all he does is deliver babies."

"And I don't suppose," I said, "that the Creasman woman is a member of the prayer chain?"

"It's good to get new members involved in church activities as soon as we can, you know that, Julia. But I would've suspected it when I heard that Binkie had to run out of court, during a trial, too, to throw up." A small frown appeared on Emma Sue's face, then she went on. "You know that I don't like to talk about people, but everybody but you knows it, which is just as well, since you wouldn't be throwing this big shindig if you did. Nobody's blaming you, even though we Christians do have to draw the line somewhere and be careful that we don't celebrate sin."

"Emma Sue," I said, just about done in by what she was saying. "I think it's a shame to go around carrying stories about people you hardly know, and that's the main reason I wanted off the prayer chain. It does nothing but pass along rumors, half of them not even close to the truth, and I resent all the talk about Binkie. She's a good girl."

"Well, we'll see, won't we? Now, I've got to be going; I still have to put the hem in the dress I'm making for tomorrow. I really got behind because I had to make that trip to the Winn-Dixie for the communion wine."

"Welch's grape juice, Emma Sue."

"You know what I mean. Anyway, it's locked in the car trunk, so you-know-who can't get at it." She slid into the car, saying, as she reached for the door, "I know the Lord'll bless you for what you're doing, Julia."

"I'm sure, Emma Sue," I said tiredly. "Thank you for bringing us supper. I'm sure we'll enjoy every bite." I stood there and watched her drive off, just sick at heart that Binkie's condition was known to the town. And I got sicker at the thought that even though Emma Sue might be willing to overlook a late wedding, she wouldn't be so forgiving if there was no wedding at all.

Chapter 26

Trying to ignore the shuffle of feet along the sidewalk as people began to gather for another night vigil, I turned to gaze at my house. A late afternoon in June, a soft light from the setting sun, the smell of freshly cut grass and the glow of white impatiens under the boxwoods, the swept brick walkway lined with potted pink azaleas, and the blessed relief of silence from the building across the street—my heart should have been swelling with pleasure on this wedding eve. My house was clean and shining, ready for guests, and the long-desired culmination of Binkie and Coleman's romance.

Instead, I slowly trudged into the house, taking little joy in the preparations we'd made.

It didn't help my state of mind to find Hazel Marie and Little Lloyd less than thrilled at the thought of eating Emma Sue's supper.

"Oh, no!" Little Lloyd wailed. "I wanted to go out."

Hazel Marie stood gazing at the chicken and rice casserole on the kitchen table. Then she said, "I bet that's been frozen a solid month. I know she makes several at a time to have something on hand for covered-dish suppers at the church. It probably has freezer burn."

Little Lloyd then suggested that we dump it all in the sink, turn on the disposal and go out, as we'd planned to do.

My heart wasn't in anything. I so wanted to tell Hazel Marie that the news was out and being broadcast, but I couldn't with Little Lloyd there to hear it, too.

Just as they were seriously considering scraping Emma Sue's efforts down the drain, Mr. Pickens called to see if he could drop by. After that, not another word was said about going out to eat. In fact, Hazel Marie busied herself with setting the table with an extra place for him, chattering away with her excitement.

"It's a good thing we hadn't already left," she said. "We'd've missed him, and he's been so busy I hardly ever get to see him. Now, Lloyd, don't be disappointed; we'll get pizza maybe Sunday night. Oh, I hope J.D.'ll like this casserole. But he will, I'm sure of it. He'll eat anything." Then she laughed, her hand over her mouth. "A good thing, too, since I'm hardly the best cook in the world."

Mr. Pickens came in with his usual air of energy and good spirits. He hugged Hazel Marie and gave her a big smack, right in front of me and the child. Then he hugged Little Lloyd, asked how he liked being out of school and promised to go hiking with him as soon as he finished Dixon Hightower's case.

"That rascal's staying one step ahead of the sheriff's department," Mr. Pickens said. Then with a rueful shake of his head, he admitted, "And me."

"That's certainly hard to believe," I said.

He rounded on me, throwing out his arms and saying, "Hey, darlin'. How 'bout a hug?"

"Behave yourself, Mr. Pickens," I said, stepping back out of hugging vicinity. "Now, let's sit down and eat."

"Miss Julia," Mr. Pickens said, as he pulled out my chair. I was glad to see Little Lloyd follow his lead and pull out his mother's chair. "I know you're a woman of some means," Mr. Pickens went on. "But I didn't know you had half the county on your payroll."

"What are you talking about?"

"That crowd out there in front of your house." He glanced at me with those black eyes, a smile at the corners of his mouth.

"Well, Mr. Pickens," I said, trying to give back as good as I was getting. "I'll have you know that after engaging you last winter, I've had my fill of the employment business."

He threw his head back and laughed. Then he said, "Sure enough, though, why're they out there? I almost couldn't get through."

"We don't know," Little Lloyd said. "Mama won't let me go out there, but I wish you'd asked them."

"In too much of a hurry to see my three favorite people," Mr. Pickens said, with a wink at Hazel Marie.

Hazel Marie smiled at him and said, "We've been too busy to look into it, but we think they're admiring Pastor Ledbetter's new building."

"Admiring's not the word," I said. "Dumbfounded at it, more likely. Little Lloyd, pass Mr. Pickens the butter."

I picked at the food, put off by Hazel Marie's observation that it had been frozen so long, but Mr. Pickens made a considerable dent in it. Hazel Marie was right; he'd eat anything.

As he took his third helping of the casserole, Mr. Pickens said, "Would anybody object to turning on the TV? I'd like to get the news."

Well, I did object, since mealtime ought to be filled with pleasant conversation without the intrusion of wrecks and wars, and first one thing and another of unsavory happenings that weren't fit to listen to while you're trying to eat. I held my peace, though, so taken up with the burden of my worries that I couldn't hold a pleasant conversation if I had to.

I reached over and turned on the television set on the counter and switched it to the Asheville station. As soon as the station stopped advertising itself, we saw that the lead story was Dixon Hightower again. The major news was that he'd not been found. Mr. Pickens grunted.

"We have late-breaking news," one of the

local anchors said with a rush of excitement, as we all turned toward the set. "The Briar Creek House of God in Abbot County has just reported the theft of a box of raffle tickets that were to be sold for a new Silverado pickup, donated by Junior Willard Chevrolet in Abbotsville. We spoke with Pastor Harold Hobbs by telephone, and he told us that any number of bingo prizes in the form of gift certificates, donated by local businesses, are also missing. We wanted to bring you a live report from Pastor Hobbs, but we're having audio difficulties. Tiffany," he said, turning to his co-anchor, "can you tell us more about this latest development?"

"Yes, I can, Kenny." The smiling co-anchor turned from him to face the camera. Then she cut off the smile and frowned at the seriousness of the situation. "Pastor Hobbs reported that no locks or windows in the church were broken, which means, and I quote, 'We have a good idea who the culprit is. And I want him to know that all our members're praying for the return of our valuable raffle tickets and bingo prizes.' Unquote. Back to you, Kenny."

"Oh, for goodness' sake," I said. "I don't

believe that. What would Dixon want with such things?"

"Probably nothing," Hazel Marie said. "You know how he is. He just picks up whatever's in front of him when the urge to take something strikes him."

"Well, I wish they'd catch him before he's blamed for everything that happens in the county." I passed Emma Sue's rolls to Mr. Pickens, as I mused aloud. "Where in the world could he be?"

The Abbot County sheriff answered me by way of an interview with a cosmetically enhanced television reporter who asked questions like: "Are the residents of the county in any danger from this desperate man?" with a dazzling smile on her face.

Sheriff Earl Frady stared at her, and I thought for a minute that he didn't have an answer. He seemed to be trying to figure out what she was so happy about. Then he said, "No, we don't see him as desperate or dangerous. My guess is he's left the county by now . . ." He had his mouth open to say something else, but she cut him off. She was looking for something more exciting and found it in several brief prerecorded interviews with county residents who'd reported sightings. One man said he'd seen a man on his roof, hiding behind the chimney. He knew it was Dixon because nobody else could climb that high without a ladder. The camera then panned around the house to show that there wasn't a ladder in sight.

"I declare," I said, "people're crazy, aren't they? They must sit around all day thinking up ways to get on television."

"That's the truth," Hazel Marie said, standing and beginning to pick up our plates. "But at least the sheriff thinks Dixon's out of the county."

"Well, he's the authority," Mr. Pickens said. "But I'm thinking that's just for public consumption. For my money, that ole boy's still around."

"You think he's still here? Close by us?" Little Lloyd's eyes were about to pop out of his head. "Oh, me, I was hoping he was gone. Now I'm going to start worrying again."

"Sorry, sport," Mr. Pickens said. "Didn't mean to worry you. All I meant was that Dixon's likely holed up in some unlikely place, but not anywhere close to you."

"Who wants dessert?" Hazel Marie

asked. "J.D., would you like ice cream on yours?"

"Sure, pile it on."

Little Lloyd shook his head. "I think I'll pass. My stomach's not feeling too good."

"Then you've made a wise decision to pass," I said, recalling Emma Sue's remark about a surprise in her dump cake. "Now calm that stomach of yours down. Dixon's not interested in us at all and there's no reason to make yourself sick over him." You do have to reassure children when their little minds are filled with worry.

"That's right," Mr. Pickens said, with one of his wicked grins. "Miss Julia knows I'm hot on his trail, so there's not a thing to worry about."

Little Lloyd managed a smile, as we, especially Mr. Pickens, concentrated on our plates. Then Little Lloyd's attention was drawn back to the news, which I'd mentally turned off. "Wonder what that is?" he asked.

"What, sugar?" Hazel Marie said.

We all turned to the television set just as Kenny said, "We'll have an update on this unusual occurrence tonight on the eleven o'clock news. Tune in then when we'll have a live report from Abbotsville."

"Well, I never," I said. "Wonder what other unusual occurrence has happened in Abbotsville? They'll probably blame that on Dixon, too. Turn that thing down, will you, Hazel Marie? They've got their sports segment on, and I have no interest whatsoever in a southern hockey team."

When Hazel Marie started rattling on about the wedding and/or party set for tomorrow, I didn't want to hear it. I could hardly bear to think of the fiasco we were facing the next day, much less sit around and discuss it. So I shooed the three of them out.

"Go sit in the backyard," I told them. "It's a beautiful evening, and Raymond cleaned all the yard furniture. So just go on out and enjoy it. I'll get the kitchen cleaned up, and I can do it better by myself."

Both Hazel Marie and Little Lloyd seemed eager to enjoy Mr. Pickens's company. He was an entertaining man, I had to admit, although he was entirely too free with his teasing and carryings-on. With the sadness weighing so heavy on me, I was in no mood to put up with him. Much better not to infect the others with my sinking feelings. Besides, it'd take me forever to clean Emma Sue's Pyrex casserole dishes and get the kitchen back to Lillian's standards. I knew she'd have something to say about its condition as soon as she stepped in the door the next morning.

As I scrubbed baked-on dump cake with a Brillo pad and worried about ruining the manicure that I'd paid seventeen dollars plus a three-dollar tip for, I couldn't help but wonder if I'd done everything possible to make Binkie see the light. Maybe sending Coleman with flowers and love notes and an engagement ring had been too little too late. Maybe my visit had hardened her heart. Maybe it'd all get on her nerves—you never know what'll upset somebody who's expecting. Maybe something else was needed.

I nearly choked with a sudden, wayward thought. What if I sent Pastor Lance Petree over there to serenade her with his guitar and questionable singing voice? The picture that came into my mind of what Binkie would say, much less do, under those circumstances was enough to bring out a quick laugh. Although it was just as quickly cut off as my throat thickened.

Giving up on Emma Sue's blasted Pyrex dish, I filled it with water and Lemon Joy and left it. Lillian would just have to fuss; I couldn't clean the thing.

Chapter 27

I went out onto the front porch, since there was nowhere to sit in the living room except in one of those tiny, backbreaking chairs from the rental place, and took my seat in one of the rockers. It was almost full dark with the streetlamps throwing long shadows across the yard. I sat in the corner behind the wisteria vine where I was shielded from the steady stream of people walking along the sidewalk. I sat there in the dark and let all the burdens on my heart come flooding over me. I thought I'd drown with the weight of them. Whatever the morrow brought, it would also bring the loss of Hazel Marie and Little Lloyd. They'd be moving out and miles away, thanks to Mr. Pickens who, if I'd known what was going to happen, I'd've never engaged in the first place. Even if it had been to find Hazel Marie when we thought we'd lost her to a fund-raising scoundrel. I'd just not had the confidence in myself to try to track her down without Mr. Pickens's professional help, when the fact of the matter was, Little Lloyd and I managed quite well by ourselves with only minor help from Mr. Pickens. And look where it'd led. Hazel Marie so much in love she couldn't see straight and ready to leave my house and home to throw in with a smooth-talking private investigator. He was handsome, though; I'd give him that. But I couldn't give him much else because he'd be taking that child along with Hazel Marie.

Maybe I should sell this house, just get out from under all the memories, good and bad, that lingered in its corners. And maybe I should convert all of Wesley Lloyd's quick-stop stores and car washes and commercial buildings into cash, and move into a retirement home where I wouldn't have to deal with the likes of Etta Mae Wiggins and her constant nagging.

I sighed, thinking that I might be able to fix it so that pushy woman would be somebody else's problem, but how would I fill my time? Sit in a rocker as I was now doing and feel sorry for myself? Since Little Lloyd and Hazel Marie had been with me, my days had been so full that the past was as if it'd never been. But when they left, I knew the bleak years would come rushing back over me like a tidal wave. Why, I can't tell you how many committee meetings I'd attended during those years, just to have something to do until Wesley Lloyd came home for supper and the six o'clock news. When the church doors were open, I was there—Women of the Church meetings, circle meetings, Sunday school meetings and any other meeting that women were allowed to attend. Then there were D.A.R. meetings, P.E.O. meetings and any other meetings anybody could dream up for idle hands and minds, except political meetings, which Wesley Lloyd deemed unsuitable for someone in my position. I carried casseroles to new mothers and shut-ins, arranged a few flowers, read a few books and tried my hand at needlepoint—everything and only the things dictated by the Lord for a woman to do and passed directly to me by way of Wesley Lloyd.

Where had my mind been? Now, here I sat, brooding on how I'd fill the empty days ahead, but determined not to let Wesley Lloyd direct me from the grave. I didn't know what I'd do, but one thing was for sure. I'd never go to another committee meeting again, especially one that Emma Sue Ledbetter was on. Imagine! Putting me and Little Lloyd on a committee that we were eminently unsuited for. And for our own good!

I leaned my head back and set the rocker going, trying not to sink down into despair at my own pitiful situation or at Hazel Marie's headlong rush into common-law living.

I stopped the rocker with a jolt. It came to me like a news flash. There was the difference: I'd done whatever I was supposed to do according to whoever was making the rules, namely Wesley Lloyd, while the Binkies and the Hazel Maries of the world were doing whatever they wanted without a thought in their heads as to the consequences. There ought to be some middle ground somewhere, but, I declare, I didn't know where it could be or anybody who'd found it.

Just look at Binkie, who'd let me plan and prepare for her wedding and, without one word to me, called it off in a flight of fancy that took no account of anybody else's feelings. If her parents had had to put up with such unmitigated willfulness from her, no wonder they'd moved to Florida. I had a good mind to do the same.

"Miss Julia?"

I hadn't heard the child as he'd come through the dark house nor could I see more than his outline as he stood in the unlit living room looking out through the screen door. My eyes weren't what they once were.

"Over here, Little Lloyd."

"You feeling all right?" He opened the screen and came to stand beside my chair.

"I'm fine. Just sitting here in the dark worrying myself sick over Binkie and Coleman. And dreading the day that you and your mother'll be moving away. I'll miss you, Little Lloyd."

"I'll come back to see you."

I patted his arm where it rested on my chair. He was a thoughtful child, sensitive and considerate. Very much like me, I was pleased to note.

"I know you will. Now, don't listen to an old woman's complaints. I'm just feeling sorry for myself thinking about being alone again. I'll get over it; don't you worry."

"You won't be alone, Miss Julia, because

you've got Lillian and, when I get old enough, I'll look after you."

Oh, Lord, my heart clenched up in my chest with the sweetness of it. I had to clear my throat before I could answer.

I put my arm around his skinny shoulders and squeezed him close. "That means more to me than anything I've ever heard. Thank you, Little Lloyd."

But, being a child, his attention quickly shifted, and I was just as glad since I'm not one to express my emotions in public.

"Look, Miss Julia," he said, pointing toward the street. "That's a WLMN-TV van! And it's stopping!"

I peered through the wisteria vine at the white van with a satellite dish and antennas on the roof. The boy was right; it had pulled to the curb and stopped, the motor still running. I couldn't see anything else but a mass of shadowy people, many more than there had been the previous night, on the edge of the property line that ran between my and Lila McCarran's side yard next door. The crowd was massed on the sidewalk for some little way and spilled out onto the street.

"My word," I said. "Why would television

people be on our street?" I grasped Little Lloyd's arm. "You don't suppose they've caught Dixon, do you?"

He trembled at the thought, then his great good sense took hold. "No'm, it couldn't be that. There'd be a bunch of deputies here, too, if it was Dixon. All I can see is a lot of people standing around like they were last night. I walked down the driveway a while ago, but they were talking too low for me to hear what they were saying. Maybe we ought to call Coleman to see what's going on."

"Well, it makes you wonder, doesn't it? I just can't figure out what's drawn them here, or why a television station would be interested."

As we watched, three people climbed out of the van, one of them a sleek blond woman holding a microphone. A man hoisted what turned out to be a camera with a powerful light onto his shoulder, while another one reeled out wires and cables onto the street. Then he began positioning the woman and directing the man with the camera. I guessed he was the director.

"This thing's getting out of hand, Little Lloyd. I don't know what's worth televising over there, but I don't like it. Let's go in and see if Coleman's on duty. If he's not, he'll be at Binkie's, and I'm not sure I want to disturb him over there. He'll be in the midst of some heavy negotiations, if he's doing what he's supposed to do."

"We could ask Mr. Pickens," Little Lloyd said. "He might could find out."

"I don't know," I said, going across the porch. "He didn't seem all that interested at supper. Got his mind on Dixon, I expect." Besides, I thought but didn't say, Mr. Pickens was probably so occupied with Hazel Marie he wouldn't know which end was up. "Though we could ask him to go out there now and find out what's going on."

I locked the front door behind us, just in case Dixon was sneaking around. Then we went to the kitchen, lit only by the light over the stove, and I dialed the sheriff's department. The dispatcher was able to put me right through to Coleman, which was unusual, to say the least.

"Just brought somebody in to be booked, Miss Julia," he explained. "What can I do for you?"

"First of all, you can tell me why you're

not over at Binkie's, talking some sense into her."

"I'll be off duty in a few minutes, and I'm going over there then. But, Miss Julia," he said, then paused for so long I thought he wasn't going to continue. Then he went on. "I was going to call you, but I might as well tell you now. I'm giving up on trying to change Binkie's mind. If I keep on at her, I might end up losing her altogether."

"Coleman! No!" Not only did I not have the bride, I was about to lose the groom as well. "Listen to me, you can't take that attitude. You've got to be positive and determined. You've got to convince Binkie that you're going to be here and that she has to be, too."

"No," he said, and I could almost see him shake his head. "I'm not going to shame myself by showing up without her. I'm sorry, Miss Julia, for all the trouble you've gone to, but it's better to let it go. I don't want to count on something that's not going to happen." He gave a short, painful-sounding laugh. "Even though she says she's still thinking about it."

"She's going to think herself right into a lonely old age if she's not careful. Now,

Coleman, you may be giving up on your wedding, but I'm not. I don't want to hear another word about it, so just get it out of your head right now." Taking a deep breath and hoping to show I'd brushed off his change-of-heart threat, I said, "Now that we have that taken care of, I need your help with another matter. We've been noticing a group of people gathering on the sidewalk outside the house for the last couple of nights, and now there're even more of them. I don't know what they're doing, but they're making me nervous. And on top of that," I added, "a television van's out there with lights and camera and everything, getting ready to put them on the news, and I want to know what's going on."

"Yes, ma'am, we know about 'em. Not about the television; that's news to me. But as long as the crowd's peaceful and not bothering anybody, there's not much we can do. It's some kind of religious vigil."

"On the sidewalk? What in the world is religious about the sidewalk on Polk Street?"

"Beats me. Just telling you what some of the other deputies told me. I'm working the south side of the county, so I haven't been over there. Maybe they're commemorating a special day. Or something."

"Well, that makes me feel some better, I guess. Maybe that's why a television station sent their truck. Human interest, you know. Well, far be it from me to interfere with somebody's way of worship. Even though it wouldn't be mine."

After hanging up, I reassured Little Lloyd that the sheriff's department had the sidewalk congregation well in hand. I kept Coleman's announcement that he might not show up for his wedding to myself. If I didn't bring it up, I wouldn't have to think about it.

Little Lloyd, unaware of my increasingly troubled mind, still had his on the sidewalk gathering. And he'd come up with some reassurance on his own. "One good thing, Miss Julia," he said. "As long as they're out there, that ole Dixon Hightower won't be sneaking around, will he?"

"Highly unlikely, I'd say. He'll stay away from crowds where somebody might recognize him." Then looking at my watch, I said, "Are your mother and Mr. Pickens still in the backyard?"

"Yessum. I just came in because I was worried about you."

"Bless your little heart. But as you can see, I'm fine. Now, let's get some lights on in here to remind them that it's close to bedtime. Why don't you go up and start your bath?"

When he left, I stood in the empty kitchen realizing that I could've shaken Coleman until his teeth rattled. What was he doing going on duty when he should've been romancing Binkie? And what was he doing even thinking of giving up when she was wearing his ring? I had a good mind to call him back and tell him to drop what he was doing and take care of what was important.

But as far as telling him *how* to take care of it, well, I'd reached the end of my rope in the romance department. But that rope hadn't been very long in the first place.

"Well," I said to the empty kitchen, propping my hands on my hips. "Maybe everything that could be done *hasn't* been done yet. So I guess I'd better get to it."

Chapter 28

"Hey, Miss Julia," Hazel Marie said as she came in from the yard. She blinked her eyes in the light of the kitchen, a little smile on her face. I noticed that her mouth looked soft and smeary, but decided not to dwell on it. "Somebody called J.D. on his cell phone and he had to leave. We thought you'd already gone upstairs, so he said to say good night for him."

"Very polite of him, I'm sure," I said. "But I wish he'd stayed. Hazel Marie, that crowd out there has grown by leaps and bounds, and now the Asheville television station has sent a van to put it on the news. And the more I think about it, the more it worries me. As if I didn't have enough to worry about already. I'll tell you this, I don't want to see my house or my church, including that nightmare of a Family Life Center, on the news for everybody to stare at."

"Well, my goodness," Hazel Marie said, going to the kitchen window to look out. "Wonder which reporter they sent? I like Kenny Kane, wonder if it's him?"

"I don't care who it is. Don't get carried away with television personalities, Hazel Marie. Now, listen," I went on, "not only do we have a problem with Binkie and whether or not she's going to be here tomorrow, we have a problem with Coleman. He's decided he doesn't want to risk being embarrassed if Binkie doesn't show. He's thinking of staying away himself."

"Oh, no," Hazel Marie cried, turning to me with a stricken face. "He can't do that! Oh, Miss Julia, they're dropping away like flies!"

"I know, I know," I said, my hand at my throat. "But *we* haven't dropped away and we're certainly not giving up. Now, Hazel Marie, first things first. We have to straighten out that problem outside. It's turning into a public nuisance.

"I checked with Coleman a few minutes ago, and would you believe he's on duty when his on-again, off-again wedding's less than twenty-four hours away? Anyway, he said those people milling around out there are on some kind of religious vigil, which was news to me. Well," I said after a pause, "I guess it's news to everybody, or they wouldn't be putting it on the air."

Hazel Marie craned her neck trying to see out the side window. "I'd kinda like to go out there. I've never seen a television camera in action."

"I'd recommend against it," I said, reaching for my purse. "Little Lloyd's upstairs, and I'm going over to Binkie's again."

She turned around, surprised. "Why, Miss Julia, it's after ten o'clock! You can't be going over there now."

"I don't see why not. Hazel Marie," I said, pressing my hand against my forehead. "I have to talk to her again before Coleman gets over there. If he tells her he's going to bow out, then there'll be no hope at all. And I can't just stand by and let that happen. According to Coleman, she's still thinking about it, so if there's anything I can do, I have to do it."

"I guess so," she said, "but I hope you have better luck than I did." She reached for a sweater that was hanging behind the door. "Better take this; it's gotten cool out there."

I stopped. "When did you talk to her?"

"I called her after you said I could tell her better than anyone how hard it is to raise a child alone. She just said that our situations weren't at all alike, since, with her job, she wouldn't be without resources the way I was."

I gasped at Binkie's effrontery. "Finances aren't the only consideration in raising a child, doesn't she know that?"

"I tried to tell her, but you know, Miss Julia, I think Binkie thinks she can do anything she sets her mind on."

"Yes, but she's past due for a comeuppance. If it wasn't for that unborn child, I'd just sit back and let her learn her lesson. But I can't, so I'm going over there again." I started for the door. "No telling when I'll be back. Be sure and lock up before you go to bed."

"I wish you wouldn't go by yourself. Let me get Little Lloyd and we'll go with you."

"No," I said, holding up my hand. "No, I can manage better by myself. I'm going to let Binkie have it in no uncertain terms, and neither you nor that child need to witness the knockdown, drag-out that it'll probably turn into. She's either going to marry her baby's father tomorrow or . . . or, I don't know what."

Little Lloyd, in his pajamas and robe, pushed through the kitchen door. His wet hair was slicked down, except for the cowlick that had dried enough to spring up. "They've got a spotlight out there now!" he said, his eyes as round as his glasses. "And a whole bunch of people everywhere."

"Well," I said, walking out on the back stoop. "They'd better get out of my way. I'm heading out."

But when I got to the side yard, I was brought up short by the mass of people on the sidewalk and the street. To say nothing of the television van that blocked my driveway as pretty as you please. The spotlight that Little Lloyd had mentioned was focused on the side of the Family Life Center, making me blink in the glare. The camera light swept across the crowd, and then centered on the blond reporter as she interviewed a member of the congregation, if that's what it was.

"Hazel Marie!" I called. "I'm going to need some help getting out of here."

When she walked out into the yard, Little Lloyd trailing along behind her, I pointed and said, "Would you look at that? The television van's blocking the driveway! If that's not the most inconsiderate thing I've ever seen, I don't know what is. And illegal, too, if I'm not mistaken."

Little Lloyd said, "I'll go ask them to move it." And off he went down the driveway in his pajamas, bedroom slippers and robe. Hazel Marie followed him halfway, while I stood by the car, fuming at the hindrance to my mission.

I saw the child go up to the cameraman and point toward the van. An action that brought no response, so Little Lloyd walked over to the one operating the spotlight. I could see the man shrug his shoulders and shake his head.

By that time, I'd joined Hazel Marie nearer the end of the driveway.

"They didn't send Kenny," Hazel Marie said with a twinge of disappointment. "It's Tiffany Hill reporting. She's all right, but I like him better."

I couldn't tell a nickel's worth of difference, except for the obvious, between one announcer and another, so I didn't express a preference.

As we watched and waited for the van to move, Little Lloyd came running back to us.

Catching his breath, he said, "They said they'd be through in a little while, but they can't interrupt a live broadcast right now. They said you'll have to wait."

"Wait!" I demanded. "Who do they think they are, telling me to wait? Hazel Marie, where'd Mr. Pickens go? Can we get him back here? Go call the sheriff, Little Lloyd. I am not going to put up with such high-handed arrogance."

"I was hoping J.D. might still be here," Hazel Marie said, standing on her tiptoes. "He left in a hurry through the back gate, but I thought he might've stopped and investigated this. He's so curious, you know."

"Oh, my goodness," I moaned. "I've got to get out of here before Coleman talks to Binkie. What're we going to do, Hazel Marie? It might be that I could say just the right thing that would change Binkie's mind, and here I am, *thwarted* from saying it!"

I began marching toward the center of the action, determined to have that van moved and moved immediately.

"Wait," Hazel Marie said, plucking at my

sleeve. "It's television. You can't just walk into a broadcast."

"I most certainly can. There's not a thing sacred about television."

And I walked up to the cameraman and said, "You'll have to move that van. It's blocking my driveway."

He didn't even have the courtesy to look at me, just kept his eye pinned to his shoulder-held camera that was aimed at the talking blonde, who was lit up like she was on a stage. "Sorry, ma'am," he said. "Can't do it now, we're taping."

"Well, you can just *un*tape! This is an emergency, and I have to get my car out."

The man who was operating the spotlight and managing the wires and cables came over. "Lady," he said, "you're going to have to stay out of the way. We're taping some crowd and background shots, then we'll do a live feed for the eleven o'clock news. We'll move the van then." He grasped my arm, almost lifting me off the ground, and walked me firmly away, all without a by-your-leave.

I was speechless with outrage. But before I could react, Hazel Marie was on him like a wildcat. "Get your hands off her! Don't you dare push her around like that!" Then she pointed down at my asphalt driveway where we were all standing. "You are on private property, and in danger of imminent arrest!"

My word, Hazel Marie, I thought, you are certainly well-spoken.

The man stepped back onto the sidewalk, off private property. Then he said, "We can't move the van until Tiffany gets through." He cocked his head toward the blonde, who was smiling and talking into a microphone and pointing behind her at the crowd and at the brick wall of the Family Life building. And all the while never taking her eyes away from the camera that was focused on her like the star reporter she was.

"And when will that be?" Hazel Marie demanded, her hands clenched in fists by her sides.

"Tiffany doesn't like to be cut short," he said, not the least perturbed that we were for all intents and purposes prevented from leaving our own home. "It's up to her and the director. Not you," he said, pointing at me, then at Hazel Marie, "or you. We'll film as long as it takes."

"We'll just see about that," Hazel Marie said, turning on her heel and heading toward the house. I'd seen that look on her face a time or two before, and I knew it boded ill for whoever got in her way.

Just then, Little Lloyd came running from the house, slamming the screen door behind him. He dashed up to us, his bathrobe flapping around his knees. I'd been so taken up with the rudeness of those who work in television I'd not noticed that the child had been gone.

"Mama!" he said, gasping and almost out of breath. "Miss Julia! I called Coleman and he's coming, and they're sending some more squad cars, too."

"Well, thank goodness," I said. "That was quick thinking, Little Lloyd." Then, seeing Hazel Marie stomping on toward the house, I called, "Hazel Marie, wait. Where're you going?"

She didn't answer, so the boy and I followed her, stopping halfway as we saw her squat down by the side of the house.

"What's she doing?" Little Lloyd asked, peering into the shadows where his mother now stood with a coil of hose in her hands.

"I have no idea," I said, as perplexed as he was. "Oh, my Lord," I gasped as Hazel Marie strode past us, dragging the hose that we watered the lawn with behind her. "Hazel Marie?"

"Stand back, Miss Julia," she said, her back straight and her eyes glaring at the obstacle in front of her.

"Mama?" Little Lloyd said as he started toward her.

"Hazel Marie?" I said again, and started with him, but she was not to be deterred.

Those television people, now that we'd been put in our place, were intent on the business at hand and didn't see Hazel Marie take aim and twist the nozzle. A stream of water spurted out full force. We'd always had good water pressure, and it didn't fail her now.

Her first poorly aimed shot went into and through the open windows of the van and out the other side. She got their attention, though, for the beam of the spotlight went wild, veering this way and that up and down the street. One man jumped from the back of the van, cursing something awful, and the crowd turned as one to see what the trouble was. The man doing the directing ran toward Hazel Marie, his mouth open in a yell and his arms outstretched to grab her. She turned the hose into his face, backing him off as he sputtered and gasped at the sudden influx. And all the while, Tiffany, the television personality, continued to broadcast, her eyes wide with the thrill of breaking news. The light of the camera swiveled back and forth between her and the wild woman with the hose.

Hazel Marie stepped to the side and, taking deliberate aim, yelled, "Tiffany's finished!" Then she soaked the reporter to a fare-thee-well, not stopping until the woman's hair was plastered to her head and her clothes were sopping wet.

And still the shoulder-held camera kept filming, turning first to Hazel Marie and then back to the saturated Tiffany.

Tiffany, with water dripping off her, screamed, "Turn that damn camera *off*!" And finally all the lights went off, and we were left with only a streetlight and the glow of candles still held by the mesmerized crowd.

Hazel Marie flung the hose down and stomped back to us. With a satisfied grin, she said, "You'll be able to get out now, Miss Julia."

Then three squad cars, their roof lights flashing blue and red, turned the corner.

One blast of a siren cleared the way, and they pulled up and stopped beside the television van. Coleman and two other deputies stepped out, as the television crew, minus Tiffany who had ducked inside the van, ran to them, waving their arms, pointing at us and lodging their complaints.

"I don't know, Hazel Marie," I said, noting that now there were four vehicles impeding my passage. "I may be stuck for good. But as long as Coleman's here, he can't be at Binkie's, can he?" Then, trying not to laugh, I said, "I declare, Hazel Marie, you certainly know how to wrap up a broadcast."

Chapter 29

Coleman and the two deputies who'd come with him calmly listened to the indignant, arm-waving director, while the cameraman stood aside with a bemused expression on his face. Gradually the tension lessened, especially when Tiffany asserted from inside the van that there was "no way in hell" she would go in front of a camera in the shape she was in. The men began gathering up their cables and wires, and placing them in the van.

When they slammed the back door of the van and climbed into the front seat, Little Lloyd said, "Bet those seats're squishy."

Hazel Marie and I smiled at each other as we watched one of the deputies direct the van through the crowd and send it on its way.

"I guess I could go on to Binkie's now," I said. "But since Coleman's here, I'll wait and try to talk him out of giving up on her. And I want to find out why this strange gathering was worth putting on television."

By that time, Coleman and the deputies were moving among the crowd, shaking hands and talking with several people they seemed to know.

As we stood to the side of the milling crowd and watched, Hazel Marie said, "Something's drawing these people here. I mean, there's got to be some reason why it's right by our house. And it's not like any kind of religious vigil I've ever heard of."

I nodded as I squinched my eyes at the crowd. "I've never seen some of these people before. Wonder where they came from?"

Little Lloyd said, "I saw some out-of-state license plates on the cars parked down the street. Some from Virginia and Tennessee, even."

"My word," I said, marveling at anybody who'd drive so far to stand around on a sidewalk. "Look over there on the other side, Hazel Marie. Isn't that the Riley family? And there's Bud Wilkins, too. And have you ever seen so many candles? It's like a Christmas Eve service. You know, if it's religious and it has candles, it's got to be something with Catholic overtones. Maybe that's why we don't know anything about it."

"But why would anybody want to celebrate anything on Polk Street?" Hazel Marie said, frowning and casting worried glances toward the candlelit gathering. "Oh, look. I think that's Norma Cantrell across the street. Well, there're too many heads in the way. I'm not sure."

"Well, it wouldn't surprise me," I said. "She has to check out everything in town. You think we can get through to her? She'd know, if anybody would."

Hazel Marie said, "I don't think we ought to try it. Too many people between us."

Little Lloyd, who seemed entranced by the street meeting, said, "Let's just ask somebody here."

"Lord, child," I said. "I don't know anybody nearby to ask."

"I don't mind asking a stranger," he said.

I raised my eyebrows at Hazel Marie, wondering if she thought we'd be disrupting a religious service, even though I hadn't seen a preacher anywhere.

She shrugged and said, "We could try.

Maybe we'd learn what's brought them here. And if they're going to leave before the wedding guests start coming."

"Don't mention the wedding to me, Hazel Marie," I said. "I'm so wrought up about it now I can hardly stand it. All right, let's see if we can find out what's going on. But keep an eye on Coleman; I don't want him getting to Binkie before I do."

"Look," Little Lloyd said, pointing toward a man in a short-sleeved shirt. "There's Señor Acosta again. Let's ask him." And he headed into the crowd.

Looking back at us, he went on. "Remember? I know his son from school. Angel."

"What?" I asked, as Hazel Marie and I frowned at each other.

"Angel. That's his son's name," Little Lloyd said.

"My word," I said under my breath. "They must be a religious family."

Hazel Marie and I cautiously followed Little Lloyd, not wanting to get too close but not wanting to lose sight of him, either.

As we approached the gathering, Hazel Marie giggled nervously and took my arm. "I hope they won't get mad at us for asking what they're doing."

"They won't get mad, Mama," Little Lloyd said, walking fearlessly into the crowd. "We just have to be respectful, like we'd be in church."

"Huh," I said. "I could be a lot more respectful if this kind of carrying-on wasn't practically in my front yard."

"Sh-h-h," Hazel Marie said, poking me with her elbow.

As we followed Little Lloyd into the crowd, I heard the low cadence of their voices in what might have been prayer. Each face was lit with a circle of light from the candles they held. Little Lloyd walked right up to a square-shouldered man who had his eyes closed. Not a fearful bone in the child's body, I thought with pride, except when it came to Dixon Hightower.

"*Buenas noches, Señor Acosta. ¿Cómo está usted?*" Little Lloyd said, surprising me at how fluent he was in another tongue.

The man turned to him, smiled broadly in the glow of his candle, and said something like, "*Buenas noches, señor pequeño.* Would you like a candle?" He offered his candle to Little Lloyd.

I hurried up beside him and whispered, "Give it back, Little Lloyd. No telling what kind of worship service this is."

The boy shook his head, and said to the man, "*¿Qué pasa?*"

The man took a deep breath and pointed toward our half-built Family Life Center and said in an awestruck voice, "*Está un milagro.*"

"What'd he say?" I whispered. "What's growing around here?"

Paying me no mind, Little Lloyd said, "*¿Que?*"

His face glowing in the light of the candle, the man leaned down to the child and said, "*¡La santa!*"

"What?" I whispered. "What'd he say?"

Little Lloyd said, "He said *la santa,* but I don't know what it means. I mean, I know what it means, but . . ."

Señor Acosta pointed at the building again, jabbing the air with his finger. "*¡En el muro!*"

"*¿Qué?*" Little Lloyd hunched his shoulders and squinched up his eyes, peering through the dark at the brick wall. "I don't see anything."

"*¡Mira!* It's a miracle from God." And

he fell down on his knees before our very eyes and began crossing his chest. Others followed his example until more than half the crowd knelt on the cement sidewalk. I'd known all along it was some kind of Catholic ceremony. Or maybe Episcopal.

"Come on, Lloyd," Hazel Marie said, as if she too had recognized the strangeness of it. "We better not bother him anymore."

"Yes," I agreed. "I've seen enough, and I still don't understand it."

"*Un minuto,* Mama," Little Lloyd said. "I mean, in a minute. I want to find out what's on the wall. I can't see what he's talking about."

He leaned down to the man, handed back his candle and said, "I can't see anything, Señor Acosta. What is it?"

The man looked up at him with a beautiful smile. "*Nuestra Señora del Muro. Está un milagro de la virgen.*"

"*Gracias, señor,*" Little Lloyd said, somewhat subdued by the answer. Then he turned and walked back to the driveway, glancing over his shoulder at that offensive building.

Hazel Marie took my arm, and we hurried after him.

"What'd he say, Lloyd?" she asked as we stopped a little distance from the crowd.

"Well," he said, frowning so that his glasses slipped down his nose. "I'm not sure that I got it all. But he said something about a miracle, and I think he said it was on the wall. Of the new building, I guess, 'cause he kept pointing at it."

"That doesn't surprise me," I said. "I told Pastor Ledbetter it'd take a miracle to get that thing built without my help."

"No'm, I don't think he meant that. If I understood it right, he said there's a lady on the wall."

Hazel Marie and I looked at each other with our mouths open. "A lady on the wall?" she said. "You mean somebody's walking around on top of that brick wall?" Then she squinched up her eyes, trying to see in the dark.

Little Lloyd shook his head. "No'm, not that. From the way he said it, I think it meant *our lady.* He said it was a miracle of the virgin."

"What!" I was shocked at the word. "How dare that man say such a thing to a child!

Hazel Marie, I'm going to tell Coleman about this. It's bad enough to see half-naked women on the TV, but to hear such talk on the street is another matter."

"Wait, Miss Julia," Hazel Marie said. "I don't think he was saying anything ugly. I think he was talking about Mary, the Virgin Mother. I wish we could get through this crowd and talk to the Rileys, so we'd know for sure."

"Well," I said, somewhat mollified. "Even if it wasn't ugly, it's pretty Catholic, if you ask me. And in a Presbyterian neighborhood, too."

The three of us stood there for a while, mulling over that theological riddle. Then I turned and stared at the Family Life Center, wondering how anybody could see a woman, even if she was a lady, on a wall of bricks in the dead of night. My attention was taken then by Coleman, who was walking with Señor Acosta toward his squad car. I gasped, thinking Coleman was making an arrest, but instead, he leaned in the car window and turned on his spotlight. With Señor Acosta directing him, Coleman wiggled the light until it was centered on the wall between the windows of the second and third floors, right where the television people had aimed their spotlight.

I leaned forward, straining to see what was on the wall. All I could see were some streaks of poorly applied mortar.

"Can anybody see anything?" I asked Hazel Marie and Little Lloyd.

They both shook their heads but, after a minute, Little Lloyd said, "I kinda think I do." Which just shows you how the power of suggestion can raise havoc in little children.

As Señor Acosta returned to his place in the crowd, Coleman walked over to us. "Hi, Miss Julia, Hazel Marie," he said, then ruffled Little Lloyd's hair. "How you doin', bud? Can you see it?"

Before we could answer, a young woman with long dark hair appeared at his side. *"Buenas noches, señor,"* she murmured, her dark eyes shimmering in the light of the candles. She was wrapped in a beautifully embroidered shawl, which she clutched around her shoulders.

Coleman turned to her. *"Buenas noches, Señora Diaz.* Good to see you again. Can you see what's on the wall?"

"Sí, she is there if you look," she said, turning toward the wall. "She has given

back my shawl," she went on, fingering the fringe. "It was lost, but it came back to me here." The woman gazed at the wall and whispered, "*Nuestra señora,* she makes a miracle."

Coleman lifted his head and squinched his eyes at the spotlighted area on the wall. "Really?"

"Oh, *sí.* The Lady on the Wall works wonders for us."

"I wish she'd work some for me," Coleman murmured, more to himself than to her.

Señora Diaz touched him lightly on the arm and said, "You are a good man; she will hear you." Then she stepped back into the crowd.

Coleman stood there, staring for the longest time at the spotlighted wall. Then he turned toward us, but before he could say a word, Hazel Marie suddenly jumped and grabbed his arm. "Coleman, look!" She pointed toward the far side of the gathering where there was hardly any light at all. "I just saw Dixon Hightower!"

"Oh-h-h," Little Lloyd moaned, taking his mother's hand. "I don't want him to be around here."

"It couldn't be," I assured him. "Hazel Marie, you must be mistaken."

Coleman motioned to one of the deputies and told him to be on the lookout because Dixon might be on the premises. "Better call it in, just in case," he said to him. Then to Hazel Marie, "You sure you saw him?"

"Well, I just got a glimpse," she said worriedly, "but it sure looked like him."

"We'll get some people out here to look around the neighborhood," Coleman said, but it seemed to me that his mind was not on Dixon Hightower. His eyes kept swinging back to the white streaks on the wall of the Family Life Center.

"Coleman," I said, directing his attention to the matter at hand. "Just what is going on here? They're all talking about a miracle, but so far I've not seen anything that comes close to one."

Little Lloyd chimed in. "Señor Acosta says there's a lady on the wall."

"That's what they're saying, all right," Coleman agreed. "An image of some kind on the bricks." He stopped, rubbed his hand across his face, then went on. "Blanca Diaz said the lady gave her shawl back to her. A miracle, she says." With a glance at me, he said, "You know her, don't you, Miss Julia? She lives in the trailer park on Springer Road."

"No," I said, "I don't believe I've had the pleasure."

Little Lloyd gasped. "That's who Miss Wiggins told you about, Miss Julia. Remember?"

"Now, child," I cautioned. "Let's not get carried away." But I felt a jolt of elation. If Mrs. Diaz got her shawl back in a miraculous way, why couldn't Coleman get Binkie back in the same way? Not that I believed in miracles, you understand.

Thrilled, though, at the possibility, I stepped closer to Coleman and peered at the wall. "Can you see anything up there?"

"I'm not sure, Miss Julia," he said. "There's something there . . . but I don't know." He moved a few steps away to get a different view, looking as if he needed time to ponder the matter.

Then he straightened his shoulders and firmed up his face. "Well, things are calm here, so I guess I'll be going."

"No, Coleman, wait," I said, pulling him aside. "Listen, you can't give up on Binkie now. I think she's teetering on the edge and, if you'll be patient just a little longer, she'll come around, I know she will."

He smiled as if it hurt him to do it. "It's not a good idea to try to talk her into something she doesn't want."

"She doesn't know what she wants," I told him. "Coleman, I've told you that women in her condition have all kinds of flights of fancy. They want somebody to tell them what to do. You just have to be firm with her."

He grinned down at me. "Be firm with Binkie? Huh, that girl'd have my hide." Then he stopped and looked off into the night. "Still, what've I got to lose? That's one thing I haven't tried."

"Then try it!" I said, giving him all the encouragement I could muster. "Maybe if miracles are going around, you and Binkie're in line for one."

"Well," he said, frowning. "She may have my head on a platter, but I won't know till I try, will I?"

Then he moved through the crowd to his patrol car, while I watched with a steadily lightening heart. Then I drew Hazel Marie close. "We may have ourselves a wedding after all."

"Oh, I hope," she said.

"No, it's a settled fact. I don't care if that lady on the wall is Catholic, Baptist or somewhere in between, Binkie told me she'd need a miracle, and, bless Pat, I think we've found her one."

Chapter 30

I came out of bed with a bound the day of the wedding and almost threw my back out. I went to the window, first thing. There were still people standing around on the sidewalk, and I could see others walking in small groups coming from downtown. I strained to see the wall across the street, but couldn't make out a thing except some pretty poor masonry work. It looked as if the brick masons had let the mortar drip down the bricks, and instead of cleaning it off, they'd let it dry in crooked patterns. Either that, or they'd used a poor quality of bricks. I'd've made them do it over, if it'd been up to me.

But whatever was over there, it had certainly turned Coleman around and that was miracle enough for me. Now if it would do the same for Binkie, I wouldn't be averse to giving a public testimonial even it meant going on television.

I glanced up at the sky—clear as a bell, not a cloud up there, shaping up to be a perfect day for a wedding. I hurried to dress, then made my bed and laid out my wedding finery on it. I could hardly wait to call Binkie, for I knew in my heart that she was going to go through with it. If, that is, there was any meaning at all in a miracle showing up in front of my house. I mean, surely the lady didn't appear on Polk Street just to return a shawl to somebody who didn't even live here.

"Lillian!" I said, as I went into the kitchen for my morning coffee. "What're you doing here so early?"

"Morning to you, too," she said, tying an apron around her waist. "You think I'm gonna stay home when they's so much to do here? No, ma'am, I got to watch out them people comin' in here do things right. James and Mr. Emmett, they both be here pretty soon an' I got to get ready for them."

"Well, I'm glad you're here. But you just remember that you're a guest, and you'll need to leave in plenty of time to get out of that uniform and get ready."

"My weddin' dress and my weddin' hat come with me. They upstairs, an' I'll get dressed here. 'Sides, you and Miss Hazel Marie gonna need my help to get ready. And Miss Binkie, too, if she show up."

"Oh, she's going to show up and she's going to get married, too." I smiled, somewhat smugly, I admit. Then I told her all that we'd learned and seen the night before, and how miracles were being passed out right and left. "I'm going to call Binkie right now, and tell her to get moving."

Lillian frowned at me. "You think that lady on the wall change Miss Binkie's mind? I don't know I b'lieve that."

"Just listen," I said, and dialed Binkie's number.

"Binkie?" I said when she answered in a sleep-filled voice. "Are you up? This is your wedding day, so hop to it. Come on over anytime, and bring everything you'll need. You can rest upstairs until it's time to get dressed, and we'll help you get ready." I rushed through, not giving her time to make excuses or put me off.

Then she surprised me, as her voice cleared and she sang out, "Oh, hi. I was going to call you. Listen, I know I've created some problems, but I just need a little more time before I actually do it."

"Do what?" I asked, suspicious, which I am by nature.

"Why, marry Coleman, of course. Isn't that what we're talking about?"

"That's what I've been talking about for a solid week," I told her. "I don't know what you've been doing. Now, Binkie, how much more time do you need?"

"Well, I was thinking a couple of weeks."

My mouth worked but nothing came out. Finally, I managed to say, "No. Binkie, no." I couldn't think of anything else to say, as the phone line hummed between us. I was just so done in that she was still playing with Coleman's affections. And mine too, if the truth be known. And where was that lady on the wall, just as I'd thought there might be something to her?

"Miss Julia?" There was a note of concern in Binkie's voice. "Are you all right?"

"Yes," I said, trying to hide my disappointment. I understood then why Pastor Ledbetter said that the age of miracles was past. "I mean, no, I'm not. I so want you to do the right thing, for Coleman's sake and for that baby. And for yours, too." Not to mention, which I didn't, for the sake of the people we'd invited and the food we'd ordered and everything else I'd planned.

"Well," she said, "let me talk to Coleman some more."

"You do that," I mumbled, and didn't try to disguise a sob as I hung up.

"Lillian," I said, turning to her, "let me have that dishcloth, please. I can't find the Kleenex."

She handed it to me and said, "She not gonna do it, is she?"

"She wants to think about it some more," I said, wiping my eyes. "Lillian, I think I'll just get in the car and go somewhere. I don't think I can face the shame of Binkie's behavior. Why don't we get Hazel Marie and Little Lloyd, and the four of us just take off?"

"You not gonna do any such a thing. Now, straighten yo'self up an' smile if it kill you."

"Well, it's likely to," I said, trying out a small one. "Lillian, I'd about convinced myself that that image appeared over there for a purpose. And I mean more than for handing out shawls. But if it did, it wasn't for the purpose I had in mind."

"That's where you get in trouble," Lillian said, as sure of her pronouncements as any preacher. "When you figure whatever you want is what the Lord want, too."

"I'm certainly getting my comeuppance, then." Before I could finish the thought, the telephone rang. "You get it, Lillian; I don't think I'm up to talking with anyone now."

Lillian picked up the receiver and handed it to me. "This a good place to start. Answer it."

Before I could say a word, Binkie cried, "Miss Julia? Is that you? Guess what? I've decided I might as well do it today as any other. I mean, you're ready and everything, aren't you?"

"Yes," I managed to get out, swallowing hard. "Yes, we're ready." I stopped, trying to reformulate my views of the miraculous. "Binkie, there're a lot of things I don't understand going on around here. But I guess I'm not one to question a miracle, if that's what it took."

She laughed. "Oh, I don't know about a miracle. It's just that Coleman and I have been talking, and I guess he's laid down the law. He said I either married him today or else. I think he's going to arrest me for committing mayhem on his affections. He said he'd carry me kicking and screaming to the altar, if he had to." Then she giggled.

"Well, I declare," I said, thinking all that talk of independence and doing things on her own had been just that—talk. All Coleman had had to do was give her some orders, a few caveman threats, and she'd turned into a giddy girl. You never know what will appeal to these modern young women, do you?

I just shook my head, then remembering that they weren't married yet, I said, "I want you over here, Binkie, just as soon as you can make it. I'm going to keep my eye on you until I turn you over to Coleman this afternoon."

"I'll be there as soon as I can. Don't worry, Miss Julia, I wouldn't miss this for the world. It's my wedding day!"

"I should say it is, and we have a million things to do. Now, Binkie, where is Coleman? He needs to be here no later than two o'clock so we don't lose him, too. And you stay away from him; you know he's not supposed to see the bride on the wedding day."

I heard the rustle of bedcovers, and the muffle of a hand over the phone. Then she giggled again.

"Oops," she said.

When I hung up the phone, I turned to Lillian. "Lord, Lillian," I said. "Can you believe this? I've been going round and round about miracles ever since last night, and had about given up on them. But this is a miracle if there ever was one, although I think it was Coleman who performed it."

"What you talkin' 'bout?"

Before I could answer, Hazel Marie and Little Lloyd pushed through the kitchen door, ready for breakfast.

"Hazel Marie, you'll never guess," I said. "Binkie's on her way, and she's going through with it. Now, what we have to do is not let her out of our sight, just in case she has another attack of hormones." Then seeing the interest on Little Lloyd's face, I corrected myself. "I mean, nerves."

"What happened?" Hazel Marie asked. "What made her change her mind?"

"Coleman put his foot down, that's what. Instead of moping around and pleading with her and acting pitiful, he just flat-out told her what she was going to do. Not that I think that's the best approach in the world, mind you. I wouldn't stand for it myself, although

I used to all the time. But it must've been just what Binkie needed."

"I wish J.D.'d put his foot down," she said, somewhat longingly. "But, oh, I'm so happy for them, and for us. It's going to be a great day. Lloyd, honey, what kind of cereal do you want?"

As the day wore on, the house rang with so much going and coming that I could hardly keep up with who was in and who was out. Harriet from The Watering Can arrived with two helpers, and they brought in one huge arrangement after another, spilling fern leaves and leaving water spots on the floor. Lillian went behind them, sweeping and mopping. Harriet stuck fresh flowers in the greenery on the arch and, pretty soon, my two front rooms looked like a garden spot.

LuAnne popped in with a large basket heaped high with little net sacks tied with pink ribbon. "Got them all done, Julia," she said, pleased with herself and rightly so. "I'll just set the basket by the front door, where the guests can get them as they go out."

"They're lovely, LuAnne. Thank you."

"It was a pleasure to have something to do," she assured me. "And besides, I got

Leonard to help me. Kept his hands so busy tying ribbons, he didn't have time for anything else." She giggled as she placed the basket by the door.

"Glad to've helped," I said, but she was already out the door, saying she had to start getting ready for the wedding.

Before Harriet was finished putting the last touches on the flower arrangements, the caterer arrived with her helpers, and they began to fill the kitchen with loaded trays, covered pans and dishes of all sorts. Lillian stood by with her hands on her hips, looking for something to complain about. They ignored her as they filled the refrigerator, checked the dining room table and arranged their party food on every empty surface. James and Emmett had come in by that time and helped them bring in the trays. In their white jackets and black bow ties, both of them looked handsome enough to join the wedding party.

During all the commotion, that lady on the wall across the street kept looming in the back of my mind. Was she real or just a fancy in everybody's mind, including mine? And what was she doing on the wall of Pastor Ledbetter's Family Life Center? You'd think she'd've found a more congenial place than a Presbyterian wall to make her appearance.

Then it came to me with certainty that she'd appeared at the very place where she'd do the most good. Something had certainly worked wonders on Coleman, then went right on through him to straighten out Binkie. I couldn't deny that a miracle of some kind had happened. I'd tried my best with Coleman and Binkie and gotten nowhere, so it stood to reason that a higher power had intervened somehow.

But miracle or no miracle, that sidewalk congregation was going to have to move on before our guests began to arrive or whatever'd happened would be all for naught.

A little after noon, just as I was beginning to worry, Binkie came bounding in, long after I'd wanted her there. She had her wedding dress draped over one arm, and a tote bag filled with shoes, hair dryer and beauty aids on the other.

"It's beautiful, Miss Julia!" she said, gazing around the living room, filled now with enough flower arrangements to start a shop of our own. "What can I do to help?"

"Not a thing. The bride doesn't do anything but rest and get ready. Take your things upstairs to my room. Does that dress need pressing? Let Lillian look at it; I don't trust you with an iron on that flimsy material. Oh, you might want to open some of these gifts that've come in." I pointed to the linen-covered table by the door piled high with presents. "Be sure and keep a record of who sent what and, if you want to get started on your thank-you notes, there's some stationery in my desk." You have to keep after young people today to do what they're supposed to do. I knew people who'd carried a grudge the rest of their lives because they hadn't gotten a thank-you note. Mildred Allen was a prime example of it, too. I always made sure I wrote her one if she so much as spoke to me on the street.

Lillian, suddenly deciding that Binkie's usual breakfast of nothing would make her light-headed and that she needed some-thing to eat, sailed into the kitchen. Katie's Kuisine had made it plain that they wanted no interference, but that didn't stop Lillian. Paying no mind to their glares, she went about her business and piled a plate full. Then she poured a glass of milk and took the tray upstairs to Binkie.

That inspired Emmett, who declared,

"That whole weddin' party need something on they stomachs. They gonna be faintin' all over the place, they don't eat." Ignoring the frowns of the caterers, he and James prepared a plate of sandwiches and a pitcher of tea. We all gathered in Hazel Marie's room to eat since the kitchen and dining room were out of bounds. By the time we'd finished, Mr. Pickens had shown up, his wedding clothes over his shoulder.

"Hey, folks," he said, going straight over to Hazel Marie and displaying some of that public affection he was so free with. "Everybody about ready? Miss Julia, you mind if I put on this monkey suit over here? I was afraid if I came any later, I wouldn't be able to get through the crowd to your door." His black eyes sparkled and I prepared myself for more of his teasing. "Kinda got carried away with your invitations, didn't you?"

"No, I did not, and you know it, Mr. Pickens," I told him. "We're just going to have to put up with them, I guess, and I'd appreciate it if you wouldn't remind me of something I can't do anything about. Now, you can use Coleman's room to dress and you need to hurry up. He's over at Binkie's, but if he's not soon here, I'm going to send you after him."

"He'll be here. I talked to him a little while ago. Lloyd, why don't you dress with us, and leave your room for the ladies? They need more space than we do."

The boy grinned, pleased to be included with the men. Hazel Marie held on to Mr. Pickens's hand, her face shining as it always did in his presence. Lord, I needed to get those two married, even if it meant losing Little Lloyd for good. But one miracle at a time, I told myself.

Mr. Pickens couldn't leave well enough alone, though. "I knew you were good, Miss Julia," he said. "But I didn't know you could start a brush-arbor revival all by yourself."

"That's not what it is," I said. Then realizing that he was teasing me again, I went on. "You make me so tired, Mr. Pickens."

"Well," he said, turning serious for a change, "the street's filling up with half the county. You've got a crowd scene out there and lots of traffic. I had to park a block away."

"Oh, my word," I said, getting to my feet. "Mr. Pickens, we've got to do something. What if the wedding guests can't get in? Call the sheriff, Hazel Marie, we're going to need some crowd control around here."

"I'll call 'em," Mr. Pickens said. "But I expect you're going to have all the help you need, since half the department'll be here for the wedding."

I went to one of the front windows in the living room and peered out. Lord, but the sidewalk was teeming with people in their Sunday best. And they'd spread out until they were right in front of the house and down past Lila McCarran's yard. Cars and pickups filled with whole families were creeping along the street, slowing even more as they passed that brick wall in front of my house. And to cap it all, there was a guitar player strolling up and down the sidewalk strumming away at some doleful Latin melody. My first thought was that it was Pastor Petree, except he wouldn't be caught dead in cowboy boots and a baseball cap, much less sporting a mustache as black and bushy as Mr. Pickens's.

"Mr. Pickens," I said, patting my chest to help me breathe easier. "I can't have this. Something'll have to be done. We found out last night that there's a miracle on the wall over there. But that's no excuse for ruining a wedding that's taken a miracle to pull off."

Chapter 31

"Huh," Mr. Pickens said, his eyes sweeping the crowd that now included whole families with children. "Come on, Miss Julia, you don't believe that, do you?"

"I don't know what I believe at this point. But Coleman saw something over there, and Little Lloyd thinks he did, too. And I declare, Mr. Pickens, something has certainly worked wonders with both Coleman and Binkie. Now," I said, looking him straight in the eye, "if something would get to work on you, I wouldn't have a doubt in the world."

He laughed as I knew he would. "Don't expect miracles, Miss Julia."

"I'm not. But that's the trouble. I think I've seen some, but it's hard to believe they could come from something on a Presbyterian structure. Especially since it has to do with a woman. Why, John Knox would turn over in his grave, to say nothing of John Calvin and Pastor Ledbetter."

"Here comes Sam," Mr. Pickens said, pointing as Sam came from around the back of the house to the front door. "Let's see what he has to say."

If anything could've taken my attention from the problem in the street, it would've been Sam in all his finery. There's nothing more handsome than a well-set-up man in evening clothes, even though he was wearing a dinner jacket long before the proper time, thanks to Binkie. He almost took my breath away, but I recovered before it was noticed.

"Hello, folks," Sam said, as he came in. "From the looks of things out there, Julia, your guest list has doubled and then some."

"Oh, Sam, what're we going to do? Those people just keep coming and coming. They're already blocking the street and creating problems."

"There'll be some deputies here in a few minutes," Mr. Pickens assured me. Then shaking Sam's hand, he went on. "What do you make of it, Sam?"

Sam gave us that tolerant smile he was known for and said, "If people're convinced there's something miraculous going on, then it's natural to want to honor it."

"Huh," Mr. Pickens said, leaning over to look through the window again. "That's the damnedest thing. Can you see it?"

"Oh, yes," Sam said, nodding his head and surprising me no end. "I can make out the outline, and it does look like a woman's head and face. You know what it is, don't you?"

"I don't," I said, not wanting him to think I'd been taken up in religious emotionalism. Regardless of how much uncertainty I had in my heart. "Surely you don't believe it's the Virgin Mary, Sam. There's nothing on that wall but some sloppy workmanship. Although I have to give it credit for getting this wedding back on track."

Sam grinned at me. "You'll take whatever you can get, huh, Julia? But no, I don't believe it's a miraculous appearance. What they're seeing is something called efflorescence, a salt deposit that seeps out on the surface of the bricks in white lines and splotches. It can happen as new bricks dry out after getting wet. And those bricks got a good soaking when rainwater sluiced down from the roof. At least that's one explanation for it. I've heard that the seepage can take some strange forms, and looks like that's what's happened here."

"Well, good," I said, pleased that we now had the means to thin out the crowd. "We can just go out there and give those people your scientific explanation and send them home. If we hurry, we'll have room for our guests to get through."

Mr. Pickens said, "I doubt a scientific explanation will cut much ice with believers, Miss Julia. They'll see what they want to see, and you'll have to put up with it." He stopped, opened his mouth, closed it, then said with a touch of awe, "Would you look at that!"

Sam and I looked over his shoulder, thinking to see some new evidence of a miracle. Instead, we saw Miss Mattie Mae Morgan, decked out in a red silk damask gown that swirled around her red pumps as she lumbered up the walkway. As she reached the steps, she hiked up the long gown to her knees, and came puffing onto the porch.

"Oh, my word," I said, my hand at my throat. "There goes Binkie's color scheme."

"Miz Springer!" Mattie Mae called as she

opened the screen door. "You ain't gonna b'lieve what's out there on that buildin'! It's Mary, Mother of God, sure as I'm standin' here. Oh, Lord! I'm gonna play that instrument like it never been played before! In the presence of a miracle, that's what I am. Hallelujah, Jesus!"

"Miss Morgan!" I cried. "Mattie Mae! Get hold of yourself. You need to calm down. Sam, Mr. Pickens, you see what's happening? The wedding's going to be ruined! I just know it is!" I could've cried right there.

Hazel Marie came halfway down the stairs and called, "Miss Julia, you better come on up and get dressed. I'm ready to do your hair, and Binkie needs you."

I turned to her, wringing my hands, then back to that spectacle on the street. "How in the world can I do two things at once?"

"Go on and get dressed, Julia," Sam said. "J.D. and I'll take care of Miss Morgan and watch things down here."

Mr. Pickens said, "Here comes Peavey. You're in good hands now, Miss Julia." He gave me a wicked grin.

I glanced out the window and saw Lieutenant Peavey walking into the yard. He was resplendent in a white dinner jacket with a ruffled shirt, bow tie and cummerbund. And his ever-present sunglasses.

"Well," I said, "send him out there. If he can't scare them off, nobody can. As for myself, I'm going to get dressed before he gets in here."

I hurried up the stairs to be greeted by the smell of burning hair. The doors of my and Little Lloyd's rooms were open, and Binkie and Hazel Marie were running between them in various stages of undress. Hair rollers and hair curlers steamed along with an iron sitting upright on the ironing board.

"Hurry, Miss Julia," Binkie said. Her hair was rolled on rollers as big as juice cans, and she was running around in a loose robe with her dyed-to-match shoes in her hand. Her face was flushed and her eyes were sparkling. "Hazel Marie! Can I take these rollers out now?"

"Get in here, Miss Julia," Lillian said as she wielded a curling iron on her own head. "I'll he'p you with all them buttons soon as I get this hair straightened."

Lord, I thought, some are curling hair and some are straightening, but all of them looked to be using the same instruments.

I went into my room and took my dress from the bed. On my way to the bathroom to undress in private, Binkie came running back in. "Is Coleman here yet? Have you seen him?"

I stopped, tried to calm my nerves, and said, "Mr. Pickens is in charge of Coleman. Don't worry; he'll be here."

I closed the bathroom door and leaned against it. Lord, where was Coleman? Wouldn't that be a pretty come off if he didn't show up? I dressed as quickly as I could, spending a few minutes on my face without looking too closely in the mirror. I find that, after a certain age, it doesn't do to spend too much time in front of one of those things. They can make you not want to go out in public.

I came out of the bathroom trying to get those endless buttons fastened. But being so anxious to get back downstairs to see if that crowd of people had been dispersed and to see if Coleman had arrived, I wasn't doing much more than fumbling with them.

"Set down right here," Lillian said, swinging a chair around. She was in nothing more than a slip, but she'd already arranged her hat on her straightened hair. "Lemme get them buttons for you. Miss Hazel Marie, you can come on in now. I got her settin' down."

Hazel Marie hurried in, as fully dressed as she was going to get in that next-to-nothing garment Binkie had chosen. She was still in her bare feet, holding a number of brushes, mirrors and little plastic containers in both hands.

"Hold still, Miss Julia," she said. "I'm going to fix your face."

"My face doesn't need fixing."

"Yes, it does. It needs some color. Now look, I'm going to put some lavender eye shadow on, just a dab or two, and darken your eyebrows a little."

As she laid hands on me, I said, "Hazel Marie, watch what you're doing! I'm not used to all that paint."

"Hold still," Lillian said, as her hands worked at the buttons on my bodice. "An' get used to it."

"Now for some blush," Hazel Marie said, swirling a huge brush on my cheekbones. "Oh, you're going to knock Sam's socks off. Binkie, where's that hair pick? I need to fluff out her hair a little."

"You're beautiful, Miss Julia," Binkie said, handing the pick to Hazel Marie.

"I doubt that," I said, resigned to their ministrations. "Hurry up, Hazel Marie, you've still got Binkie's hair to do, and I need to get downstairs."

"Okay, a little mascara and some lip gloss and we're done. Now turn around and look in the mirror."

They all gathered behind me and looked over my shoulders. I couldn't help but smile. It was a transformation, if I do say so myself. Maybe it was a day for miracles in a number of ways.

"That's remarkable, Hazel Marie," I finally said. "I just hope the powder doesn't get clogged up in all these wrinkles."

Hazel Marie cocked her head to the side, considering her handiwork, then said, "Binkie, what do you think? My Joy or your Giorgio?"

"She could wear either. Whatever you think."

Hazel Marie reached for a bottle and said, "The Joy, then. But I warn you, Miss Julia, don't get too close to J.D.; this stuff makes him wild." And she giggled.

Then she dabbed perfume behind my ears and on my throat before I could tell her that Estée Lauder's bath powder was already doing the job.

"Enough, Hazel Marie," I said, getting to my feet. "I have things to do. Lillian, do you need help with your dress?"

"No'm, I got it right here, an' I'm fixin' to get in it soon's we get Miss Binkie in hers."

"Well, I'm going downstairs and try to do something about that mess outside. But first, I'll make sure that Coleman's here. Thank you, Hazel Marie, for your help. I just hope I'm recognizable." I started out of the room, holding up my gown, but stopped as I saw Binkie sitting in the open window. "Binkie, get out of that window! People're going to see you and they're not supposed to until you come down the stairs. And you're not even half dressed!"

"Oh, shoo, Miss Julia. I'm having too much fun watching all those people out there, and I think I see that miracle they're talking about."

"Where?" Hazel Marie said, dropping a brush and heading for the window.

"Where?" Lillian said, running behind her with her dress half zipped.

"Well, tell me, too," I said, following suit. "I'd like to see some real evidence."

"Okay," Binkie said. "Look real close at that wall, right between the middle windows. See all those white lines on the bricks? If you start on the top level and follow the lines on the left side down past the second story and on down to the first, you'll see that they form sort of a half-profile of a woman's face. Now go back to the top and follow the lines on the right side, and you'll see what looks like a shawl or a cowl, or maybe it's her hair. Look where the face should be, and there're your eyes, nose and mouth."

"Oh, my Lo-o-rd," Lillian said, her eyes popping out of her head. "I see it! Sweet Jesus, I see it plain as day!"

"I do, too," Hazel Marie said, her voice choking with emotion. "You think we ought to pray or something?"

"We ought to pray for some sense," I said, not wanting to admit that I'd begun to believe in *something* on the wall, even though I couldn't make out a face for love nor money. "I don't see a thing but some mighty poor construction work. I declare, you're all as bad as those people in Atlanta who saw Jesus in a plate of spaghetti on a billboard."

Lillian lowered her voice and said, "Lotsa people saw that, and the Reverend Oral Roberts saw Him astraddle of a hospital, big as you please. It don't do to question ever'thing, Miss Julia. You miss a lot, if you do."

I rolled my eyes. There was a lot I didn't mind missing.

"Yes," Hazel Marie said, "and I heard that eight thousand people showed up to see Jesus' image on a garage door. I think it was in California."

"California." I sniffed, still trying to make out what they were seeing and failing on all points. "What do you expect?"

Binkie turned a mischievous face to me. "Well, what about the Mother Teresa cinnamon bun? I've seen a picture of it on the Internet, and it looks just like her."

"Oh, Binkie, quit encouraging them. Now get out of that window and get dressed. Look, some of the guests're beginning to arrive. Wouldn't you know Mildred Allen'd be the first one, and more than an hour early? Wants to look things over, I expect."

I started out of the room. "Hazel Marie, if Little Lloyd's ready, send him on down so he can begin seating people."

I closed the door on the dress-strewn, perfumed air of the room and hurried to tap on Coleman's door. Without waiting for an answer, I stuck my head in just enough to get a glimpse of his brief-clad bottom. Considerably relieved to see even that, I quickly withdrew, murmuring, "Sorry, just making sure you're here."

Then I hastened downstairs, intent on putting an end to miracle-watching, at least until after the wedding. But that was before I saw Sam's awestruck face.

"What's the matter with you, Sam?" I said. "Don't tell me you've seen the woman on the wall, too."

"No, Julia," he said, coming over to take my hand. "I've just seen the woman on my heart." His smiling eyes searched my face, my hair and my attire.

I turned away, uneasy with such close scrutiny. "Oh, Sam. Don't get carried away."

He leaned close and whispered, "I'd like to carry you away."

Before I had to answer, Mr. Pickens raised his eyebrows and gave me what we used to call the once-over. "Sam," he said, "is this woman yours or is she for the taking?"

Just then, Miss Mattie Mae Morgan struck up a resounding chord and launched into the pre-wedding music with plenty of extra trills and rumbling bass notes. Just as well, because I could pretend I didn't hear Sam when he said, "Oh, she's mine, all right. Keep your distance, Pickens."

Chapter 32

Just then I was struck dumb by the entrance of Etta Mae Wiggins from the Hillandale Trailer Park, her arm draped through the crook of the arm of a tall, tan-skinned man who could give Mr. Pickens and Coleman, both, a run for their money in the looks department. Miss Wiggins was dressed fit to kill in a black sundress, barely held up with more of those spaghetti straps Binkie was so enamored of, with sequined white flowers across the bodice. It ended a good deal north of her knees and, as far as I was concerned, was totally inappropriate for the occasion. I mean, black? For a wedding?

"What is she doing here?" I whispered to Sam and Mr. Pickens.

Mr. Pickens turned to look, then he waved to the couple, and answered, "That's Bobby Lee Moser from the Delmont sheriff's office, and I'd guess that's his date with him."

"Etta Mae Wiggins," Sam said, taking my hand again and running his thumb over it. "You remember her, don't you, Julia?"

"I remember her, all right." Thinking I'd have to make the best of it, but somewhat reassured by Sam's present lack of interest in her. Or so it seemed.

I said, "More people're coming up the walk, and it's more than an hour before the ceremony. Where're the ushers? Where's Little Lloyd?"

"Here I am." And there the child was, as handsome as he could be in a miniature dinner jacket and black trousers with satin stripes down the sides. "What do I do?"

"Just go to the door and escort people to their seats. Hold your arm for the ladies like I showed you, and remember, bride's guests on the left of the aisle and groom's on the right. Mr. Pickens, you need to get on the job, too."

"Come on, sport," Mr. Pickens said, putting an arm around the boy's shoulders. "We can do this."

"Just a minute, Mr. Pickens," I said, plucking his sleeve. "Who're those people standing around on the front porch?" All I could see were broad-shouldered men with mustaches and military haircuts clustered by my wisteria vine.

"They're all deputies, Coleman's friends," Mr. Pickens said. "Probably keeping an eye on the miracle-watchers."

As he and Little Lloyd walked toward the door, Miss Wiggins flounced over to Sam and me. I stiffened as she approached, thinking that if she said one word about that trailer park, I was going to pinch her curly head off.

"Oh, Mrs. Springer," she gushed. "I'm just so thrilled to be here. I couldn't believe it when Bobby Lee asked me to come with him. Oh, this is Bobby Lee Moser; he's an old friend."

"How do you do," I said, offering my hand to the smiling, but silent deputy, which you wouldn't know unless you'd been told, because of his dress suit and tie. His suit was a summer-weight charcoal, his shirt a blinding white against his tanned complexion and his tie a conservative red with a gold pattern.

Very nice, I thought, until he was close enough for me to make out the gold designs—tiny handguns all over the thing. A dangerous man, if I was any judge, of the ilk of Lieutenant Peavey.

"Is there anything I can do to help, Mrs. Springer?" Etta Mae said, her eyes darting around, taking in everything. "I'd love to help, if I can."

"No, thank you," I told her, wanting to say that I'd had all the help from her that I could afford. But she was a guest in my home, so I refrained. "Everything's well in hand . . . except, oh my goodness." Panic overtook me at my lack of foresight. "Flowers," I gasped. "I forgot the flowers!"

"Lord, Julia," Sam said, "you've got flowers everywhere."

"The bouquets and the boutonnieres. For the bridal party."

"Where are they? I'll get them," Etta Mae said, slinging the chain of her purse over her shoulder.

"Oh, thank you, Miss Wiggins. They're in the refrigerator in the kitchen. Mr. Pickens and Little Lloyd and Sam get the pink rosebuds, and, well, you'll see the bouquets for Binkie and Hazel Marie. And Coleman, don't forget his. Everybody's upstairs, if you don't mind running them up, but don't let Coleman see Binkie." As Etta Mae eagerly hurried off to the kitchen on her errand, I suddenly clasped Sam's arm. "Oh, Sam," I cried, "the photographer! Where is he? Or she? Or whoever Hazel Marie got. Oh, my goodness, what if we don't have one?"

"It's a he," he said, "and he's here. I saw him a minute ago lugging in his cameras. Said he had to walk a mile from where he had to park."

"Just so he's here," I said, breathing a sigh of relief. "I hope he's competent."

Sam just smiled and, if I hadn't been struck with another thought as Miss Wiggins started up the stairs with a box of bouquets, I'd've taken note of it.

"Let's go up with her, Sam," I said. "I want to pin Coleman's boutonniere on and have a word with him. And you're his best man. You should be up there helping him."

We went upstairs together, waylaying Etta Mae to get the rosebuds for Coleman's and Sam's lapels. As we went toward Coleman's room, we heard Binkie and Hazel Marie welcoming Etta Mae with squeals over the bouquets.

Sam tapped on the door, then opened it. "Coleman? You decent?"

"Yeah," Coleman answered, as we walked in. "Hi, Miss Julia, Sam. How's it going downstairs?"

I declare, I'd seen a bait of good-looking men that day, but Coleman took my breath away. So handsome in his wedding apparel that set off his broad shoulders and blond hair—in spite of the sheen of sweat on his brow.

"Coleman," I said, "Binkie's a lucky girl. I just want to wish you both a happy life together."

"Thanks, Miss Julia. Is she all right? She's not going to leave me at the altar, is she?" He wiped his face with a handkerchief.

"Binkie's having the time of her life," I assured him. "Although she is paying entirely too much attention to that apparition on the wall over there. Hold still now, I want to pin this rosebud on your jacket."

Coleman got that far-off look he'd had the night before, as I began sticking the pearl-headed pin through his lapel and the stem of the flower. "It's still over there then?" he asked.

"Apparently so. I haven't seen it, myself. But people are still flocking around, looking at it and kneeling and crossing themselves,"

I said, unpinning the flower and going at it again. "You were absolutely right when you told me they were holding some kind of religious vigil. But Sam knows the truth of it. Tell him, Sam."

So Sam went through the scientific explanation again, intriguing Coleman enough to make him forget for a while to worry and sweat over Binkie's previous intransigence.

"Now, Coleman," I said, suddenly fearing that science and reason would overcome his faith in a miracle, which after all was what had set this wedding in motion again. "It doesn't matter what it is—seepage or shoddy bricklaying or handwriting on the wall—if it works, we just accept it and go on with our business."

"That's what I aim to do," Coleman said. "Though I don't mind admitting it shook me up last night when I saw that woman as clear as a bell." He frowned, thinking about it. "Couldn't see it so well when I came in a while ago, though.

"Oh, well," he went on with a smile. "It's done the job so far, if it'll just hold out awhile longer. And listen, Miss Julia, don't worry about the crowds; they won't bother us.

This is the happiest day of my life, and I don't mind sharing it. Besides, what better time to see a miracle than on our wedding day?"

"You're as bad as Sam, Coleman, with all that tolerance," I said. Then picking up the other boutonniere, I turned to Sam. "Hold still now, and let me get this pinned on you."

While Sam bent his head to watch me as I pushed the pin through fabric and flower, I bit my lip with the effort. "Careful, Julia," Sam said, smiling. Then, sniffing, he said, "My, you smell good."

"That's this flower you're smelling," I said somewhat sharply, reminded of what Hazel Marie'd said about the perfume she'd been so free with on my person. Then, my mind switching back to more immediate concerns, I whirled around. "Coleman! What about your car? Will you be able to get through that mass of people when you and Binkie're ready to leave? Sam, that's your job, to see that they have a getaway car. And what about your suitcase, Coleman? Did you pack for your honeymoon?"

"All taken care of, Miss Julia," Coleman said, reassuring me considerably. "Sam put my suitcase in the car this morning, and we parked it where nobody'll think to look."

"But how're you going to get to it? Coleman, I'll tell you," I said, getting more concerned by the minute. "I've heard of some terrible things being done to grooms in bygone weddings—things like putting a ball and chain around their necks and throwing away the key, or carrying a groom off and leaving him to walk for miles to get home. Now, I know all those deputies down there are friends of yours, but friends're the worst kind for mischief such as that. There's no telling what they'd be capable of if they got their hands on you. I mean, there're some dangerous-looking men among them, especially Lieutenant Peavey and that Deputy Moser with handguns all over his tie."

"Julia, Julia," Sam said, in that soothing way of his. "We've got it all arranged. A special car with a special driver will pull up to your front walk when Binkie and Coleman're ready to leave, and it'll take them right to their car. Give us some credit, woman, we've thought of everything."

"Well, all right. Now all I have to worry about is if *I've* thought of everything."

Chapter 33

"I'd better go see about those girls." Then, overcome with the high seriousness of what he was about to enter into, I turned back to Coleman. "Coleman," I said, smoothing his lapel and giving his bow tie a tweak. "I can't tell you how much I've enjoyed having you in my house, and how much I appreciate all you've meant to me, just by being here." I snatched a Kleenex from the box on his bedside table. "This is a momentous time for you, a highlight of your life, but I want you to know that I'm always here for you. You've been like a son to me, and, well, I guess I hate to see you go." My eyes began to fill in spite of my relief at getting him and Binkie married.

"Julia," Sam said, putting his arm around me. "Remember, now, this is what you've been working toward for so long. Let's be happy for them."

Coleman moved closer and displaced Sam. He put both arms around me and pulled me close. "Don't cry, Miss Julia. I'm not going far, you know, and I plan to be around so much you'll think I'm still living here."

"Well, I know, Coleman," I said, wiping my eyes and wondering if Hazel Marie's mascara was the waterproof kind. "But I'm just trying to be a mother to you, and mothers're supposed to cry at weddings." I straightened my shoulders. "Well, enough of that. Sam, what time is it?"

"Getting close to three-thirty."

"Oh, my goodness, we're running out of time. I'd better check on Binkie. Sam, you stay here with Coleman and keep him entertained. At a quarter till, you two go down the back stairs and wait in the kitchen. Then a minute or two before four, come out to the living room and take your places in front of the arch. Pastor Petree will already be there, so he'll make sure you're in the right place. Coleman"—I sniffed as my eyes teared up again—"this is one of the happiest days of my life."

I left then, pulling the door closed behind me, to be greeted by a blast of chords from the blessed hands of Miss Mattie Mae Morgan at the piano downstairs. I headed down the hall to my room where the female contingent of the wedding party was congregated. Giggles and laughter from Binkie and Hazel Marie and Miss Wiggins blended with an unfamiliar voice giving instructions to stand here, to smile or to look this way. As I reached the door and looked in, I was stunned at the scene before me. Clothes, stockings and shoes were strewn over the bed and every chair; open cosmetics cases on the dresser overflowed with one beauty aid after another, a Styrofoam cooler filled with ice and soft drinks sat in the corner, and Binkie was still in her robe and bare feet.

That was all bad enough, but the photographer was a redheaded man wearing baggy shorts and a tee shirt. And work boots of all things. There he was in my bedroom, like it was the most normal thing in the world to be in the presence of women in various stages of undress, and not a one of them turning a hair about it. Except Lillian, who was flapping a robe in front of Binkie. The whole unsuitable scene stopped me cold.

While I stood at the door, watching, the man hopped around, giving orders and putting hands on first one and another. "A little closer," he said. "Okay, that's good." Then a snap, flash and whir of the camera. "Now let's have the bride sit at the dresser, while the bridesmaid fixes her hair. Look back this way. Good." And another snap, flash and whir.

"Seem like that's a Lord's plenty," Lillian said, frowning at the photographer.

Etta Mae Wiggins couldn't stay out of the picture. "How about one of Binkie sitting in the window?"

"That'd be good." Binkie laughed, and crawled onto the windowsill. "Then I want some with you, Miss Julia. Come on in. This is Rusty Reid. You probably know him, he's the sports photographer for the newspaper."

"It's past time for you to be ready, Binkie," I said. "How much longer is this going to take?" Then I was blinded as the redheaded, freckled photographer flashed the camera in my eyes. Blinking away the afterglow, I snatched up Binkie's wedding dress and held it toward her.

But Binkie had her attention on the spectacle in front of the house. "Good grief," she said, leaning her forehead against the window screen. "They just keep coming."

All of us—Rusty the photographer, Hazel Marie, Miss Wiggins, Lillian and myself—were drawn to the window where Binkie sat and to the one beside it, straining to see. Not only had the crowd grown on the sidewalk and the street, but my front yard was full of wedding guests, as well. To say nothing of the cars lining both sides of the street and, if a turned collar meant anything, a Catholic priest. I gasped at the nerve of him, for he was studying the streaks of mortar or whatever it was on our Family Life Center with a pair of binoculars. I had a good mind to go out there and let him know that Pastor Ledbetter had no ecumenical leanings at all.

"Miss Julia?" I turned to see Little Lloyd standing at the door, wringing his hands. "Miss Julia, I don't know what to do."

Walking over to him, I said, "What's wrong, honey? I showed you how to seat people."

"That's just it," he said, looking up at me through those thick glasses. "They don't want to be seated. They won't even come in the house. They're all out in the yard, looking at that lady on the wall. And Miss Mattie Mae Morgan says she can get 'em in, so she keeps playing louder and louder."

"Where is Mr. Pickens?" I demanded. "Isn't he helping you?"

"Well, no'm, not much," he admitted. "I mean, he's trying, but I think he wants to see that lady, too. So he's out in the yard with the rest of them."

"I declare, that man! Hazel Marie," I said, turning to her. "Look out there and see where Mr. Pickens is. If you can get his attention, tell him to do the job he's assigned to do, and help this child get . . ."

I was interrupted by a clatter of shoes on the stairs and a breathless Emma Sue Ledbetter calling, "Julia! Oh, Julia!"

"What now?" I mumbled, then called: "In here, Emma Sue."

Emma Sue hurried to us, her flowing floral chiffon whirling around her. "Julia," she panted. "I can't find Lance Petree anywhere. Have you seen him?"

My hand went to my throat as my breath caught. "Why, no. I just assumed he was downstairs. I mean, whoever heard of a preacher being late for a wedding? He put it on his calendar. I saw him do it." Turning to the bride, I said, "Binkie, do you see Pastor Petree in the yard?"

"No, ma'am, I don't, and I've got a pretty good view."

"Oh, my word," I said. "Where can he be? Maybe he's praying in his office at the church and lost track of the time. I've heard that can happen."

"No, I've already looked there," Emma Sue said, as she moved farther into the room, looking around at the chaos. She cut her eyes at me, then said, "My Larry's always at a wedding an hour early, so he can counsel the wedding party if anybody has second thoughts. It's too bad, Julia, that you couldn't wait until he returned from the Holy Land."

"Too bad he had to take off just when I needed him, too," I said. "Hazel Marie, do you see Mr. Pickens?"

"Yessum, he's right down there, talking to some deputies. But I can't get him to look up here." She pushed against the screen and called, "Yoo-hoo, J.D.! J.D.!" To no avail.

"Little Lloyd," I said, turning to the child. "Run down there and tell Mr. Pickens he's needed up here. We're in dire need of a preacher, and I want him to find Pastor Petree right away, even if he has to get the sheriff's department after him. Oh, and when you do that, go look in the kitchen. Preachers are known to be where the food is."

"Yes, ma'am, I will." But before he hurried off on his mission, the boy added another possibility to the mix. "Maybe that ole Dixon Hightower's got the preacher."

"What in the world would Dixon do with a preacher?" I said, waving him on his way. "Not that he couldn't use one. Hurry now, and get Mr. Pickens up here."

As the boy left, I began to pace the floor. "What're we going to do?" But I might as well have been talking to myself. Emma Sue was fascinated with the bottles and jars and plastic containers spilling out of the cosmetics cases, while Binkie and Miss Wiggins were still entranced by the goings and comings down on the lawn. Hazel Marie had her head almost poked through the screen, trying to get Mr. Pickens's attention, and only Lillian seemed to reflect my worry about the legal aspects of a wedding without a preacher.

"Miss Julia," she said, a deep frown on her face. "What we gonna do if that preacher be lost somewhere?"

Rusty snapped another picture before I could look away, and the flash blinded me again. And downstairs, Miss Mattie Mae Morgan came down hard on a hymn I recognized—"Bringing in the Sheaves," which I certainly hoped she could do.

Holding my hand against my eyes to prevent another blinding, I said, "He's got to be somewhere, Lillian. What time is it?" I glanced at the clock on my bedside table. "My Lord, it's a quarter till! We've got to find him!"

A flash exploded again, as Rusty moved from one side of the room to the other, getting his candid shots.

"Enough pictures," I said, holding up my hand toward him to ward off the eye of the camera. "We don't have time for any more. Why don't you get set up in the living room, but, remember, no flashes during the ceremony. If we have one." And I began to wring my hands again. First, we had no bride, then almost no groom, and now we had no preacher. "Now, Mr. Reid, I know you're used to snapping pictures of uniformed boys running around on a field, but keep in mind that this is a wedding. We won't need any action shots. Lillian," I said, turning to her. "Where can that man be? I should've known not to depend on an associate pastor; they don't have enough experience in these matters. What're we going to do if he doesn't show up at all?"

"Maybe—" Lillian started, but she was interrupted by a squeal from Etta Mae Wiggins.

"Binkie!" she screeched. "I almost forgot! You need something old, something new, something borrowed, something blue. And a dime in your shoe. Have you got 'em all?"

"Oh, shoo," Binkie said, laughing. "I've been too busy deciding whether to get married at all to think of that."

"You have to have them. For luck, you know. So it's a good thing I brought this." Miss Wiggins reached into her purse-on-a-chain and brought out a blue garter. "Now, this," she said, dangling it in the air, "has seen its share of weddings, and it's been lucky for some of them. If you don't have one, I'd love for you to wear it. And don't forget to take it off and let Coleman throw it to the men right after you throw your bouquet to the women."

Both Binkie and Hazel Marie oohed and aahed over the little pink flower attached to the blue elastic thing. I held my tongue, determined to restrain myself from throwing cold water on Binkie's enjoyment, even if it did involve a much-used garter getting into the hands of a bunch of male guests. She was entering into her wedding preparations with all the enthusiasm I could ask for, in spite of her earlier vacillations. If a blue garter added to her pleasure, then so be it. Not that I held with superstitious signs and omens and good-luck charms like those people out in the street, but who was I to say they didn't work?

"Put it on, Binkie," I said. "From the way things're going, we need all the luck we can get. And I'd already planned this anyway, but I want you to wear my single strand of pearls." I opened a drawer and took out a velvet case. "They were my wedding pearls."

I didn't mention that they'd not done much good for the course of my marriage, but pearls are pearls.

I fastened them around Binkie's neck, as

she fingered them, her face glowing. "Thank you, Miss Julia. I'll take good care of them. Okay, I have something blue and something borrowed, and they're both old. Now what about something new? Oh, I know. My engagement ring!" She held out her hand, wiggling her fingers so that the stone in its setting sparkled in the sunlight.

"Here's a dime for your shoe," Emma Sue said, rummaging in her purse. "Although I don't believe in such things."

Emma Sue went to the window and stood looking out at the mob scene down below. "If Larry were here," she said, shaking her head at the sorry sight, "he wouldn't put up with this so close to the church. Even if they are on a public street. I don't understand why the sheriff doesn't send them on their way. I mean, what're they doing out there, anyway? Are they planning to march or protest or something? They're just milling around and carrying on; it's a disgrace, if you ask me."

"Why, they're worshiping, Mrs. Ledbetter," Hazel Marie said.

"Worshiping what? I mean, who?" Emma Sue craned her neck to look closer.

"That woman's face over there. See, on

the wall of the new building? They think it's some kind of saint or maybe Mary."

"Oh! Oh!" Emma Sue began panting, her breath coming in short gasps. She felt behind her for a chair and sank into it. "Oh! Not a Catholic image on our church. Oh, no, the Lord wouldn't do that to us! Where is Larry when we need him?"

"That's what I've been asking," I said. "Get yourself together, Emma Sue, we can't help what's going on outside. Our worry is about what's going on inside. Like not having a preacher."

"We've got to pray about this." Emma Sue gasped.

"Don't you dare touch that telephone, Emma Sue," I said, for fear she'd start the prayer chain and be on the phone throughout the ceremony, if we had one. "Besides, most of the prayer chain's out there in my yard."

"Lloyd's bringing J.D. in," Hazel Marie said, hurrying in from the hall. "He'll find Pastor Petree for us."

"An' what if he don't," Lillian said. "Or can't?"

"Oh, Lillian," I said, leaning against her. "My beautiful wedding's all messed up, and all for want of a preacher. Unless . . . ," I said, straightening up. "Maybe we could ask that Roman priest out there. But, no, that wouldn't work. I don't imagine he'd do it, and if he did, Binkie and Coleman might have to raise all their children in the Catholic faith, and Emma Sue would have a heart attack. Oh, Lillian, what're we going to do?"

"We still got the Reverend Mr. Abernathy of the Harvest House AME Zion Church, if you want him."

Relief flooded my soul. "I certainly do want him. He'll be an answer to prayer, if you ask me. Call him, Lillian, right now and I'll send Mr. Pickens to pick him up. The ceremony will just have to be late, but better late than none at all." As she went to the phone by the bed, I began to pace the floor again in my agitation.

"I'll tell you this, though," I said to anybody who was listening, "Pastor Petree's going to have a lot to answer for when I get my hands on him!"

Chapter 34

"Hazel Marie," I said, as I heard heavy foot-steps on the stairs. "Go tell Mr. Pickens to wait out there in the hall. He can't come in here, since Binkie's not dressed." As she went to meet him, I tried to organize a plan of action. Seeing Lillian hang up the phone, I turned to her, hoping for good news. "Can Reverend Mr. Abernathy do it?"

"He puttin' on his weddin' suit right now," she said. "He be ready when Mr. Pickens get there."

"Thank the Lord," I said, throwing my head back in relief, "for preachers who take their duties seriously. Lillian, why don't you go with Mr. Pickens and show him the way. How long will it take you?"

"He live next door to the Harvest House Church, so ten, fifteen minutes."

"Well, get back here as soon as you can. Mr. Pickens ought to get some of those deputies swarming around down there to give him a police escort.

"Miss Wiggins," I went on, "if you'd like to be useful, I'm going to put you in charge of getting Binkie dressed. Binkie, listen to me now, your groom is probably already downstairs waiting for you, so get out of that window and into your wedding gown.

"Emma Sue," I continued, turning to her. She was still sprawled in a chair, fanning herself with last Sunday's church bulletin. Her moans blended with the chanted prayers of the crowd outside, both of which were gaining in volume. "Get up from there, Emma Sue, and get yourself together. I need your help getting the guests in the house. Come on now."

She struggled to her feet, her face pale with the shock of a miracle appearing on a Presbyterian wall. With tears brimming in her red eyes, she said, "How can the Lord let this happen to us?"

"His ways are not our ways, Emma Sue," I reminded her, taking her arm and moving out into the hall. "Now put your mind on this wedding and forget that apparition on the wall. First things first, I always say."

As we went down the stairs, I saw Mr.

Pickens and Lillian hurry out the door, on their way to pick up a preacher. Little Lloyd stood in the almost empty living room, still wringing his hands. Miss Mattie Mae Morgan was filling the air with hymns played in a most uplifting tempo, her huge body swaying from side to side, while Lieutenant Peavey stood as stiff as a board next to the piano.

Raising my voice to be heard above the din, I told the two of them that the ceremony would be delayed, but only until the Reverend Abernathy arrived. "In the meantime," I shouted, "we're going to get the guests inside. As soon as they begin to come in, Lieutenant Peavey, you can entertain them with one of your solos. Maybe that'll keep them from that spectacle outside."

He looked down at me, I think, since he still had on those dark glasses, and nodded. "I'll do as many as it takes. Mattie Mae, let's start off with 'Baby, I'm Amazed By You.'"

And, as I was being amazed by the selection, which didn't sound like any wedding music I'd ever heard, Miss Morgan swung into a tune with enough extra ruffles and flourishes to sound like a full-fledged orchestra. I threw up my hands, unable to manage another crisis, much less a musical one. I grabbed Emma Sue's arm and headed out the door.

"Little Lloyd," I said as we passed. "Stand right here and seat people as we herd them in. Remember to save places for Lillian and me on the front row, and for Miss Wiggins and her friend, too, since she's being so helpful."

"Save one for me, too," Emma Sue said as I marched her out on the porch and surveyed the yard, teeming with guests who'd forgotten why they were here.

"Go over that way, Emma Sue," I told her, "and tell them we're ready to start."

She tottered off, her high heels sinking into the lawn, but her eyes were drawn to the object of veneration and wonder across the street. I headed toward a group of deputies whom I recognized, in spite of their civilian clothes, by the similar mustaches they sported.

"Time to go in, gentlemen," I said, as two of them stubbed out cigarettes on my front lawn. "If you'll start, I think the others will follow."

Just then Lieutenant Peavey's voice, amazingly lifted in something close to a breathy, tremulous soprano, floated out to us, and the whole crowd—wedding guests and street worshipers, alike—turned as one toward the sound. Several of the worshipers fell to their knees on the sidewalk, and I was tempted to do the same. It seemed another miracle for such a high, quavery voice to emanate from the muscular throat of Lieutenant Peavey.

One of the deputies murmured, "There he goes. Gives me goose bumps every time I hear him."

Lieutenant Peavey gave me goose bumps too, every time he opened his mouth in my presence.

As the deputies moved toward the porch, I went around the yard, urging, cajoling and inviting our guests into the house. They went, easily enough, but with backward glances at the image on the wall. I couldn't see it myself, but I guess it was all in your point of view.

LuAnne Conover, with Leonard close behind her, paused on her way in and whispered, "I declare, Julia, Leonard is about to drive me crazy. Weddings give him all kinds of ideas."

"Keep him in check, LuAnne," I whispered back, not wanting to witness any of his ideas in action. "But I wish you'd hidden that medication from him, today at least."

She smiled a satisfied smile and whispered, "Oh, I wouldn't want to interfere with his medical treatment."

I rolled my eyes, but she'd joined the guests as they crowded onto the steps and up on the porch, waiting to get in. I turned and motioned for Emma Sue to follow them. Tearing her attention away from the Family Life Center, she came over to me.

"Julia," she said, wiping the tears from her face. "What're we going to do? That thing's a desecration, and there's even a priest over there who'll report it to the pope as a miracle. First thing you know, that popemobile of his will be parked by our church, and I just can't stand the thought. You're going to have to excuse me from the ceremony, for I'm being led to witness to those poor souls who're lost in superstition."

"Emma Sue," I said, grabbing her arm and giving it a shake. "Don't you dare! Those people aren't bothering anybody. Well, except for drivers trying to get through, but you leave them alone. I've got a wedding to put on, and I don't want you stirring up trouble and disrupting it."

"Well," she said, as she yielded to my leading. "I guess I could wait till after the wedding, but my head's going to be bowed in prayer all the way through."

"Good, and you might as well mention the rest of us while you're at it." I was in dire need of some prayer myself.

"Oh, thank goodness," I said, as Mr. Pickens's car screeched to a halt in the middle of the street, and Lillian and a short, thin and very ebony man disembarked. "There's the preacher."

"*That's* the preacher!" Emma Sue came to a standstill. "Julia, you can't!"

"I certainly can and, furthermore, I certainly will. That's the Reverend Morris Abernathy, and I thank the Lord for him. Now, go on in, Emma Sue, and let me speak to him."

Tears flooded her eyes as she looked at me with shock and deep disappointment. "I don't know that I can be a party to this. What's Larry going to say?"

"I don't care what Larry Ledbetter says. And as far as you being a party to this, do what you want. But I'll tell you this, Emma Sue, if you start proselytizing those people and creating a disruption to this wedding, I'll move my letter to the Episcopal church. Then see what happens to the church budget."

"Oh, Julia," she said, her eyes peering at me through a film of tears. "You wouldn't! Why, Episcopalians're almost Catholic with all that incense and carrying on."

I sucked in a breath between my teeth. "Go in, Emma Sue, or go home, I don't much care which. Now, excuse me, I have to meet the Reverend Mr. Abernathy."

I left her then, and walked over to Mr. Pickens and Lillian. "Mr. Pickens, hurry on in and help Little Lloyd get everybody seated. He's probably running his little legs off."

Mr. Pickens gave me a wink and a small salute. "Yes, ma'am," he said. "On my way."

Turning, I said, "Lillian, thank you a million times. I am so relieved to have a qualified minister at last. You run on in; Little Lloyd's saving you a seat on the front row next to me."

I gave her a hug for coming through for me again, then she introduced me to the savior of the wedding. "This here's the Reverend Morris Abernathy, Miss Julia, an' he say he happy to be of service to you and the Lord. He gonna get them two married good an' tight, don't you worry." She straightened the veil on her hat, and walked with regal grace in her hot pink silk to take her place among the guests.

Turning to the not-very-tall man standing beside me, I was somewhat taken aback at his get-up—striped trousers with spats, of all things, and a morning coat with tails almost to his ankles. Yet, in spite of his outdated attire, there was a serenity about him that put my mind at ease. He came barely to my shoulder, and I had to look down on his head of frizzled white hair. His deep brown eyes were milky with age, and his small hand trembled as he held a limp and well-worn Bible.

"Reverend," I said, extending my hand. "I'm Mrs. Julia Springer, and I thank you from the bottom of my heart for coming at the last minute. You are a lifesaver."

A small smile lit up his eyes, as he grasped my hand. "Mrs. Springer, that's the business I'm in. Now, you just show me where you want me, and I'll join that young couple in holy matrimony. Let not your heart be troubled any longer. My," he said, looking around at the dwindling crowd on my front porch and the burgeoning crowd on the sidewalk. "This is a big wedding."

"Well, no, not exactly. That crowd over there are here on another matter."

"Ah, yes, Miss Lillian was telling me about it. I'd certainly be interested in seeing what they're seeing."

"You won't see a thing, I promise you." I took his elbow and turned him toward the house. "But you can look all you want, just as soon as the ceremony's over. Come this way, Reverend. We'll sneak through the back. Oh!" I stopped with a sudden piercing thought. "It's just that it's easier to get to our makeshift altar through the kitchen and the dining room."

His kind eyes crinkled, as he took my hand and patted it. "Don't trouble yourself, Mrs. Springer. I been goin' through kitchens for these many years now, an' it don't never bother me as long as it lead to the altar of the Lord."

Standing there in the midst of confusion on both sides, I put my other hand on top of his, as a sense of peace came over me. "Perhaps we could talk sometime, Reverend Mr. Abernathy. But for now," I said, leading him toward the side of the house, "we've got a wedding to get through."

Chapter 35

As I hurried the Reverend Mr. Abernathy around the side of the house, I heard Hazel Marie bang her hand against the window screen overhead.

"Miss Julia! Miss Julia!" she hissed, trying to get my attention without alerting half the town. "We need you up here. Binkie's sick!"

"Oh, my word," I said, clutching the Reverend's arm. "We have to hurry, Reverend. That's the bride she's talking about!"

I hurriedly opened the kitchen door and urged the preacher in. Sam and Coleman stood by the swinging door to the dining room, waiting for the signal to enter. Since I was the one who was supposed to give the signal, they were in for a long wait. Coleman was white around the mouth in spite of his tanned face. He shifted from one foot to the other, as nervous as a cat. I don't care how much a man wants to marry, when it comes right down to the doing, he'd probably just as soon bypass it. Sam looked as easy as he always did, smiling and assuring Coleman that it would all be over in a few minutes. The caterer's helpers leaned against the kitchen counters, waiting for the time to serve the food. They were taking a great deal of interest and amusement in Coleman's pre-wedding jitters.

I introduced the Reverend Mr. Abernathy to Sam and Coleman, wondering what their reaction would be to the ministerial substitute. Coleman didn't turn a hair. In fact, he was in such a daze that I don't think he noticed the difference between the Pastors Petree and Abernathy. Sam surprised me, greeting the minister by name, shaking his hand and asking about his family. But then, Sam knew just about everybody.

"It'll be just a few more minutes," I said, not mentioning the current crisis with Binkie, for fear of distressing Coleman more than he already was. I patted his arm. "The guests are slow getting seated, since they lingered so long outside. Coleman, you need to sit down and rest. Reverend, you come out when Mr. Pickens lets you know the last guest is seated. You'll know who he is, he's got an exceptionally full mustache. And, Sam, you bring Coleman out right after Little Lloyd walks me to my seat."

"We'll wait for the high sign, Julia," Sam said, pulling out a chair for Coleman, as James put a glass of ice water in front of him. "You run on and get started," Sam went on. "Coleman's going to be a wreck if we have to wait much longer."

As the Reverend Mr. Abernathy suggested a word of prayer, I eased out into the dining room and poked my head around the door to scan the rapidly filling living room. Our guests were arrayed in all their finery, patiently waiting for the long-delayed moment of truth, while Miss Mattie Mae Morgan regaled them with her unique artistry at the piano. Lieutenant Peavey waited by her side for his next rendition. I saw Mr. Pickens escort the sheriff's wife to a seat on the groom's side, his black eyes sparkling as he said something he probably shouldn't have to her. Little Lloyd made me proud as he walked tall and somewhat stiff with Emma Sue Ledbetter on his arm.

I caught Lillian's eye and motioned her to follow me upstairs. As she was seated on the front row, everybody noticed her leave. I saw the whispers start behind some hands, and a few smiles as I gathered up my long skirt and we both scurried up the stairs.

"What's the matter?" Lillian asked, breathing hard as we reached the top of the stairs. "Is Miss Binkie's mind changed again?"

"Lord, let's hope not," I said, hurrying toward my room. "No, Hazel Marie said she's sick, so we've got to get her un-sick in a hurry. On top of that, Coleman's downstairs looking ready to throw up, too. Lillian, those two are getting married today, if I have to hold a bucket in front of them."

Hazel Marie greeted us as we entered the room. "Oh, Miss Julia, she's a mess. She's already thrown up everything, her lunch and all, and now she's just heaving and heaving. Etta Mae's trying to help her. She's a nurse, you know."

Well, not exactly, I thought, but near enough. Lillian headed for the bathroom, where Binkie, still in her robe and bare feet, knelt by the commode. Miss Wiggins stood over her, holding her head.

Lillian took over, giving her diagnosis immediately. "It's the excitement," she pronounced, knowing exactly what to do. "She need a cold washrag on her head."

"What she needs is a good whipping for getting herself in this condition in the first place," I mumbled, standing outside the bathroom for fear of a sympathetic response to Binkie's alimentary spasms.

Lillian wrung out a washcloth in the sink. "She didn't do it by herself, so quit fussin'. We got to get her up from here." But Binkie's stomach heaved again, and Lillian pressed the washcloth to her forehead.

"Be careful," Hazel Marie said, watching as I was from the door. "Don't mess up her hair."

Then Hazel Marie drew me back into the bedroom. "I didn't want to say anything to the others," she whispered, "but I think I saw Dixon Hightower again."

"No!" I gasped at the thought. "No, Hazel Marie, he couldn't be that foolish. Not with half the deputies in the county in our living room. Are you sure?"

"Well-l-l." She frowned, thinking over what she'd seen. "I guess I'm not. It sure looked like him, though, slithering and scooting through that crowd with nobody but me noticing him. I guess it could've been a child." She didn't sound too sure about it.

"Well, I can't worry about him now."

I looked past Hazel Marie to see Miss Wiggins give way to Lillian, who lifted Binkie to her feet. "I'll get her a cold drink," Miss Wiggins said, as she headed for the cooler in the corner of the bedroom. "That might help settle her stomach."

As Lillian led Binkie to the bed, I said, "Don't let her lie down. We don't have time. Binkie, how're you feeling now?"

She gave me a weak smile, her face slightly on the green side. "I'm all right. I think. Where's Coleman?"

"He's downstairs with Sam. They're just waiting on you, as is everybody else. Take some deep breaths, Binkie."

She did, then sipped from the icy drink Miss Wiggins held for her.

"Nibble on this," Miss Wiggins said, giving her a saltine cracker. "Just nibble, now. No big bites, just enough to put something on your stomach. It'll stay down, I promise."

Binkie, like a little girl, obeyed, biting carefully into the cracker and sipping the cold drink.

"I'm feeling better," she said, taking a

deep breath and smiling with some assurance.

"Let's get her dressed, Hazel Marie," I
said, taking the gown from its hanger. "If her
stomach'll hold off for ten minutes, we'll
have this wedding over and done with.
Where're her shoes?"

With Binkie still sitting on the bed, Hazel
Marie settled the dress over her head, being
careful of her hair. Miss Wiggins knelt and
put Binkie's shoes on her feet. As Lillian
zipped up the dress, Hazel Marie loaded a
brush with enough rouge to bring a healthy
color to the face of a corpse. Then she laid
on with lipstick and lip gloss until Binkie was
ready for public viewing. They helped her to
her feet, and she only swayed a little bit.

"All right," I said. "Let's get this show on
the road. Hazel Marie, don't you leave
Binkie's side. I want you to be ready to
catch her if she stumbles on the stairs.
Binkie, pay attention now. You stand right
behind Hazel Marie at the bottom of the
stairs. As soon as Little Lloyd seats me,
Sam and Coleman will come out and stand
in front of the arch where the minister will
be. Then Hazel Marie'll come out and walk
toward the arch. Slowly, Hazel Marie,

remember that. When you get there, Miss Morgan will strike up the wedding march and that's when you come out, Binkie. Walk right up, but real slowly, and stand beside Coleman. Everybody clear on what they're supposed to do?"

They all nodded, then Binkie asked, "What if I get sick again?"

"You're not going to get sick again," I assured her, and if willpower had anything to do with it, she wouldn't. "But if you do, there's a big vase of flowers by the arch. Just lean over and throw up. But you stay right there until you've said your vows. The Reverend Mr. Abernathy'll understand. Oh, by the way, don't be surprised at the last-minute change of ministers; the one we have is better qualified than the one you're expecting. Now, Hazel Marie, give us five minutes to get around the house and into the living room. Oh, and don't forget your bouquets; be sure Binkie has hers."

"Yes, ma'am," Hazel Marie said, her eyes already on her watch. "I'll look after her and get her down there on time."

Miss Wiggins, Lillian and I hurried down the back stairs, coming out into the kitchen to the surprised faces of Sam and Coleman.

The Reverend Mr. Abernathy remained un-
perturbed, probably because he'd officiated
at so many weddings, nothing surprised
him anymore.

As the three of us rushed out the back
door, I called, "As soon as we're all seated,
Sam, get Coleman out there."

Lifting my skirt, I ran after Lillian and Miss
Wiggins, turning the corner of the porch to
the amazed stares of the mob of people
who were momentarily distracted from the
object of their worship.

Breathing hard, we climbed the steps to
the porch where Mr. Pickens and Little
Lloyd waited for us. Everyone else had been
seated, and the rustle from inside the house
let us know they were getting restless.

"What's the holdup?" Mr. Pickens said, a
smile lurking around the corners of that
bushy mustache. "You have trouble getting
dressed, Miss Julia?"

"No, I did not. But there's been plenty of
trouble, which you don't need to know
about. Mr. Pickens, we don't have time for
your foolishness. Now take Miss Wiggins
down the aisle and get back out here for Lillian as quick as you can, then Little Lloyd
will escort me."

"Ah, one little question," Mr. Pickens said, lifting one eyebrow. "Do you know who's standing in the arch, looking for all the world like a man of the cloth?"

"He *is* a man of the cloth. That's the Reverend Mr. Abernathy, and don't you say one word, Mr. Pickens," I said. Then, looking him straight in the eye, I went on. "Just do your job and let him do his. Now, as soon as I'm in my seat, give Sam the signal to get Coleman out there. Escort Miss Wiggins in now, and step lively."

Anxiety knotted up my stomach until I began to fear that I'd have Binkie's problem, but with a lot less cause for it. I wrung my hands as Mr. Pickens and Miss Wiggins entered the house. He was on his best behavior, holding his arm in the correct manner for Miss Wiggins to cling to. Which she did, smiling brightly.

"It all goin' now," Lillian said, patting my back. "You don't need to worry no more. You jus' walk in there an' take yo' place like they not a flustration on yo' mind. Hear me, now."

"I hear you, Lillian, and thank you. If we can just get through the next few minutes without a catastrophe, I won't ask the Lord for another thing. I'll even sign back up for the prayer chain."

Little Lloyd grinned behind his hand, as Mr. Pickens returned and held the screen door for Lillian. "Let's go, Miss Lillian," he said, crooking his arm. "I've already escorted you down once, but it's my pleasure to do it again."

Lillian's face glowed as she accompanied him on her second march down the aisle. Little Lloyd and I were left alone on the porch, well, except for the surging crowd on the sidewalk that couldn't decide which was of more interest—us or the lady on the wall. I squeezed his shoulder. "Won't be long now," I said. "At least, let's hope it won't."

Mr. Pickens opened the screen door, smiling at us. "Ready, Miss Julia?" he said. "Last call."

He gave Little Lloyd a pat on the back, as the boy held his arm in the approved manner for me to take. We stood in the doorway a moment as I gathered myself, then we walked sedately down the aisle toward our seats and the beatific presence of the Reverend Mr. Abernathy in the flower-filled arch.

Chapter 36

I straightened the folds of my dress and breathed deeply as I settled into my seat beside Little Lloyd. Lillian reached across him and patted my hand. Seeing the Reverend Mr. Abernathy's complacent smile as he faced his audience reassured me that the service was in good hands. There was nothing else I could do now.

A brief silence descended as Miss Mattie Mae Morgan changed her sheet music and nodded to Lieutenant Peavey. He stood to his full height and filled his impressive chest. Then, as she began the music, he commenced to hit notes that I'd never imagined him, or anybody of his gender, capable of, from the extremely high tones to a breathy whisper. He sang about somebody's wedding day, which I thought most appropriate, if he could've managed it in a normal range and without an excess of qua-very high notes.

Little Lloyd leaned over, his eyes big with wonder, and whispered, "He sounds just like Barry."

"Who?" I whispered back.

"You know. Barry, with the Bee Gees. That's a Bee Gees song, too."

"You don't say," I said under my breath, feeling a rush of chills run across my back as Lieutenant Peavey sang most movingly of husband and wife being taken to heaven. I wasn't sure the song was all that spiritual, but the sound of it was so sweet that, I de-clare, my heart clenched up on me.

Then, as Lieutenant Peavey ended on a tremulous whisper, Coleman and Sam emerged from the kitchen and made their way down the improvised aisle that wound through the seated guests. Coleman looked remarkably improved, now that the moment was at hand. He walked with confidence, a smile twitching at the corners of his mouth, to the arch, then turned to face us with Sam at his side. As tears started in my eyes, I saw the Reverend Mr. Abernathy rise up on his tiptoes and whisper some encouraging words to the groom. Coleman clasped his hands in front of him, nodded and relaxed his shoulders. Sam beamed with pleasure, having accomplished the important job of getting the groom where he was supposed to be. He turned his head slightly toward me, and winked.

Lord, I hoped he had the wedding ring. What with all I'd had on my mind, that was the one thing I'd forgotten to check on. Well, if he didn't, it was too late to worry about it. I slipped off my engagement ring and loosened my wedding band, readying it to hand to Sam if he needed it.

There was a stir in the crowd as Miss Morgan began a more traditional selection, and people turned in their chairs when Hazel Marie stepped off the stairs and into our view. Moving with grace, a bridesmaid's pride glowing on her face, she carried her bouquet at her waist as she glided along the winding aisle between our guests. She turned her head toward Mr. Pickens, who stood at the back of the room, and I thought her heart would jump out through her eyes. She looked lovely—in spite of that skimpy dress that would probably have Emma Sue fanning the air again.

I heard Little Lloyd suck in a breath as he

whispered, "Mama." I patted his knee, as she walked beside us to her place opposite Sam. She smiled at Little Lloyd, then at me, and I hoped it was an assurance that Binkie was able to make it to the altar alone.

Oh, Lord, I thought, we should've had somebody give Binkie away, in spite of the harsh words she'd had to say about the practice. At least, she would've had somebody to lean on in her weakened condition. Too late, though, for Miss Morgan struck up the wedding march with all the power at her command, which was considerable, for I saw the vases on my mantel shake with the vibration. If that didn't get Binkie moving, I didn't know what would.

The guests turned with one accord as Binkie appeared, sighing at the sight of her. She was beautiful, glowing as if she'd never had a second thought in her life. Hazel Marie had done wonders with Binkie's hair, to say nothing of the makeup that hid all the signs of her earlier indisposition.

Binkie tottered briefly as she started through the guests, then she lifted her head, locking her eyes on Coleman. Joy lit up her face, and her steps steadied as she seemed drawn to him alone. I glanced at Coleman and was struck by the wide smile on his face, so remarkably different from the usual grim and serious demeanor of grooms I'd witnessed heretofore. I was looking at a happy man, and it did my heart good, considering all I'd gone through to get him to that point.

As Binkie approached the arch, the guests turning with her as she passed, Coleman held out his hand and gathered her to him. At last, I thought to myself, Coleman has her. He'd take care of her, and I could breathe easy for the first time since it had all started a week before.

It was all so affecting that I had to dab at my eyes again, and Lillian, stirred by the same tender emotion, blew her nose.

Binkie was so intent on Coleman, and probably on another internal threat, that she forgot to hand her bouquet to Hazel Marie. Hazel Marie had to reach over and take it from her, but that was only a minor hitch in the proceedings.

Still, though, there was a nagging worry in my mind that something else would go wrong. And to that end, I could've smacked Lieutenant Peavey to kingdom come when he rose to regale us again with song. If I had thought of it, I'd've told him to limit himself to pre-wedding singing so the ceremony could continue apace. Every minute counts when you're trying to get something to move along. Instead, I had to grit my teeth and listen to him warble something about everything starting from this moment on.

Little Lloyd leaned close and whispered, "That's Shania Twain."

Well, hardly, I thought, but I nodded in response. Frankly, I didn't care who it was as long as Lieutenant Peavey finished in a timely manner so the Reverend Mr. Abernathy could get on with it.

At last, the lieutenant and the piano came to a stop, and the Reverend Mr. Abernathy beamed up at the expectant—and expecting—couple. "Dearly beloved," he said, his voice clear and confident, not at all intimidated by the preponderance of Presbyterians in the audience. "We are gathered together to join this man and this woman in holy matrimony. Let us rejoice in this moment that the Lord our God has seen fit to bring about."

Thinking that the Lord hadn't been the only one working to bring the moment about, I bowed my head. The reverend continued in prayer, blessing the long-awaited union of Binkie and Coleman. I don't know whether it was the power of his prayer or the culmination of all I'd been through to get to this moment, but my heart lifted at the thought of a mission finally accomplished, and relief flooded my soul.

"Deputy Coleman," the reverend intoned, "do you promise before God and these witnesses to take this woman to be your wedded wife, to love and to cherish, to have and to hold in plenty and in want, in joy and in sorrow, and in sickness and in health, till death do you part? Say, I do."

Coleman looked down at Binkie, tightened his arm around her, and said firmly, and with all the love in the world, "I do."

"Miss Binkie," the reverend said, as I cringed at having forgotten to tell him that her name was Elizabeth. No matter, I hoped, since the powers that be knew who she was. "Do you promise before God and these witnesses to take this man to be your wedded husband, to love and to cherish, to have and to hold in plenty and in want, in joy and in sorrow, and in sickness and in health till death do you part? Say, I do."

Binkie looked up at Coleman, and my

heart skipped a beat at the glow of happiness on her face. Then, her smile faded as she began swallowing hard. I leaned forward, yearning to answer for her, watching as she swallowed again. Oh, Lord, I thought, she's going to throw up all over Coleman and the Reverend Mr. Abernathy.

Instead, a crescendo of moans undulated from the crowd outside, surrounding us with waves of sound, and above it all a single voice bellowed a spate of indecipherable words. A shiver ran down my spine at the strangeness of it. Every guest in the room turned toward the door, shifting in their chairs, and Mr. Pickens and some of the deputies moved quickly to see what was going on. Binkie and Coleman turned, too, distracted from their primary purpose. Even the Reverend Mr. Abernathy looked somewhat sidetracked, as the din increased in volume and intensity.

I jumped up from my chair and grabbed Binkie, turning her toward the reverend. "Say I do, Binkie," I urged her. "Forget what's going on out there and say it." I gave her a shake, hoping I wouldn't dislodge anything.

She nodded, looked from the minister to

Coleman, then said, loud enough to be heard over the rustling and whispering of our guests as well as the rising rumble of the crowd outside, "You bet I do." Then she grinned, as I sagged in relief, still holding on to her arm and Coleman's.

"Pronounce them, Reverend," I urged. "For the Lord's sake, pronounce them before something else happens."

The Reverend Mr. Abernathy smiled a slow smile, raised his hand in benediction, and said, "Before God and this congregation, I now pronounce you man and wife. Be fruitful and multiply, and may the Lord bestow His grace upon you."

No need to tell them that, Reverend, I thought, as I collapsed in my chair, released from my burden at last.

Chapter 37

As if the pronouncement were the signal, a number of guests rose from their seats, their faces strained with concern, as they prepared to hurry outside to see what the disturbance was.

"The ring, Sam!" I said with some urgency.

But Sam was already handing it to the Reverend Mr. Abernathy, who, seeing the imminent loss of witnesses, said, "With this ring, I do thee wed." Which I thought the groom was supposed to say, but Coleman repeated it and put it on Binkie's finger where I hoped it would stay forever and ever, amen.

Then the reverend raised his voice over the stirring and scraping of chairs as the guests began to push into the aisle. "Ladies and gentlemen, I present to you Mr. and

Mrs. Coleman Bates. God bless you, each and every one."

I leaned across Little Lloyd and Lillian, and waved to get Miss Morgan's attention, which was on whatever was happening outside. "Play!" I said. "Get some order back in here!"

And did she ever. She swung back to the piano, and I'd never heard such an exhilarating recessional as she produced. Hazel Marie thrust Binkie's bouquet into her hand, just as the bride and groom all but ran down the aisle, happier than any newlyweds I had ever seen.

As they went through the door and out onto the porch, the proceedings lost the last vestiges of the high and serious purpose I had intended. The guests began to push and shove, anxious to follow the couple and see what was causing the commotion outside. Chairs fell over in the crush, voices were raised in the tumult and I heard Mildred Allen screech "That's my foot you're stepping on!"

I bowed my head, leaning it on my hand, so overcome with relief at getting that unborn child a legitimate father that I was hardly disturbed by the general uprising inside and out.

Hazel Marie took Sam's arm to follow the wedded couple, as they were supposed to do, even though the aisle was now mobbed with wedding guests.

Sam leaned over and said, "You and Little Lloyd get behind us, Julia. Lillian, take the Reverend Mr. Abernathy's arm and don't let him get run over. Everybody stay close, now."

As Lillian, Little Lloyd and I rose from our seats to follow Sam and Hazel Marie, Lieutenant Peavey vacated his spot by the piano and came over to us. "I'll go in front," he said. And even with those ruffles on his shirt, his authority asserted itself to a marked degree.

"That'll certainly help," I said as his massive body slid in between us and the mob of people still trying to get out the door. "And I want you to know I enjoyed your singing ever so much. You have a remarkable voice."

I don't think he heard me, for he didn't acknowledge my compliment. Of course, there'd never been much he'd ever acknowledged from me, given the fact that he rarely gave me the time of day.

Slowly but firmly, Lieutenant Peavey exerted some crowd control, clearing the door and directing the guests onto the porch and out into the yard where there was room to spread out. As I emerged from the press and onto the porch, I saw long shadows stretching across the grass, thrown by the afternoon sun. Even though the yard had plenty of shade, it was still, in Mr. Pickens's words as he mopped his face and took Hazel Marie's hand, "hot as hell."

Binkie and Coleman were standing, hand in hand, at the edge of the yard, gazing intently at the spectacle across the street. The roiling, moaning crowd of miracle-watchers now included more local residents brought out by the continuing live coverage of another television crew. A reporter and a cameraman were staked out on the opposite side of the crowd, as far away from the hose hooked up to my house as they could get. Tiffany, I noticed, was not among them. The wedding guests, drawn by the television camera and the hoarse cadences of a preacher in full cry, merged into the crowd, forming a melting pot on Polk Street.

We finally stepped out onto the lawn, and I came to a dead stop, my hand clutched onto Little Lloyd's shoulder. "Thay Lord!" I gasped, overcome with the unnerving sight that greeted me.

An extension ladder was propped against the wall of the Family Life Center and, holding on for dear life with one hand, was Pastor Lance Petree at the very top of it, some two and a half stories above the concrete sidewalk. With his free hand, he wielded a long-handled brush as he scrubbed at the white lines of the alleged image. A hose, running full-stream as water gushed down the ladder and onto the street below, was draped over a rung of the ladder. Pastor Petree had obviously made free use of the hose, for not only was the wall of bricks dark with water, he'd soaked himself from head to toe. His hair, usually blow-dried to a fare-thee-well, clung to his head in wet strands, and his face was red with exertion and righteous indignation.

At first I couldn't understand a word coming out of his mouth, so stunned was I and so unsettling was the moaning of the crowd as they watched Pastor Petree scrub and scrape at the woman on the wall.

As I watched, Pastor Petree's words began to make sense. Well, I'm not willing to go that far, but at least I began to make out their meaning. "A desecration! That's what it is! It's not a miracle! Listen, people! This is not of the Lord; it's Satan's work, put here to mislead you and to profane the house of the Lord. It's a sacrilege, I tell you!"

Lord, the man was beside himself, especially since the wetting of the wall and all his scrubbing hadn't made a dent in the white lines of the image. If anything, his efforts had brought the lines into even greater relief. I could almost make out the woman myself, but I didn't believe in such things.

"Sam," I said. "Get that fool down before he breaks his neck."

"He's got a head of steam, Julia," Sam said, standing there shaking his own head. "I think we're going to have to let him run his course. Actually, he's probably safer up there than if he came down."

By this time, Lieutenant Peavey and a group of deputies had moved out among the murmuring people, reassuring them and keeping them contained across the street from the ladder that swayed with every push and pull of Pastor Petree's brush.

Emma Sue Ledbetter dashed across the street and leaned against the foot of the ladder to steady it. "Bless you, Lance Petree," she yelled. "The Lord bless you for your efforts! I'd be up there helping you if I didn't have on a skirt."

My eyes rolled up in my head at the thought of her climbing a ladder. It hadn't been often in the course of our relationship that I had longed for the presence of Pastor Ledbetter, but I did then. At least if he'd been with us, he'd have done things decently and in order, as the Book of Church Order recommends we conduct ourselves.

"Come on, Little Lloyd, Lillian," I said, moving across the yard. "Let's get the guests back inside for the reception. We need Binkie and Coleman for the receiving line. Where are they? This is supposed to be a wedding, not a three-ring circus."

But in spite of our urging, nobody would budge, not even Binkie, who said she wasn't about to go inside. The show was too good to miss, even for food.

"What're we going to do?" I wailed to Lillian. "All that food's going to waste!"

"Least you got 'em married," she said. "Thank the Lord for that blessin'."

"Bring the food out here, Miss Julia," Little Lloyd said, with the great good sense he often surprised me with. "You've got all those card tables in the garage, and we can have them set up out here in no time."

"Then that's what we'll do," I decided, determined to make the best of the situation. "Get Mr. Pickens and Miss Wiggins's boyfriend to help you. And whoever else you can round up. Sam, show them where to put the tables, over there near the crape myrtles where there's some shade, I think."

As Little Lloyd ran to get Mr. Pickens, who was busy telling Hazel Marie she looked pretty enough to kiss and he had a good mind to do it, I hurried into the house to instruct James and Emmett. Momentarily struck with the waste of my beautiful table in the dining room, I nonetheless told them to load the silver serving pieces and commence taking them outside. They were eager enough to join the fray, since all the kitchen help had been watching events from the back. I ran down the hall to the linen closet and grabbed several white sheets to serve as cloths for the card tables I intended to string together.

I thought to myself that with an AME Zion

wedding conductor and a Presbyterian pastor-turned-street-preacher the last thing I needed was a Baptist dinner on the grounds. But it couldn't be helped. I took out Harriet's magnificent centerpiece to grace the tables and, before long, guests began to fill their plates and eat with a ringside view of the show Pastor Petree continued to put on.

Soon the tension began to ease off, so I hurried over to Lieutenant Peavey and urged him to let his deputies, who were off duty after all, come and fix their plates.

He shook his head. "We're in the midst of crowd control, Mrs. Springer," he said, scanning the crowd over my head.

Following his eyes, I saw Raymond standing by the hedge that lined the sidewalk. "I believe I can help with that," I said and walked over to invite him and his friends to the table.

They were reluctant at first to abandon the miracle on the wall to Pastor Petree's ministrations, but as it was fairly obvious that the pastor was making little headway, they could safely leave him to it. Still, they seemed hesitant to partake of a wedding feast they'd not received a formal invitation to.

"Tell them, Raymond," I said. "Tell them they're more than welcome. You go first while I invite some of these out-of-staters."

He gave me that shy smile of his and nodded, especially when Little Lloyd came over to us and added his two cents in Spanish. Soon some of the crowd formed an orderly line, still keeping their eyes on Pastor Petree, while Lillian started piling their plates full. Binkie and Coleman, laughing and chattering in broken Spanish with Raymond, stood at the head of the table seemingly having the time of their lives.

Mr. Pickens stood to the side, his arm around Hazel Marie, laughing in his usual disrespectful manner. Knowing him, he'd never let me live this down, but I didn't care. In fact, as I watched, wedding guests began to mingle at the tables with the newly invited, filling their plates like they hadn't eaten in a week. I saw Sam pick up a little boy dressed in his Sunday best, and take him and his plate to the porch steps where he could eat in comfort. I looked over the blended crowd that filled my yard, and felt my heart fill with goodwill. Binkie had wanted a wedding that was informal and fun, and that's exactly what she was getting. Although Pastor Petree's continued exhortations from the top of the ladder weren't adding to my sense of fun.

I'd about had enough, so I walked across the street to crane my head up to look at Pastor Petree, who'd lost most of his congregation to the wedding feast. Still, he was preaching his head off and scrubbing the stubborn stains as if his life depended on it.

"Pastor," I called. "Wrap that up and get down from there. I've had enough of street preaching for one day." And standing clear of the free-flowing hose, I reached over and shook the ladder so that it wobbled against the wall.

But he was caught up in some spirit-filled exuberance, scouring the wall and expounding at the top of his lungs on the evils of superstition, and paid me no mind.

"I'll not tell you again," I shouted when he stopped to get his breath. "Either get off that ladder and behave yourself, or I'm calling the fire department to bring you down!"

Chapter 38

I stomped back across the street, deciding he'd come down when he got tired enough. Either that or he'd fall, which would certainly put an unexpected climax to my beautifully planned wedding. I gritted my teeth at the thought.

By this time, all my guests were busily eating or resting.

"Lillian," I said to her as I approached the tables. "Where did the Reverend Mr. Abernathy get to?"

"He right over there enjoyin' himself." She nodded in the direction of the sidewalk, where I saw the reverend ensconced in a wicker chair from my porch.

Satisfied that the reverend was being well attended, I asked, "What about Miss Morgan? Has she had anything to eat?"

"Yessum, she come out a while ago and got herself a plate. But don't be surprised at what gonna happen next." She smiled broadly, her gold tooth sparkling, and pointed to the porch.

I saw a squad of deputies, Lieutenant Peavey and Miss Wiggins's boyfriend prominent among them, moving the piano out onto the porch. Miss Mattie Mae Morgan directed the proceedings, then when they had it where she wanted it, she sat herself down at it and commenced putting out some of the most foot-tapping music I'd ever heard this side of the TV channel Little Lloyd watched. I mean, she was rocking back and forth on the piano bench, banging on the keys for all she was worth. I heard Miss Wiggins comment that Miss Morgan reminded her of a three-hundred-pound Little Richard, an oxymoron if I'd ever heard one.

Drawn by Miss Morgan's pounding on the keys, the Mexican guitarist drifted closer to the porch and began to add his brand of music to the general racket. One of the deputies urged him to join them, and the guitar player stepped right up and began to blend in with that rock-and-roll music.

"Who is that playing the guitar?" I asked, hardly expecting an answer.

Mr. Pickens, who'd come up behind me, said, "That's Jesus."

"Hay-who? How do you spell that?"

"You don't want to know, Miss Julia," he said, laughing at me with those black eyes.

Before I could pursue the matter, my attention was taken by Binkie and Coleman, who were dancing on the paved driveway. He was swinging her around enough to create concern for the state of her health. She didn't seem to mind, having forgotten, apparently, her earlier queasy condition.

Then, as I watched, several more couples joined them, including Mr. Pickens and Hazel Marie, and Miss Wiggins and her deputy with the astonishing tie. Even Leonard Conover led out LuAnne, holding her close enough to put my errant imagination to work. Soon some of the Hispanic couples took up the beat on the sidewalk. Others, searching for more space, moved out into the street, swinging, dipping, twirling and dancing to beat the band. An unsuspecting motorist turned at the corner, then quickly backed up and sped away.

And still, Pastor Petree preached on.

As the afternoon lengthened into dusk, a spotlight from the television crew bounced around, then centered on Pastor Petree, re-vitalizing his efforts. Flashes from the sports photographer's camera lit up first one side of the yard, then the other. He was single-mindedly making his way through the melee, caught up with capturing memories for Binkie and Coleman. Although I doubted they would need any special reminders of this wedding.

I walked over to the redheaded sports photographer, where he squatted to reload his camera, and asked if he'd taken any for-mal poses of the wedding party.

"Sure did," he said, rising to his feet. "Not very many, though, since they wouldn't stand still long enough. Too much going on. I tell you, Mrs. Springer, this is the damnedest wedding I've ever seen. And I'll tell you something else." He leaned close to share a thought. "I got some terrific shots of that preacher up there. They'll be front page, for sure."

"Oh," I gasped, as my knees nearly gave way. It wasn't enough to have Pastor Petree on television where he'd be here today and gone tomorrow. He was going to be in the newspaper where his picture could be cut out and put on bulletin boards and in scrapbooks. Our church was going to be a laugh-ingstock, but before I could protest, the photographer had scampered off into the crowd.

As I began to look for Sam to see if he could stop the presses, I was stopped in my tracks by the racket coming from the porch. Miss Mattie Mae Morgan began hammering down again on the piano, while Lieutenant Peavey and several deputies gathered around her singing about somebody driving them crazy. I'd never seen such bodily movements that accompanied the driving beat, but deputies are usually in good enough physical shape to manage the most strenuous exercise. Too much of such music would drive me crazy too, but it stirred even Mildred Allen and the sheriff to take to the floor. Well, the pavement. Soon my driveway, the sidewalk and the street were a bouncing mass of whirling dervishes. If I hadn't known better, having specifically ordered sparkling grape juice, I'd've thought them all intoxicated.

I found a gilt chair someone had brought outside and sank into it. Lillian brought me a plate, saying, "Eat!" Then she pulled up a chair beside me and began to sway with the music.

And still, Pastor Petree preached from the rooftop.

Mr. Pickens, no longer constrained by coat and tie, suddenly appeared at my side. His shirtsleeves were rolled up on his brawny arms, and the sight of all that hair made me slightly uneasy.

"I've been cut in on," he said, looking back where Little Lloyd was engaged in gyrations with his mother. Then he held out his hand to me. "How 'bout it, Miss Julia? Dance with me?"

"Oh, Mr. Pickens, you know I don't dance. I'm a conservative Presbyterian." Besides, I wanted to add, I hardly know how since Wesley Lloyd had not been a dancing man.

He threw his head back and laughed, those white teeth gleaming under his black and bushy mustache. Gaining control of himself, he said, "I tell you what. I won't tell anybody, if you won't. Come on now. This is the only way I'll ever get to lead you."

"Go on, Miss Julia," Lillian urged, taking my plate from my lap. "This might be yo' last chance 'fore Miss Hazel Marie take him away."

Feeling foolish and awkward, I let Mr. Pickens lead me to the driveway. "I declare, Mr. Pickens, I can't dance to that tune. It's much too lively."

"Bet you can," he said, smiling at my hesitancy. "Look, just stand there and sway till you get the rhythm, then move with it. Don't worry about the steps; just stay with the beat."

And before I knew it, he was pulling me this way and that, whirling me in a slow spin and catching me in his arms. I declare, it was exhilarating, if somewhat out of the ordinary for one of my usual decorous manner. Especially when Little Lloyd called out, "Look, Mama, Miss Julia's dancing!," which brought several couples to a halt to stare at us.

To my dismay, an audience spurred Mr. Pickens on to greater exertions and I had to avert my eyes from the swiveling of his hips. Thankfully, the tune finally wound down, with Mr. Pickens giving me a final twirl.

As he wiped his sweating face, I commented that he might consider his age before engaging in such vigorous activity again.

"Tell that to Hazel Marie," he whispered in my ear, as he breathed a wicked laugh and gave my waist a squeeze.

From behind my back, Sam said, "Go get your own woman, Pickens. It's my turn with this one."

Grinning, Mr. Pickens gave a mock bow and said, "Thank you for the dance, Miss Julia."

I brushed the air with my hand, having had enough of his teasing. "Sam," I said, turning to him. "I am worn out from all this exertion."

"It's good for you, Julia," he said, taking my hand and pulling me close. "Besides, I've put in a special request for a slow one. Now dance with me, woman."

Unable to leave without creating a scene or, rather, *another* scene since we'd had the Lord's plenty of them already, I submitted to Sam's leading. And, sure enough, Miss Mattie Mae Morgan swung into a fairly sedate melody, although accompanied by an inordinate amount of additional notes that I tried to ignore.

I suffered through that so-called dance,

knowing I was stiff and awkward, and self-conscious because of it. But toward the end of it, I realized that it had gotten too dark for anybody to notice my lack of grace. And Sam was light enough on his feet to cover my missteps. I was grateful to him, and gradually let myself go loose in his arms. That brought up another problem, for I could feel him breathing and that didn't do much to bring about a sense of ease.

"Sam," I said, stepping away from him as the music drew to a close, "we should see about Binkie and Coleman. It's past time for them to leave for whatever honeymoon they're going to have."

"All taken care of, Julia," he said, his arm still around my waist as if there wasn't a crowd of people to see it. "The car they're leaving in will be here in a minute, but I don't know if Binkie and Coleman can tear themselves away. They're having too good a time." He leaned down then and went on. "You've outdone yourself, Julia. This wedding beats all anybody's ever seen; it'll be the talk of the town for years to come."

"Well, if you mean that as a compliment, I'm not sure it is one. Besides, everything that'll make it memorable was not of my doing. I'd've preferred something a good deal more solemn. Still," I said, brushing the hair off my forehead and looking around, "I guess people're having a good time, and that's what Binkie wanted."

As we walked onto the grass, away from the resumption of what passed for dancing, Lillian came up to us.

"Miss Julia," she said, "them caterers has fixed a great big basket of party food for the bride and groom to take with 'em, an' it ready to go soon as they are. An' I tole Little Lloyd to pass out them little bags an' tell everybody to get ready to th'ow birdseed when they leave."

"Oh, Lillian," I said, "what would I do without you? Here, I've been out there dancing and leaving you to keep things moving."

Before she could answer, a loud *whomp, whomp* pierced the air, bringing even Miss Morgan to a sudden halt. We all turned to look down the street where the racket was coming from.

Threading its way down the dark street, through the double-parked cars and street dancers, a sheriff's patrol car eased toward us, roof lights flashing and siren whooping loud enough to stop the music and draw attention away from even Pastor Petree. In fact, as I watched the car approach, I saw the pastor's foot slip as he turned to see what had interrupted his sermon. He had to grab on to the ladder to save himself from a sudden descent.

As the patrol car slowed to a halt in front of my house, its lights flashing red and blue streaks across the gathering crowd, its siren blasted out again, then died away in a long, piercing wail.

"What is that thing doing here?" I gasped, wondering what other crisis was at hand.

Sam grinned. "That thing's going to start Binkie and Coleman on their honeymoon."

Chapter 39

I was still gaping at the couple's unlikely conveyance when Little Lloyd ran up, gasping for breath. "It's gone, Miss Julia! It was there a minute ago, and now it's gone!"

"Slow down, child." I put my hands on his shoulders, feeling them heave with excitement. "Now what's the problem?"

"That . . . that," he got out between gasps, his eyes so big they were about to pop out of his head. Pointing toward the porch, he finally managed to say, "That basket of Mrs. Conover's, the one with the birdseed bags that I was supposed to hand out. It's flat gone!"

"Oh, it couldn't be," I said, straining to see through the milling guests. "It just got moved aside when they brought out the piano. Let's go look for it."

"No need, Miss Julia," Little Lloyd said, shaking his head firmly. "I've looked all over, and I've asked everybody, even Miss Mattie Mae Morgan, and nobody's seen it since Mrs. Conover set it out there."

"Well, who in the world could've taken it?"

"I know who did it," the boy said with a dark frown. "I bet it was that ole Dixon Hightower."

I tried to reassure him that Dixon would not be mingling among so many people, but in my heart of hearts I was beginning to wonder. Twice Hazel Marie had thought she'd seen him. Maybe she had. Maybe Dixon was another uninvited guest, but one who was making free with a basket of birdseed bags.

About that time, I was distracted by the crowd turning with an audible sigh and a few catcalls, as Binkie and Coleman appeared on the porch. They were still in their wedding outfits, Binkie's bare shoulders splashed with intermittent streaks of red and blue lights from the patrol car. A spotlight aimed by the driver of the car suddenly found them, lighting them up like movie stars, and I saw the television camera turn toward them. Coleman stood there in the glare, grinning with delight, his arm around Binkie as they acknowledged the crowd's benediction. Even the worshipers of the woman on the wall drifted closer, smiling and waving at the happy couple.

As Binkie and Coleman came down the steps, I noticed the guests looking around for something to throw. Even though nothing was forthcoming, Binkie ducked and Coleman put an arm over his head. Yells from the deputies and, I'm sorry to say, from some guests who should've known better, urged them on to the culmination of their marriage, although in terms I'm unwilling to repeat.

As Binkie passed me on the way to the car, she stopped and hugged me. "Miss Julia, this has been the best wedding anybody could ever have. I wouldn't've missed it for the world."

She didn't give me a chance to answer, for she was quickly on her way. But I thought to myself that if it'd been left up to her, she certainly would have missed it.

"Wait! Wait!" Miss Wiggins yelled, hurrying toward the car. "Put this in their basket." And she thrust a large ribbon-decorated bottle through the window to the driver, who I saw was Deputy Moser.

I pursed my mouth at the nerve of her, but

there was little I could do about it. I comforted myself that maybe Binkie and Coleman wouldn't partake, thereby spoiling their wedding night with a stimulant.

Hazel Marie called, "Throw the bouquet!" When Binkie reached the open door of the car, she turned her back to the crowd and flung her bouquet high in the air. Hazel Marie ran to get under it, but that pushy Etta Mae Wiggins leaped up and came down with it. Hazel Marie backed off in disappointment, but Mr. Pickens whispered something to her that picked up her spirits.

"Where's the garter?" a group of deputies called out. "We want the garter!"

And before my very eyes and those of a hundred people or more, Binkie hiked up her dress and disencumbered herself of the blue garter with a little pink flower on it. Coleman stood there laughing, not at all disconcerted by his wife's public display. He took it from her and whirled it around his head a few times, then slung it far and wide.

As it began to fall, deputies scattered away, yelling in mock terror, none apparently wanting to be the next to take a wife. I noticed Mr. Pickens laughing and cringing behind Hazel Marie, who was trying to be a good sport about it. I could've whipped him.

A laugh erupted from the crowd as the garter floated down and came to rest on Lieutenant Peavey's rigid shoulder. He'd been standing on the side, above the fray so to speak, but the blue elastic fell on him like it had singled him out. Though I couldn't see that any woman would want him, he was so unbending and set in his ways. Imagine living with such a man, I thought. Then I realized that was exactly what I'd done for some forty or more years.

As we laughed at Lieutenant Peavey's discomfort, a louder noise than we'd heard before emanated from the throats of the worshipers behind us. I turned to see them running out into the street, their attention turned to some new occurrence. Their hands were stretched out, reaching up in the air as they shouted and jumped and snatched at the small, large and odd-shaped things that were floating down from the top of the Family Life Center. As I watched, openmouthed, I felt a sprinkling like raindrops, only not at all wet, on my head and face. Brushing away whatever was raining down on us, I found my hand covered with birdseed. Birdseed! Falling through the air and strewing across the ground.

Hosannas or hallelujahs began to drown out the wedding festivities. The whole marital event threatened to become unhinged, as the crowd seemed to be going into a state of ecstasy or something. I looked around for Little Lloyd.

Coleman quickly pushed Binkie into the car and tried to close the door to keep her safe, but she popped back out, determined to see what was going on.

Lieutenant Peavey and his deputies, professional faces restored, began to spread out to see what was happening.

"Sam," I said, clutching at his arm. "What is it?"

"Don't know, Julia," he said, frowning with concern. Then: "Look! What in the world is that?"

Then we all saw a sight that brought gasps and screams from the guests in the yard. In the soft light of early evening, the glare of the television lights and the colored streaks of the patrol car, bits of paper and streamers and shiny banners were flickering through the air, as birdseed peppered on and around us. Down past Pastor Petree it all came, falling into the outstretched hands of the crowd below.

Our guests milled around, bride and groom forgotten in this new attraction, watching and wondering at what clearly seemed a miracle you could put your hands on. In fact, some of the guests ran out to join the worshipers and began snatching at the fluttering objects raining down from the Family Life Center, like they believed manna was falling from heaven.

Before I could grab his collar, Little Lloyd dashed out into the street to join the general melee, where I saw Binkie's flower-bedecked head bobbing up and down in the crowd.

"Sam!" I cried. "Oh, Sam, go get her. Where's Coleman? She's going to do herself some damage out there!"

"He's right behind her," Sam assured me. "See, he's pulling her away."

Relieved that Coleman was on the job, I shifted my concern to the source of the paper-and-birdseed shower. "Where's that stuff coming from? Sam, can you see anything?"

"Looks like it's coming from the roof."

Sam stretched to try to see over the heads of the mob. "Here comes another downpour. See it?"

Yes, I did, for what looked like an armful of papers, large, small, long and slender pieces whooshed up in the air above the roof of the Family Life Center, then came drifting down to the eager hands below.

Little Lloyd came running back to us, his eyes big with wonder and his hands grasping a few pieces of the airborne treasure. "Miss Julia!" he cried, fear, wonder or awe vibrating in his voice. "Look what it is!"

Sam took a shiny paper from him and held it up. My knees nearly buckled under me as I read PRAY WITH US. "My Lord!" I cried, clutching Sam's arm to keep myself upright. "It's one of Emma Sue's bumper stickers!"

"Yessum," Little Lloyd said, nodding his head and trying to catch his breath. "But look at this," he added, holding up a much smaller piece of paper. "It's not Mrs. Ledbetter's."

I took the paper and read: GOOD FOR ONE FREE LUBE JOB AT P & J'S PIT STOP. "It's a gift certificate!" I drew in my breath sharply. "Oh, my goodness, remember that church that had all their bingo prizes stolen? How many of these things are there?"

"Lots of 'em!" Little Lloyd assured me. "I heard people yelling about groceries and movie passes and free gas! It's a miracle, Miss Julia!"

"Well, I guess it would be, if I believed in such things. Still," I said, marveling at the sudden appearance of that which had been taken from the backseat of my car, as well as from the Briar Creek House of God, "how could these things come out of the blue like this?"

"Oh, for goodness' sake," Sam said, laughing and pointing to the top of the building. "There's your answer."

I looked up to see a jumping, yelling small figure scampering along the ledge of the roof right above Pastor Petree's head. The figure reached down and threw out another handful of papers to the waiting hands below. At the sight of him, half a dozen deputies dispatched by Lieutenant Peavey swarmed to the door of the building, intent on rounding up the perpetrator of, well, I didn't know what. Littering, maybe.

Pastor Petree seemed oblivious to the antics above him, for he'd turned on the ladder to face the crowd, making his perch somewhat problematic, to say the least. He held one of Emma Sue's bumper stickers, a look of wonder on his face.

Then the figure above him leaned over and dropped a double handful of small, brightly colored objects onto the pastor's head, and I thought the poor soul was going to go into a rapture of some kind. Miss Wiggins screamed as she snatched at the objects. "My candy! It's my candy!"

Then, from the midst of the shouting, shoving crowd, I heard Binkie's clear voice. "That's my client!"

When a cackling laugh floated down from the ledge, I too recognized the source of the miracle of the coupons. "It's Dixon Hightower!" I yelled. "Sam . . . !"

"Dixon!" Little Lloyd yelled, jumping up and down. "It's that Dixon Hightower! Oh, my word, he's here amongst us!"

I reached out to calm him down, but something dark and feathery brushed my shoulder and I jumped a mile.

The air was suddenly filled with a mighty rushing of wings amid the scattering and cries of wedding guests, as a swarm of pigeons from the steeple of the church swooped down on my lawn. They flew in and around us, coming to skimming halts around our feet, then waddling and pecking at the grass.

Little Lloyd's arms flailed as another bevy of flapping wings swooshed past his head. "Help!" he cried. Then, seeing what they were after, he yelled, "It's the birdseed! Look, Miss Julia, they've come for the birdseed!"

"Oh, Sam," I said, almost collapsing on his shoulder. He put his arm around me and held me close. "What else can go wrong?"

Plenty, as it turned out. Coleman hustled Binkie to the waiting patrol car and, as they climbed into the backseat, Deputy Moser released the trunk latch and a rush of balloons escaped into the air. Children ran to catch them as the balloons wobbled and floated up, passing the flecks of paper floating down, and disturbed by the commotion, the pigeons rose in a fluttering mass. Then they circled and rushed down again. Just as they began to settle on the yard, Sergeant Moser eased the car down the street, trunk lid flapping as the last of the balloons zoomed out like a comet's tail. Then, with

Binkie and Coleman waving from the windows, he set off that whomping siren again.

At the sound of it, the pigeons swooshed up again with a great fluttering of wings to circle above the heads of the guests. Then, shedding feathers as they came, they dived among us, landing on heads and shoulders and between feet, so that people were stumbling and tripping over them. I heard the sheriff yell out, "Dad-blame the dad-blamed cussed luck!"

Sam was shaking so hard that I wondered if he could hold me up. When I looked at him in sudden concern, I saw he was laughing his head off.

"Sam Murdoch!" I said, drawing myself up. "How can you laugh at a time like this? My beautiful wedding is ruined!"

"Ruined? Oh, Julia," he said, wiping a finger under his eye as he began to control himself. "Look what you've done. You've gotten Binkie and Coleman married; you've taken strangers to your table; you've brought in an escaped prisoner and you've provided a feast for the birds of the air." He stopped and smoothed his hand across my face. "I'd say that this wedding is far from ruined."

"Well, if you put it that way . . ." I began to smile, thinking that no one would ever be able to outdo me when it came to putting on a wedding.

"Besides," Sam whispered, "if you don't like the way this one turned out, I can think of another one you can work on."

Chapter 40

But by the time that day had ended, I'd had my fill of weddings and miracles, too, if the truth be known. Unless, of course, Hazel Marie managed to drag Mr. Pickens to the altar, which would be a miracle in itself. If that came about, I would have to take a hand in it, just to make sure he didn't run out before it was over. But a wedding between those two didn't look to be happening anytime soon, much to her sorrow.

Well, sorrow is not quite the word. Exasperation, maybe, for she took a lesson from Coleman and laid down the law. Although, to my mind, it was a law with no teeth in it. What she told Mr. Pickens was that she and Little Lloyd would move in with him for the summer, and if by the time school started in the fall, he hadn't become more amenable to making the arrangement permanent, they'd move back home. If I'd have them, which, of course, I would, and gladly too.

"I told him," she said to me, "that three months was long enough for him to make up his mind. And I mean it, Miss Julia, I told him it'd be either put up or shut up."

I was proud of her for taking a stand, but I'd've been even prouder if she'd turned down even a trial period and let him suffer for a change. Still, you take what you can get, so I didn't point out the inherent danger of putting herself in Mr. Pickens's seductive hands. I'd seen him in action.

Besides, she already knew where I stood when it came to cohabitating without benefit of matrimony. Then she gave me even more reason to hold my peace because, after ranting to me about his recalcitrant ways, she went all soft and dreamy at the thought of that man and asked if Little Lloyd could stay on with me a couple of weeks.

"Just so we can get used to each other," she said, having the grace to blush. "Sort of a honeymoon, you know. Time for ourselves for a little while. Though I guess it won't be a real honeymoon since we won't be married."

"I guess it won't," I said. "But of course

Little Lloyd can stay with me. He can stay all summer if you'll let him."

In fact, as done in as I was at the improper way she was conducting herself, my heart lifted at the thought of not losing the boy, at least for a while.

So, in the week following Binkie and Coleman's wedding, Hazel Marie took her suitcases and hair rollers and shopping bags full of shoes and went off with Mr. Pickens.

I didn't discuss the situation with the boy, not wanting to criticize his mother, or approve of her actions either. Better to leave well enough alone, I thought. Besides, what a child doesn't know won't hurt him. Although I expect it's highly likely that a child knows more than you think he does.

The two of us found plenty of other situations to discuss, the main one being that apparition on the wall across the street. Every afternoon after supper, we'd sit on the front porch and talk over the changes that were slowly taking place. Whatever had caused the white lines on the bricks, whether it was salt deposits as Sam said it was or poor workmanship as I suspected or even some mysterious hand writing on the wall as the worshipers believed, it was still going on. Little by little, changes in the design were taking place. Not two days after the wedding, the two eyes had blended into one white splotch that was now spreading down to the mouth. Soon there'd be no features at all, which was fine with me. If you want a sudden start to your day, just wake up in the morning and find a woman's twenty-foot face staring at you through your window.

As it was, the town of Abbotsville narrowly escaped the calamity of becoming the Myrtle Beach of North Carolina, for people continued to pour in from all over the place. I thought I was going to have to move just to be able to get to the grocery store, but Little Lloyd set up a lemonade stand in the front yard and made a killing.

Well, when that woman on the wall started dissolving into something else, the mayor, the town commissioners and the chamber of commerce met in an emergency session to see what they could do to keep people coming and spending their money locally. One of the commissioners even suggested hiring a painter to preserve the woman in living color. Emma Sue Ledbetter took it upon herself to tell them that if we wanted a mural on our Family Life Center, we'd pick a subject better suited to what our church stood for. Which was family values and, to her mind, a strange woman's face didn't come close to measuring up.

So nothing was done and the woman continued her disappearing act. The number of spectators who had been attracted to the image began to dwindle down, as well. A few cars still drove by, slowing so the passengers could look out, but before the month was out, it would've taken a unusually active imagination to make out anything other than a brick wall that badly needed a paint job.

"Wonder if it really was a miracle," Little Lloyd mused. I was in a wicker rocker on the porch, and he sat on the steps making a chain of dandelion stems. Although it was getting along toward dusk, bees still hummed in my abelia and snowball bushes.

"I don't know," I answered, rocking softly and thinking over all that had happened. "Could be, I guess. Or if it wasn't, it served the purpose. At least we got Binkie and Coleman married, and if the woman on the wall had anything to do with that, then I'm just as grateful as I can be to her."

The boy thought that over for a few minutes, then he said, "You think since she's fading away, it means we don't need any more miracles?"

"I expect we need, and probably get, more than we think we do." I stopped and twisted my mouth, considering what to say to him. "Still, there's one thing you should remember, Little Lloyd. The Lord giveth and the Lord taketh away, and we don't have much say about either."

He didn't have much to say after that, which is what I notice usually happens when you quote a Bible verse to somebody.

———————

Both Sam and Coleman helped entertain the boy so he wouldn't miss his mother too much, and of course she called every day and came to visit. Bringing that insufferably pleased-with-himself Mr. Pickens with her. I let him know just what I thought of their arrangement, believe me I did, and more than once, too. But all I got from him was the suggestion that I make the same arrangement with Sam.

"Do you good, Miss Julia," he said, "and help you sleep, too."

"My sleep doesn't need help, thank you," I told him, and right sharply, too. But little got through that hard head of his.

It wasn't long after getting the house straight after the wedding that Pastor Ledbetter returned from the Holy Land with a newly inspired fire for preaching and a sunburn. I don't know who all told him what'd happened while he'd been gone, but I was sure Emma Sue had filled him full of her version. I saw him several times walking up and down the sidewalk, studying the remnants of the woman. It was fairly plain to me that he couldn't see it himself. He'd come to a stop, plant his hands on his hips and shake his head.

I took it on myself to go over to his office a few days after he got back to suggest that he see to Pastor Petree's welfare.

"That young man needs to go back to seminary for a refresher course," I told Pastor Ledbetter. "Maybe a remedial course would be better. Just don't inflict him on another congregation without warning them that he's apt to lose his composure on occasion."

Pastor Ledbetter listened to my advice with a calm, though severely peeling face, assuring me that it was all being handled. I didn't press him, for I was sure that he was still suffering from shock at the mess he'd returned to.

Emma Sue had taken the young preacher home with her after the wedding, but it had taken an athletic deputy to climb the ladder and talk him down. Pastor Petree'd been wet and exhausted, and so hoarse from all that yelling and carrying-on that he'd hardly been able to manage on his own. Emma Sue'd put him in her guest room, and he'd stayed there in bed under her constant ministrations until Pastor Ledbetter returned, after which the pastor wasted no time rectifying the situation. Before the day was out, he had Pastor Petree transferred to a ministerial retreat for burned-out preachers, of which I learned there was an unsuspectedly high number.

When Coleman returned from his brief honeymoon, he took Little Lloyd for a tour of the sheriff's department, which was an entertainment I decided I could do without. At other times, I kept the child busy with overseeing the fence installation at the Hillandale Trailer Park, going over the bills with him and showing him the rental income, as well as pointing out the discrepancy between the two.

"Well, see, Miss Julia," he said, after studying the figures, "in a couple of years we'll recover the cost of the fence and the paving of the street. Then we'll have a better investment."

That was such perceptive reasoning that I didn't point out that an investment is only as good as what a buyer is willing to pay for it. If we were willing to sell, which we weren't. Still, paving the street and putting up a fence was little enough to do in order to put a stop to Miss Wiggins's complaints.

It frosted me, though, that as it turned out, Dixon Hightower had been responsible for all the thefts in her neighborhood, as well as in mine. And since he was back under lock and key where he belonged, we hadn't needed to spend that money at all. I only went through with it to show Little Lloyd some business management practices.

And speaking of Dixon, Binkie came back

from her honeymoon and swung full steam into his defense. Since he'd been taken safely into custody on her wedding night, she hadn't needed to worry about him getting hurt while she was gone. Sam came by and picked up Little Lloyd and me so we could go to the hearing, and that was an entertainment worth attending. I declare, listening to the witnesses, from the jailer who let Dixon escape to the psychologists and social workers who examined him, made me realize that it's all in your point of view. You can pretty much tell what a witness is going to say if you know which side of the fence he's on.

During the testimony about his state of mind, or lack of same, Dixon sat beside Binkie taking it all in. He smiled and laughed at some of the stories told about his escapades, delighted at being the center of attention. Several times he'd turn around and scan the spectators, waving to those he recognized and, in general, enjoying the limelight.

The testimony was fascinating, I must say, for we learned that Dixon had hidden the fruits of his labors deep in the Family Life Center, down in the shaft that would eventually accommodate an elevator. I was reminded that Pastor Ledbetter had always told Dixon that the church was open to him at all times, and Dixon had taken him at his word.

Deputies had found Emma Sue's tortoiseshell hairbrush, Lillian's can opener, a child's plastic toy—Big Wheels, they called it—and empty snack-food wrappers from the Hillandale Trailer Park. That wasn't all, though. When the prosecutor started laying out the odds and ends from Dixon's cache, we all leaned forward, amazed at the sorry lot that had drawn Dixon's eye.

The bailiff wheeled out a bicycle with a flat tire and propped it against the table. And the exhibits kept coming, drawing gasps from the spectators as they recognized their belongings. But when the prosecutor held up a Game Boy, Little Lloyd pulled his Game Boy from his pocket. His head suddenly swiveled toward me. "I thought . . . ," he whispered. Then he squinched up his eyes. "You bought me another one."

I patted his knee. "I didn't want you to worry. Now you'll have two, so you can give one to Mr. Pickens," I said, thinking the man needed something to keep his hands occupied.

In all the tawdry display presented to the court by the prosecutor, the only thing of monetary worth was Pastor Ledbetter's clock with the little brass balls, the appearance of which caused Emma Sue to overflow with an avalanche of tears in thanksgiving. Between sobs, she murmured, "It's a miracle!"

I pursed my mouth at that, thinking that the greater miracle was the fact that she wasn't in jail for falsely accusing Norma Cantrell.

Then the prosecutor set an almost empty corked bottle on the evidence table. I could see the word "sacramental" on the fancy gold label. The prosecutor shook the bottle, showing us the few dregs of a deep red, suspiciously grape-juice-looking liquid in the bottom of it. "We don't know where this came from," the prosecutor said. "But he had almost half a case of it."

The courtroom spectators, including the judge, erupted in laughter when Emma Sue sprang from her seat and cried out, "That's the First Presbyterian Church's nonalcoholic communion wine! I'd recognize it anywhere!"

Eventually, the judge decided to take Binkie's plea for treatment instead of incarceration under advisement, whatever that meant, and Dixon was to be kept in our local jail until the judge made up his mind. After a deputy took Dixon out in handcuffs and shackles so he couldn't run again, we waited in the hall for Binkie. When the courtroom emptied and she still hadn't come out, we went back in to see what was delaying her. We found her crawling around under the defense table looking, she said, for her favorite fountain pen.

"I can't find it anywhere," she told us. "And I just had it. It has to be here somewhere."

Sam and I looked at each other and laughed.

Little Lloyd grinned and said, "I bet I know where it is."

Binkie got to her feet and started cramming papers in her briefcase. Although done in by the theft, she was undeterred from her mission. "All the more reason to get treatment for him," she said. But she grumbled to herself as we walked out together.

On our way to her office, she settled down enough to smile at the irony of defending a thief who'd stolen from her. I thought to myself that marriage was having a mellowing effect on her. But on second thought, I decided it might well be due to the hormones stirred up by her expectant state. Already her waistline had thickened to a noticeable degree, a matter of some concern to the prayer chain, I'm sorry to say. Binkie had begun wearing tunic tops to cover the evidence, for all the good they did. I was reminded that she'd chosen a wedding dress with an Empire waist that would allow for expansion. She'd been smart enough to pick a dress with hardly a stitch on top so as to draw attention away from her midsection.

As much as I hated to admit it, it was probably a wise choice. Although I still thought she could've chosen something with more coverage for Hazel Marie, since she didn't have anything to hide.

———

"Well, Sam," I said, as we strolled along the sidewalk after leaving Binkie at her office. Little Lloyd walked on one side of me, playing with one of his Game Boys, while Sam walked on the side by the street, putting me in the middle.

"Well, Julia," he said, raising an eyebrow.

"Well, I just realized how pleasant it is to rest up from doing a good deed. I thought I'd be feeling down, what with the exertions of the week and, especially with, you know, the change in a certain person's living arrangements." I gave Sam a knowing look and cocked my head toward the boy, not wanting to come right out and refer to my displeasure with Hazel Marie and Mr. Pickens.

"Instead," I went on, "I find that I have a sense of peace about everything. Maybe I'm finally learning to accept things as they come, and not let myself get all bent out of shape by trying to influence matters. Why, can you believe that, not too long ago, I was thinking of selling my house? That just shows how upset I was, and all because people I cared about weren't doing what I thought they should do. But now that I've gotten Binkie and Coleman married, I've learned to just let well enough alone."

Sam took my hand and squeezed it. Then he smiled down at me and said, "Hard lesson to learn, Julia. Hard for all of us."

We turned the corner and walked toward Main Street, the three of us enjoying the afternoon, as well as the anticipation of a fountain Coke at the drugstore.

"Yes," I went on. "I've decided to just enjoy life and quit trying to convert everybody to my way of thinking and doing. Of course, we do want to see Hazel Marie and Mr. Pickens follow Binkie and Coleman down the aisle."

At Sam's grin, I hurried on. "But that's up to them. As long as I have my business partner here," I said, putting a hand on Little Lloyd's shoulder, "I couldn't ask for anything more."

We walked in silence for a while, nodding at people we passed on the sidewalk. Then, out of the blue, Sam said, "Seems a lot of miracles have taken place, wouldn't you say?"

"I guess so," I said, nodding in agreement. "Although the real ones may've been those we can't see."

"Exactly what I'm talking about, Julia. They give me hope that there'll be another one real soon." He brought my hand to his lips and kissed it. Right there on the sidewalk in full view of the public.

Little Lloyd glanced up at this untoward demonstration of emotion, then back down at his toy. "You better watch out, Mr. Sam. Miss Julia says she's a changed woman these days."

"Not too changed, I hope," Sam said, his eyes smiling at me as he turned my hand over and kissed the palm. "I like her the way she is, but I'll take her any way I can get her."

"Oh, Sam," I said, pleased in spite of myself and maybe with a tinge of color on my face. Then I came to myself, aware that a public sidewalk was no place for such intimacies. I freed my hand from his. "Behave yourself," I said, feeling my face getting hot.

"I will," he said. "For now. But miracles do happen, so you better watch out. Another one might sweep you off your feet any minute now."

"Well," I said, not daring to meet his eyes. I looked away and smiled to myself. "I guess you never know, do you?"